LEGACY:

The Treaty of Little Big Horn

Rejoice
Celebrate life
I did

Ward C. Ganing

LEGACY:

The Treaty of Little Big Horn

by

Ward C. Garing

Based on an idea **by Scott Baron**

Easy Break, First Time Publishing
Royal Oaks

TREATY (*noun*): A formal agreement or contract, duly concluded and ratified, between two or more sovereign states.

SOVEREIGN (*adj*): Free, independent, and in no way limited by external authority or influence; as, a *sovereign state.*

Legacy is dedicated to:

Marissa, Vesta and Alvin
Children's Village,
Pine Ridge, South Dakota
The future of the Oglala Lakota

Acknowledgements

Legacy took the author to another time, another culture. I am deeply indebted to the following individuals and institutions.

Fred Menard, Sioux Museum, Rapid City, South Dakota for assistance with Lakota language.

Michael Marshall, Brule Lakota and U. S. Ranger at the Little Bighorn Battlefield National Monument, Montana for assistance with understanding of the Native Americans involved in the battle and U.S. Army battle tactics.

Brother Simon, Red Cloud Indian School, Pine Ridge, South Dakota for assistance in understanding the reservation, current education, challenges and changes through the years.

Also the staffs at the following locations for their assistance in answering even the dumbest questions:

Fort Laramie National Historic Site, Wyoming
Fort Robinson State Park, Nebraska
Sioux Museum, Rapid City, South Dakota
Little Bighorn Battlefield National Monument, Montana

Of course, there would be no book without a story and Legacy would never have been written if Scott Baron had not entrusted me with seeds for the plot. Thanks Scott.

Special thanks for the original cover art by Will Northcutt who worked and reworked the images to give them life.

I am also grateful for the warm reception of the Oglala Lakota people at Pine Ridge reservation who treated me with kindness and invited me into their ceremonies.

I have stood among the tourists at the Little Bighorn Battlefield National Monument and contemplated the events memorialized there. I have also stood alone at sunset in another, lesser known and rarely visited battlefield, Wounded Knee. One site is a memorial to a battle, the other to a massacre. Though vastly different, both reflect great tragedy.

I would also like to acknowledge my family-especially my wife Gloria, and mother, Verl, for their unqualified support in this effort.

The Treaty of Little Big Horn

I. PRELUDE   1

II. MANHUNT   27

III. NEW BEGINNINGS, 1875-76   139

IV. A GOOD PLACE TO DIE   211

V. LEGACY   303

CHARACTERS & GLOSSARY   309

NATIVE VOICE
Published by The Native American Nation
Issue 4, Volume III   March 5, 2018

Our Pride! Our Downfall!

We, the oppressed peoples of North America, became disenfranchised beggars in our own land largely because of events beyond our control. Historically we were not civilizations that made technological advances—nor did we make great advances in producing machines of war. We neither invented nor imported gunpowder or steel. We did not make great voyages of discovery. We did not combine our might to face an adversary. When faced with those who did these things, we were at a decided disadvantage.

The Lakota secured that which was necessary to sustain life from the land we occupied. Historically, within the culture there was no pressure to conquer until the white man came and pushed us from our ancestral lands. No inventors of note arose to bless The Lakota with laborsaving devices. Statesmen made no grand treaties with neighboring nations, freeing us from later breaking solemn promises. We faced our world and fought it on even terms.

All of this was irrevocably reversed when we were faced with a numerically superior civilization well versed in the arts of war, the practice of conquest and the artifices of peace. Like small children we attempted to contest the limits imposed on us by those who *appeared* superior. For our efforts we were rebuked and punished. We found we were not equipped to fight and win. Nor were we ready to succumb to virtual enslavement in our own land. We were like children. Like children we were treated.

It did not need to be this way.

Unfortunately, our greatest triumph was our greatest downfall. Until June 25, 1876, there was a chance for peace between The Lakota Nation and the United States of America.

Although there had been many unfortunate incidents between our nations, *there were those who spoke for peace and had the power to make a lasting treaty—on both sides.*

Tatanka Yotanka is revered today as a man great in war and strong in peace. Until the day he was assassinated, he had the strength to force a settlement between the two nations. Had he but used the great mass of Lakota and Cheyenne as a tool to force talks, instead of a sword to destroy 265 soldiers of the United States of America, our history might be much changed. Today we could control our own destiny. We would certainly control more of our ancestral lands. Unfortunately, the destruction of George Armstrong Custer and the men under his immediate control embarrassed the military and civilian leaders of a nation still forming an identity. "The loss" could not be tolerated. Even today, we are punished for our greatest victory.

Could only one day in our history be altered—June 25, 1876—our entire existence would be enhanced. We would be powerful and feared. We would be: **The Lakota Nation!**

(Signed)
Wiyaka Sapa, Lakota
(Black Feather of the Lakota)

PRELUDE

Saturday, July 3, 2021. Weston, Maryland.

"Randy, hurry up! We'll be late."

"Coming, mom." Reluctantly Randy switched off the hologram viewer and watched the images of his football heroes fade from the center of the room. He impatiently tugged a Washington Redskins cap over his unruly hair and darted out the door of the study.

In the kitchen, Kimberly Caldwell finished assembling the picnic lunch, adding cold drinks to the insulated bag. Wine coolers for herself and Jamie—a popular sports drink for Randy. She paused in front of the mirrored refrigerator door to smooth a wrinkle in her summer-weight jumpsuit. The white, tailored outfit set off her tan and showed her long, slim legs to perfection. "Not bad for thirty-two," she muttered. She brushed aside an errant auburn curl from her forehead as Randy burst into the kitchen.

"Mom, do I really have to go?" he asked.

"Darling, you know how much Jamie wants to have us there. He especially asked that you come. It'll be fun. You'll see. Here, grab the picnic basket for me."

Kimberly picked up her purse and led them to the door. She slid her magnetic entry/exit key through the scanner and the door slid open admitting them to the hall of the condominium complex. The door whispered shut behind them. In the garage Kimberly paused for a moment to admire her new Electra 440 before unplugging it from the meter. The bubble top flipped up when she inserted the magnetic key. She and Randy slid easily into the formed seats as the top closed and seat belts automatically enfolded them. The car moved silently to the barred gate that slid open, releasing them into light Saturday afternoon traffic. *What a relief*, thought Kimberly. *I guess most people left for the long weekend last night. It'll be an easy drive today.*

Randy produced a pack of his football cards and began to reorganize them for the umpteenth time. His silence gave Kimberly time to analyze her feelings.

Analysis was what Kimberly did best. When her husband, David, was assigned to Japan four years ago as a military liaison officer, Kimberly landed a job at the American Embassy in Tokyo in the statistical department. Her degree in International Relations had been the key. She enjoyed the challenges of sifting through tangled reports, locating key information and bringing it to the attention of her superiors. Her greatest coup occurred when she pieced together a puzzle which led to the discovery that the Japanese were seriously pursuing research to unlock one of man's fondest dreams—time travel. Her work was later verified by experts, leading to the United States stepping up its own efforts. Although she was no longer privy to information in that field, she shrewdly guessed research was still proceeding at one or more "black" sites in the United States.

Less than two years had passed since David was killed while on joint military exercises in South Korea. "Friendly fire," and "unfortunately, an incident that could have been avoided" were phrases she had come to loathe. She sometimes wondered about little boys playing cowboys and Indians and their fascination with guns, a fascination that could lead to men like David being killed with real weapons.

Then, she thought, there's the other side. *Why do women fall for shiny brass buttons, spit-polished shoes and snappy uniforms?*

And now I'm on my way to meet another tin soldier. Is this what I want? Or worse, could I survive another loss like David? When David was killed, she was devastated. The quaint Japanese villages along the Inland Sea they loved to explore lost their charm. Only heartache remained. The bustling atmosphere of Tokyo became unbearable. She applied for a job in the analysis department of the Defense Intelligence Agency in Washington, D. C., and was immediately accepted. Her work in Washington was demanding but rewarding, and had the advantage of placing her near her childhood home in Virginia. Her work at the DIA also brought her into contact with Lieutenant Colonel H. Jamison Partridge the Third. Jamie's assignment as Assistant to the Commander of Weapons Research and Intelligence meant the two of them often attended the same briefings and analysis sessions. Jamie was considered one of the most eligible bachelors in the higher middle echelon of command in Washington. Kimberly's status as an attractive young widow made an eventual coupling almost inevitable. Mutual friends, however, left nothing to chance. When they were introduced to each other for the third time in two days and invited to the same two intimate dinner parties, they accepted it as fate.

The early weeks of the relationship were wonderful. Jamie took to Randy immediately, although the boy was somewhat reserved in his judgement of the man in his mother's life. However, it helped that Jamie was also a devoted Redskins fan.

Jamie and Kimberly discovered they had many common ideals and aspirations. Both loved their work and had progressed in their jobs with flair. Jamie was twelve years older, an initial stumbling block to Kimberly, but was trim, fit and looked years younger. He was devoted to his native Montana in the same way Kimberly loved Virginia.

Since his graduation from West Point in 1998, he had seen varied service including the Macedonian Incursion, Second Balkan Campaign and Desert Thunder. His degree in chemical engineering led to his posting with a chemical warfare containment unit in Iraq and a position in the airlift command for Bosnia, which often handled exotic chemical weapons, the existence of which was yet to be released to the public.

Like Kimberly, Jamie enjoyed traveling throughout the world, although he almost always chose Montana, Idaho or Wyoming for vacations.

"There's just something about returning to the peace of the mountains," he said. "I guess you could say I escape to a different place and time when I shed the uniform and ride into some remote valley where fish don't recognize a baited hook. I feel a deep peace, a kinship and belonging that I never experience anywhere else."

Escaping to another time was what he'd be doing today. As a member of the First Maryland Volunteers, a group of Civil War buffs, he would lead a cavalry charge of Union troops against their Confederate foe in a reenactment of a skirmish that took place at an insignificant bridge in the Virginia countryside in 1862. The staging of battles from the Civil War was the primary reason for the existence of the First Maryland and similar units. Although 160 years had passed since the original battles, the public still flocked to the engagements whenever they were staged.

Kimberly was almost certain today was also the day when Jamie would broach the subject of their continuing relationship. He had been hinting, not too subtly, that he had an important question to ask her. Just thinking about it made her throat dry. Jamie was intelligent, attractive, caring and devoted to her. When they made love he was tender and responsive to her needs. He made her feel whole, warm, loved. The thought of their intertwined bodies quickened her pulse. She swallowed hard to regain her composure. *Yes, he is wonderful. He would be a loving father to Randy. A twelve-year-old boy needs a father and maybe there would be more children. But–but, what?*

But I'm being stupid, she thought. Sure, there were still thoughts of David and an ache which had faded but not disappeared. Eleven years of a happy marriage didn't fade into oblivion in two years. But there was something more nagging in the back of her mind. Jamie was a military man, through and through. He'd already been in three conflicts and now there were ominous signs that China had combined its strengths of population and new technical skills to become a super power to be reckoned with. If they followed their current policies, it was only a matter of time until they might try to flex their muscles in the Far East. If that happened, it would be the Mother of All Wars. Jamie was sure to be in danger. *Could I stand the thought of losing another husband? How great is the risk? Why—why am I so afraid?*

The little bridge had been rebuilt several times since the Civil War, but was still on an out-of-the-way back road in the mixed timber and fields of rural Virginia. Kimberly followed other arriving vehicles to a temporary parking lot in a field out of sight of the bridge. She and Randy shared the load of the picnic basket as they strolled with the crowd down the dusty lane through the trees. Bleachers were set up in an open area near where the action would take place. They found seats in the shade and Kimberly pulled out her video recorder. The 12-to-1 zoom would bring the action right to her. Beneath the trees in the distance she could see men in blue and gray uniforms and horses tethered nearby.

When all was ready, a squad of Confederates thundered in on the near side of the creek. With them was a four-horse team pulling a howitzer and caisson. The actors jumped from their horses as the howitzer rumbled to a halt before the bleachers. Two troopers collected the horses and moved them out of sight. The howitzer was quickly unlimbered as a dashing officer bellowed orders. The spectators watched, fascinated, as the big gun was set facing them. Loaders hastened to ram powder and a paper cartridge in the barrel. When all was ready the howitzer was fired directly toward the spectators. Randy covered his ears just before the roar of the explosion. The muzzle flash, shock wave and streams of confetti filled the air. A large smoke ring moved lazily toward the crowd.

"Wow!" exclaimed Randy as the spectators wildly applauded.

"Good afternoon ladies and gentlemen," came a voice over concealed loudspeakers. The disembodied voice went on to explain what would transpire over the next hour. Union forces from the right would attempt to dislodge Confederate defenders on the left. "The finale will be an ill-fated charge by Union cavalry of the First Maryland Volunteers!" he concluded.

Kimberly and Randy found themselves drawn into another world as they watched the forces maneuver. Men and horses fell with uncanny realism. Rebel yells punctuated the air. Clouds of dust obscured the scene until driven away by errant breezes. The smells of gunpowder, horses and sweat mingled with the dust and smoke.

Then it was time for the Union charge. Twenty mounted troopers wheeled out of the woods. Jamie led the charge with sabre held high. Kimberly focused on him through the video recorder, following his every move. He was focused—intent. He hunched forward slightly and moved with his horse as if they were one. She realized she was seeing the primordial warrior, personified. He was in battle and this was what he was bred to do. She sensed the fierce exultation in his eyes. For him, this was more fulfilling than any other activity. She had never seen him so excited.

Unconsciously, she squirmed in her seat and licked her lips. She felt her passion rising, her pulse quickening. Her skin tingled; the touch of fabric became a soft caress.

Riveted to the eyepiece, she groaned when he was cornered. Rebel horsemen moved closer, hemming him in. Suddenly he slumped in the saddle and his horse moved to the side, out of the melee. Jamie slid from the saddle and lay still on the battlefield. A fierce shout of victory erupted from the surviving Confederate soldiers.

Kimberly held her breath. It was over. Her palms were sweaty. She could hardly hold the recorder, still focused on the prone figure before her. She almost collapsed as he rose, removed his hat and began to beat off the dust. Weak with relief, she stopped recording. It took her several moments to get her breath and stop shaking.

Beside her, Randy was whooping with delight. All around them, spectators were jumping up and applauding wildly. In the meadow, "dead" troopers rose, threw their arms around each other and began to celebrate.

"Mom…Mom! Can I go see the colonel? Please, Mom!"

"Sure, Randy, but…" He was already off and running. "Be careful!" she shouted after him.

Kimberly used the few free minutes to compose herself before picking up the picnic basket. She joined the crowd moving onto the "battlefield." The only emotion she felt was relief. *Her* man was alive.

"That," stated Jamie, "may just be the best lunch I've ever eaten." His smile flashed, showing strong, even teeth. His eyes sparked a bright blue, full of merriment.

Kimberly returned the smile. *Just like the conquering hero home from the war,* she thought. Only he was not the winner. Today his forces were defeated, but it was only a mock battle. *He's just excited by the battle itself,* she thought. *The joy is in the fighting.*

Jamie sprawled comfortably on the blanket at the base of a massive old hickory tree. Kimberly was easily the most beautiful woman at the gathering—and she was his woman. *This is just like the old box lunch socials,* he thought. *My great-grandparents may have courted this way.*

"Kimberly, while we have a few moments alone, I have something to ask you."

Kimberly realized Jamie was no longer as relaxed. Her heart began to race. *This is it,* she thought. *What will I say? What do I really feel? Oh dear.*

Jamie had imagined this scene countless times in recent weeks. He knew this would be the perfect place, the perfect time. He didn't notice Kimberly's reluctant attitude.

Raising himself to one knee, he put his hat over his heart and grasped her left hand in his. "Kimberly Caldwell, will you do me the honor of becoming my wife?"

There. The words were out. In spite of herself, Kimberly smiled. He was so—so, sincere—and, she had to admit, he made a dashing figure in his blue and gold uniform. She decided to adopt an attitude suitable to the day.

In her best southern drawl, she replied, "Why, Suh, y'all do this Virginia belle great honor. Ah swear, Ah'm overwhelmed." She fluttered her free hand in front of her face, as if holding an invisible fan. At the last moment she remembered to bat her eyelashes outrageously.

Jamie's heart pounded. He felt flushed, unbelievably relieved. His smile flashed. "Then you will?"

The look on her face told him all was not as he expected. The smile froze.

"Jamie, I—I truly am honored. I'm flattered. I'm—I guess a little shocked." She dropped her eyes. "I'm also not sure," she whispered.

Jamie swallowed hard, twice. "Not sure? What, or I mean, why?"

Kimberly took a moment to collect her thoughts. When she spoke, it was softly, but clearly.

"I can't really tell you for certain. I've known this moment might come and I've tried to understand why I'm hesitant."

She raised her eyes to his, seeing the pain there. This just wasn't coming out right.

"Jamie, it's not that I don't care for you. I do. I care very much. You're a wonderful man, the most wonderful I've met since—since David died."

There. The words are out, she thought. *David is dead. Yes, but not in my heart. And what if you were to die, you gallant soldier? What then? Can I really say that to you? No, I can't. At least not now.*

"Jamie, I need some time. Please give me time to sort out my feelings. I care for you so much that I must be sure. I don't want to make a mistake with the rest of our lives."

Jamie was struck dumb. He continued to kneel before her without moving.

"Please," she barely whispered.

The spell was broken as Randy crashed into their reverie.

"Wow! Mom! This is wild! One of the men let me ride his horse! He even made it run a little! I got to hold a real sword, too! This is better than a trip to the space station!"

As fast as he roared in, he raced away, leaving the disconsolate pair in the same position.

Jamie was first to speak. "You know I love him, too."

"Yes, I realize that. Please give me some time. It's just too much for me right now."

Jamie forced a smile. "Sure, I know you delicate southern types," he joshed.

A faint smile returned to her face.

"Until Thursday? Do we still have a date?" he asked.

"Of course, you silly Yankee." She tried to be light, but it was only partially successful. "I don't want this to change what we have."

Later, as she drove to visit her parents, she wondered why she considered the next five days a reprieve. "Oh well, five days is a lifetime. Lots can happen in five days."

"What, Mom?"

"Oh, nothing, dear. I was just thinking out loud."

Tuesday, October 5, 2021.

The droning of a fly, circling near the windows, blended perfectly with the droning of Miss Larson. Randy lazily watched the fly circle and escape through the window into the mild October afternoon. Outside it was one of the last perfect days packed between the hot, sticky summer and the frigid days of winter to follow. *It isn't fair to have to sit in school on a day like this,* thought Randy.

"Mr. Caldwell! Am I interrupting your nap?"

Randy snapped his head around to find the whole class looking at him and grinning.

"Uh—no. I—I was just thinking," stammered Randy.

"I see. Well possibly you could think about the question I just asked."

"Sure, Miss Larson. Um. What was the question again?"

Several of the students were openly giggling by this time. Randy felt his face turning red.

"Ah, yes, the question. The question is, 'Can you name two of the main Indian leaders at Little Big Horn and name their tribes?'" Miss Larson folded her arms and rocked on her heels.

Wildly, Randy scanned the page in the book on his desk. The words were a blur. They made no sense to him. Panic set in. Words raced through his mind and suddenly the answer appeared.

"Yes! Raging Bull and Cochise!"

The immediate peals of laughter from the class alerted him to his error. A red flush zoomed to his hairline.

"Perhaps, Mr. Caldwell, you would do better to listen in class and read your material instead of gazing out the window," intoned Miss Larson.

Mortified, Randy hung his head and studied the picture in the open book on his desk.

The caption under the old, grainy photo read, *Custer and his officers prepare for action with the Sioux.* Four men, arrayed behind their leader, posed rigidly in full uniform. Slightly to the front, George Armstrong Custer peered haughtily at the camera. As Randy concentrated on the photograph, details began to emerge. Although the picture was black and white, Randy realized the uniforms were actually deep blue with gold trim. *Gee,* he thought, *those uniforms are just like the ones the colonel wears when he goes out to do those Civil War battles. If the colonel were here, he'd show everybody. I'll bet he knows everything about Indians and soldiers. Why did mom say he wasn't coming back? He'd show all these stupid kids—Miss Larson, too.*

TWO

June 29, 1863

My Dearest Brother,

Greetings from your wandering brother. Since I last wrote I've traveled far distances and seen much bloody killing. Mother of God, I believe 'tis the luck of the Irish which has kept me from harm. All round me I've seen death at close hand, but have bin spared even a scratch. All Saints be praised.

I'm on the move again. I've bin assigned to General Buford's staff and we've crossed the Potomac into Maryland chasing Gen'l Lee. Word is that Lee's moving north, possible into Pennsylvania, and we're suppose to catch him, but still protect Washington City—a very nervous place. We've had several hot little skirmishes with the Rebs, but, so far, no decisive action. I pray this condition continues. I've a new command and most of my men are green boys from the farm. I also don't know Gen'l Buford, or how he fights.

The country thro which we're passing is pleasant enough, tho hot. It reminds me of the home

*of our birth, tho my memories of that place are dim. I
do laugh occasionally when we travel thro what
passes for mountains here. My men do not totally
believe my stories of how great are our Rockies. How
I do miss them, and you!*
    *Here I must stop. A rebel patrol's been
reported and we must move. Lord bless the people of
this region who are so faithful in reporting the enemy
to us. More later.*

"You're lookin' a little peaked, Major."
    It was true. Major Matthew O'Shaunessey was sagging
in the saddle. His woolen blouse clung to his sweaty body. His
face was streaked with dust and sweat to form a thin, muddy,
slippery coating.
    Straightening his sagging shoulders, he forced a tired
smile. "Sergeant, 'tis true that I'm hot, tired and more than a
little dirty. However, I will survive this purgatory, Lord willin',
and still be ready to face Johnny Reb. 'Course, we got to catch
'im first."
    "Oh we'll catch him, sir. That we will. Question is, what
we gonna do with 'im when we got 'im?" Without waiting for
an answer, the sergeant pulled his horse to the side of the road
to check the line of troopers behind them.
    Major Matthew, "Matt," O'Shaunessey was the new
man. Two years had passed since he left the mining region of
Colorado with a dozen other men who answered the call to
arms. Two years of fighting and frustration. Now he was the
sole survivor of the First Colorado Volunteers. After
Chancellorsville, he was the last man from "The Rocky
Regiment," as they had called themselves, left alive in the
Union forces. The orders bringing him to Buford's staff had
been a surprise. He felt lonely among these strangers.
    Matt's shoulders sagged anew as thoughts of his
companions from Colorado pushed into his mind. Ahead and
behind, the Army of the Potomac stretched like a long blue
snake through the farm country. *And this is only part of the army,*
thought Matt. *As far as I can see, there's no man who knows me
well. I'm a stranger among strangers. There's no man in this long
line to call friend. 'Tis a sad day for the Irish.*

Wednesday, July 1, 1863. Near Gettysburg, Pennsylvania.

It appeared the chase was over. Leading elements of Buford's cavalry had encountered stiff resistance on the road to Cashtown. Matt listened as messengers reported to Buford that their units had been pushed back to the south, through the small village of Gettysburg, where they were finally meeting with infantry reinforcements. Confusion reigned as firing from both sides increased in intensity.

The Union forces established hasty defensive positions at the base of a low ridge dominated by a Lutheran seminary. Before them, rocks and trees had been cleared by farmers on the level ground. Across the planted fields, Confederate troops fanned out behind the cover of low fences on the brushy plain.

The cavalry units left their horses behind the crest of the ridge and squirmed into the line of defenders. It was the beginning of a long, hot day.

A shower of leaves, twigs and small branches made Matt pull his head lower between his shoulders. Confederate artillery was finding the range.

"Damn, them rebs!" he muttered.

"Be better if'n we can find us a hole a mite deeper, Major. I reckon they got lots more grape shot they plan to send our way."

"Be even better if they'd just come at us, Sergeant," responded Matt. He raised his head and shoulders for a better view through the smoke hanging between the lines in the still air. He was rewarded with a whistling akin to an angry bee by his right ear. The sound was followed immediately by a sharp, stinging pain. Instinctively, he slapped his palm to the side of his head. He was amazed to see his hand splashed bright red with blood. "Damn! They got part of my ear!"

The sergeant didn't hear him. Matt looked at him and was shocked to see a messy, jagged hole in his temple. His head was cocked at an angle, his eyes wide open as if in amazement.

Angry now, Matt drew his pistol and fired futilely at the enemy, seeking to punish the man who had drawn his blood and to repay the one who ended the life of the man closest to him.

Through the afternoon, the weight of numbers slowly forced the Union troops to abandon their positions along Seminary Ridge. Matt was among the last to retreat over the crest. Below him, in a shallow depression, the sergeant was one of many casualties abandoned to the Confederates.

By late afternoon, Matt was once again crouched in a hastily scooped-out hole in the Pennsylvania soil. Three-quarters of a mile away, across a fertile valley, Rebs occupied the ridge abandoned earlier. The new Union positions were on Cemetery Ridge. *An apt name,* thought Major O'Shaunessey.

The opposing armies began fortifying their lines as the sun set. Supplies were brought forward. Artillery caissons clanked to new sites where they would be more effective on the morrow, should battle continue. Occasional sharpshooting from both sides kept men alert. Gritty and tired, they labored on or tried to sleep. Occasional artillery fire denied sleep to all but the most exhausted.

July 1, evening

My Dearest Brother,

I must hasten to finish this letter to you. I believe we've found General Lee, or, rather, he's found us. We've passed this day in heated battle.

Perhaps my mood tonight is just a reaction to being under fire for most of the day, but there are things I must say, for I feel quite low.

I'm the last of the boys who left so long ago to fight. Until today I've not been touched by the enemy. Now I have a nice nick in my ear to remind me how close I've come to death. Saints preserve me, it was too close. The man next to me was not so lucky, for he is dead.

We've retreated a short distance from where we were this morning, but this battle is not over. Tomorrow we shall begin again. Even now the big guns from both sides are not still. I fear there shall be a great killing here.

It is possible I shall not survive this battle. If that be the case, I leave all I have to you. Actually

*there is precious little to leave to mark my thirty-one
years. It would be better that I survive to build a
larger estate for my younger brother.*

*But I ramble without purpose. Perhaps this is
but a mood and will change in the morning. I will
seal up this letter now and decide later whether or not
to post it.*

*Work hard, Tim. The mine is our future.
Pray for me, an Irish lad too far from home.*

Affectionately,

> (signed) *Matthew O'Shaunessey, Major of
> Volunteers.*

Friday, July 3, 1863. Gettysburg, Pennsylvania.

Rebel resistance was crumbling. Two days of concerted,
bloody attacks against the tight defensive positions of Union
forces left thousands dead. Even more lay wounded in
makeshift field hospitals or mixed among their dead comrades
in the no-man's land between the almost static lines.

As the noon hour passed—with only sporadic,
desultory firing from exhausted troops—the heat of the day
intensified. Along with heat came an increasing tension along
Union lines.

Colonel Augustus Bowes, with Matt in his wake,
snaked his way among the men along the crest of the ridge.
"Stay alert. Keep an eye peeled there. I figger Johnny Reb's
gettin' ready fer somethin' here."

Shortly after one o'clock, 122 Confederate cannons cut
loose with long range shot, making the air sing and the earth
jump. Dust and smoke mingled with furious sound to pound
the senses of the defenders. Colonel Bowes was among the first
to be cut down by the deadly shot.

The fury of Rebel guns was answered almost
immediately by 77 Union cannons. The fields between the lines
disappeared from view in smoke hanging in the still, hot air.
The greatest artillery duel in United States history was under
way. Major Matthew O'Shaunessey, an erect target among men
dug into the hill behind any protection they could find, threw

himself prone, wriggling his body deep into the bucking earth, his hands clasped protectively behind his head.

Before long there were ominous signs for the Union forces. Fewer and fewer cannons belched flame and smoke behind the dug-in defenders. The weight of Confederate artillery seemed to be reducing Union guns to rubble. New fear rose among the huddled men. They were losing this battle. Confederate shelling suddenly eased. Matt had lost all track of time. His eyes watered, his throat was parched. Covered with dust and sweat, ears ringing from constant explosions, he raised his head and faintly heard the fearsome rebel yell swell beyond the hazy fields. Numbly he fumbled for a discarded rifle while trying to focus his bleary eyes. Only sound penetrated the smoke. There were no targets.

Up and down the line of Cemetery Ridge, from the Devil's Den and Little Round Top on the left, to Cemetery Hill on the right, the popping of rifle fire swelled. Still there was no sign of the enemy before him. Then, as if they were ghostly visions materializing from the smoke, there were hundreds of butternut gray uniforms emerging in his field of vision.

"Mary, Mother of God, protect me. Forgive me, for I have sinned." The words came unbidden even as he sighted and fired again and again. At some point he said a prayer for the new Spencer carbine which freed him from reloading after each shot. Before him, like a relentless wave, came the rolling rebel line. Those who fell seemed not to be missed. The wave was boundless.

Now Union cannons, which had been silent and seemed doomed, pounded a furious, booming counterpoint to the musket fire. Ragged holes showed in the human mass approaching the first line of defenders. Undaunted, the rebs rolled over fences and walls. The fighting below Matt became a confused tangle of blue and gray locked in individual duels. The gray wave rolled up the slope, ever closer to the ridge. Finally, even the crest of the ridge itself was no barrier. Matt prepared to rise. Soon he would be face to face with the enemy. In the corner of his eye he saw a thin wave of blue scaling the top of the ridge and disappearing behind him. He was now the front line.

Jethro Robbins was a lanky farm boy from Alabama. He was amazed he was still alive, still moving forward. He was hoarse. His rebel yells were now mere croaks. Before him, the top of the ridge was being swept clean. He eagerly searched for a target. The bright gold insignia of an officer caught his eye. The man was just rising to his feet.

Two steps. Just two steps and Jethro would have himself an officer. As he swept his bayonet forward, he locked eyes with the Yankee. In them he saw reflected the fierce desire of his own eyes. Conquer—win—live—fight again.

The bayonet was backed by all the force the scrawny, one hundred-thirty pound farm boy could muster. Matt knew, even as he swung his rifle to parry the blow, that he was too late. There was a flash of pain as the steel bit through his tunic and ripped into his belly. His own forward movement assisted to impale him on the blade. His own rifle dropped as he raised his hands to attack the freckled face with the gap between the front teeth, now exposed in a grimace of triumph. Matt's hands clawed for the skinny neck, then fastened like a vise. Surprised, Jethro tried to pull away. The gleam of delight in his eyes changed to clouded uncertainty and fear. Locked together, the two men swayed and twisted atop Cemetery Ridge.

A blinding flash and concussion terminated the struggle. The rebel shell probably should have carried farther, or perhaps the gunners didn't realize just how far their forces had surged in the battle. When the smoke cleared, two charred torsos lay in an eternal embrace.

Sunday, July 5, 1863.

The greatest battle of the Civil War was over, the Union victorious. Rebel prisoners were paired off and assigned to sweep ahead of wagons carting away the detritus of battle. Along ridges and across valleys, men moved slowly, heads bent to their grisly task.

"Yo, Sarge. We've got sumfin ovah heah." The voice came muffled from behind a scrap of cloth covering the prisoner's nose and mouth.

He, and his partner, were standing at the edge of a shallow crater on the crest of Cemetery Ridge. From the crater an angry swarm of flies rose from their feast, revealing the blackened meat and tattered bits of cloth where they had been feeding.

Two rifles, two pairs of boots with stumps of legs protruding and two torsos lay entwined. A Union sergeant hustled up and took in the scene. Although hardened by two years of war, bile rose in his throat as he studied the remains. "Okay, let's see what we got here." One of the rebel prisoners bent over and nudged the corpses with his gloved hand. "Looks like we got us one of our'n 'n' one of your'n." A bit of gold braid on dark blue serge was revealed below. "Mebbe your'n was an officer." "Could be. We'll never know for sure the way them two is blown to bits. Git the wagon over here 'n' load 'em up."

On the board he carried, the sergeant added two hash marks—one Confederate, one Union—in the column marked "Unknown."

As the bits and pieces were lifted from the depression, a scrap of paper fluttered loose and floated to the ground at the sergeant's feet. Idly he picked it up and glanced at it. As he smoothed it, he could read: *"My Dearest Broth...."* He crumpled it, dropped it and moved ahead when another team called.

Monday, August 10, 1863. Near Leadville, Colorado Territory.

Elijah Stone looked up from the ore he was sorting. An ominous rumble and slight tremor through the ground had distracted him. As his eyes swept the rocky slope, he saw the billow of dust from the shaft entrance to The Irish Rose. Not ten minutes earlier he'd waved to Tim O'Shaunessey as Tim disappeared into the mine.

Elijah dropped the rocks he was working and ran across the talus slope to the entrance. Choking clouds of dust stopped him from entering.

"Tim! Tim O'Shaunessey! Can you hear me?" Vainly he waited for an answer.

By dusk a group of miners cleared the worst of the cave-in. One of the smaller men squeezed through the narrow opening they'd created. Just beyond the pile of rubble he saw Tim's legs emerging from below the mound of rock and earth. In the flickering candlelight the legs seemed to be moving. He slid his hand up under the pant leg. The skin was cold; the leg stiff. There was no need to hurry now.

Three days later, Timothy O'Shaunessey was laid to rest in the rocky soil near the lean-to shelter just below the mine entrance. The Irish Rose was boarded up to await the return of the other owner—Matthew O'Shaunessey.

12:30 a.m., June 23, 1876. Rosebud River, Montana Territory.

A chill wind fanned the flames of dying fires throughout the encampment. George Armstrong Custer sat alone on a folding chair, wrapped in his campaign coat, lost in private thoughts. The motion of a passing officer roused him from his reverie.

"Lieutenant!"

"Yes, sir?"

"A moment of your time?"

"Of course, sir."

"You seem restless tonight, Lieutenant." Custer leaned back in his chair, boots to the dying fire. "You ever do any Indian fighting before?"

"No, sir."

"But I heard you came from the west, before the war, that is."

"That's true, sir, but my brother and I had a gold mine in Colorado. I wasn't in the army then."

"A gold mine? How come you're here if you have a gold mine?"

"I don't have it anymore, sir. I found out after I returned to Washington that my brother died thirteen years ago, may he rest in blessed peace, and the mine is no longer my property."

Custer eyed the Lieutenant speculatively. "Ah, yes, your miraculous resurrection and return to duty. Fascinating." He reached a decision. "Lieutenant, I'm detaching you from the pack train. I want you to act as my adjutant for this campaign. Although you haven't fought Indians, I can always use a man with pluck and luck close to me. Besides, I liked your attitude at the briefing this evening. You're obviously spoiling for a fight, as am I. If everything goes as I suspect, we'll make history on this campaign. More than enough glory for all and they'll still be writing about our exploits a hundred years from now. Report to me in the morning."

"Yes, sir!" Lieutenant Matthew O'Shaunessey saluted sharply and turned away, his face a wooden mask, his thoughts jumbled.

THREE

Thursday, June 17, 2021. Berkeley, California.

The persistent pulsing of the wrist telephone roused Lincoln Long from a deep, peaceful sleep. The luminous clock on the nightstand read 4:37. Linc fumbled for the button to answer the call. The pulsing stopped as he mumbled, "Hullo."

"Hey Long," came the jovial response. "Shake a leg. Up 'n' at 'em Injun."

"Damn it," yawned Linc, "I've told you not to call me that."

"Yeah, yeah. Listen, Johnson wants you at the lab, and I mean pronto."

"Does he know what time it is?"

"Nope, and he don't care. He says get you—now."

"What's the big deal?"

"He wants those reports you're working on. I think he's solved the variable magnetics problem, but you have all the latest data. The computer copy here is no go."

"Jesus, Jerry, if that's all he wants, I'll put it on the modem and go back to sleep."

"Nice try, pal, but he wants your high powered personal computer here. Two brains are better than one, right? Quit arguing and get dressed. I'll see you here." There was a click and the line went dead.

Linc yawned and shook his head to clear the cobwebs. Mumbling softly he rolled off the mattress and padded to the bathroom. His roommate, Bill, snored softly in the other bed.

Linc and Bill were both graduate students at the University of California at Berkeley. Linc's specialty was sub-atomic physics while Bill's field was molecular biology. Both had been tapped as assistants by Professor Demetrius Johnson, often referred to as "Einstein's Perfect Pupil, a man who could now teach the master." Johnson was renowned for his many accomplishments in the fields of mathematics, physics and chemistry. He was also well known for his unorthodox methods and schedule. Occasionally he'd been known to work for 72 hours at a time when he was hot on a promising lead. By the time most people would be considered technically brain dead from lack of sleep, Johnson would reach his sharpest peaks. The early morning call was not unusual.

Linc debated whether or not he had time for a quick shower. "Yes," he mumbled. "Johnson can wait." Chances were good the session might last until the sun set once more.

Revived by the shower, he studied his reflection as he combed his shoulder-length black hair. He found it amusing that people seldom placed his ancestry. They would study his black eyes, broad face with prominent cheekbones and his full lips. The straight black hair, often worn in a ponytail, combined with a skin tone usually described as "copper colored" just didn't fit with the name Linc Long. The guessers usually pegged him as a south sea islander or Malaysian.

They might have had better luck if they knew Linc's full name was Lincoln Long Trail, or if they could see the elaborately fluted white arrowhead on a chain around his neck. Even then, it was a stretch to place him as a Lakota Sioux. Berkeley was a long way from Pine Ridge Reservation, South Dakota.

Linc fingered the arrowhead on the chain and raised it and brushed it against his lips. "Luck," he mumbled. It was a daily ritual. He considered the relic of another age his personal talisman. It had been passed from father to son for so many generations that now nobody was sure when it started. He did know that an ancestor acquired it from a dead Indian—reputedly a powerful Lakota Medicine Man. The unusual part of the tradition was that the shaman died while visiting the Great White Father in Washington D.C. in the long, lost past. Linc often wondered about the circumstances surrounding the death. Who was the shaman and why was he so great?

With a final twist to the neat ponytail, Linc crossed to the computer and began stuffing reports and computer disks into his backpack. The first gray of a foggy dawn greeted him with a damp chill as he went to the garage behind the old Tudor house on Bancroft Way. The once elegant home had long ago been transformed into student apartments. The garage that once housed elegant automobiles was now home to six motorcycles and a dozen bicycles. Linc's old Kawasaki gave a satisfying roar before settling into a well tuned idle. He gunned the bike down the drive. "If I gotta be up," he muttered, "everybody does."

The streets were practically deserted. He rolled through stop signs and sped toward the Lawrence Laboratory, perched high on a hill overlooking the campus. The lab was originally built to study atomic and sub-atomic particles. The old cyclotron was seldom used these days, but many important breakthroughs in atomic theory had been made in this complex. The laboratory was now used by the Federal Government for top secret experiments. The project Linc was involved in—Project T—was headquartered at the lab. Other components of the project were scattered from Houston, Texas, to Syracuse, New York.

Two gate guards greeted Linc by name as he parked the bike to be scanned. He obediently removed the contents of his pack and submitted to a body scan before pressing his palm on the mirrored surface of the entry door.

"Hello, this is Lincoln Long," he said to the door. Upon confirmation of the voice and handprint, the door slid open. His motorcycle was rolled through the gate. He mounted, gunned the motor and headed toward the lab building.

"About time, Long. Where you been? You have the files?" Professor Demetrius Johnson wasn't known for his communication skills. His style and timing were better suited to super-computers than mere humans.

"Yes, sir. Sleeping, and yes I do." In a pinch, Linc could match the old professor, word for word.

"Well? Where are they?" When the professor was agitated, his chin moved as far forward as his jaw would allow. His eyes sparked below the shock of graying uncombed hair. Sometimes, as now, he leaned his spare frame so far forward it appeared he would topple.

Linc whipped off his backpack and dumped the contents on the nearest workbench.

"Hmmm—no—no. Aha! Yes!" Like a conquering hero, the professor brandished a report above his head as he spun on his heel and made for the nearest computer terminal.

His mission apparently completed, Linc glanced around the lab. Jerry Silver, the assistant who had telephoned, was deeply involved on another terminal across the room. The table next to the plexiglass screen, used to display equations such that everyone in the room could see them, was littered with balled up pieces of paper and empty coffee cups. Behind the plexiglass, the readout on the wall-mounted scientific calculator blinked a message: "Calculations complete. Turn me off." Obviously, it had been some time since the professor used it.

"Long, get over here!" barked Johnson.

Involuntarily Linc cringed.

"Yes, sir!" Mechanically, Linc walked to the table.

"These changes must get to Stockton immediately! Program the fourth equation, first. Make sure the magnets are set on auto. Don't set any safety stops."

"Couldn't we just phone them?" asked Linc.

"They'd screw it up. Just take it! I have other problems."

Linc looked dejectedly at the notes in his hands. The professor was already striding away to his next challenge.

Linc decided it would be easier, and almost as fast, to take BART to Stockton. It would give him time to relax and study the notes.

BART had been a grand design in the last century to link all major cities of the San Francisco Bay area with one rapid transit system. The idea had failed. The voters in two counties, San Mateo and Santa Clara, had not seen the wisdom of the system and wouldn't participate. Ultimately, lines were extended to Sacramento and Stockton instead of to San Jose. The resulting downfall of the Silicon Valley was partially caused by this lack of foresight of the citizens.

Of course, at one time, the land values in the San Jose area were so high there was no chance that the SSLA (Stockton Super Linear Accelerator) would have been built there anyway. Earthquake faults, voter objections and high building costs also contributed to the accelerator being developed in the sprawling farmland of the Central Valley.

One mile wide and sixty miles long, the super accelerator cost seventy billion dollars. Part of the cost was shared with NASA when it incorporated the Low Earth Launch Orbital Facility above the underground accelerator. Now the only complaints were from residents far to the south whenever a shuttle blasted off.

Additional billions of dollars were secretly "appropriated" from other budgets to construct a tube parallel to the atomic accelerator. The existence of the Project T facility was known by less than two thousand people. If the project failed, there would never be any admission of its ever existing.

Linc used time on the train to study the notes he'd been given. He knew there was one seemingly insurmountable problem facing Project T. For months, the entire staff had been directing its efforts to overcoming the complex problem of adjusting magnetic strength in the accelerator to accurately place a traveler in the selected time period. It was a whole new concept. Magnets moved around magnets at high velocity creating an energy wave with unnatural properties. The wave could "bend" matter, creating a funnel effect. An object inserted into the funnel was instantly capable of being transported to another location. The most intriguing aspect of the energy wave was that it created negative time, therefore, it could be programmed for precise terminal velocity to move an object both to another location and to a previous time period.

Seemingly more complex problems, such as accurate placement of the subject at the correct elevation in the coordinates designated, at the time chosen, now seemed to be simple exercises. Like the best of inventions, once you discovered the principle and built the apparatus, it was no longer a mystery.

One of the super-computers assigned to the project had been tackling the magnetic strength problem exclusively for two months. The three disks with theoretical solutions could now be tested. Linc studied the accompanying printout, but was soon lost in the jumble of equations. By the time the train left Brentwood station for the last sprint to Stockton, he was lost in thought, watching the farmland roll by.

If this works, he thought, *maybe, just maybe, we can make use of it. I'll have to let Charlie and Ruth know how close we are. I can use a pay phone in Stockton. No way to trace the call. It could happen. We could make it happen. His pulse raced with the thought.*

Charlie Teague was a quiet man. Certainly he would not be called garrulous, however, he was commonly known as "Charlie Talks Too Much." His mother worried that he would never learn to talk, but when he did, he wouldn't stop. She hung the name on him and it stuck.

Charlie was unemployed—again. Even in good years, the unemployment rate at the Pine Ridge Reservation hovered near thirty percent, and this was not a good year. Charlie had been employed only briefly during the spring round-up and branding on nearby ranches. His current state left him many hours to sit in his ramshackle mobile home. Lonely and alone, he escaped with beer, when he could afford it, and dreams.

His dreams revolved around plans, which were always brewing, to make Lakota lands a separate nation. Charlie was a member of The Native American Nation (NAN) which grew out of the American Indian Movement of the last century. Members of NAN continued to lobby in Washington for their goals, but without success. Small gains within the Bureau of Indian Affairs did little to change the sad conditions of reservations. Frustrations occasionally boiled over in violent confrontations with the authorities. Charlie was currently under indictment for assaulting a federal officer during a march in Washington the previous summer. There was no doubt NAN was becoming increasingly violent and radical in its quest for freedom. State and federal law enforcement agencies were stepping up their efforts to quash the organization. Now there were rumors that the militant arm of NAN had been infiltrated. Charlie shared the fear of many others that there could be a raid any time. If the cache of weapons was located....

His thoughts were interrupted by a knock on the door.

"Charlie, you in there?"

Charlie recognized the voice of Old Ed, proprietor of the Lower River Trading Post next door.

"Yeah, I'm here. Whad'ya need?"

"You got a phone call over to the post. Long distance."

"Okay." He belched noisily and dragged himself off the beat-up couch that doubled as his bed. He dragged on his boots and walked to the telephone mounted on the wall of the post.

"Yeah, who wants Charlie?" he asked.

"Your western cousin," came the reply.

"Oh, hello, Cousin. How's the weather?"

"Hot. It looks like it'll be even warmer soon. Can you possibly make arrangements to come for a visit on short notice?"

"Mebbe. Sis has been wanting to make a trip, but we already have another vacation planned soon."

"That may have to wait. I'll only have a few days when I can travel with you. It could be any time now."

"Okay. Let me know. See ya."

Charlie hung up and meandered back to his shack. *That crazy assed Black Feather,* he thought. *Of all the ideas to get a Lakota Nation, his is the weirdest. Maybe I'll be here when he calls and maybe I won't. The trip I have planned will get us some attention. In fact, it just may shake the tree hard enough that a few apples will fall around here.*

Fifteen minutes later, Charlie was snoring peacefully on his sofa. He'd already discounted Linc's plan. It was just too far-fetched.

MANHUNT

ONE

Thursday, July 8, 2021, Lincoln, Nebraska.

Midday sun, burning in an azure sky, bounced heat from the tarmac. Charlie and Ruth Teague arrived early to secure positions where they would have a clear view of the vice president and the secretary of the interior when they arrived. Now the crowd had swelled and they were sandwiched between a police barricade and a communications van belonging to one of the networks covering the arrival.

Charlie appeared somewhat sinister in his Levi's, boots and leather jacket. The placard he carried would be plainly visible to the men as they left the plane. In bold black letters, it proclaimed:

**KILL MY PEOPLE NO MORE
JUSTICE NOW !!!**

Charlie wore his beer in a prominent belly, his hair in braids and his round, flat face and beaked nose were already showing the effects of too much alcohol. Purplish veins gave him an appearance of more than his twenty-six years. His eyes rarely betrayed emotion or inner thoughts—just black holes absorbing but not revealing. His mouth, a thin straight line, was more apt to curve down than up. Smiling did not come naturally, although Charlie's closest friends were aware of his well-disguised sense of humor.

Ruth appeared diminutive next to her two-hundred-fifty pound brother. It wasn't until you got close that you noticed she was 5' 9" tall. She was well proportioned, but large. She discovered long ago that scales were not her best friend, so she was uncertain how much she weighed. Her driver's license said 130 pounds, but she knew that was a lie. Her black eyes appeared intense, but were softened with a sparkle that hinted at mischievous behavior. High cheekbones, a slender nose and full lips in her oval, copper-toned face combined to make Ruth most pleasant to behold.

Ruth worked hard to keep a trim figure and preferred to wear her hair hanging loosely almost to her waist. She was twenty-five this summer, unmarried and bored with life on the land still known as Pine Ridge Reservation. Although she had continued her studies after high school at Oglala/Lakota College and was accredited as a paralegal, there was no work in her field so she worked in a restaurant in Kadoka, up on Interstate 90. She suspected that the owner hired her as a novelty for the passing tourists—a real Indian serving them their authentic buffalo burgers (beef occasionally, but who knew the difference?). Then, too, the greasy s.o.b. never stopped trying to cop a free feel. If it weren't for the excellent tips during the tourist season, she'd have heaved a flaming pan of hot grease in the general direction of his hyperactive crotch a long time ago. *Someday*, she often thought, *I'll save enough money to go away, like Linc did, and Mr. Hot Rocks will have his flame broiled.*

Ruth wasn't carrying a sign today. She was content just to be here, along with more than 300 people from nearby reservations, to see the two men from Washington who would spend the next three days meeting with leaders from NAN and other Indian organizations. Tribal leaders from twelve nations were on hand to meet and discuss grievances spanning 300 years.

Not since the early '90s, when then-President Clinton appointed a Native American to lead the Bureau of Indian Affairs, had hope for real change been so high. President Thomas Bowles appeared to be genuinely concerned about the plight of Native Americans. This trip by the vice president and the secretary had his personal blessing.

The people of Lincoln were also out in large numbers to welcome their native son who had attained the second most powerful job in the United States. A few among them carried messages opposing the ones carried by the Native Americans. Others were openly sympathetic. Most were simply there for the spectacle.

All the local television stations were represented, along with CNN and rival American News Network ("The ONLY news compatible with your hologram viewer."). The ground was littered with snaking cables, and cameras were poised to capture the moment from every angle.

There was a stir among the throng as the sleek aircraft was spotted on its final approach. Restive movement swept along the barricades. Posters and placards were raised. Security personnel—Secret Service, FBI, local and state police—anxiously surveyed the crowd. The guards would not see the distinguished guests until later—on the news.

Most of the news cameras focused on the plane as it taxied toward the open area where microphones were set up for remarks by the distinguished visitors. A few of the cameras zeroed in on the crowd to get intimate shots of joyous people welcoming their heroes.

Charlie and Ruth leaned against the barricades in anticipation. Charlie was pumping his placard up and down when the plane rolled to a stop. They were in a perfect position to see the vice president and secretary when the door opened. The dignitaries would descend the ramp only a hundred yards away. They couldn't help but notice the sign directly in front of the ramp.

Minutes passed before the door was opened and the two men appeared at the top of the ramp. A wild cheer swelled from the crowd as the vice president stepped into the sunshine with his hands clasped above his head. The tall, lanky secretary was only a half-step behind. He immediately raised his right hand and waved wildly, a huge smile on his face.

The first gunshot was lost in the din. The vice president suddenly doubled over. His hands arced down to clutch his mid-section. He staggered back, bumping the secretary who continued to smile and wave.

The second shot hit the vice president in the neck. His head flew back. His body seemed to be snatched into the plane's dim interior.

Before the third shot was fired, the adulation of the crowd began to turn to terror. A deep, animal wailing and incoherent screaming filled the air. Finally, the secretary became aware of what was happening. He half-turned and attempted to catch the vice president's body. Two more shots, in rapid succession, spun the secretary even further. He grabbed frantically for the open door of the plane. The last shot slammed him against the door. It also severed his spine. As he slid, lifeless, to the deck at the top of the ramp, the spectators collectively decided to run. The slow and weak were trampled. Each person chose a path to safety, though they had no idea where it might be safe.

Charlie had enjoyed hunting ever since his grandfather gave him a .22 when he was seven years old. He killed his first deer on a trip to Wyoming when he was ten. He knew the sound of a gunshot.

He was looking directly at the vice president when the first shot hit. By the time he heard the second shot, he had whipped out the old .45 he almost always carried tucked in the back of his waistband under the heavy leather jacket. Ten feet away an FBI agent saw the motion and reacted.

Charlie had barely leveled his pistol when he saw the agent reaching for his shoulder holster.

"My God! What's happening?" screamed Ruth.

For Charlie, time slowed to a crawl. He barely heard Ruth screaming next to him. Shots were being fired. Charlie's instinctive reaction was to protect himself and Ruth. The pistol appeared in his hand as if by magic. Dimly he heard the last two shots. In his peripheral vision he noticed the secretary sliding, in slow motion, to the top of the ramp.

Now the nightmare began.

The FBI agent had light-blue eyes above lightly freckled cheeks. Charlie locked his sight on the agent's eyes just as he blinked. The pistol in Charlie's right hand described an almost lazy arc as his brain directed the motion toward this source of possible danger. Slowly the agent's eyes blinked open. The black butt of an automatic pistol was appearing from under his jacket. The hand gripping the pistol was freckled, like the face, and firm on the butt. Like a tape unwinding, the action suddenly speeded. The barrel of the pistol emerged and whipped toward Charlie. Still Charlie's hand moved with agonizing, maddening slowness.

The burst of flame and kick of the pistol shocked Charlie back from the place where time almost stood still. A neat red hole appeared just above the left eye of the man sworn to protect the vice president of the United States. The agent's shot was a fraction of a second too late. The bullet made a whacking sound as it tore through the metal van just behind Charlie.

"... the hell are you doing!"

Ruth grabbed for his shoulder even as she turned to her right and stepped toward the corner of the van. "Put it away! Come on!"

Charlie numbly turned and followed her around the end of the van as he quickly slipped the pistol back into his belt.

Rick Harker was low man on the totem pole. As the cameraman with the least experience on the ANN News team, he'd been assigned to a bulky, old-fashioned tripod camera placed on the roof of a van. With his face buried in the hood behind the camera and headphones over his ears, his world was reduced to the view through his lens. He'd spent the last twenty minutes making sure he'd be able to pan through an interesting segment of the crowd below him. His attention was drawn to a large contingent of Indians pressed against the barricades directly in front of the place where the plane would taxi to a halt. They would be in perfect position to flash the messages on their placards at the vice president.

Finally, the plane had taxied into position. Even through the bulky headphones, Rick could hear the whine of the jets as they wound down to a murmur.

Moments later, the whine was replaced by the din of hundreds of people shouting greetings in anticipation of the dignitaries. In his lens, Rick could see the greetings from the Indians were less than approving. Some just stood stoically, their faces frozen in malevolent glares.

"Damn, this is good stuff," muttered Rick. "Hell, it'll probably end up in the shit can, though."

When the shots came, they were muffled in his ears. His hands on the camera never wavered. From the reaction of the group in his picture, Rick knew something had happened. He started to tear his eyes away to check what was causing the excitement.

"What the fuck?" A motion in one corner of his picture froze him in place. There was no doubt that a big man next to the barricade had pulled a pistol.

Without conscious thought, Rick's hands moved to center the image and zoom in at the same time. Before the actions could be completed, the pistol swung in the direction of the camera and bucked. A tongue of flame erupted from the barrel. A man in a suit with his back to the camera seemed to jump slightly, then crumpled to the ground. The shot was perfectly centered in the lens.

Someone reached from behind the man with the pistol and dragged his arm down. Without a backward glance, the shooter faced away from the camera and quickly disappeared behind a storage van. Still clutched in his left hand was a boldly lettered sign. Rick caught just two words: JUSTICE NOW!!!

Even as he continued to record the scene, Rick's incoherent screaming joined with those below. Through the lens he could see only the grotesquely sprawled figure in the tan suit, who lay on his back, unseeing eyes fixed on the bright blue canopy above. Around him swirled bits of paper and trash, caught in a light breeze. His head was lying in a bright red liquid halo slowly spreading and mixing with grease and dirt on the tarmac.

There were thousands of pictures, from every angle, of the vice president and secretary as they spun out of this life, but only one camera recorded the death of FBI Special Agent Timothy Johns. One camera caught an assassin in the act. This was the image that would truly shock a stunned nation and world, triggering one of the largest manhunts in history.

8:30 AM, the same morning. Conference Room, SSLA, Stockton.

Professor Johnson impatiently hushed the gaggle of scientists and assistants in the room. "Okay, okay. Pipe down." Around the room, eyes lifted to the podium. Those who were lucky enough to get chairs, leaned forward expectantly. Lincoln Long and his roommate were lowly graduate assistants, relegated to standing in the rear along with lab technicians from the SSLA. Lincoln cradled his coffee and stifled a yawn. For sixteen hours he'd been studying the latest computer information, checking and rechecking the data. Although he didn't rank with the noted scientists sprinkled in the crowd, he knew what this announcement would be. He smiled wearily as he watched. Professor Demetrius Johnson was about to turn the world on its ear.

"Right. You all know we've been fighting a major problem: variable magnetics." Johnson paused and leaned forward. "Well, we've licked it."

Linc was expecting an ecstatic reaction. The announcement, however, was greeted by total silence. *Maybe everyone's as tired as I am,* he thought. Finally someone did stir. Dr. Talbot, from Cal Tech, had a privileged seat at the conference table. Very quietly he asked, "Are you sure, Demetrius?"

Professor Johnson favored his colleague with one of his stony stares. "Course I'm sure. Wouldn't be here if I wasn't."

At that point, the pandemonium Linc was expecting broke loose. A half dozen questions were shouted at once from different parts of the room. Several people jumped up and clapped their neighbors on the back. One rebel yell, from another lowly assistant, split the air. It was several minutes before order was restored.

Dr. Talbot again managed to ask a question. "How soon do we test?"

"Soon as we want," answered Johnson. "Question is, what do we test it on?"

"I'll volunteer," came a voice from the lab staff.

"Nope. No humans yet—maybe never," replied Johnson. "Animal, yes. Large animal. Approximate mass of a human. Only way to be sure."

Manhunt 33

"Why not send a telemetric device?" asked one of the electronics technicians. "We could pre-set it to send a signal to be picked up by one of our satellites from, say five years ago. We could program the message to hold and release to us in the next week or so."

"Won't work. Explain it to 'em, Long."

Linc was shaken from his reverie when he heard his name.

"Oh, yeah. Sure, Professor." Linc strode to the front of the room, feeling the penetrating eyes. "According to the computer, we have a window of time we can access. The conversion of the time and location of the matter involved is, for all intents and purposes, instantaneous. However, even using the minimum energy necessary places any object at seventy years, plus or minus two years, in the past. Since no satellites capable of retrieving and storing a signal were launched until the late 1970s, we'd have to wait until around 2040 to be assured of success. About the best year we can hope to hit for now is 1950. More likely, 1948."

"Are you saying," asked Dr. Talbot, "that our margin of error is that wide? Two years is a long time."

"No, Dr. Talbot. That differential only applies at the thresholds of the time span we can access. Our lower limit is sixty years. The other end of the spectrum is 148 years, or about the year 1873. It's a function of energy. The closer we move to the center of the spectrum we can access, the more accurate placement becomes. At most, we miss a targeted date by three to five days."

Professor Johnson spoke up. "Face it. The only way we know it works is if we send an animal. Got to send one approximating a human."

"A chimp?" asked someone.

"Possible. Probably the best choice." Johnson was stroking his chin and glaring at his audience.

"How the hell do we know it got there? Or what kind of shape it was in when it does arrive?"

There was a short silence.

"Newspaper." The single word hung in the air.

"Eh, what are you saying?" asked Johnson.

The woman who had spoken stepped away from the wall. "Newspaper," she repeated. "It's simple. Send your voyager back to a populated area, like Washington, D. C., where it's sure to be noticed. A chimp suddenly appearing on a street near the White House in 1950 would certainly be reported in the newspaper. All you have to do is check the archives at the *Washington Post* to make sure the story appeared. It would probably even tell you what shape the chimp was in when it was found."

"That's crazy. If someone found a chimp strolling down Pennsylvania Avenue in 1950, they'd just assume it escaped from a zoo or ran away from a private owner. About the only mention it might get is in the personals. 'Lose your chimp? Call this number.'" The speaker crossed his arms in apparent satisfaction.

"No, no it may not be crazy," said Dr. Talbot. "Suppose, just suppose that instead of a chimp, which is fairly common, we send some more exotic animal. Maybe a —"

"Kangaroo?" suggested Linc.

The suggestion was greeted with giggles and wide smiles.

"Sure! Why not?" said Talbot. "It makes sense. A large kangaroo should approximate the mass of a human. Also, it's much less likely to be wandering around loose, especially—especially if we dump it in, say, 1880 instead of 1950. They had newspapers then. No sense sending it cross country either. We can dump it right here in Stockton."

"One problem," interjected Johnson. "Would we be able to find the papers from 1880? Didn't have microfilm yet."

"We could call the *Stockton Record* and see if they have an archive," suggested Linc.

"Are we really serious about this?" Roger Graham, Senior Vice-President of McDonnell/Lockheed had been silent to this point. His company was the major contractor for the transport pods for Project T. "Are you really going to use a $30 million vehicle to transport a—a kangaroo?"

"Looks like it," replied the professor. To Linc he said, "Check the newspaper angle. Go!"

"Yes, sir!" he might just as well have added "slave" to the command.

Two hours later the primary decisions were in place. Concrete planning for a trial within a week was proceeding. There was an air of unreality in the room. Every so often one of the planners would sit back and shake his head. They were really going to attempt to accomplish one of man's oldest dreams. Soon, time travel might be as common as trips to the space station.

The meeting was suddenly thrown into disarray as the door burst open. A breathless secretary gasped the news. "The vice president's been killed! It's on TV!"

A murmur swept the room, Professor Johnson flicked a control button at the dais. The screen on the wall behind him popped to life.

"... the scene just moments ago as the vice president and secretary of the interior crumpled at the top of the ramp." The announcer's voice was obviously strained as the dramatic scene unfolded. Linc caught only fragments of the description as the same tableau was repeated from various angles. "... just landed at Lincoln ... to meet Native American leaders ... big conference ... many shots ... possibly others injured."

Linc felt a cold knot deep in his guts. Although there had been no hint as to the identity of the assassin, the fact that so many of his people were gathered there made it almost certain Indians were involved. *Oh God*, he thought, *what if it gets tied to NAN? What if someone I know pulled the trigger? What if....*

His thoughts were interrupted by a new tone in the announcer's voice. "This just in. An FBI agent has apparently been killed also. We're just getting video now."

The image was confused as the picture of the crowd near the barricades showed people throwing themselves to the ground or running in obvious panic. As the camera moved and zoomed in, a big man with a pistol dominated the center of the screen. Linc gasped. The tension in his guts exploded as he recognized his cousin. *No, no*, he screamed silently. *Oh no, not Charlie!*

Nobody noticed Linc's distress; they were too mesmerized watching the event unfold. Only rarely had an actual murder been captured on film as it happened. The raw action, the finality, the knowledge there was no director in the background to call "Cut!" made this scene irresistible to every viewer. Later, reruns would show, in dramatic stop motion, every frame. The outcome never varied, but millions continued to watch the replays in fascination.

By the time the grisly scene faded, Linc was in a state of shock. He'd just watched his cousin calmly execute another man. Although his image was only visible for two or three seconds, it would be enough to identify him and condemn him. Charlie Talks Too Much was a walking dead man. Only the back of Ruth's head was visible, but Linc was certain the authorities would quickly tie her to her brother. Overcome, Lincoln Long Trail collapsed into a nearby chair.

Evening. Weston, Maryland.

The day's events cast a pall over the dinner. Kimberly wanted this evening to be special, reassuring to Jamie. She had dressed with care, chosen a special wine and taken extra pains with the meal, but it was difficult to rise above the specter of the double assassination.

Over dessert and coffee, they finally brought the conversation to a personal level.

"Jamie, I know I've disappointed you," Kimberly began.

"No, no. You haven't..."

"Yes, I have, but I want to explain. It's not that I'm not fond of you. I am. In fact I find you to be an exciting, loveable man, but you have to remember I wasn't on a manhunt when we met. David is dead. I know that. But I'm not quite ready to make another commitment."

Jamie wished there was some way to end the conversation, to bury the pain, stop the fascination he had watching her lips, but there was no easy way to escape.

"On the other hand, Randy needs a father and he certainly likes you. I can see that the two of you could be very good together. I like that."

"Then our problem is, what? Time?" asked Jamie.

"Time is part of it, but there's something else. It's hard to explain. I—I worry about losing you. If there was another war, you'd want to be where the action is. I saw the thrill, the exultation, last Saturday. You're a warrior and that bothers me."

Jamie took time to collect his fractured thoughts. He stood and slowly walked around behind her chair. He placed his hands on her shoulders and softly massaged the base of her neck.

"Kimberly, I only know one thing for sure. I love you and want to spend the rest of my life with you. I'm willing to wait, willing to make some changes, if necessary. Just let me know I have a chance."

Kimberly rose and faced him. "Hold me. Love me." Jamie folded her in his arms. Their embrace was total. His hands moved to slip the dress from her shoulders. She didn't resist. Tears slipped onto her cheeks, but her body pressed against his. She buried her face in his neck, gripped him fiercely and surrendered herself to their common need, each for the other.

Jamie clutched her tightly and smiled through his pain. In time he knew they would be together. They just needed time.

TWO

Monday, July 12, 2021. Berkeley, CA.

The phone was ringing when Linc opened the door to the apartment. He set a bag of groceries down and grabbed the receiver. "Hello, Linc here."

"Hi, Cousin."

Linc's heart skipped a beat.

"Ruth—er—Oh hi." His mind raced. One of the most wanted people in the United States had just surfaced in his ear. For three days the news had been filled with pictures of Ruth Teague and her notorious brother, Charlie. The sharply defined film clip of the shooting in Nebraska had replaced the old, grainy shot of Jack Ruby killing Lee Harvey Oswald as the most famous on-camera homicide ever. Linc had stopped watching the news. He was afraid he would have to sit through a protracted shoot-out with holed-up terrorists, who happened to be distant cousins, one of whom shared his first kiss. In his mind it was a foregone conclusion that Ruth and Charlie were as good as dead.

"You still there, Cousin?" Her voice sounded calm, untroubled.

"Uh—yeah. I just hadn't expected to hear from you. Nice surprise." Linc strained to make his voice sound normal.

"Well, we've been on vacation, but we're hoping to have a chance to see you."

Linc waited for her to continue. When she didn't, "Oh, I see. I'm not sure this is a good time. I'm real busy these days." A new picture floated in Linc's mind. Three bodies being removed from the scene of a shootout—in his apartment. This could be very dangerous.

"That's right. Your mother told me you're working on a project, very secret, and it's looking real good. Must be exciting."

"It's just work, but it keeps me occupied." *How do I find out what they want? Where are they? What if they come here?*

As if she were reading his mind, Ruth continued. "I'd really be disappointed if we can't get together. I'll be camping in the place you showed us on the last trip. I'll be there tonight. Why don't you stop by for awhile? We can catch up on the news from home."

Immediately Linc pictured the spot she was describing. The camp was a primitive site in Redwood Park, not far off Skyline Boulevard in the Oakland hills. A rough fire trail passed through the camp by a small stream. Although the site was seldom used for overnight camping, it was popular with day hikers. Linc could think of lots of places more remote, better for the fugitives. His heartbeat quickened. It was just after 8 o'clock. The sun would set before he arrived.

"Well, maybe I can get away for a little while."

"Good. It'll be wonderful to see you" He could hear the relief in her voice. "And Linc, could you bring something for dinner? I haven't had time to shop."

"Sure, see you there." His hand was trembling when he replaced the receiver.

The camp appeared deserted when Linc rolled his motorcycle silently into the redwood grove. Skirting park rules, he had inched the bike past the barricade on Skyline Drive when he felt sure he was not being observed. The fire road ran mostly downhill and he coasted with the engine and headlight off, praying he wouldn't meet a stray hiker. On the uphill portions, he dismounted and pushed the bike, sweating in the warm evening air. He saw only a pair of deer crossing the trail.

A barely audible whistle from the brush to his left caused him to whip his head in that direction. He set the kickstand and released his tightly wrapped fingers from the handlebar. Charlie loomed up silently only a few paces away, his bulk huge in the gloom.

"Evening, Cousin. Any problems?"

Linc gulped and tried to relax. "Nope. Didn't see anybody."

Out of the shadows another figure appeared. "Hi, Linc. It's been a long time." Ruth tried to remember how long. It must have been five years since she visited Berkeley with her mother. Part of that trip had been an afternoon hike in this park and Linc had shown her this spot where he camped and fished, illegally, on occasion. He had matured into an attractive young man from the previous time she had seen him.

When he had left for college there was a big family gathering. The occasion attracted all members of Linc's *tiyospaye*, the extended family, including Ruth and Charlie. Everyone at the party was making approving noises about this rising star of the reservation, especially Ruth's mother. Although he was only two years older, he seemed so mature, so sure of himself. She remembered walking along the river with him and how surprised she was to find out he was really very shy. He held her hand, but she almost had to corner him before he kissed her. Before the celebration ended there were more kisses and vows to write. She was the better correspondent, but he had remained true to her through the long separations. His success also helped put more pressure on her for her last year of high school and college on the reservation. She was curious to see how he looked now, but it was hard to tell in the gathering darkness.

"Did you bring some food?" she asked.

Linc motioned to the box strapped to the rack on the bike.

"I hope you got somethin' in there we can eat cold. I'm starved." Charlie moved forward as he spoke. Involuntarily, Linc retreated a step. Charlie didn't seem to notice. He was focused on the box of food.

"We haven't had a thing to eat since yesterday," said Ruth. "Once they I.D.'d me, we didn't dare show our faces."

"How the hell *did* you get here?" asked Linc.

"Drove," replied Charlie around a mouthful of bread. "You drove? Just like that? Every cop in the country is looking for you, and you just drove your car from Nebraska to California?"

"Not my car," mumbled Charlie. "You got any beer?" Linc gestured to the box. Charlie continued talking as he groped in the box. "My car was busted when we went to Lincoln. I sort of borrowed one from Old Ed. He must have about fifteen sittin' around the post. He probably don't know it's gone yet."

"We stayed pretty much on back roads," said Ruth. "I drove. Charlie mostly hid on the floor in back. We kept listening to the radio and it never sounded like the law had a clue to where we were. We just kept driving until the car ran out of gas in Colorado. We dumped it in a gully and swiped a truck. That lasted 'til somewhere in Nevada. We walked most of the night and found another car the next morning. We've got it stuffed up a dirt turnout on a back road about a mile from here."

"Where'd you get food?"

"Busted up a few vending machines in closed gas stations," answered Charlie. "Shit, I'm sick of candy bars and potato chips. They ain't got no beer machines either." He punctuated his remark with a healthy belch and opened a second beer.

As they talked, the gloom deepened. Gray fog crept through the redwood grove, muffling sound and making even close objects blurry. Linc began to shiver, but knew a fire was out of the question.

"So, what now?" asked Linc. "You can't just keep stealing cars and running forever."

Charlie set his beer aside. "That's where you come in, Cousin. How's your project coming?"

"You mean the time travel?"

Charlie nodded while studying Linc.

"We don't know yet. We're planning to test it this week." Realization suddenly lit his eyes. "You're not thinking—?"

"You're the one who first said we should do it, Cousin."
"Yeah, but—but—I mean you told me I was crazy. Remember?"

Ruth spoke up softly. "Linc, that was then, this is now. Everything's crazy now. You're right. If we stay here we're dead. Charlie didn't mean to kill that man and we didn't know anything about the assassination before it happened, but nobody—and I mean nobody—will ever believe that."

Charlie nodded agreement. "Besides, Black Feather, I—"

Linc stiffened. "Don't call me that," he hissed. "If anyone finds out about that, I'm cooked. All the work, everything I've done, everything I'll ever do—it'll all be gone."

"As I was saying, Cousin, you've made believers out of lots of people. You're the only one who'll ever have the opportunity to change our history—to find out if you're right."

Ruth spoke calmly. "It was your idea, remember? Think about it Linc. You told us about how it could all be done. We know you can do it. We trust you. Besides, we don't have lots of choices."

Linc sat heavily on a nearby stump, his mind whirling. Finally, he spoke, slowly and softly. "I do believe I may be right. Until the very day of the battle there were people on both sides who counseled peace. Custer disobeyed orders when he attacked. He could've just as easily disobeyed his orders and talked peace. Tatanka Yotanka might have proposed talks—with the right encouragement. It might have been different. I've spent time studying everything, but I might be wrong."

The light was gone now. Ruth's voice floated out of the deep blackness surrounding them. "Think on it Linc. Go back to your warm room and your work. Think about what we could do. What we could do for The Lakota. If you're right, what occurred last week will never happen. Three men who died wouldn't have been there. No conference would have been necessary."

Linc was silent for several moments. "Of course you realize *you* wouldn't be here if it weren't for what happened. We wouldn't be having this conversation." He rose and paced for several moments before facing them. "What makes you think history *can* be changed? Are we God?"

Charlie rose and placed his hand on Linc's shoulder. "There's only one way to find out. Go. Do like Ruth says. Come back tomorrow night with more food. We'll talk again."

"I don't know," replied Linc. " Maybe we're all crazy."

"Linc, before you go, think about this. If we don't try, *nothing'll* ever change," said Charlie. "Just get it done, Cousin." As Linc prepared to leave, Ruth moved close and stopped him. "Bring more food tomorrow, and some gas. The car is about out."

"And beer," said Charlie. "Bring lots of beer."

Ruth wrapped her arms around Linc's neck and kissed him. He held her closely, his heart beating wildly, then she turned and followed Charlie into the trees.

Linc stood still, the vision of her imprinted in his mind. He felt flushed, excited by her presence. "Get a grip, Injun," he muttered, then, smiling foolishly, pushed the motorcycle into the night.

The trail rose sharply just beyond the camp, then dipped down to follow the canyon to a back road just over a mile away. Linc breathed easier when he found the road deserted and kicked the engine to life. It was almost midnight when he reached his apartment.

Tuesday, July 13, 2021.

"Hey, where were you last night?" asked Bill.

"Oh, uh, I was feeling kind of like I needed some time to myself. I just went out and rode the bike around." Linc felt naked, exposed. He was only wearing his shorts, but he felt uncomfortable with the knowledge of his evening with the fugitives.

"Well you'd better get your shit together today. Johnson is calling for the whole crew to be in Stockton tomorrow. Big day. Test time, baby."

"Already?"

"Nothing to it. Johnson got the test animal, everything checks out. Why wait?"

"Bill, doesn't this bother you at all?" asked Linc.

"Why should it? This is what we've been working for. It's crunch time. The age-old dream is about to come true."

Linc couldn't sit still. He rose and paced the room. Unconsciously, he plucked at the arrowhead hanging around his neck.

"What is it with that arrowhead? You always play with it when you're nervous."

"Oh, it's just a habit. My grandfather gave it to me. Said it was good luck. He told me his grandfather took it off a dead man who changed our history. He told me, well, he told me to never lose it. Nothing important. Now it's ethical questions that bother me. Should we be doing this? What if someone goes back and screws up our entire history?"

"Not to worry, chum." Bill sat with his hands clasped behind his head, totally relaxed. "First, who's crazy enough to take a one-way trip to wherever, even *if* they could get through the security?"

"Lots of people are *just* that crazy! There're freaks out there who'd just love to test their pet theory of how to change the world. What if someone who worshiped Adolf Hitler went back and advised him? Maybe someone who'd make sure Germany developed the atomic bomb before the United States. You think the world would be the same if the Germans had bombed New York and Chicago?"

"Hey, Linc, don't get all worked up about this. What we're doing is strictly scientific. We're advancing knowledge, not changing history."

"You can't really be that naive."

"Naive? Me?" Bill looked stunned. "Look, I'm a scientist, you're a scientist. We have the opportunity to prove that time is a medium that can be conquered. Sure, there may be applications—someday, but we won't be around to see 'em."

"You're wrong! If the experiment works, someone will use it. Count on it!"

"Well, it'll have to be someone with authorization and I can't think of anybody less than the President of the United States. Even *he* would need the approval of Congress."

"I don't understand how you can so easily discount the wackos and nut cases running around out there. When word of what we've done gets out, there'll be a rush to be the first to make a trip."

"Linc, you're the one who's naive. First, you have to get through the security. Nobody—and I mean nobody—is going to get within shouting distance of the transporter without being triple checked. One slip, bingo, go directly to jail, do not pass go.

"Second, what would someone do if they did get all the way to the control room? Without the correct computer codes they couldn't even access the program for Project T, and if they did access it, they'd never figure the steps necessary to activate the system, set the magnets, insert the coordinates, and on and on. There are what, maybe six of us in the whole world who can make that baby hum. Even on a good day it'd take me two hours to set it up. By that time an entire army would be sitting on top of the SSLA. One little hole, one little magnet knocked off balance and all you have is a broken toy. I tell you it just ain't possible."

Linc stopped pacing in front of the window. He contemplated his reflection in the glass. "Then, if you're right, only one of *us* would have a chance."

Bill cocked his head and studied his friend for a moment. "Linc, you got something on your mind?"

"Me? No. Just thinking out loud."

"Well, I think you should leave security to the pros. Our job is to make it happen, not worry about how it could be misused."

"Sure, you're right. Think I'll get some shut-eye. We may have a couple of long days coming up."

Bill felt uncomfortable. Something was bothering Linc. It was almost as if he knew a present danger existed. Maybe he should say something to Professor Johnson.

Washington D.C., Office of the Director, FBI Headquarters.

Jordan Phillips replaced the gold receiver in the cradle gingerly, as if it might explode if too much pressure was applied. "I guess I don't have to tell you who that was. The Man is not happy. He's about as hot as the asphalt on Pennsylvania Avenue. It sounds like you're sitting on the same griddle, Payne, if you didn't know it."

"Jesus, Jordan, you're not nearly as close to the fire as I am. He's so damn mad he's stopped even talking to me. If we don't catch us a shooter soon, the Secret Service will have a new director."

Kenneth Payne rubbed a hand through his grizzled short hair and heaved an exaggerated sigh. "Hell, he knew I was coming here this morning. This is just his way of getting at me without having to talk to me. So what's up? You said you may have something."

"Well, it's thin, but we have a lead on Charlie and his sister. An agent poking around on the reservation finally got some cooperation. Seems the old guy who runs the trading post next to Charlie's trailer suddenly discovered one of his cars was missing. He's apparently got a veritable junkyard of old clunkers out back. A 1998 Chevy Camaro, unregistered, unlicensed, black and gold, just disappeared. Strangely enough, a car matching that description was found in eastern Colorado on Saturday by the Colorado Highway Patrol. Same day, a pick-up truck was reported stolen from a ranch about a mile away. The pick-up was located yesterday near Elko, Nevada. You see a pattern developing here?"

"Well, like you say, it's thin. It would help if another vehicle was reported stolen about the right time in Elko."

"Today's your lucky day. Seems we have a missing Volvo, Model 2000, Nevada license AVB-459. It was taken sometime night before last from west of Elko."

"California, maybe? They're heading for California. Why?"

Phillips shrugged. "If we knew that, we'd be on 'em like stink on shit. As it is, we've got every law enforcement agency in Nevada, California and Oregon, just in case, looking for the Volvo. We find it, we got ourselves a shooter."

"Which will solve maybe half our problem. We've still got to nail the sniper who got the VP, and I don't have a clue on that one."

Jordan Phillips sat back and let a small smile play across his face. "I may have something on that one too."

"So, give."

"The rifle was wiped clean, no prints, no nothing."

"I know that!" exploded Payne. "Tell me something I don't know!"

"Okay. How about this. We have a picture of the rifle. One of my men found a photo in a house we were searching, along with a lot of Native American Nation literature. Just this morning we got a search warrant for the place and tore it apart. Under the barn there was a secret cellar just piled with rifles, ammunition and explosives. Enough stuff to blow the windows out of every building for two miles if it all went up at the same time. Now we have a couple of redskins on the griddle and they don't like the heat. I expect we'll have name, rank and serial numbers of everyone involved before the sun sets. One thing we know for sure. The guy holding the rifle in the picture was not our shooter."

"Okay, I'll bite. Why not?"

"He's dead. Got himself knifed outside a bar six months ago. Somebody else inherited that rifle. I'll bet you ten to one when we find out who that someone is, we'll have our shooter."

Ken Payne sat quietly, deep in thought. "One thing I don't understand."

"What's that?" asked Phillips.

"Why California? Why the west coast at all? Everything I've seen on this guy indicates he tends to stay pretty much at home. Why wouldn't he head for the place he knows best? Or even jump across into Canada? We'd play hell trying to flush him out of some of that country, so why California?"

"Dunno. Maybe he figures to lose himself in the big cities on the coast. Could be he's trying to jump a ship—get out of the country."

"Could be something else. Maybe our good ol' boy from South Dakota knows someone in California. Lots of rugged country out there too. With help he could lose himself somewhere in the Sierras, for instance."

Phillips shrugged his shoulders. "Who knows? When we find the car, we'll have some answers. I'll tell you one thing, there aren't many of his Sioux brothers in California. NAN is pretty much a Dakotas thing."

"Just the same, you might have your men see if they can dig up anything on the reservation. Maybe, just maybe, he has a friend out there."

Jordan Phillips let out a long breath. "Okay. I'll tell the teams to check it out. Shall we get word to The Man about what we know?"

Ken Payne was rising to go. "No, not yet. Let's see if we can get something more concrete first. He'd talk with the chief of staff, and you know what a blabbermouth he is! The fewer people know about this, the less chance we'll have a leak. The last thing we need is to tip off our shooters. I want to nail those bastards!"

Evening, Oakland hills.

Linc was puffing hard from the effort. The motorcycle was unwieldy with the load of gas and food strapped on the back. Once again the trail was deserted, for which he was thankful. It would be difficult to explain the supplies to any curious hikers.

The meeting at the camp was short. Charlie headed for the cold beer like a man crawling out of the desert.

"Any news, Linc?" asked Ruth. She sat with her back resting against one of the smaller redwoods in the grove.

"No, nothing new. The news people keep stirring the same items. It sounds like everyone's getting frustrated. Listen, I'm on my way to Stockton. I have to be there in the morning. We're going to run the test tomorrow."

Charlie wandered up in time to hear the last comment. "So, what happens in this test?"

"We're going to try to send a kangaroo back."

"A what? Shit, why do that? I don't get it."

"The kangaroo approximates the weight of a man. We send it back to where it'll be sure to be noticed. Hopefully, if it works, it'll be written in the newspaper. Then all we have to do is check the old newspapers to see if a story shows up."

"Shit, sounds crazy to me," said Charlie. "Why don't you shove a stiff in and send it back. You'd get a big headline when some guy is found dead in the middle of main street somewhere."

"One thing wrong with that, Charlie. If the guy's already dead, we won't know if the trip would've killed him."

Charlie took a slug of beer while he thought about it. "So, what about us?"

"Just lay low here. I brought you enough food to last a few days. Also, gas up the car. I'll get away as soon as I can. We may have to move fast."

Ruth had been sitting quietly. Now she rose and joined the men. "Linc, we may have to move out of here before you get back. Is there a place we could meet you near Stockton?" "You're probably safest right here. It's hard to hide in a big, flat valley." "We're safest here until someone spots us. Then what do we do? Kill again?" There was a flicker of pain in her eyes. Linc found her face, her eyes, her hair suddenly very attractive. She seemed so vulnerable. He considered for a moment. "Okay, I've got an idea. When the SSLA was built, some of the locals sued to have the government buy their properties because they didn't want to live near it. SSLA bought lots of properties up and down the valley. Some of them are still vacant. There's one big place not far from the main gate. Here, I'll show you." He pulled out a piece of paper and drew a map for her. "When I head back, I'll check there." He flashed her what he hoped was a reassuring smile, holding his eyes on hers for an extra heartbeat. He was rewarded with a shy, tentative half-smile.

As he pushed the motorcycle away from the camp, Linc heard another pop-top click. Charlie was making short work of the beer.

THREE

Wednesday, July 14, 2021.

It had been a tense night in the dormitory wing of the headquarters building at the SSLA. Almost everyone was up and dressed long before the 5 a.m. wake-up call. Now the hard work of programming the "shoot" was coming to an end. On the monitor on the far wall of the control room was the eerie sight of the large joey, well tranquilized, seated uncomfortably in the transparent ovoid module which would soon catapult it through the magnetic tube to history.

Linc and Bill sat at their consoles as Professor Johnson started the final check.

"Module seal?"

"Airtight. Pressure checks," came a disembodied voice from behind another computer station across the room.

"Vital signs?"

"Heart and respiration normal. Temperature, normal. Brain patterns, reduced to 60%."

"Magnets?"

Bill glanced down at his display. "Calibrated. Showing 100% power available."

"Coordinates?"

"Locked and loaded," replied Linc.

"Elevation?"

"Twenty-four feet," answered Linc.

Linc leaned back and tuned out the balance of the check-off. Primary and back-up systems continued to report full readiness. The capsule was programmed to go automatically at 8:30 a.m., less than 20 minutes from now, unless halted by Professor Johnson.

After much discussion, the decision had been reached to make this first "shoot" right here in the Central Valley. If all went as planned, the kangaroo would land just west of the center of Stockton, in level delta country, on May 1, 1875. The margin of error, according to the computer, was plus or minus six days. The virtually level, treeless plain made an ideal landing site.

Within two minutes of touch-down, the entire capsule would evaporate as a result of changes in molecular structure of its components. All that should appear to any curious soul happening on the site would be a slightly drugged kangaroo and a microprocessor chip, which was the only component that wouldn't disappear completely. At least, mused Linc, this was the theory. By this afternoon, they should know.

On the monitor, the kangaroo appeared calm. His head nodded occasionally and his eyes were unfocused. The veterinarian had set the dosage to last just beyond the 8:30 shoot time. If there were delays, the capsule would have to be destroyed to remove the joey. There was a strong incentive to make the shoot on time.

Linc roused himself from his musings long enough to make his reports on the second check. All systems reported ready. With six minutes to spare, there was nothing to do but wait. Tension in the room mounted with each passing minute. Everyone present realized that what was happening here would irrevocably alter man's perception of time. A large spectrum of the past would be open for exploration. Would it be only a matter of time, wondered Linc, until the team would perfect a system that would allow travelers to return from the past? His thoughts turned dark as he contemplated the possibility that he might be removing himself from this team if today's experiment was successful. Suddenly, he dreaded the thought.

"T-minus one minute," announced an automatic recording. Around the room, faces strained as everyone concentrated on the large screen. The recorded voice continued to count "T-minus twelve... eleven... ten...." Professor Johnson's right hand hovered above the abort button, his intense concentration focused on the visual image. "...nine... eight..." The kangaroo began to stir. One hind leg kicked feebly, a front leg twitched. "seven... six... five..." There was no doubt about it. The head moved, the eyes appeared to focus. "Come on," muttered Linc. "Let's go. Go." Unconsciously, his fingers had poked under his shirt and extracted his arrowhead. He nervously fingered his personal talisman. "Make it happen," he whispered.

"Two... one...." The screen went blank. The kangaroo was gone.

Quickly, Linc jerked his gaze to his digital display. Almost before he could focus, the display registered 'magnetic function complete.'

One theoretical item was immediately confirmed. The capsule and its cargo had been converted to another location, and hopefully, to another time.

Linc realized he'd stopped breathing. He stared numbly at his screen. When Bill slapped him on the back, he almost toppled into the computer.

"Wheee! We did it!" screamed Bill.

Linc sucked in a great gasp of air and turned a silly, lopsided grin to his roommate. All around the room a great cheering noise swelled. Only the professor sat immobile. He stared at the monitor as if waiting for a reappearance of the kangaroo. When he finally did turn away, he was all business.

"Long! Crawford! Get your butts over to the *Stockton Record* office. They're expecting you. Don't come back until you find a story about a kangaroo!"

Still grinning foolishly, Bill and Linc jumped up and ran from the room. Behind them they could hear Johnson restoring order. A victory party would wait until Linc and Bill returned with proof. Until then, there was work to do as the post-shoot analysis began.

11:55 a.m. (EDT) - FBI Headquarters, Washington D. C.

"Mr. Phillips, San Francisco for you on three."

Jordan Phillips set down his briefcase. Lunch could wait. Maybe this was the call he'd been hoping for. He stabbed the button for line three. The image of Walter Reynolds, special agent in charge of the San Francisco office, snapped onto the screen. "Yeah, Walt. What you got?"

"We got the Volvo."

"Damn! That's great. Anybody with it?"

"No."

Jordan's face fell, his jowls sagged. Experienced agents recognized these signs of displeasure and usually shied away when they saw the look of disappointment now blanketing the director's face.

"But the news isn't all bad. It doesn't seem to be abandoned. There are two empty gas cans in the back seat. Just below the gas filler there's a damp spot on the ground. It looks like the car's been gassed up in the last twenty-four hours."

Jordan's features softened. If the car hadn't been abandoned, they still had a chance. "Where's the car?"

"Hidden in some brush on a dirt turn-off from Pinehurst Road in the Oakland hills. You should be getting an e-mail with map and pictures about now."

On cue, his personal computer began to spit out the images. Quickly Jordan scanned the photos of the car, heavily camouflaged with brush. The Nevada license was clear. This was the right car.

"Any sign of our subjects in the area?"

"We found one beer can. Still some beer in the bottom."

"Fresh?"

"Yeah, flat, but fresh. We left it there—left everything just the way we found it. I've instructed the agents who found it to make themselves scarce until we decide what to do."

"Good, good. We don't want to spook our shooter, but get more teams staged ASAP."

"Already doing it. Six teams en route. We've got Oakland P.D. and S.F.P.D. SWAT teams on alert, too. They'll be ready to mobilize in less than half an hour. Three choppers are on stand-by at Oakland International. They can be over the area in eight minutes from lift-off."

"Okay. What's the area like? Any likely hiding places close to the car?"

"It's heavily wooded terrain. Redwood, eucalyptus, pine and brush. There are no structures visible within a half-mile of the car. They could be anywhere in the trees and brush. It'd take days to comb the area."

"Hmm. Okay. Stay on the line." Phillips mashed the intercom button. "Rose, get me General Wright at the Pentagon. Priority. No excuses."

Phillips' mind raced as he waited for the general. Maybe they were in luck. If the agents hadn't been spotted by the fugitives, and if they planned to use the car again, they were dead ducks. On the other hand, if they stole another car in the bay area, it might be days, if ever, before authorities would be able to sort out which car they'd stolen. His thoughts were interrupted by the intercom.

"General Wright on five."

Savagely, Phillips punched the button. "General, what do we have over northern California in the next hour that could take some pictures and heat sensitive shots?"

"Nice to talk to you too, Mr. Director. What's the rush?"

"This is classified, but we have reason to believe we've isolated one of our shooters from Nebraska. I want to nail 'em before they move again."

Suddenly the general was all business. "Hold on. Let me see what I've got. Where in northern California?"

"Top secret—no leak—Oakland, Berkeley, S.F."

"Whew, hard area to search. You'll get heat readings from everywhere."

"Not from the area we're primarily interested in. I'll have exact coordinates for you in a few minutes. What've you got?"

"Okay, looks like Lanstaat 12 in…um…twenty-three minutes. What have you got for cloud cover in the target area?"

"Walter, you hear that?"

"Yes, sir. We've got about 5% coverage. Visibility about twenty miles with haze."

"No problem," replied Wright. "We'll have your shots in one hour. Just get me the exact coordinates. We'll do the rest."

Phillips could see his agent in San Francisco hand the note to an assistant before he spoke to the general. "We'll e-mail it to you within three minutes. Thanks, General. I'll get back to you." Phillips turned his attention back to San Francisco. "Walter, before we have that photo pass, can you get a man back in there and plant a silent alarm on the car? I want to know the minute someone touches it."

"Can do, sir."

"Okay. I'm leaving now for Andrews. I'll order up a hop and be there in three hours. I'll have all data forwarded from the satellite pass to you directly. I'll stay in touch from the air. If anything changes, I want to know, stat! Understood?"

"We're on it, sir." The screen went blank.

"Did you get all that, Rose?"

"Yes, sir. Voice and video. We're on line to Andrews now."

"All right!" Jordan Phillips rubbed his hands together with satisfaction. In his mind, he began to construct a net which would trap a minnow. A whale the size of Charley Talks Too Much would certainly brush against one strand of the net.

11:30 a.m. (PDT) - Control Room, Super Linear Accelerator.

The look of expectancy on the faces of the scientists in the room faded when Linc and Bill entered. Without uttering a word, they dropped the level of noise to almost zero.

Professor Johnson was the first to speak. "What? Nothing?"

"We checked three weeks before and three weeks after our expected date. Nada, zilch, zero. No mention of a strange creature hopping around town. We compared each page to the ones you had copied. No variation."

A deep gloom settled over the room. One of the technicians moaned, "What could have gone wrong?"

"Several thousand things, you nitwit," snapped Johnson. "All of you, out of here. Let me think."

Nobody wanted to be around the professor when he was in a mood like this. Within thirty seconds, everyone had scuttled out of the room.

"What do you think?" asked Bill as they headed back to their room.

"Damned if I know. Bet you a dollar Johnson will come up with something. We'll probably get a 3 a.m. wake-up call when his brain finally warms up." Privately, Linc felt depressed at the apparent failure. If the project was, as now seemed possible, worthless, his job and his chance to test his theory, were history. Without the possibility of using time to escape, it would not be long before the authorities would catch up with Charlie and Ruth. *Hell*, thought Linc, *I might be implicated as an accomplice. For sure I'd lose my top-secret clearance. My future won't be worth a damn.*

Then again, he was relieved. Now he wouldn't have to put himself into danger, even possible death. Life would go on as it always had. There would be other projects for a bright, young physicist.

Deep within his mind a thought formed. *I might be better off to cut my losses. Maybe it would be best not to get close to Charlie and Ruth. I should salvage as much as I can.* Another part of his brain teased him. *And abandon Ruth?*

12:10 p.m. (MDT) - Over Colorado.

The F-34 streaked just above the crests of rising super-cumulus in a deep blue sky. The pilot, riding in the second seat just behind the FBI director, scanned his instruments. Although people below were obviously in for a violent afternoon of thunderstorms and possible twisters, the automatic pilot in the fighter kept the plane straight and level at 2.3 times the speed of sound.

Jordan Phillips was too busy to enjoy the view. He'd just terminated his call to Kenneth Payne with the latest details. They decided it was time to let the President know that progress was being made. Still, the fear of a leak kept Phillips from disclosing everything about the current operation.

Before Phillips could punch up a call to San Francisco, Rose came on the net. "Sir, I have a report for you from the reservation."

"Put it through, " ordered Phillips.

"Sir, Fishbein here. We have information on the rifleman."

Phillips listened as the agent described how the NAN activists had finally cracked and disclosed the name and hiding place of the man who assassinated the vice president and the secretary of the interior. The shooter had fled to Canada and it would involve some sticky negotiations between the FBI and Canadian authorities to make a nab, but Phillips knew time had just run out on the killer.

"Great, good work. Give your team a 'well done' from me. Rose? You still on the line?"

"Yes, sir."

"All right, copy that last call and send it by courier to Ken Payne. One copy, eyes only. Get Jefferson on the horn with his opposite in Canada. Make arrangements for Fishbein and his team to be in Canada tonight. Any problem with the Mounties, call me. Got that?"

"Yes, sir."

Phillips clicked off and allowed himself a moment of reflection. The fighter had cleared the crest of the Rockies. Ahead, clear skies revealed the great desert basin of Utah and Nevada. A smile played briefly across his face. *We've come so far,* he thought. At one time this great desert was large enough for a man to hide out for a century. Now there was virtually no place in the world for a fugitive to hide. Global cooperation between police agencies was almost universal. Only fundamentalist Muslim governments in the Middle East and Africa posed problems. Now it made no difference—deserts, mountains, forests—all could be penetrated. In fact, it was amazing the fugitives had lasted this long. It would soon be over. They couldn't hide forever.

"Mr. Phillips, please tighten your harness. We'll be landing soon."

Jordan almost laughed out loud at the pilot's words. He couldn't resist replying. "Major, I wonder what our ancestors would think about this."

"Sir?"

"Can you imagine what someone in a wagon train in the 1800s would think of strapping themselves to the seat in Utah for a landing in California?"

"Can't say I ever thought about it before," replied the puzzled pilot.

Jordan Phillips felt too good to worry about a pilot who couldn't see the humor in the situation. He decided not to call Walter Reynolds with his latest plans. They would meet soon enough.

The fighter slid through 40,000 feet on its way to Oakland.

Reynolds himself was seated behind the control yoke of a sleek new Mustang on the taxiway when the fighter rolled to a stop. Phillips unsnapped his harness and scrambled out of the cockpit as soon as the canopy was raised. As he hustled across the pavement, he waved Reynolds back into his seat.

"No formalities, Walt. Let's hit the road."

Phillips slid into the passenger seat as the bubble top came down and the Mustang roared to life. Now that the boss was here, Reynolds wasted no time.

"So, what did we get from the satellite pass?" asked Phillips.

"We got thirty-one hot spots within a mile and a half," replied Reynolds. "We've already eliminated fourteen as vehicles on the roads and four were occupied buildings. Two may be campfires, they're real bright, and the remaining eleven are either humans or large animals. There may be some cows or horses in the hills, and there certainly are deer. The photos have been analyzed. They don't give us any information on the eleven possibles."

"Is the car wired?"

"Yes, sir. Anyone touches the car, we'll know it."

"Okay. Have we got the area blanketed?"

"Nearly. All trails, roads and some obvious ways out of the hills are under observation."

"How soon before we can close it up. I mean *really* close it up?"

"About two hours. No problem."

As they talked, the car roared onto the East Cross Toll Road and headed toward the command post on Skyline Drive.

Jordan Phillips felt his adrenaline pump. He hadn't realized how much he missed being in the field. *This is where the rubber meets the road,* he thought. *This is living!*

"Charlie, sit down. You're driving me crazy."

"Can't help it. Something's wrong. I got a feeling someone's lookin' down my neck." Charlie continued to pace, his massive hands clenched as if for a fight.

"Nobody's been close for days. What makes you think—?"

"I don't know! Shit! I'm getting the heebie-jeebies sitting around here."

"Maybe it's the firewater, redskin."

Charlie stopped pacing and glared at Ruth. "Okay, you've made your point!" Charlie contemplated the half-empty beer. "Maybe you're right. Still, I have a bad feeling. Let's check on the car. Maybe it's time to get out of here."

Ruth heaved a sigh. Charlie wasn't always the easiest person in the world. Maybe the best course would be to humor him. "Sure. I can use the exercise. Lead on, noble warrior." She jumped to her feet and bowed deeply to him while waving her arm toward the trail.

"Aw hell, sis. You know how I like t' spout off." Charlie dropped his head and slouched against the nearest redwood.

"Yeah, I know. I also know you have good instincts. Let's check the car. Okay?"

Somewhat abashed, Charlie motioned Ruth to lead.

Phillips and Reynolds were nearing the command post when the speaker on the dash came to life. "Contact! Contact! We got positive on the vehicle!"

"How far?" croaked Phillips.

"Two minutes," answered Reynolds.

"Step on it!" Phillips whipped the mike from its clip. "All units! All units! This is Jordan Phillips. Close! Close, now!"

The Mustang leaped ahead, the siren activated and headlights flashing. At the Oakland Airport, three Apache III jet helicopters roared to life. From the command post, six cars raced to be the first to the scene. Camouflaged agents in the hills near the car broke from cover. The race was on to nail the man who had gunned down one of their own. It was not a time for mercy. The director was here, in person. There would be recognition and promotion for the man who brought down the killer.

There was only room for one car in the dirt lane leading to the hidden car. The two leading cars of the strike force both tried to make the turn. One had to lose. It ended up in the creek alongside the road, both agents snarled in air bags.

"I don't know, Chuck. Maybe we shouldn't be playing around here. What if the owner comes back?"

"Quit being a sissy. Nobody's gonna come. This baby's probably been abandoned for five years. It's like treasure, 'n we found it." Chuck was only fourteen. It would be two years before he could drive. Ignoring his brother's whining, he eagerly gripped the wheel of the old car and imagined himself racing down the road.

Reality returned when he looked through the windshield and saw a shiny new car coming straight at him. The car skidded to a stop. The doors flew open and men with guns—big guns—flew out.

"Oh God," wailed Chris, "It's a drug snuff! We're dead!" He covered his eyes and shrank down in the seat.

Chuck gripped the old fashioned steering wheel and stared.

"FBI! Drop your weapons now!"

Overhead the "whup-whup" of rotors from a helicopter could be heard. Another car slammed to a stop behind the first. Men in forest camouflage seemed to materialize from nowhere in the surrounding woods.

Chuck Wheeler fainted. Chris raised his hands and wailed.

Just to the south, on a ridge densely covered in eucalyptus and poison oak, two shadowy figures melted into the undergrowth and disappeared.

FOUR

Thursday, July 15, 2021. Pine Ridge Reservation.

The knock on the door was not unexpected. Since the assassination, men in suits and ties had been crawling over the reservation.

Marie Long Trail turned off the water and dried her hands. The dishes would have to wait.

When she opened the door, one man was holding a badge. They both appeared uncomfortable in suits and ties.

"Mrs. Long Trail?" asked the suit with the badge.

"Yes. Who are you?"

"FBI. Can we come in, please?"

Marie had nothing to hide, but these men were strangers. They were representatives of the white man's government. Like all Indians, Marie had a strong distrust of "white justice."

The agents were becoming accustomed to frosty receptions. The people they contacted were polite, for the most part, but remote and faintly distrustful. The "G-Men" were learning that they were working in a closed community. Information was freely given—up to a point. Inevitably, a porous wall developed between the parties. Only some of the requested data filtered through. The people on the reservation seemed unusually well informed about what might be asked. Evasion, deceit and outright lies were the basis of most answers. By now most agents had accepted the fact that anyone not a member of the society was an enemy. Still, they had to try.

"Certainly. Make yourself to home." At forty-eight years old, Marie Long Trail had been alive long enough to see great changes in the relationship between whites and Indians. From the time of her birth, in 1973, she'd witnessed a Native American rising to a pinnacle of power in the United States. Like many Native Americans, she adored Ben Nighthorse Campbell, Speaker of the House of Representatives. She'd been an idealistic young woman when he was first elected. As a mother, she held out his achievements to her children and was rewarded when her son rose to the challenge and was accepted at the University of California on a full scholarship in physics. Her daughter, Amy, would be leaving soon to pursue her dream of becoming a doctor. Princeton University lured her with another substantial scholarship. However, over 180 years of distrust made her cautious. The men facing her represented a government incapable of keeping its promises. Her home was open. Her guard was up.

The agents found themselves in a simple, clean, frame house, well shaded by cottonwood trees in the shelter of low hills to the west. The woman reflected her home. Clean, erect, simply dressed with an air of refinement. She would never be mistaken for other than what she was: a Native American. The straight black hair, high cheekbones and copper coloring identified her immediately.

"Sorry to bother you, but I guess you know we have some questions to ask. We'll try to be brief."

"I've been expecting someone. Would you like some coffee?"

"No, thank you." The agents appeared as mirror images. Tall, crew cut, matching gray suits and innocent, open faces. Their demeanor was designed to put people at ease, but it wasn't working on the reservation. "Please bear with us for a few minutes."

Marie nodded her head.

"Is your full name Marie Long Trail?"

She nodded again.

"I understand from tribal records that your husband is deceased. Is this true?"

"He's been dead for five years," she answered.

Crew cut number two scribbled the answer in a notebook. "And what was the cause of death?" continued crew cut number one.

"Hunting accident."

"Oh, sorry." The agent was mildly surprised. He'd discovered that alcohol and suicide were the almost universal causes of death among young men on the reservation. Almost automatically he questioned whether the death was an accident or a carefully staged suicide. It really made no difference. The vice president hadn't been shot by a Sioux man dead for five years. "I see also that you have two children, Lincoln and Amy. Is that correct?"

Another curt nod.

"Can you tell me where each of you were last Thursday from 11 a.m. to 1 p.m.?"

"I can tell you where Amy and I were. Same place we are every Tuesday and Thursday at that time. We were at the emergency clinic. We volunteer there. I guess you'd have to ask Linc where he was. He's away at college."

"College?" This was a new idea to the agent. Somehow he didn't think about Indians going to college. "Where does he go to school?"

Marie's chest swelled with pride. "University of California. He's doing important graduate work with a famous scientist."

A small alarm echoed in the agent's mind. *California? Why was California important?* Then he remembered. "That sounds wonderful, Mrs. Long Trail. Where in California is he doing this work?"

"I told you, University of California."

"Yes, but they have campuses all over the state. Which campus?"

"Why, Berkeley, of course."

Bingo, thought the agent. *Time to change tacks. Don't let her know this might be important.*

"Just a few more questions. Are you familiar with the organization, Native American Nation?"

Marie's features clouded perceptively. The agents recognized the familiar signs of an open face closing to them.

"I've heard of it ... some."

"Do you personally know anyone associated with the organization?"

Her negative shake of the head was a standard response. Everyone knew the organization, but nobody had ever met anyone associated with it. The blue sky existed, but no one had ever seen it.

"Do you know Charlie and Ruth Teague? He is commonly known as Charlie Talks Too Much."

Marie chose her answer carefully. *Did these men know Charlie and Ruth were distant relations?* "I've seen 'em around some."

"Are you aware that they are members of Native American Nation?"

Again the negative shake of the head. Unconsciously, Marie rubbed her sweaty palms against her skirt.

A few more questions and a polite farewell finished the session. Marie stood behind the screen door and watched the two men slowly drive down the dusty lane to the main road. She wasn't sure why, but she felt somehow she'd helped the government agents. She chewed her lip as she tried to decide what she could have said to help them.

"Oh boy, oh boy," exulted the senior agent. "Time to get to a secure phone. I think we got us a California connection and I'll swear she knows more about the Teagues than anyone we've talked to."

Once out of sight of the house, the car leaped forward. It was a long way to a secure land line.

9 a.m. (PDT) - Stockton Super Linear Accelerator.

Linc was pleasantly surprised to awaken to sunshine. The dreaded middle-of-the-night call never came. He stretched luxuriously before the memory of yesterday's failure, and its consequences rushed in. Immediately, he felt a rush of conflicting feelings over the failure. The buzzing of the intercom interrupted his thoughts. He crossed to the desk and punched the answer button. Professor Johnson's face appeared on the screen.

"Long. Get back over to the newspaper. Go through everything one more time."

Linc almost groaned out loud, but caught himself. "Okay," he said resignedly, "But—why? I mean, we've done it."

"Just do it. I'm leaving for Berkeley now. Call me when you're done."

"Yes, sir." Linc clicked off the intercom before flipping the bird at the blank screen. Bill was out somewhere, so the whole job would fall on him. Linc uttered a string of curses as he headed for the shower.

9:40 a.m. - FBI Regional Office, San Francisco.

Jordan Phillips was in a towering rage. Anyone crossing his path was liable to leave either singed or charred, depending on how badly the headlines were effecting the boss at the moment.

The bungled apprehension the previous afternoon had been too large an operation to escape media notice. Within minutes of bursting into the remote mountain lane, before adequate security could be set up, the first newsman arrived.

Now CNN, ANN, ABC and all the rest were baying at the doors. The street outside resembled a parking lot, with vans and trucks parked everywhere. Each sported an antenna fixed on the point in the heavens where a satellite could pick up every byte of information. Black cables extended from the vehicles to stationary cameras poised on vehicles, sidewalks, steps—anywhere a tripod could be mounted. Massed around the entry doors, hordes of mini-cams and microphones sprouted from the men and women of the fifth estate. The scent of blood was in the air. This was news!

Walter Reynolds sat glumly across the desk from Jordan Phillips. He restlessly rubbed the stubble on his chin and passed his hand across bleary eyes. The headline of the *San Francisco Chronicle*, large and very black, mocked him. **FBI MISSES SUSPECT. OOPS!** The article compared the FBI attempt to Keystone Cops antics of a century earlier. Somehow the suspects came off the heroes with the cops playing obliging clowns. The director was not amused in the least.

"Where are they?" Phillips hissed. "I've never wanted a suspect worse in all my years with the bureau. The agent he gunned down had a wife and two kids. We owe them!"

Phillips walked to the window, but retreated hastily when he spotted long lens cameras focused on the window from the street.

Ever since the missed opportunity the previous afternoon, all efforts had been concentrated on sealing off the mountainous area and combing every inch. Choppers ferried FBI agents, local and state police and army units into the area, dropping them in remote spots to converge toward the primary target area. Every opportunity had been taken to photograph and image the hills with passing satellites. So far the massive effort had turned up only four illegal pot farms and a half dozen transients who were probably wanted for minor crimes. Charlie and Ruth remained at large.

11: 30 a.m. - Stockton Record Office.

He almost missed it. There really wasn't much information, but as soon as Linc started to read, he knew. He knew this was it! The experiment had worked. Linc read it three times to be sure.

"Constable Norris reported yesterday that he investigated a suspicious incident on the Trafton farm in the AM. A worker on that place reported a strange animal which suddenly appeared and made several leaping jumps before dropping dead in a potato field. Constable Norris found the beast to be a large kangaroo, native to Australia, but never seen in these parts. He is at a loss to explain the incident. When pressed to produce this creature, the Constable reported the unfortunate animal was reduced to stew meat and fed several families last evening."

Linc searched for the date in the masthead. Wednesday, May 10, 1875 - only nine days off from the programmed date. He shakily pressed the record function. The printed paper slipped from the side of the machine. He picked it up and read it again. Here it was, in black and white. He was holding proof that history had changed.

He flipped through the stack of previously printed copies, searching for the same page printed only yesterday. A comparison revealed that the new article had replaced a small advertisement for "Dr. Deans Mineral Rub: Guaranteed to Provide Instant Relief From..." The list was long, largely in Latin.

"Well, Dr. Dean, it seems that you've been rubbed out," mused Linc.

Just to be sure, he ran another copy of the page, then a third. The kangaroo remained. Linc sat stunned, staring at the page.

12:15 p.m. - East of Stockton.

The house was just as Linc had described. A small, frame house, partly concealed by a barn and corral fence. Cottonwood trees arched in the light breeze, providing welcome shade over the house. From the entrance drive, only fields and walnut orchards could be seen. There were no other cars on the side road. Ruth spun the wheel and gunned the engine. They stopped long enough for Charlie to scratch a large "X" in the dirt at the head of the drive. Linc would recognize the signal.

They pulled up behind the barn and waited, listening for any sound. There was only the stirring of the leaves on the trees.

"Let's get this in the barn," ordered Charlie.

Ruth held her breath as Charlie first fiddled with the chain and lock on the massive door to the barn, then resorted to beating on it with a rusty hammer he found in the weeds. He finally wedged the handle of the hammer into the chain and bore down with all his weight. A weak link popped with a sound like a pistol shot. Then the door was open and she drove in.

The interior was gloomy, with a distinctly musty air. A few broken tools littered a workbench along one wall and there was a pile of mildewed hay bales in a corner. The sights and smells were familiar. Ruth started to relax for the first time in over twenty-four hours.

Charlie peered through a crack in the door. "All clear," he announced. "Looks like nobody saw us. Let's get in the house—see if they left us anything to eat. I'm starving."

"You and your stomach," sighed Ruth. "What about him?" She jerked her thumb toward the trunk.

"He'll keep."

"He'll stink pretty soon, Charlie."

"Hell, nobody here to smell him. What do ya want me to do? Bury him?"

"No, but I want him out of there. I don't want to smell him when we take off again."

"Won't be usin' that car again anyways. By now he's probably been reported missing and every cop in the state is lookin' for his car."

"Damn you, Charlie! Get him the hell out of there. We may not have a choice. How do you think we're getting out of here?"

"Link'll—"

"Link's got a motorcycle. How long do you think it would take a cop to pull over a motorcycle with three people on it?"

Charlie rubbed his face, wearily. "OK, OK. Where do I put him?"

"I don't know. Maybe over there under the hay."

Ruth didn't want to look, but found herself unable to draw her eyes away from the corpse. He was a pleasant looking man, maybe sixty years old. His slacks and shirt were good quality, although the slacks were messy now. He'd died horribly, with Charlie's massive hands tight around his throat. It had been so easy.

They'd found a place near a seldom-used paved road. From their vantage point they could see the road for several hundred yards in both directions. They kept one eye trained on the sky for helicopters criss-crossing the ridges and valleys, dropping sensors as they passed. Charlie had quietly pointed out one of the devices to Ruth. When they were a safe distance away, he whispered in her ear. "Sound and motion detectors. From now on, no talking and move slow. When you see one, tug on my sleeve."

It was early morning before they found the place on the road. The first three cars they saw were marked police units. The fourth was their ride out of trouble. Ruth quickly scrambled down the bank to the road. She started to walk along the shoulder with a noticeable limp. As the car approached, she gave a beckoning wave just before collapsing in a heap. The driver never even considered passing her, or using his cellular phone. As he knelt by her side, Charlie grabbed him from the rear. From the ground, Ruth watched in horror as Charlie dragged the man up while clamping his fingers firmly over the windpipe. Seconds ticked by and still the man clawed and kicked. Then it was over. Ruth had to grab his feet to help Charlie carry him to the back of the car.

They stayed on secondary roads as much as possible, alert for roadblocks. Surprisingly, there were none. By the time they reached Lafayette, they joined the main stream of traffic on the freeway. Huddled behind the front seat, Charlie read a map and gave instructions. The drive went smoothly, but Ruth found her hands ached now from gripping the wheel so tightly.

The body had stiffened and Charlie had little trouble dragging the corpse by the collar to the hay bales. Ruth shuddered and felt sick as she watched Charlie rearrange the pile to cover their victim.

The house was much easier to enter than the barn. Someone, kids or a transient, had pulled plywood off a back window. The glass was shattered. It crunched under their feet on the carpet. The semi-dark interior was cool after the mid-day heat. Charlie headed straight for the kitchen through the vacant rooms. Ruth heard his cry of frustration when he found it as bare as the rest of the house. Her own stomach was rumbling, but she was still too upset over the latest murder to eat anyway. The emptiness in her body matched a new emptiness in her soul.

Now there was nothing to do but wait.

3 p.m. (CDT) - Pine Ridge Reservation.

Over the years, the river had carved multiple channels across the flat lands of the prairie. The back roads of the reservation often dipped on concrete aprons to span the channels, which were almost always dry. It was much cheaper than building bridges, which would only be used by a few Indians anyway. Between the home of Marie Long Trail and the nearest town, there was only one small river to cross. The road dipped, then rose onto a small island, before dipping again to reach the opposite bank.

In the clear, hot, sunny afternoon, only one car was visible for miles on the road. It belonged to the U. S. government and contained two FBI agents. It was sitting on the island between two raging torrents. The flash flood was the result of a heavy thunderstorm many miles to the west. Although the water was rising rapidly when they reached the first ford, the agents had breasted the water before their engine died and left them stranded on the island. By the time they restarted the engine, the second ford was impassable.

It would be some time before they reached a phone with the information about an Indian student named Lincoln Long Trail in Berkeley, California.

3:30 p.m. (PDT) - Stockton Super Linear Accelerator.

Linc was still finding it hard to concentrate. His call to Professor Johnson had been a revelation.

"Professor," he began giddily, "it's there! The article's there! I don't believe it. I could have sworn there was no mention of it yesterday."

"There wasn't," replied the professor. His face appeared totally deadpan on the screen.

Linc was caught off-guard. "But—I mean, you don't understand. It's there! Right where it should be. The kangaroo made it."

"Of course it did. Knew it would." Still no expression. "But you don't understand. There was no mention of it yesterday."

"Couldn't have been anything yesterday."

Linc found he was getting frustrated with the professor's short, superior answers. Here he was, calling with the most stupendous news the world would ever hear, and all he was getting were supercilious answers from some kind of a superior know-it-all. In his excitement, Linc blurted, "What the hell are you talking about?"

If the professor took umbrage, he disguised it well. "Think about it, Linc. When you work through the possibilities, there is only one answer."

Linc's fevered brain listened, but he found himself unable to connect Johnson's words to anything which made sense. Yesterday there was no mention of what they had done. Today there was. This was logical to Johnson; it was Greek to Linc.

"Are you still there, Linc?"

Linc realized Johnson was watching his reactions closely. He took a deep breath before answering. "I'm here, but I have no idea what you're talking about."

"That," continued Johnson, "is why you are the student and I am the professor. It is quite logical, when you think about it."

Linc was tired of playing games. He let the silence drag. "Linc, when did we send the subject back?"

Linc took a deep breath. It didn't seem like a trick question. "Yesterday, Professor."

"Very good. Now, when did we look for the results of our experiment?"

Again, an easy answer. "Yesterday."

"Good. Now do you see the problem?"

Linc decided it would not be productive to scream into the phone.

"Sir," he said softly, "I am a dull-witted graduate student. I seek only the wisdom which you can give me."

Linc had never before heard, or seen, the crusty professor chuckle. "Linc, you are one of the brightest I've ever taught. You're working too hard for an easy solution. The answer's so simple, it's stupid. Until yesterday, there had been no change to history, as we know it. Correct?"

"I'll buy that," responded Linc.

"So, what changed between yesterday and today?" continued Johnson.

"We sent a kangaroo back in time?"

"Ah, yes, we did that. Now does it make sense?"

Suddenly, the proverbial light bulb came on. "Of course! Yesterday what we did couldn't have been reported. It wouldn't appear until at least one day later in the newspaper! When I was looking yesterday, the story was being written…so it could appear today! Right?"

"Full marks, Long." There was no disguising the elation in the professor's voice. He was vindicated. The experiment had worked. Time travel was a reality.

Linc's head was spinning too. Only now he remembered the rest of the news. He almost took joy in bursting Johnson's bubble.

"Only one problem, sir."

"Eh, what's that?" A worried furrow appeared on his forehead.

"The kangaroo died."

There was a prolonged silence at the other end. "What happened—specifically?"

"According to the newspaper, an eyewitness saw it take a few hops, then it keeled over. It was dead when the man got there."

Again there was silence as Johnson absorbed the news. "Did they find out why it died?"

"No. They ate it."

Linc almost burst out laughing at the look on Johnson's face.

"They—What?—Ate our experiment?" The professor was spluttering, his face contorted. "Don't they realize? No, of course not. They couldn't know." He quickly composed himself. Linc could almost feel the intensity of the thoughts through the phone. It was instructive to watch the great intellect whir through the possibilities. "Right. Here's what I want you to do."

Linc scribbled furiously while the professor outlined the steps to be taken. Inwardly, he groaned. A full day's work piled up in a few moments. By the time they disconnected, Linc was totally absorbed in the data to be analyzed. The world outside the lab ceased to exist.

FIVE

Thursday, July 15, 2021. 7:30 p.m. - East of Stockton.

The setting sun cast golden light through cracks in the weathered plywood covering the western windows. Dust motes, stirred up by the fugitives' presence, danced in the light. In the back bedroom, an oblong of yellow light covered the floor near the window where Ruth and Charlie had entered the house. Ruth was seated in the light, dreamily listening to a tractor working in the distance. Her hands slowly stroked the hair of an ancient Barbie doll she'd found.

The doll was not special. It was dirty, the clothes torn. Apparently it had been thrown up on the shelf in the closet and the owners overlooked it when they packed. Ruth turned it over in her hands, wondering about the little girl who had owned it. It resembled a doll she dimly remembered.

Rosie. She had named the baby Rosie. Rosie was the one person who understood all the problems. For years Rosie had been her confidante; sometimes her only friend. Rosie had never deserted or disappointed Ruth. That was not something she could say about most people she'd known.

Daddy certainly deserted her—big time. A large, lumbering man with powerful hands which could be so delicate when they worked with leather or beads, he had grown despondent over his inability to hold a decent job. Too often his pay disappeared into a bottle. The bottle made him temperamental, quick to anger, then deeply sorrowful when the effects wore off. It was during a period of anguish that he went to the mountain alone. Charlie, and a few friends, found him four days later. One bullet through the roof of his mouth had quieted his pain forever.

Mama wept for days before she turned to liquor to deaden the pain. It took her four years to drink herself into the clinic. The doctors pronounced that there was nothing to do for her. They turned her out to come home to die. She left Charlie and Ruth to fend for themselves. Though only fourteen years old, Ruth took on the duties of caring for her older brother. At least he had not deserted her.

A gentle snoring disturbed her thoughts. She rose and walked into the living room where Charlie lay, full-length, on the living room floor. A lighter patch of carpet with four deep indentations at the corners indicated where the sofa had been placed in the room. Like a homing pigeon, Charley had unerringly located the spot and chosen it for his bed. An empty beer bottle, the last they had, lay by his head.

Ruth contemplated his serene face and wondered. Through the years he had stuck by his little sister. He'd saved her from hurt and harm on the reservation. He'd tried to provide for her, but faced the same difficulties which confounded their father. The jobs never paid well, nor did they last long. There was always the lure of the liquor store when spare change rattled in his pocket. The sofa in the old trailer was often more attractive than another day spent washing dishes or herding cattle. Charlie just sort of wandered from one thing to another. All that changed last week. Now the entire world knew who Charlie Teague was. He was now the most famous Sioux since Sitting Bull. His days of casual loafing were over.

Ruth turned back to the bedroom. Another thought was nagging at her. *Where is Linc? Has he deserted us also? He must know by now that we've left the camp. Why hasn't he come looking for us?* With sudden dread, she thought possibly he'd been found out—linked to them some way. She leaned against the window frame, trying to draw strength and reassurance from the sunlight. Still, a stone lay on her heart. She clutched the doll closer as long shadows crept across the land.

Linc pored over the computer printouts again. It was absolutely silent in the lab, where there had been so much excitement only two days before. A copy of every piece of data he was studying had been forwarded to Houston, where others searched for some key. Why? Why did an apparently healthy kangaroo, in the prime of life, collapse almost immediately after the transport? Until this question could be answered, there would be no advancement on Project T. There might not even be a job for him.

"Give it up, Injun," he mumbled. "You have some shopping to do."

The last glow of sunset was the only light he needed to see the "X" in the dust of the driveway. He continued slowly past the property until he could ease the motorcycle off the road into dense willows along a drainage ditch. He crouched next to the bike, his heart racing while he waited for the night sounds to start. He could see only one light from a farmhouse in the far distance. A frog croaked nearby and was answered. Crickets chirped in the high weeds of the field bordering the ditch.

He shouldered a box of groceries and crept through the weeds to the house.

"Ruth," he hissed. "Charlie, you in there? It's me, Linc."

"Pssst. Over here, Linc." Ruth leaned out the window and took the groceries. Linc stepped over the sill and melted into the house.

"Hullo, Cousin." Charlie was an imposing black shadow. "You bring food?"

"Yeah, in the box. Glad to see you got here."

"Hasn't it been on the news?" asked Ruth.

"Hasn't what been on the news?" responded Linc. "I haven't seen a newspaper or TV all day. What happened?"

Ruth looked a little sick. It was Charlie who answered.

"Wasn't easy. Feds found the car."

"What!" Linc was alarmed. "Jesus, if they found the car, how'd you get here?"

"Stole another one," replied Ruth softly.

"Damn! Now they're lookin' for that car," said Linc.

"Yeah," responded Charlie, "and the guy who was drivin' it."

Linc felt lightheaded. "You didn't....I mean you—"

"Yeah, Cousin. 'Fraid so."

Linc was ready to explode. There was an icy fear in his gut. Suddenly Charlie was an ominous shadow, a murderous black apparition—and Linc was implicated. His mind whirled.

A new thought leaped at him. *Cut your losses—one call to the FBI—that's all it would take. Think about it.*

"Linc. Linc." Ruth was shaking him.

"Huh. What? I can't believe—"

"Forget it, Linc. It's over. What's more important is what happened with the experiment?"

"No!" exploded Linc. "The experiment is not more important than murder!"

"Linc, listen to me." Ruth gripped his shoulders with desperate strength. "It's not our fault the FBI agent pulled his gun and aimed at Charlie. The killing really was an accident but no matter what we do, we'll be convicted of murder and you know it."

Linc looked into her eyes and clearly saw her pain, her fear. "It's wrong, terribly wrong, to kill innocent people. Don't you realize that?"

"Yeah, Cousin. We know." Charlie was a brooding shadow in the far corner of the room. "Believe me. I wish it was different, but it ain't, so deal with it."

Ruth dragged Linc's attention back. "Linc, we're doomed if you can't help us. So tell me, did the experiment work?"

"Yeah, I guess so."

"What d'ya mean, you guess so?" asked Charlie.

"Well, it worked, but it didn't. I mean the kangaroo made it. We found the article in the papers, but it died almost immediately."

Ruth dropped her hold on Linc's shoulders and slumped against the wall. "Great. If we stay here, we're dead. If we follow your plan, we're probably just as dead. Some choice."

Linc's mind was starting to function again. "We don't know. I mean we don't have any idea what happened. There's nothing in the computer to indicate any malfunction. Maybe it was just shock. We may never know, but it does mean there won't be any experiments for awhile. Things are pretty quiet at the accelerator."

"Well, that's good for us," said Charlie. "Won't be so many people around when we go."

"You still want to try it?" asked Linc. "Jesus, Charlie, the thought scares me to death."

"Yeah. Death, d-e-a-t-h. As in d-e-a-d. That's what we are. Listen, Cousin, I don't give a damn about your grand theory about Custer and all. I always thought it was kinda nuts anyways. All I want is for you to put me in one of your toys and send me somewhere where there ain't nobody lookin' for Charlie Teague. If I die on the other end, so what? It's better than waitin' here for the shit that's gonna come down on this Injun."

The idea of calling the FBI returned. Linc was scared. He decided he'd just have to tough it out for now. Once he was out of the house, he'd have time to consider his options.

"Okay. Okay. Let me think," Linc said. He took a deep breath. This had to be convincing.

"I've got it all figured out, I think. If you guys are going, we may as well stick to the plan. I already have most of the things we need and I can get the rest tomorrow."

"What kinds of things are you talking about?" asked Ruth.

"Clothes, money, weapons."

"We already got all those things," said Charlie. "Might be a good idea to hit a bank for more money though."

"You moron," hissed Ruth. "How much good do you think your twenty-first century money is going to be where we're going? You'd look pretty stupid in those clothes too, Injun. Remember, back then our kind wore skins and moccasins and carried bows and spears."

"Well, that wasn't quite what I had in mind," said Linc. "Look, I've been working as a volunteer for the last two years at the California Native History Museum in Sacramento. Most of what they have is from California tribes, but across the street at Fort Sutter, they have rooms full of stuff they don't have space to show. I've spent a lot of time cataloguing the excess and I managed to sneak out some stuff we can use. I've got it stashed in a storage place in Berkeley. The clothes I have could have come from anywhere in the 1870s. I've got shirts, pants, boots, dresses—even underwear. Everything we wear or use has to be from that time."

"Bullshit," stormed Charlie. "I don't go nowhere without this." He pushed his pistol near Linc's eyes. "And how the hell we supposed to get by lookin' like whites?"

"That's easy," replied Linc. "By the 1870s lots of Sioux had traded with white traders. Some wore white man's clothes, but I've got a better explanation. You tell everyone you were found, apparently abandoned, by a white family when you were kids. They raised you and that's why you speak English and dress the way you do. Now you've decided to come back and live with the tribe. No problem. As for the gun, I've got two pistols and two Sharps carbines. They're authentic. Nobody'll question them."

"How'd you get those?" asked Ruth.

"Bought 'em from collectors. No problem. I got a couple of knives the same way, and some money. There is one problem, though. I couldn't find much ammo for the pistols, but I figure to dump you near a trading post along the Oregon Trail and you can buy some."

"You keep saying you have these things for us," said Ruth. "What about you? Aren't you coming?"

"Yeah, I guess so, but I won't be with you—at least not right away. I'm going to Washington, D.C. first. While you plant the seeds among the tribes, I'll be priming the pump with the politicians. By June, 1876, both sides have to want the peace we're going to offer."

11:30 p.m. FBI Offices, San Francisco.

"Mr. Phillips? Uh, Mr. Phillips, Mr. Reynolds wants you."

Jordan Phillips shook off the cobwebs and sat up on the cot in the storage room. He lumbered to his feet and followed the agent back to the office.

"What have you got, Walt?" he asked.

"Call from the reservation. Thought you'd want to see it."

Phillips looked at the conference screen on the wall. He didn't recognize the agent, who looked rumpled and tired.

"Okay, I'm listening."

"Yes, sir. I think we found a connection between the reservation and California."

"Yeah?" Phillips was still exhausted and exasperated.

"It's like this, sir. There's a woman we questioned this afternoon who has a son going to the University of California at Berkeley."

"What?" roared Phillips. "You questioned her this afternoon and now it's after midnight there and you're just calling?"

The agent looked panicked. "We got trapped by a flash flood before we could get to a secure phone. We just now got here."

"Jesus, God damn! Why didn't you use the car phone?"

"Uh, too many red ears around here. We have reason to believe our cellular calls are being monitored all over the reservation."

Phillips slumped and spoke more softly. "Yeah, right. Okay, so who's our man out here?"

"Name's Lincoln Long Trail. Doing graduate work at Berkeley. Also, we have a feeling he knows the Teagues."

"Long Trail? Like it sounds?"

Yes, sir."

"One word or two?"

"Two, sir."

Phillips turned to his S.F. chief. "Okay, Walt. Get on it. Let's dig up our friend Long Trail and see what we got." He turned back to the screen. "You two roust out a judge and get a search warrant. I want everything on this guy and I want it yesterday! Get me photos ASAP."

"You mean get a judge now, sir?"

"Right now! Any flack, have him call me. Understood?"

"Yes, sir!" The screen went blank.

"Walt, I need everything on this guy from Cal—DMV, Social Security, military, police—anything. I want to know when he shits and what color it is and I want to know now."

"Yes, sir. I've got a team on it."

"I don't suppose we've had any other luck since I crashed."

"Maybe one thing, but it's slender."

"I don't care if it's miniscule. I want everything."

"Well, Contra Costa Sheriff's Department issued a missing person alert this afternoon. Some guy who lives in Moraga, that's near where we've been searching, didn't come home last night. His wife reported him missing today."

"You think he was up there in the woods with his secretary, or something?"

"No, he commutes to San Leandro and uses the back roads sometimes. His wife knew he'd be working late last night and didn't realize he hadn't come home until she got up this morning. He wasn't home. His car wasn't there and nobody's seen him."

Phillips sat down heavily. "Okay. So this missing person just *might* have used roads in the area last night after we busted the kids. *Maybe* our pal Charlie found out his car was hot, so he and his sister *somehow* got our guy and his car." Phillips scratched his head, yawned and blinked. He was very tired. "Okay, okay. Could be. Look, let's do this. Get with the sheriff out there and have him play this up big. Lots of news coverage. Plaster the picture of the guy and his car on every newscast—lead story. Same with the newspapers. Page one, color photos. Just maybe someone saw something." Another thought popped up in his fuzzy brain. "Any chance this guy's car's got a GPS locator?" Global Positioning System Locators were optional equipment on later model cars and often standard equipment on luxury models.

"Apparently not, sir. I'll get on the rest immediately."

"But, Walt, keep our connection out of it. Just make sure we get everything they do."

Jordan Phillips had a feeling everything was connected. Long Trail, the missing car, the fugitives. *Just a little more time, that's all we need.*

Friday, July 16, 3:00 a.m.

Linc was exhausted. It was after midnight before he left Charlie and Ruth to return to Berkeley. When he stopped for gas, he debated calling the authorities but decided he needed more time to think. He was still undecided.

Luckily, he thought, *Bill's in the dormitory at the SSLA tonight, so I don't have to answer any questions about where I've been or why I'm pacing the floor. There are two choices: call the cops or rent a car in the morning and finish shopping.*

He flopped in his bed and stared at the ceiling. He hadn't made up his mind when he fell asleep.

"Nothing? We've got nothing?" Jordan Phillips black scowl dominated the room filled with the team assigned to track down Lincoln Long Trail.

Walter Reynolds went down the list one more time. "Phone book, zilch. Police, nothing. DMV and combined U. S. military records, nada. He does have a South Dakota driver's license and a motorcycle with Dakota plates, but the license doesn't have a picture and there are over three million motorcycles in California. We'll probably get something from the university, but the records office doesn't open 'til eight."

Christ, get somebody out of bed and open it up. If I'm up, I want lots of company."

"We tried, but the registrar is the only one who can release records and she, uh, doesn't seem to be sleeping at home tonight," Reynolds finished lamely.

Phillips heaved a deep sigh. "Great, just great. What about the reservation?"

"We had a call an hour ago from a highly pissed off judge. He said we'd get the warrant when he was damned good and ready. I guess he decided he was ready, 'cause one of the agents reported a half hour ago that he had the paper and was on the way to the house."

6:30 a.m., Pine Ridge Reservation.

This time there were four suits on the stoop when Marie opened the door. There were no polite questions, just terse directions.

"You can't go in there!" yelled Marie. "My daughter's asleep."

"Well, you better wake her up, 'cause this warrant's good for her room, too."

Everyone froze when the door slammed open. Amy Long Trail was holding a shotgun in a manner suggesting familiarity with weapons.

"Hold it, Miss. We're FBI and we've got—"

"You hold it, whitey, or I'll blow your brains all over the wall." Amy's voice left little doubt she might, indeed, pull the trigger.

"You don't want to do that," replied the agent. "It's a federal crime to even threaten us."

"I'm not threatening you, asshole. I'm promising you. Now, get out of here."

"Amy, they have a warrant. Maybe you should—"

"Maybe I should shoot, Momma. They can't come in here like this and—"

The nearest agent struck like a snake. There was a deafening explosion as he wrenched the shotgun from Amy's hands. The other three agents threw themselves on the floor as buckshot ripped through the roof. Amy staggered and lost her balance, falling to her hands and knees. Two agents pounced on her and pinned her to the floor.

"Cuff her," snarled the agent with the shotgun. "Read her her rights and throw her in the car—gently."

"No!" screamed Marie. "She didn't mean it. You—you surprised her, that's all. Let her go, please."

"She goes to the car, Mrs. Long Trail, and if there's any more trouble, she goes to jail. Understood?"

Marie watched helplessly while Amy was handcuffed and led out the door.

"Tell 'em to go to hell, Momma. Don't worry about me."

When Amy was safely deposited in the car, the agent in charge of the search wasted no time telling Marie what would happen to her daughter if Marie didn't cooperate completely.

The house and outbuildings weren't large. An hour later the agents carted away five boxes of evidence. Marie and Amy watched them go from the stoop. Amy massaged her chafed wrists and silently swore revenge. The humiliation of being disarmed and wrestled into handcuffs was compounded by the revulsion she experienced when the agent putting her in the car roughly groped under her nightgown and cupped her breast with his hand. He laughed when she spit in his face. They had the shotgun, but there were lots of guns on the reservation. Through narrowed eyes she watched them leave. One of them was a walking dead man.

"We need to warn Linc," said Marie.

"We need to kill them, Momma. Dead men don't tell tales."

"No! Amy, where are you going? Stop!"

Amy raced into the house and grabbed the keys to their beat-up old farm truck. "I'll be back, Momma," she yelled as she jammed the truck into gear and sent gravel flying in her race down the drive.

"Sweet Jesus, did you hear that?" asked the agent in the passenger seat.

"Yep," replied the driver. "At least we know the bug's working."

"Well, step on it. I've suddenly got a strong inclination to leave the reservation behind. Maybe you could find a nice, peaceful police station with lots of armed cops around."

"It's a long way to a police station. Might be better to stop and get this hot stuff on the horn to Frisco."

"Fuck 'em. They can wait 'til we put some distance between us and Annie Oakley."

SIX

Friday, July 16, Berkeley, 6:20 a.m.

Linc didn't want to answer the phone. The last thing he needed was Professor Johnson to give him some assignment today. He let it ring until he couldn't stand it.

"Yeah," he didn't try to disguise his exhaustion and bad temper.

"Linc? Linc, is that you?"

"Mom? Mom, it's—it's six a.m., what—"

"Linc, they have everything. They know all about you. Amy's trying to kill them!"

"Mom! Slow down! You're not making sense. Who has what? Who's Amy trying to kill?"

"Government! Agents! Came here with a warrant. They took everything! Amy went after them."

Linc's mind went blank. He didn't hear the words. The room was spinning. He felt like throwing up. It was all over. There wouldn't be a shining future with glowing accolades for Doctor of Physics Lincoln Long Trail. He was stone cold dead.

"Mom! Mom! Stop! Tell me again what's happened, slowly."

Three minutes later, thoroughly shaken, Linc knew the worst.

"Mom, listen to me. It'll be all right. I'm going to be okay, but I'm going away and I won't be back. Where I'm going they can't catch me."

"Where, Linc? Where are you going?"

"I can't tell you, but you must believe me when I tell you everything'll be fine. This whole mess never had to happen. I can make sure it never happens again. Mom, no matter what happens, I love you. I'll miss you and I thank you for everything you've done for me. Without your help, I wouldn't be in a position to do what has to be done. Believe me, it's all going to be different next time."

"Linc, I don't understand, and what about Amy?" Marie sobbed.

"She'll be all right, mom. I promise you I'll make everything right. I'm the only one who can."

"But…"

"I have to go. I'll always love you, no matter where I am."

6:32 a.m., San Francisco.

"Run it again."

"The whole thing?"

"No. Start with the part where he says: 'where I'm going, they can't catch me.'"

Jordan Phillips and Walter Reynolds concentrated on the tape received from Washington only a minute earlier. It was obvious the agents on the reservation had penetrated the Long Trail home and inserted a tap on the phone. Satellite relays gave them the information in minutes.

When the tape ended, they were left with questions, but no answers. What was "they took everything" and what could he possibly mean when he said "they can't catch me" and "it'll be different next time?"

"Christ on a bloody crutch," screamed Phillips. "The agents who raided that place better be on the horn immediately! Have we got a trace on the call? What the fuck's happening?"

"The dope on the call's coming in now, sir."

"Okay! I want Berkeley P. D. on the line. Tell 'em to roll everything. We got anybody over there?"

"Two agents standing by at Cal."

"Get 'em! Tell 'em to keep the locals from fucking this thing up. I want this redskin alive and yakking."

Linc was drained. Movement was almost impossible. *How could they know? What did they find?*

The distant wail of a police siren galvanized him to action. He frantically looked around the room and grabbed a few things he needed—keys, wallet, jacket. He fled the room in a panic.

"Mr. Phillips, this is agent Barnes. The room was empty. The door was open and the bed was warm. He can't get far."

"Ha! I've heard that line before!" stormed Jordan Phillips. "Look, tell the P. D. to put out an all points on a motorcycle, South Dakota plates, Edward-Sam-4-2-3-8. Tell 'em I want him alive! Then get your ass back up to where you were and get me everything the university's got on this son of a bitch."

"Yes, sir!"

7:20 a.m., El Cerrito.

"Thanks for the good times, old paint. I'm gonna miss you."

Linc patted the saddle affectionately. There wouldn't be any high-performance machines like this one where he was going. Now he needed four wheels and storage capacity. The rental car wouldn't outrun the cops, but, hopefully, it would be awhile before they discovered the change of vehicles. *At least I paid cash*, thought Linc. *No credit approval to trace.*

Two blocks from the rental agency, Linc pulled into a parking lot. In a secluded corner, he slipped under the car and spent several minutes disconnecting the GPS Locator.

"Even if you find the bike and trace the car you won't have much luck with the locator beacon out of commission," he muttered.

He used his magnetic entrance key at the storage facility. Nobody was around to see him load the trunk with several boxes and two rifles.

He stopped at three grocery stores in the next half hour. When he left, each one was out of stock on jerked meat and dried fruits.

He was wearing dark glasses and his long hair was pulled up under a baseball cap when he headed up I-80 towards Sacramento. Just a few more items to pluck from displays in the museum, then a quick trip south to Stockton. With a little luck, nobody would get close.

8:10 a.m., U. C. Berkeley.

"Thank you, Ma'am. You've been very helpful. Would you mind leaving the office a minute so we can make a call?"

"Is that a request, or an order, Mr. Barnes?"

"Since you put it that way, it's an order. I'm sure you understand."

"Not likely." The registrar made sure to close the door harder than necessary when she left.

The call to San Francisco was anticlimactic. The only new information of importance was the name of the instructor Lincoln Long Trail was working with—Professor Demetrius Johnson.

"Find him and bring him in," snarled Phillips.

10:30 a.m., San Francisco.

Jordan Phillips and Walter Reynolds contemplated the portable blackboard. Notes and connecting arrows covered the surface. A pile of faxes from the agents at the reservation had filled in gaping holes in the relationship between the Teagues and Linc. Included were the articles Linc had written for *The Native Voice*.

"Well, Walt, what've we got?"

Reynolds scratched his head and took a deep breath. "I'd say we've got ourselves a real bright boy who wants to overthrow the U. S. government. He reminds me of some stories I've heard from back in the Cold War days, you know?"

"You mean like a mole?"

"Yeah something like that. I mean this guy's got two personalities—Lincoln Long Trail, straight-A student in mathematics and physics, and Black Feather, raving revolutionary."

"I wouldn't be so quick with that raving part. This stuff from the reservation was written a few years ago and it's certainly revolutionary, but it's got some pretty good reasoning," responded Phillips. "I doubt that government policy would've been different if Custer hadn't been wiped out, but it's true the army never quite got over that spanking, and they did tend to overreact after that."

"Yeah, maybe he's not so raving, but where's his thinking gone from there? I mean, since he can't change something that happened over a hundred years ago, did he put his talents to work to snuff the VP? He's got to be pretty deep in NAN."

Phillips rubbed his jaw thoughtfully. "Think he might be the brains behind it?"

"Makes sense to me. He's got a perfect cover. He hasn't made many mistakes since we got onto him."

"Don't remind me. We're beginning to look like Laurel and Hardy and the Three Stooges all rolled into one. If we don't tree a possum pretty soon, it's going to get real, real ugly."

"Maybe we'll get something from his professor."

The clanging alarm startled Linc. He was still reaching for the carbine in the display case when the bell shattered the silence. He had waited until he was alone in the side room, but the din was sure to draw security personnel and a crowd. He had to move fast.

He ripped the rifle out of the shattered case and raced to the next display. A fine collection of silver and gold coins and paper bills were stoutly protected with shatterproof glass. Three smashing blows with the butt of the rifle separated one corner of the display. Linc grabbed the steel frame pieces and managed to bend them enough to reach into the case. He scooped up as much as he could and jammed the coins and bills into his pocket.

The sound of feet pounding in the corridor told him his time was up. He grabbed the rifle and headed toward the nearest emergency exit. Rounding the last corner, his feet slipped and he crashed into another display case then slid across the floor. As he scrambled to his feet, a guard came into sight. For just a moment their eyes locked, then the guard saw the rifle. He almost fell over himself as he retreated around a corner.

Linc rose and threw himself at the emergency door. Another alarm screamed to life, then he was on the street, racing for his car. A few pedestrians scattered to let him pass. The sight of the rifle was enough to keep them from interfering.

He threw himself into the car, then had to wait until the bubble top sealed before starting the engine. He was aware of prying eyes and knew they were taking note of make, model and license plates. When the engine caught, Linc tore at the control yoke in an effort to put as much distance as possible between himself and the museum. Traffic was light all the way to the on-ramp to I-5 south and he was soon lost in the mass of vehicles heading out of Sacramento towards Stockton.

"Shit, shit, shit," Linc yelled. "I'll never make it! That son of a bitching guard recognized me, I know he did. Shit!"

South of Sacramento, he turned off the freeway and followed a maze of side roads through fields ripe with grain, grapes and fruit. With each mile, he gained confidence, but his heart still beat a furious rhythm in his chest.

"Don't panic. Don't panic," he mumbled. "Yeah, at least not 'til you see red lights and hear a siren. Then, panic!"

10:45 a.m., San Francisco.

"That was the university. They still can't locate Johnson." Walter Reynolds hung up the phone and cringed, waiting for Phillips to explode.

"What else is new?" yelled Phillips. "All we've done is chase ghosts ever since I got here. Nobody! And I mean nobody, is ever where they're supposed to be." Furiously, he pounded his desk. "Just once I'd like somebody to see a real, live, monkey-assed fugitive. We've got Long Trail's picture in the hands of every damned cop in California. Every cop in the damned nation has had pictures of the other two for days. I don't get it. Are they invisible?"

Reynolds welcomed the ringing of the phone and reached for the receiver like a drowning man reaching for a life-preserver.

"Reynolds here. What? Wait, let me put you on the speaker."

The wall video blinked on. The caller was in police uniform.

"This is Lieutenant Sanchez, Sacramento P. D. We just responded to a 211 at the California Native History Museum. The security guard says he recognized the robber. Says it was this guy Long Trail you put the posters out on earlier."

"Where is he? Did you get him?" exploded Phillips.

"No, sir. The suspect escaped in a late model Tiara, brown over white, license 8-Charles-Peter-Charles-4-7-2. A citizen trailed him to I-5 south, but lost him at the on-ramp. We have an APB out on the vehicle. We've checked with DMV. The car's a rental from, hold it a minute ... yeah Skyway Leasing, El Cerrito. We got the code for the GPS, but so far, *nada*."

"Shit!" Phillips' choleric face became even more mottled. "Okay...Okay. Shit, so close. All right, listen up. I want every unit—city, county, state—to make that vehicle the number one priority."

"Walt," he stabbed a finger at his S. F. chief. "Put this info out to every unit we've got in California. Get some choppers up. Work a grid with Sacramento at the center and blanket the road net."

"Sanchez, what's south of you on I-5?"

"Not much, sir. Farms, a few small towns. The next big city is Stockton."

"How far?"

"About forty miles."

Phillips though for a moment. "Walt, have someone get a detailed map of Sacramento and vicinity up on display." Then to Sanchez, "Where else could he head from where he hit the freeway?"

"Well, just about anywhere. He could catch 50 east or I-80 east or west, or he could double back and head north."

A map of the Sacramento area popped onto another wall screen. Phillips studied it while he idly listened to Reynolds giving instructions for the helicopter grid he was organizing. "Walt, hold it a moment on those choppers. See what you think about this. Our boy might go north. Not much up that way, right, Sanchez?"

"No, sir. Small towns, open country, like to the south."

"Right. Not much chance he'd go that way, besides, it'd take time to double back and he knew he didn't have much time. He'd probably make a beeline for wherever he's headed." "Reynolds nodded. "Probably true."

"Okay," continued Phillips. "East?"

"Sierras," said Sanchez. "Lots of places for someone to get lost up there."

"Makes sense," added Reynolds. "It's the kind of country he and the Teagues could use to advantage."

"Couple of problems, Walt. If he was planning to meet 'em up there, why'd they come all the way to the Oakland hills in the first place? Besides, we're not sure the Teagues managed to get out of the area. No, I doubt he's headed east, but put a chopper on the main roads and alert rangers in any park areas up that way. So, we're left with south and west, right?"

Nobody answered the rhetorical question.

"No special reason to think south," commented Reynolds. "Open land, not much there."

"True," replied Phillips, "but I think we ought to blanket that quadrant, at least as far as Stockton. It looks like there're lots of secondary roads bending west. He could sneak back down into the area where we've been searching. He knows his place in Berkeley is blown, but he'll probably head for somewhere he knows, and that adds up to the bay area." He made his decision. "We'll concentrate in two arcs. One along I-5 south and the secondary roads heading west as far as Stockton and the second on I-80 west and parallel roads to the south. He's almost got to be in that quadrant."

"He might have cut back to old Highway 99, sir," interjected Sanchez. "It runs down to the east side of Stockton about ten miles east of I-5."

"Hmm. Not likely, Sanchez. He'd have to cut back west and cross 5 somewhere, but let's put a chopper over there in case. One more thing, Walt. Anybody spots our boy, I want to know immediately. I want surveillance only 'til I give the word. God help any bright-eyed hero who takes independent action. We play it right, our pigeon'll lead us right to our shooter."

Phillips had another thought. "By the way, Sanchez, What'd Long Trail get from the museum?"

"Well, we don't have a complete list yet, but we know he got a rifle and some old coins and bills."

"What? I don't get it. I can understand the rifle, but why not find someplace where he could get a brand new one? But, old coins? Bills? What's he doing, starting a collection?"

"Don't know, sir," replied Sanchez. "The guard says Long Trail's been working here as a volunteer for a year or so. He should know his way around. I don't imagine he took stuff he didn't want."

A puzzled Jordan Phillips ended the conversation and concentrated on the intense manhunt.

11:20 a.m. South of Lodi.

Linc chafed as he followed the lumbering farm truck at less than the posted 35 miles-per-hour, but he didn't want to draw attention to himself by speeding up to pass on the narrow road. Only a few more miles and he could cut east, cross Highway 99 north of Stockton and then turn south to the farmhouse. Maybe twenty minutes and he could rest.

Movement to the west caught his eye. Four helicopters were flying parallel to his course in stately formation. As he watched, one peeled away to the west and another followed less than a minute later.

Jesus, they're already here. I should've thought about air search. Hard to hide from those bastards.

He scanned the sky through the bubble top, half expecting to see a chopper hanging above him. He relaxed for a moment when the sky appeared clear, but caught his breath when he spotted another probing helicopter several miles to the east. *East and west. They have me bracketed.* Suddenly, he was certain they knew right where he was. *They're toying with me. They want me to lead them to Charlie and Ruth.*

An awful thought came to him. "The professor! He's told them where to find me. He'd know where I'd go! Shit! I'm trapped!"

Certain now that he was leading the authorities right to Charlie and Ruth, he turned onto a dirt lane and parked in a wide spot next to a towering old oak. Shielded from the sky by the leafy canopy, he raised the bubble top and prepared to run at the first sight of trouble. Tensely, he waited for any sign of pursuit, ready to flee. "Run where, you idiot?" he thought out loud. "Mighty redskin outruns police cars and helicopters?" No, he realized, there was nowhere to run. He waited to be captured.

Ten minutes passed like hours. The only sounds were from birds and insects. Two cars passed on the road he'd been traveling. Neither one slowed or seemed to notice the car in the lane.

If they know where I am, why don't they come and get me? He began to think more clearly as his fevered brain calmed. Linc was trained in the scientific method. His mind turned to the problem at hand. Two minutes later he'd located his lap-top computer in the trunk. He plugged into the computer jack in the dash and tapped into the Internet. Five minutes later, he was fairly certain the authorities didn't know where he was. The bubble top came down and he swung the car around. It was time to find a better hiding place.

2:30 p.m. San Francisco.

"I don't get it." Walter Reynolds looked rumpled. His desk was a mess. Faxes and e-mail continued to pile up, but at a slower rate than earlier as each search unit reported negative results. The motorcycle had been recovered, but it told them nothing. "I'm beginning to think you were right when you called these guys invisible."

Jordan Phillips wore a resigned, sad expression. His anger had boiled, simmered, boiled again and finally passed. He needed all his energy to concentrate on the evidence they had and to piece together some string which would tie it in a bundle and lead them to the fugitives.

"It's here, Walt. The answer's staring us in the face. We just don't have the key to fit the lock. Obviously, our boy is one bright cookie. He's probably bright enough to know how to disable a GPS locator. That's why we don't get a signal. He's had enough time now to get where he's going." Anger briefly flared again. "And he's probably laughing his damned head off right now!"

An assistant popped his head into the office. He knew better than to expose his whole body to the pissed-off chief. "Berkeley just called. They found Johnson."

"Who?" barked Phillips.

"The professor, sir. You remember?"

"Oh, yeah. What line?"

"Four."

Phillips stabbed the button. "What you got? Where is he?"

Agent Barnes answered the terse questions and received his orders, happy to hang up with his head still attached to his shoulders.

"They found him holed up in the science library," Phillips said. "Seems somebody finally got bright and checked their master computer to see who was logged on. Our professor's been sitting at the computer all day a block away from our team. They'll pick him up and bring him in. Maybe we can get some answers to our questions."

Walter Reynolds heaved a sigh. "That'd be nice, but he probably won't even know Long Trail. You know how it is in those big universities. He could have a thousand students."

"I don't think so, Walt. Our boy's been doing some kind of graduate work with Johnson. I'll bet he knows his grad students pretty well. He probably knows *exactly* what Long Trail's working on and where he hangs out. My hunch is that the professor holds the key we've been hunting for." The director of the FBI allowed himself a tight smile. *Now, the fun begins*, he thought.

SEVEN

Friday, July 16, 7:00 p.m. Pine Ridge Reservation.

The old pick-up was upside down, a tangled wreck at the bottom of a steep slope. It was obvious to the two police officers that the driver had been an attractive young woman, but her body was already swelling and clouds of flies hovered above their bloody feast.

"God, I don't think I'll ever get used to this," commented one of the troopers.

"Yeah, it still gets to me too. What really pisses me off is when it's a young one, like her. This never had to happen." The second officer shook his head, appalled at the waste.

"Think she was drunk?" asked the first.

"Naw. When her mother called in she just said they had a big fight this morning and wanted us to find her. She just drove off mad, I guess. You better get on the horn and let the office know. They'll probably send someone out to tell Mrs. Long Trail."

The tribal police were used to domestic disputes. They sometimes led to disaster. They had no reason to question Marie Long Trail's version of events. The officer shook his head again. "This shouldn't have happened," he repeated.

5:00 p.m., San Francisco.

Jordan Phillips felt his anger rising again. Professor Demetrius Johnson was crusty, obdurate, ornery and downright uncooperative. What was worse, he seemed to enjoy his role.

"Professor, let's do this one more time," said Phillips calmly. "You know Lincoln Long Trail very well."

"Yep."

"You know what he's working on?"

"Of course."

"But you won't tell me?"

"Can't."

"Can't? Last time you said you wouldn't."

"Same thing."

Jordan Phillips leaned forward on the table, his face only inches from Johnson's. "No, Professor. It's not the same. When you say you *can't*, you mean you *won't*, and if you *won't* tell, *I can* charge you with accessory after the fact and obstruction of justice. In fact, I'm thinking about doing that anyway. How would you like a vacation in a four-by-six room with bars on the window?"

The professor looked mildly amused. "Sorry. I don't have time for a vacation right now. Lots of work to do."

Phillips felt his blood pressure rising. An experienced agent in the bureau would recognize the signs and beat a hasty retreat. He took a different approach. He studied Professor Johnson the way he would study any hard-to-solve puzzle.

"Professor, why can't you tell me what Lincoln Long Trail is working on?"

"You don't have clearance," replied Johnson easily. "Nobody gets information on the project without clearance." Phillips stopped himself before striking the smug face in front of him. Maybe this academic misanthrope really was so disconnected from the real world that he didn't realize who he was talking to. Earlier in the interrogation he'd insisted he was unaware of any assassinations or any manhunt. He confessed that he never watched the news. It was too gloomy, too sensationalized. He preferred scientific reading, scientific computer updates and scientific programs on holovision—if he bothered to watch holovision.

"Professor Johnson, I am Jordan Phillips, Director of the Federal Bureau of Investigation. I am often briefed personally by the President of the United States of America on any and all matters pertaining to the internal security of this country. I have clearances you have never heard of. I know secrets you will never know." Phillips lost it. "What the hell makes you think I don't have clearance?"

Johnson appeared unruffled. His tone didn't change. "I know who you are and I also know you're not on the list of individuals cleared on this project."

"What the hell makes you so sure?" Phillips pushed his flushed face an inch from the professor's nose.

Walter Reynolds gulped and spoke hesitantly. "Uh, Mr. Phillips, sir. Um, maybe we should take a break."

"Shut up, Walt!" With visible effort he controlled his voice, but never relaxed his stance. "Well, Professor. I'm waiting."

"It's very simple," replied Johnson. "I made the list. You're not on it."

Reynolds made a Herculean effort to withhold a smile. "Mr. Director, may I have a private word?"

Phillips was breathing heavily. He was locked in mortal combat with an implacable foe and was reluctant to back down. "Johnson, I'm going to talk with Mr. Reynolds. If you move a muscle while I'm gone, I'll have you castrated!"

He stalked from the room with all the dignity he could manage.

Demetrius Johnson smiled and gave his impression as soon as the door closed behind the two men. "Damned unpleasant fellow. Probably doesn't know who his father was."

"Walt, I'm going to strangle the bastard. He knows *exactly* where Long Trail is and *exactly* what he's up to. Did you see his eyes light up when I told him what Long Trail stole from the museum? Shit, his whole body glowed. He knows what the rifle and old money are for. This narrow-minded son-of-a-bitch thinks Long Trail is some kind of modern day Billy the Kid, or something."

"I agree," replied Walters calmly. "Trouble is, he's got you so wound up you can't see how to handle it."

Phillips stopped pacing and glared at his subordinate. "So, you have a solution?"

"Maybe."

"Professor, I apologize if I was in any way uncomplimentary or rude. You're free to go."

Johnson savored the words as he crossed the bridge to Oakland in the back of the director's personal limousine.

They think I'm a fool. No, that's not quite right. They think I'm an absolute fool. It was all too easy. There is the apparent solution to the equation and the unseen collateral equation which really controls the experiment. The solution I see equals the solution they want me to believe. What I don't see is what they're really planning. You'd better think this one over very carefully, Demetrius. Yes, very carefully indeed.

"Nice car," he said to the crew-cut driver. "Very comfortable."

"Put a blanket on him, Walt. If he twitches, I want to know it."

"It's already done. We've got the GPS code for his car, a tap on his phone, and an agent in the apartment next to his. Another team is staking out the place. He won't go anywhere."

"If he moves, call me. I'm going to wake a few people up in Washington. That son-of-a-bitch is going to find out real fast who has authority around here. I'll be on his list before he gets home."

8:30 p.m. East of Stockton.

"Charlie," hissed Ruth. "Charlie, did y̲o̲u̲ hear something?"

A contented snore came from the front room. Ruth sat up and pressed her back against the wall. The sound came again—crunching gravel, a rustle in the leaves. She raised the pistol with both hands and steadied it on her knees. It was pointed squarely at the oblong of lighter darkness framed by the window.

"Psst. Charlie? Ruth? You in there?"

"Linc?"

"Yeah. I'm coming in."

Ruth relaxed as Linc dropped two bulky packages through the window then levered himself over the sill.

"Where's Charlie?" he hissed.

"Asleep."

"Well, wake him up. I need help getting this stuff in here and I've got to hide the car."

Minutes later they were seated near the window. Linc told them about the phone call from his mother and his botched escape from the museum. "I hid out all afternoon, but I didn't see any more helicopters. I think I got here without being seen."

"I didn't even hear you drive up," said Ruth.

"I turned off the engine at the road and coasted as far as I could, then pushed it the rest of the way."

"So, what happens now, Cousin?" Charlie was in a foul mood. The beer was long gone and Linc hadn't brought any more.

"I don't know. Hell, I'm blown sky high. They've probably got everything they need from Johnson. We probably won't be able to get within a mile of the accelerator. All they have to do is change the access codes and I won't even be able to get in. I'd say our best chance is to give up."

"Great! That's real easy for you, Cousin. You're not the one they want to blow away. You got nothin' to lose."

"You dumb ape! I've already lost everything. They know about me and NAN. They know I robbed the museum. My security clearance just went down the toilet. I won't be able to get a job teaching retards to spell. It's all over." Linc's voice trailed off to a whisper.

"Maybe not, Linc." Ruth leaned forward and spoke earnestly. "Maybe they don't know everything yet and it'll take time to change access codes and that stuff. Maybe if we move fast enough, we can still be out of here before they know we're gone."

Linc shook his head. "Naw. No way. They've got to know by now."

"Linc—we have to try. We've come too far." Her voice fell to a whisper. "We're in too deep."

Linc heaved a sigh. Even though he knew it would be pointless, he couldn't think of a better alternative. "All right. We'll try, but we have a lot to do. If we're going to have any chance at all, we'll have to get there before daylight."

He emptied the contents of the packages he'd brought and sorted the material in the dim light.

"Okay. First, clothes for everybody. You'll have to change and leave everything else here. I won't be able to change until I'm inside, so you'll have to bring my stuff with you."

"Wait a minute, Cousin. How come you're goin' in and we aren't?"

"Because I have a clearance to be there, you don't. The security guard wouldn't let you in."

"Hell, we just blow him away. By the time—"

"Charlie! Shut up. Let Linc finish."

"Look. I'm going to drop you on the other side of the accelerator, about a half-mile from the end of the building. There are emergency exits every half mile. Once I'm inside, I'll tap into the security program and scramble the alarm system, then let you in. Okay?"

Charlie grunted. "Just don't leave us with our asses hanging in the breeze too long."

"Next," continued Linc. "Rifles, pistols, some ammo—we'll need to buy more 'cause some of this stuff is hard to find."

"Where we gonna get more?" asked Charlie.

"Trading posts, forts, people on the trail. I plan to drop you near Fort Laramie. You'll be right on the main trail along the Platte River. There should be plenty to choose from, there, before you move off to make contact with the tribes."

"Linc, exactly what is our story? What are we supposed to do?"

"Yeah, and where will you be?"

"We'll go over that later. First, let's get finished with what we have to do now. I got all the dried meat and fruit I could find. You'll need something until you can buy food or kill some game. I got some money so you can buy the things you need."

"I've got money," said Charlie.

Ruth looked exasperated. "We already went over this. How good do you think your money's going to be? You think some dummy's going to accept money that won't be printed for over a hundred years?"

"That's right, Charlie. Like I said, we leave everything—I mean everything here except for what I give you to take. You understand?"

"Not my pistol. I keep that gun."

"Wrong. It'd be no good anyway. They don't make ammo for that pistol in 1875. Leave it. You'll just have to get used to the weapons I got for us."

Linc rummaged through another box. "I did bring some stuff they didn't have in 1875. Ruth, this is for you."

"What is it?"

"Magic. You're going to be a Shaman, a seer, a prophetess to the tribes. I scavenged a bunch of simple magic tricks from a novelty store. They all have instructions. They're simple, but impressive. Lots of things that go boom or make colored smoke. You should be a big hit."

"What about me? What am I supposed to be?"

"This is for you." Linc held up a long sleeved shirt with a high collar.

"A shirt? What's so damned special about a shirt?"

Linc controlled himself with an effort. "This isn't just any shirt. It's magic too. Wear it and you're practically bulletproof. It's the latest thing in protective material. It might not stop a solid hit from a rifle, but it'll sure as hell stop a pistol shot. Just wear it under your clothes all the time."

"In case someone shoots me?"

"For when you invite them to shoot you."

"Cousin, you're nuts. Why would I ever be dumb enough to invite someone to shoot me?"

"Because, that's what you have to do. If Ruth can't convince the leaders that she's a great medicine woman, you may have to finish the trick. Oh, one thing. The material can be cut, so don't depend on it to save you from an arrow or knife." Charlie appraised the shirt skeptically. "Well, at least the guys shootin' arrows are on our side."

It was after midnight before they finished planning, and Ruth and Charlie had changed clothes.

"Hey, these boots don't fit worth a damn, Cousin. This damned magic shirt you gave me ain't too comfortable either."

"Charlie, quit complaining and get some sleep. You can get new boots when we get there." Ruth was losing patience with her brother. "I wish you were going with me instead of him," Ruth whispered to Linc.

"Don't worry. I'll join you as soon as I can."

"How will you find us?"

"If you're doing your job, it should be easy. Everybody will be talking about the 'Holy Woman' and the 'Man Who Turns Bullets.'"

Linc couldn't sleep. He rested his head on the pack of clothes he would wear and wrapped himself in his blanket, but couldn't shut out the terrible feeling that it was too late.

"Linc? You awake?" whispered Ruth.

"Yeah, afraid so."

Ruth propped herself on an elbow, only a few feet from Linc. She had braided her hair and looked attractive in a gingham-checked dress that appeared gray and black in the low light. "Linc, are you scared?"

"Hell yes. I know they're on to me. I'll never get in the accelerator, and even if—"

"No, I don't mean that. I mean aren't you scared of this—this whole thing? I mean, what if it doesn't work? What happens to us?"

"You mean if we're wrong about being able to go back in time?"

"Yes. What if we, like just disappear, or something?"

"I don't know. We know it worked with the kangaroo. There's no reason to think it won't be the same for us."

"But the kangaroo died, didn't it?"

"Yes, but we don't know why. I just don't have answers for you. Either it works, or, well, I don't know."

Ruth sat up and folded her arms around her knees. "Linc, I'm terrified. I'm not sure I can do this. Maybe it'd be better to turn myself in. I'm not even sure I want to live like our ancestors, even if it works."

Linc smiled and slid over next to Ruth. He threw his arm over her shoulder. "Hey, listen. If we make it, you'll be the most famous Indian woman ever. Forget Sacajawea and Pocahontas. You'll be famous in song and story as the incredible Raven Woman, *Hecala Win*, the Lakota medicine woman who united the tribes in peace."

"Raven? Where'd you dig that up?" In spite of herself, she smiled when she said it.

"Well, you have to have a name. It sounds better than Ruth."

"I'm kind of partial to Ruth, if you don't mind."

"Okay, then your white name will still be Ruth. Since you and Charlie were supposedly raised by whites, it's natural that you'd have a white name, too."

"If I live that long," said Ruth glumly. "What's it going to feel like? Will it hurt while we're in that pod thing?"

"Nope, you won't feel a thing. It'll be over faster than you can blink. One instant you're here, then you're there. You won't even know it happened."

Ruth was quiet for a moment. "Linc, tell me how this time machine works."

Linc chuckled in the darkness. "What do you know about super-conductors, diamagnetics, and magnetic field motion theory?"

She turned her face to him, wanting to trust him, but terribly afraid she would fail. "Hold me, Linc. Make me feel good. Tell me some more about how famous I'll be. Please, make me believe you."

They settled under one blanket, bodies tightly pressed together. Linc stroked her hair and promised her fame, fortune and love in her new life.

"I want love now, Linc. I want you." Her lips pressed hard against his mouth. Under the blankets she fumbled with her clothes.

Linc forgot his anxieties and rushed to match her pace. They coupled eagerly, frantically gripping each other with wild abandon. It was so natural, so easy. They crossed from distant relatives to interlocked lovers in moments. There was no going back.

Long minutes passed while their breathing returned to normal, their hearts slowing to a comfortable pace. Ruth still clung tightly to Linc, as if he would vanish if released. She burrowed her face into his neck and shoulder, relishing his scent.

Her terror had abated, but new questions assailed her. Who would she need most on the plains? Charlie would be with her, his presence a deterrent to physical danger, but his bull-rush tactics and short temper—especially if coupled with liquor—could get them killed. Charlie was powerful and devoted to her, but dull and unimaginative. He didn't even have enough imagination to be scared. She could hear his contented snoring in the next room.

Linc wouldn't be there, at least not for some time. And what qualities would he bring? Brains, resourcefulness, a commanding presence…and love. *I'm in love*, she realized. *I really am.* She smiled and squirmed against him lightly. She felt him respond.

"It's time to go," he said softly.

Ruth slowly relaxed her arms and legs and raised her face to his. Her eyes were moist and she swallowed hard, but when she spoke, her voice was firm. "Remember this night, Black Feather. If we survive, no, when we survive, you must return to me. I love you. Promise you'll find me."

Linc felt giddy and hopeful and sad and happy. "Trust me. I'll be there. We'll only be apart a short time. Nothing will keep me from you, but now we must go."

"A few minutes more," she pleaded. "Love me again. It makes the terror go away. What difference can a few minutes make?" She smothered his lips with hers before he could reply.

Saturday, July 17, 3:45 a.m., San Francisco.

"Prof's on the move," shouted Walter Reynolds to a dozing agent across the office. "Find the chief and get him up here on the double."

Jordan Phillips was already on his way to Reynolds' office when the agent found him. It had taken much longer than he expected—Professor Johnson had been home a long time before Phillips got the answer he was seeking. He had to wake up the most powerful man in the world, but it was worth it.

"Johnson's in his car," Reynolds announced when he saw Phillips in the doorway. "Doesn't look like he's headed for his lab. Could be he's—"

"Never mind, Walt. I know where he's headed," interrupted Phillips. "Whistle us up a chopper and we'll be there first."

"A chopper? Where?"

"Stockton."

"What's in Stockton?"

"You wouldn't believe me if I told you—which I can't. Just shake up a ride for us and meet me in my car."

Phillips was gone before Reynolds could pick up the phone.

3:55 a.m., East of Stockton.

Edith Williams was exhausted. The baby was finally dozing off. She sat in the rocker by the window and gratefully rested her head on the high back. A flicker of motion across the fields caught her eye and then a light winked briefly.

"Damn," she muttered. "Damned homeless jackasses are over at Bentoni's place again." The baby stirred in her arms. "Don't worry, sweetheart. This time I'm gonna sic the cops on 'em before they get away."

The dispatcher assured her a deputy would be there almost immediately.

Edith returned to the window, eager to see the arrest of the worthless tramps who occasionally plucked food from their vegetable garden. "It'd be all right if they'd come up and ask for it," she had told the nice person who answered her 911 call, "only they never do, and I'm damn mad about it."

"Jesus, Charlie! Close the trunk," hissed Ruth.

"Aw hell, sis. Ain't nobody gonna see that itty-bitty light out here at this time. Just throw the stuff in."

Ruth quickly tossed the packages in the trunk and slammed the lid. She jumped when Linc ran around the corner of the barn with the last of the supplies.

"Okay, that's it. Let's go," Linc whispered.

Ruth slid into the back seat and Charlie dropped wearily in the passenger side. Linc sat in the driver's bucket seat and wished the bubble top would close faster.

In the confines of the barn, the purring of the four-cylinder engine sounded like a low-earth-orbit shuttle igniting on the upper level of the SSLA. Linc threw the car into reverse and whipped it out into the drive. He accelerated rapidly on the twisting drive to the road.

"Hey, Cousin, give us some light," implored Charlie.

"No light 'til we're well gone from here," replied Linc.

"Linc! Look!" yelled Ruth.

Linc eased up on the control yoke. The car slowed in the lane.

"Where? What?" he asked.

"Over there! East!"

Linc looked right and saw the distinctive yellow and blue revolving lights of an emergency vehicle coming north on a parallel road to the east. As he watched, the lights blinked out, but the headlight beams showed the vehicle was turning left. It was turning onto the road that passed the farm. Linc assumed it was a police car. Somehow they had been discovered.

Linc thrust the control yoke forward. Spewing gravel, the rental car leaped ahead. He was barely able to control the left turn onto the paved lane. The rear view camera showed bright lights only a quarter-mile behind.

"Fly, baby, fly," Linc whispered.

He knew it was no good. Four cylinders against eight. Acceleration, a function of power and distance, against a radio. One vehicle, crammed with fleeing fugitives, against the concerted might of every law enforcement agency in the country. It had never been a fair fight. Now, it seemed the race was lost. There was no more acceleration left in the rental heap. The lights behind were getting bigger, brighter.

But, suddenly, the car behind them slowed and Linc watched it turn left into the drive to the house they'd just vacated.

Linc looked back to the road just in time to see the bridge abutment.

In the sheriff's car, gravel from the drive slamming against the body drowned out the smashing of metal on metal—less than a half-mile away.

EIGHT

Saturday, July 17, 4:35 a.m., Altamont Pass.

Demetrius Johnson was among the few people who truly appreciated the Interstate Guidance System. Slipping down the east side of the Altamont at 95 miles per hour, the professor was able to let his mind concentrate on important matters. Since the advent of the magnetic strips in the pavement, linked to the internal computer in a car, the driver had become a passenger. Johnson was taking full advantage of the travel time.

A blinking memo in the upper right-hand corner of his lap-top informed Johnson he had only 20 minutes to complete his work before reaching the SSLA. Furiously, he input the data to solve the complex equation.

Long Trail = Black Feather.
VP dead = Long Trail (AKA Black Feather) involved.
Long Trail involved in NAN.
NAN > revolution.
Revolution = Violent overthrow of govt.
therefore: Long trail (AKA Black Feather) wants war.
therefore: Long Trail (AKA Black Feather) is a revolutionary.
> Long Trail not to be trusted.
therefore: He MUST be stopped?

Johnson raised his glasses and massaged his eyes. For a moment, he felt his age.

There was a time when a simple problem like this wouldn't have bothered me. Now, it's a question I need to consider more carefully. You must be getting old, Demetrius.

The computer display indicated 14 minutes to destination.

Jordan Phillips had two smiles. The first was reserved for formal occasions. It was mechanical. Crank in the angle of lift reserved for the individual he was facing, and the lips responded automatically.

His second smile was spontaneous. It appeared when he was unexpectedly faced with a beautiful woman. It also appeared when he solved a complex problem, generally related to criminal activity, and he knew he would win.

The instrument lights of the Nighthawk Attack Helicopter illuminated the second smile of the director of the FBI.

"Make sure we have coverage on the linear accelerator," he shouted into his microphone.

Walter Reynolds nodded. The message had come through loud and clear in his headphones. Teams were already en route. Besides, he thought, the display shows we're passing over Johnson's car right now. We'll be at the accelerator about the time he arrives. With a little luck the San Francisco bureau chief will capture some limelight and, possibly, a promotion when the brains behind the NAN assassination is whiffed.

Reynolds' smile was genuine, but then he only had one.

5:02 a.m.

The car wheezed and clanked with every rotation of the tires. It threatened to shake itself apart at any speed over twenty miles per hour, but it was still running. Charlie looked gruesome with a blood-soaked towel pressed against his swollen forehead. Linc was nursing a sprained wrist and Ruth had complained of shooting pains in her back.

"This is the place," Linc announced. "I should open the door over there in about twenty minutes. If I don't show, it'll mean I didn't make it in." He looked directly at Ruth. "Then I guess you'll be on your own."

Ruth smiled. "You're going all the way, and we're going with you. See you soon."

Ruth and Charlie hopped out and swiftly grabbed the packs. They disappeared into heavy shrubbery next to an abandoned building across from the block wall of the accelerator.

Linc wished he could share Ruth's confidence. His stomach was tied in knots when he parked the car and this affected his courage to approach the main gate. "It's now or never, buddy," he chided himself. He took a deep breath and walked toward the circle of light at the gate.

The security guard behind the thick glass was a regular. He showed no emotions as Linc went through the entry procedures. Palm print, voice recognition, magnetic key card—all confirmed. The door slid open. Linc was thirty paces down the hall before his stomach stopped churning.

"One pigeon in the coop," commented Reynolds. "Shall we go in and take him down?"

"No, not yet. Let's see if we get lucky. Besides, I want to make sure all our teams are here and ready. We'll give it a half hour or so."

Lincoln Long Trail might be the brains behind the assassination, but Jordan Phillips wanted the shooter above all else. "I have a feeling, Walt. This whole thing's about ready to come down. Before long we'll have all the answers."

"You think Johnson's in on this, too?" asked Reynolds.

"Anything's possible. He wasn't exactly cooperative and it looks suspiciously like he and Long Trail had this meeting set up. Time'll tell. Neither one's leaving that place without a personal escort and a nice pair of bracelets."

"Come on! Come on! Click, baby." Linc was frustrated and confused. After signing on the computer, nothing worked. Every command got the same response; "INVALID ENTRY. CHECK YOUR ACCESS CODE."

"Morning, Linc. Having trouble?"

Linc shot out of the chair like a scalded cat. "Professor! I ... I. Uh, I didn't know you were here."

"Um, yes, I assumed you wouldn't be expecting me—Black Feather."

The air went out of Linc in a rush. His knees collapsed and he sat heavily in the chair. "I guess the authorities got to you?" Linc asked weakly.

"Yes. I had quite an interesting time with a Mr. Phillips and a Mr. Reynolds. They showed me some rather amusing material they claim you authored. Were they correct?"

Linc nodded his head, too drained to speak.

"Then they are also correct in their assumption that you are a revolutionary, bent on the overthrow of the United States, and the brains behind the recent assassinations?"

"What?" Linc sat bolt upright. His brain rushed to assimilate this information. "What? What are they talking about? No! Absolutely not! I do not advocate the overthrow of the government. I advocate a Lakota Nation created from within the borders of the United States, and I want that accomplished peacefully. I knew nothing about the assassination."

"Hmmm. But you do know this Charlie whatever, and his sister?"

"Yes. They're distant cousins. But, Professor Johnson, they didn't know about the assassination either. Charlie just sort of panicked when the shooting started and ... he didn't mean to ... I mean it wasn't planned ... what he did," Linc finished lamely.

"What he did, as I understand it, was gun down an FBI agent. Mr. Phillips seemed more than a little irritated about that, and he was astonished when I said I hadn't heard of the shooting. He was kind enough to show me the tape of the murder. That's what it was, wasn't it? A murder?"

"No, an accident. A terrible accident, but no one will believe that now."

"Mr. Phillips believes there may have been at least one more 'accident' since then. There's a man and a car missing." Johnson let the accusation hang in the air.

"Yes, that's true. It's a terrible consequence." Linc felt dejected once more. There was no question that the second murder was just that—murder. And the knowledge that the FBI believed he was responsible for the whole thing left him reeling.

"And what about you, Long Trail? Stealing from a museum? Running down the streets waving a gun at people? Just pranks?"

"No, it was stuff we needed."

"For?"

The word hung in the air.

"Well?"

"You know, Professor. We needed them for tonight. For now. Where we're going, we'll need those things."

"Ah, yes, I see." Johnson acted as if the idea was new to him. "You were planning to take a little vacation? Possibly a side trip to the past somewhere?"

"It—it never had to happen. We can fix it. This," he waved his arm at the transporter pods, "is a cure for everything. We can change it so there will be no need for the vice president to visit the tribes. If there was already a Lakota Nation, there never would have been this tragedy. None of us would be here now. Professor, we can fix it."

"I find that hard to believe, young man. I'm not at all sure you can change what has happened, or even try."

"We *have* to try. It's the only chance we have."

Johnson studied his student closely. He was inclined to believe that Linc had no part in planning the assassinations. It was possible that everything he said was true. It was also possible that he was lying.

"And your relatives? They planned to go with you?"

"Yes. They're waiting for me to let them in one of the emergency doors, but I can't access the security program."

"Ah, my little scrambling of access codes slowed you down then?"

Suddenly it was all clear. The professor had locked him out of the computer. Even though he had the pre-programmed disks for the transporter, he would have no way to activate the program. So close, he thought. We were so close. Then came a new thought. *No, don't give up. Maybe there is a way.*

"Professor, I know this is a strange request, but would you allow Charlie and Ruth to come in here? Let them talk to you?"

"You mean put a gun to my head and make me open the computer, don't you?"

"No. I mean let them talk to you. You could go in the control room and use the speaker. That room's bomb-proof, and we don't have bombs anyway." Linc watched the professor. He seemed to be wavering. "Please, sir. Just talk. We're helpless if you don't listen."

"Damn! Something must have gone wrong." Charlie huddled in the bushes and studied the access door intently, willing it to open. "It'll be light soon. If we don't get in that building, we're dead meat."

"Give it a few more minutes, Charlie."

Ruth was almost beside herself. Even though they were related, it was not immediate family. After the first afternoon when they kissed, there had been other brief times together when Linc visited the reservation, and the one time she had come to Berkeley, but Linc was shy and their relationship had progressed slowly with gentle prodding on her part. Now, that was all changed. She felt a glow she had never experienced and knew he felt the same... *We've really just discovered each other, and it could already be over,* she thought. *Linc, please. Please be all right. Open the door.*

A motion up the street caught Ruth's eye.

"Psst, Charlie. Look."

A car was rolling slowly down the street toward them. The lights were out, even though it was still pitch black with only an occasional streetlight. Ruth and Charlie huddled deeper in the shrubs.

The car was unmarked. The two men inside peered intently at the storefronts, alleys and vacant lots as they passed. Ruth held her breath, willing them to hurry on.

The car was just past them when a sliver of light appeared in the blank wall. The security door was opening.

No! No! Ruth was screaming in her mind. *Linc! Hear me. Close the door!*

Almost as if he had heard her, the door closed. When it opened again the light was off.

"That's it," hissed Charlie. "Let's go!"

"No! Wait," whispered Ruth. "Let the car get further away."

Thirty seconds later they sprinted across the street and disappeared into the wall.

"San Joaquin Sheriff's dispatcher on the phone, sir." The driver handed the phone back to Phillips.

"Jordan Phillips here. What've you got?"

He listened intently with only an occasional, "Yes. Go on," and finally, "Thank you very much. Please send the completed report to our San Francisco office. I'll detach one of our teams to the property ASAP. Ask your deputies to remain at the scene. We'll take over, and, by the way, do you have any units in the vicinity of the SSLA?"

He seemed satisfied with the answer. "Let them know we have a possible situation here. We may call for assistance and we would appreciate a fast response."

"Well?" asked Reynolds. "Anything important?"

"Yeah, real interesting. One of their units just answered a call to a deserted property about two miles from here. Neighbors reported transients moving around. Guess what they found?"

"Hell, I don't know. What?"

"Well, we got us a real stiff corpse, reported missing near Oakland, buried under some hay bales, and, you won't believe this, we got us a pistol and clothing belonging to one Charlie Teague."

"Holy shit! What about Long Trail and Ruth?"

"Nope, but we also got some clothes that most likely belong to her—right down to bra and panties. Maybe we're lookin' for a couple of naked Indians. We can add indecent exposure to the rap sheet!"

Jordan Phillips seemed to derive huge delight from the idea.

The radio squawked to life.

"Base, this is three."

The driver grabbed the microphone. "Go ahead three."

"Yeah, we got some movement on the east side of the building about a half-mile from the entrance. We think it might have been two individuals; one male, one female."

"Let me have that," said Phillips.

"Three, this is Phillips. Have you got them in sight now?"

"No, sir. They disappeared along the east wall. There are security doors every half mile or so. We think they ducked into one."

"Bingo!" chortled Phillips. "Three pigeons in the coop." His smile was definitely a big number two.

"Walt, get on the phone to the sheriff. I want every unit he can spare, code three. I want this end of the building sealed off."

He punched the button on the microphone savagely. "All units, this is the director. I want units one, three and four to hold your positions. Units two, five and six move to the front door. Move it now! We're going in."

By the time he, Reynolds and the driver sprinted to the door, the other cars converged with screeching tires. Doors flew open as they braked to a halt. Behind the security glass, the sleepy guard leaped to his feet, his eyes bugging out.

"FBI!" screamed Phillips as he flashed his badge. "Open the door!"

"I ... I'm not sure. I need authoriza—"

"Open it now or we'll blow it to pieces. There are federal fugitives in there. Do it!"

The door slid open, the agents rushed through. As they passed, Phillips demanded, "Where's Johnson's lab?"

"Uh, down that—"

"Show us!"

The balding, overweight guard hustled ahead, casting nervous glances over his shoulder. "There. That door."

"Right. Get back."

The phalanx of agents formed a semi-circle at the door, weapons cocked, eyes blazing. Behind them they heard the first sirens from arriving reinforcements.

"Okay, go!" Phillips yanked the door open. The agents went through in a rush, fanning out and seeking shelter inside the lab. Their eyes raked the room, weapons waving to cover the corners.

Demetrius Johnson sat at a console in front of a glass wall on the far side of the room. He appeared unruffled by the intrusion.

Jordan Phillips stalked into the room, pistol drawn. A quick scan showed no obvious places where three fugitives could hide. Beyond the glass wall he could see a steel tube and several ovoid glass modules. Again, there appeared to be no place to hide.

"Where are they, Professor?" he demanded.

"I presume you mean Lincoln, Charlie and Ruth?"

"You know damned well who I mean. We know they're here. We saw them come in. It'll be a lot easier for everybody if they just come out."

"I'm afraid you're mistaken, Mr. Phillips. They aren't here."

Phillips was ready to explode. Then he spotted a pile of clothes at the end of the console. A hasty check confirmed them to be the clothes Linc had worn into the building.

"Your assistant running around naked in here somewhere, Professor?" He held the pants and shirt inches from the professor's face.

"No, I'm afraid you're mistaken. You see, they're not here."

"Professor, I've had it with your damned attitude. You're in—"

Suddenly, Jordan Phillips knew. There was no doubt. Demetrius Johnson was telling the gospel truth. Lincoln Long Trail, Charlie Teague and his sister Ruth were somewhere beyond the clutches of the FBI.

"Walt, get everybody out of here. Seal the building. Search every office, nook, cranny and closet."

"Yes, sir, but I don't get it."

"You don't have to get it. Just leave us alone. Close the door on the way out and don't let anyone—and I mean anyone—in here."

Phillips holstered his pistol. He took a chair next to the professor and studied the console and the equipment beyond the glass wall.

"So, this is it. Are those the transporters?"

"Ah, it seems you have been asking questions about my project."

The thought rankled Phillips anew. "Oh yes, Professor. I had a very nice chat with the President a couple of hours ago. He wasn't very happy about losing his beauty sleep, but he was very informative. Project T. Travel through time. Oh yes, I got a quick but thorough briefing." He studied the professor, trying to decide if the man was a nutty quack or a raving genius. He was beginning to believe the latter.

"Tell me. Does this thing really work?"

"It would appear so, yes."

"So they're gone? Gone into the past?"

"Apparently."

"And you let them go?"

"I sent them."

Phillips scratched his head and released a long sigh. "Then, I'm afraid you're in a lot of trouble, Professor. At the very least you've aided and abetted federal fugitives. At the worst, you are a co-conspirator or even the mastermind behind the assassinations. I'm sure the trial will be quite interesting, and it will keep you away from your work for an extended period, I would imagine. Like, maybe twenty years."

"Oh, I doubt that, Mr. Phillips. I'm certain this will all blow over before noon today."

"You are one conceited son-of-a-bitch, aren't you?"

"Not really. I'm just a realist. You see, I had nothing to do with any murders and neither did my assistant. I'm certain you will find that to be true as you continue your investigation. Also, after speaking with the Teagues, I'm quite sure he is guilty of murder and should be convicted. She, however, appears to be innocent of any crime."

"You are still guilty as hell, Professor. You helped them escape."

"Did I? Long Trail was competent enough to handle that without my assistance. He was much brighter than even I gave him credit for."

"You mean to tell me that one person can do this alone? How the hell does someone put themselves in one of your things there and then take care of everything else in here? It can't be that easy."

"Ah, but it is. At least it is that easy if you are Lincoln Long Trail. You see, he had all the information pre-programmed on these disks."

Johnson brandished the computer disks in front of the director.

"Once the disk is inserted, like this, everything is virtually automatic. The pods can be self-sealed. The program originally contained a delay factor to allow the last one to be entered. Actually, the addition of humans to the process is redundant."

"You mean those disks tell us where they went?"

"Precisely."

"Then we could pursue them!"

"Possibly, yes."

"What do you mean, possibly?"

"We have no guarantee they will arrive, shall we say, in good health. In fact we really have no idea what will happen to them. And, it's a one-way trip. Do you wish to go, Mr. Phillips? This disk contains the information which will lead you to Mr. Long Trail. All I need do is insert it and activate the program. Shall I, Mr. Director of the FBI?"

Jordan Phillips stared at the tiny disk, mesmerized. God, it was tempting. Worse, it was the most frightening situation he could imagine. No. There was no way he could send a man to that unknown fate. He knew there was no man who would do it. It was over. The hunt was ended and he had lost. It was a bitter pill.

"Just out of curiosity, Professor, where did they go?"

"Judging by the coordinates Long Trail used—that's how we program the destination—I would think he went to an area in northern Virginia. The others went to another place. Somewhere in western Montana or, perhaps, Wyoming. I'll be able to tell you exactly when I have time to check the coordinates."

"Two places? They split up? Why?"

"I'm sure I don't know. I do know there is a plan, but I have no idea what it is."

"What year?"

"1875. August, to be precise."

Johnson was correct. Long before noon he was released from custody. Jordan Phillips, frustrated and still angry, cast a baleful glance at his only prisoner as Johnson scooped up his belongings and prepared to leave the San Joaquin County Sheriff's office—again in the director's personal limo by presidential order.

"Two questions, Professor."

"Yes?"

"Why'd you do it? I mean, why didn't you stop them?"

First, I am not the police. Second, scientific curiosity, of course! We have the technology, but we may never know if it works as the model says it should. This was a test which conducted itself, and, if they die, they have no one to blame but themselves. And your other question?"

"Will they succeed? Can they change history?"

Demetrius Johnson studied the question for several moments.

"No, Mr. Phillips. I doubt they can accomplish their goal. However, just by being there, dead or alive, they've already altered history," he paused for a moment. "Haven't they?"

NINE

Sunday, August 1, 2021. Weston, Maryland.

The dinner wasn't going well. Kimberly watched Randy and Jamie making 'man talk' about the Redskins. The conversation was incomprehensible to Kimberly. Football was not her sport, but it was fun to see how well her son related to Jamie. It made what she had to do tonight even more disturbing.

"Randy, I hate to intrude on your conversation, but didn't you promise to clear the table and do the dishes?"

"Aw, Mom. Do I have to?"

"Hey, Tiger. No problem," said Jamie. "Here's the deal. You be the quarterback and I'll be the running back. Grab the plates and hand them to me in the kitchen. I'll put six on the board and your mom'll lead the cheering section. Okay?"

"Yeah! Only I'm Halverson, not Cosworth. He sucks."

"Done deal, Number Six. Let's blow Jacksonville away!"

Kimberly watched her normally stubborn son fall into the game with Jamie and shuddered. This was what Randy needed. This was what Jamie could put in their lives. *Why?* she asked. *Why can't I let it happen?*

You know why, she reminded herself. There were still the memories of David, fading now, but not forgotten. Then there was the dream. It was crazy, but twice in the last week she had awakened in a cold sweat.

Jamie was in uniform. It wasn't his regulation uniform. It was the one he wore for the Civil War skirmishes. She could plainly see him among many other mounted men, only the scene was not under the cool trees of the Virginia countryside, it was on a knoll covered with deep yellow-brown grass under a bright yellow sky. There were no trees in sight. As the drama unfolded, the orderly formation shattered. There were hundreds of shots from an unseen enemy. Men and horses wheeled in confusion, then began to fall. Screams from injured mounts and troopers filled the air. Jamie tumbled off his horse, then rose, firing his revolver. A keening cry from the unseen enemy drowned out the din of dying. It wasn't a rebel yell. It was entirely different.

Each time Kimberly awoke at the same instant. Jamie was hit and crumpled into the mass of bodies on the ground. What Kimberly couldn't understand was why Jamie had an arrow buried in his chest.

If this wasn't enough of an omen, her brief meeting with the director of the DIA this morning had decided her course of action.

Jamie kept up a lively banter with his quarterback while he loaded the dishwasher. *I couldn't ask for a better son if I made a special order*, he thought. *Then why am I so gloomy? Kimberly hasn't said no. She seems to be having a good time. But ... but she isn't with us. I'm being closed out. I know it. Why?*

"Good night, Number Six. We whipped those Jaguars like they've never been whipped before. Right?"

"Yes, Sir, good night."

This was it. As soon as Kimberly kissed Randy and tucked him in, they would have time to talk. Jamie went to the kitchen and poured himself a stiff brandy. His sense of foreboding made him tense and irritable.

"Hey, pour me one of those, will you?"

"Oh, sure. I don't remember you having an after-dinner drink before."

Kimberly licked her lips and tried to hide her agitated hands. "Um, sometimes I do. I think I need it tonight."

Jamie handed her the balloon glass. This was it. "Something you want to tell me?"

Kimberly couldn't look him in the eyes. She was chewing her lower lip. "I—I think you know, Jamie." The glass moved restlessly in her shaking hands.

"Maybe," Jamie said softly, "but I'd like to hear it from you."

"All right." There were glistening sparks in the corner of her eyes as she looked up into his face. "I'm sorry. I just can't marry you."

"Do you need more time, or is there something—"

"No, Jamie. I can't marry you now—maybe never. It's just the way it is. I'm sorry. I need to do other things with my life. I need—"

She broke off, her resolve failing, and fled the room.

The brandy tasted like stale sweat. Jamie glanced around the neat home, a home he wanted very much to share.

Somehow Kimberly's explanation was inadequate—not quite complete. His uniform jacket felt like there were lead weights in the pockets. He strained to slip it on. He wanted to say good-by, but maybe she already had.

Kimberly studied her distraught face in the bedroom mirror. Tears streaked her cheeks. She appeared older, harsher. A warm spark inside burst into flame. *I can't do this. I don't care what they said, I love him.*

She thought back to the brief meeting this morning with Darrin Dealey, Chief of the DIA. He, and a man from the FBI had asked her questions about Jamie – about his loyalty, habits, friends. There were intimations, but no direct accusations. An investigation was in process and she was to say nothing. There were hints that it might be wise to distance herself from him. No amount of probing could answer her questions.

Screw them, she thought. She dabbed her eyes, squared her shoulders and headed for the living room.

He was gone. His glass of brandy was on the table by the door. There was only the lingering scent of him to remind her he had been there. She started for the door to the hall, but her resolve failed. She leaned her back against the door and let the tears flow.

"Mommy, where's the colonel? Why're you crying? Did he hurt you?"

Randy wavered in the hall. Kimberly saw him through misty eyes—a forlorn little Redskins fan. "No, Darling. He didn't hurt me, but he's gone away and he probably won't be coming back."

"Why, Mommy? I thought you liked him a lot."

"I do. I do, but this was something I had to do."

Long after Kimberly put Randy back to bed, she lay in her own cold bed in torment. *There's still time. I'll give it a day or two. Somehow I'll have to explain why. Maybe I should just tell him the truth. The plain truth—I couldn't stand to lose him.*

She finally dropped into a restless sleep, secure in her decision to talk to Jamie again later this week and try to make it right.

Monday, August 2, 2021. DIA Headquarters.

Jamie felt like death. He had given up any thought of sleep in the deep middle of the hot night. He proposed arguments, then discarded them. He hatched schemes, but they were no good. Several times he picked up the phone, but Kimberly had given him an answer and he couldn't think of words to change her mind. Frustrated and grumpy, he paced his apartment until dawn. Two hours at the office hadn't improved his temper. Unbidden memories: the soft feel of her skin, the scent on her hair and the mumbled words of love when their bodies were intertwined. Jamie groaned aloud.

"Um, Colonel?" His secretary cautiously stuck her head through the door, ready to flee if he snapped too loudly.

"Yes," he said, too sharply.

"You got a message on the E-Net about ten minutes ago. The boss's waiting for an answer."

"What? Oh, I haven't been watching the screen. Okay, I'll take care of it."

He flicked the message switch on his keyboard. The message matched his mood—gruff and terse.

TO: Lt. Col. H. J. Partridge
FROM: Darrin Dealey
Report to my office 1130 hours. Special briefing. Reply.

"Damn. Two minutes," Jamie snarled. He punched his acknowledgement into the computer, grabbed his hat and coat and raced for the elevator.

Dealey greeted Jamie in the hallway as Jamie emerged from the elevator.

"Sorry, Partridge. I should've told your secretary. We're meeting downstairs."

Jamie held the door and started to punch the button for the mezzanine conference room.

"Hold it," ordered Dealey. He produced a key card and inserted it below the elevator buttons. Three red lights appeared on the console. Dealey placed his thumb firmly on the lowest light. There was a pause while the computer scanned his thumbprint and matched it before the door slid shut and the elevator dropped toward the third sub-basement—the Black Room.

Jamie swallowed hard. He knew the room existed, most senior analysts knew that much, but the space was restricted to personnel with much higher clearances. A bead of sweat ran down Jamie's neck as he tried to conceal his rising tension. Dealey seemed to take no notice of Jamie's discomfort, and did nothing to relieve it.

The door slid open to reveal a short hall and double doors. A sentry rose from his desk and snapped to attention. While Dealey again inserted his card and repeated the fingerprint test, Jamie wondered how effective a lone guard with a stun gun would be if headquarters were penetrated to this point.

"Any enemy attempting to remove this sentry is in for an explosive surprise," commented Dealey.

Christ, he really can read minds, thought Jamie. His apprehension increased.

Three men were seated around an oval conference table in the briefing room. Jamie recognized the FBI chief, Jordan Phillips, and the man in uniform with the three stars of a lieutenant general looked familiar.

"I'm sure you recognize Mr. Phillips, and this is General Oglethorpe, special advisor to the President." Jamie nodded to each. "And this is Doctor Demetrius Johnson." Johnson barely looked up from a yellow pad covered with indecipherable scribbles.

"Have a seat, Colonel, "continued Dealey. "Relax, while I bore you with your résumé."

Relax? I'm as nervous as a cat with a long tail in a room full of rocking chairs. He sat facing the others while Dealey paced behind him and rattled off a rapid-fire history.

"H. Jamison Partridge, the Third. Born, Helena, Montana. West Point, 1998—fourth in class. Service in Bosnian Airlift, Macedonian Incursion and Desert Thunder. Also, Pentagon staff and current assignment, weapons research and intelligence assistant, DIA. His specialty is chemical and exotic weapons."

Doctor Johnson raised his head and cast an appraising glance at Jamie. "Bio Group 4 and laser radiation?"

Jamie nodded. The doctor was obviously "in the loop". Only a handful of people knew of these projects.

Johnson went back to scribbling as Dealey picked up the narrative. "Special talents for this mission include hunting, fishing, survival skills, and experience with First Maryland Volunteers, a Civil War reenactment unit. He is therefore familiar with weapons, tactics and general living conditions of the era."

Jamie's mind tumbled in circles. *What on earth could my familiarity with the Civil War have to do with a current assignment?*

Johnson piped up. "Colonel, as a native of Montana, I presume you are familiar with Wyoming and the Dakotas?"

"Yes, I've traveled all that area, and more."

"And your role in these Civil War things?"

"A cavalry officer, sir."

"So I take it you're an accomplished horseman."

"Relatively. I've ridden all my life."

The professor seemed satisfied and returned to doodling.

"Finally," continued Dealey, "Colonel Partridge has no living relatives and no immediate family. A recent liaison with another member of the DIA staff was abruptly terminated two days ago."

The blood rushed to Jamie's face. He swiveled in the chair and half stood, ready to blast his boss.

"Sit!" barked Dealey.

Jamie collapsed in his seat.

"It is my business to know everything—I repeat, everything—about the lives of my key people. That includes their most private and intimate personal lives, Colonel. For instance, the last book you read was *The Chinese Riddle: Exploring the Treaty With Japan,* and you didn't think much of it. Miss Caldwell, however, thought it very insightful, didn't she?"

Jamie nodded dumbly. He felt numb and betrayed. *How could Kimberly have done this?*

"Don't blame Miss Caldwell, Colonel. As I say, it's my business to know these things."

Doctor Johnson raised his head, his eyes boring into Jamie. "Any physical limitations, especially heart and respiration?"

Jamie opened his mouth, but Dealey pounced on the question. "Nothing to hamper his suitability. Any other questions?"

"Yes!" roared Jamie. "What the hell is going on here? Sir."

"We're coming to that, Colonel."

"I have a question for the colonel," interjected Oglethorpe. "As a military man, familiar with tactics, what do you think of the actions taken by George Armstrong Custer at Little Big Horn?"

Jamie could only think: *My name is Alice and I've fallen down a rabbit hole.* He waited for the general to turn into a Mad Hatter.

"Colonel? Did you understand the question?" asked Dealey from behind him.

"What? Yes," mumbled Jamie. "Custer ... Little Big Horn ... command wiped out by Indians ... huge blunder. This is ridiculous! You brought me here to take an ancient history test? Or was it just to let me know Big Brother is watching? I—"

"Perhaps we should slow down a bit," interjected Jordan Phillips. "I must admit I would find it difficult to approve these tactics by my field agents." The FBI chief smiled and spoke directly to Jamie. "I'm certain this is quite confusing, Colonel. May I call you Jamie?"

Oh great, good guy, bad guy. I've seen the movie.

"As you wish," replied Jamie stiffly.

"Colonel, ah, Jamie, I'm certain you are aware of the murders of the vice president and secretary of the interior two weeks ago."

Lucky me. We go from ancient history to current events. He nodded.

"And I'm certain you know the fate of Charlie Teague and his accomplices involved with the death of one of my agents."

Jamie nodded again.

"What, as you understand it, was their fate, Jamie?"

At least there was no trick question here. "They were cremated," responded Jamie. "They were trapped in the Oakland hills and napalmed. We watched it happen on holovision in 3-D, living color. Poof! Exit bad guys—and girls."

"Exactly," beamed the FBI director.

"Well," said Oglethorpe, "if that's his read on the situation, it answers a question we've been debating at the White House. If a senior assistant at the DIA believes the story, I don't think there've been any leaks."

"Wait a minute! Hold it right here," Jamie stormed. "I've obviously been locked up in this room with a tree full of certified nuts!"

"Sit down, Colonel!" snapped Dealey. "Please."

Jamie was in no mood to cooperate, but there was something in Dealey's voice that touched a nerve.

Jamie glared at the assembled nuts, but slowly took his seat.

"Colonel Partridge is right. It's time to cut to the quick." Smoothly, Dealey took control of the meeting. "Before I can explain, Colonel, I need to ask one more seemingly irrelevant question. All right?"

Jamie took a deep breath. "Sure. Shoot."

"Colonel, in your capacity with the DIA I know you deal with some of the most exotic possibilities we might ever have to face. To do this, you have to stretch your mind and occasionally consider the seemingly impossible. True?"

"Yes, sir. I do hear some pretty strange stuff. Of course, most of it turns out to be just that, real strange stuff."

"But, occasionally, something weird turns out to be not only possible, but useful. It steps from theory to practice. Right?"

In spite of himself, Jamie began to be intrigued. "Yes, sir. Occasionally." Jamie let the word hang.

"Professor, perhaps you should explain."

"Certainly." The professor was all business now. "However, before I begin the explanation, I wish to explore another area." He turned his eyes, highly focused now, to Jamie.

"Colonel, when you were growing up in Montana, did you have any contact with Indians?"

Jamie smiled. It wasn't the first time some ignorant easterner had asked the question. "Not really, Professor. You see the Indians were mostly dead and buried by the time I was born. The few remaining were, and are, pretty much segregated. Mostly by their choice," he hastened to add. "They kind of stick together."

Johnson nodded. "And what is your opinion of Indians?"

Jamie was caught off-guard. "My opinion? In what way? I mean they're people. They live pretty much in their own sphere—not a lot of contact with whites."

"What did you think when the vice president and the secretary were killed? Was it justified?"

"Justified? Murder? No, sir. A little sad, maybe. I thought the government was maybe ready to right some past wrongs, but the killings put an end to that."

"So," Johnson pounced, "you believe the government has been wrong? You think we owe the Indians?"

"I've seen the way they live. It's not that great, but I don't know how much can be blamed on the government. Maybe we do owe them. Maybe we don't. That's not my field."

Jordan Phillips was gaining new respect for the professor. *He handles an interrogation as well as my agents*, he thought.

Johnson bored in again, very intense. "Colonel, what if I told you that the three fugitives in California aren't dead? What if I told you they got away—scot-free?"

Jamie glanced at the other men in the room. They were all studying him intensely. Maybe they were all crazy. Then an alarm went off in his head. "Wait a minute! You're not—you're not saying this is some kind of a cover-up? Are you?"

A glance confirmed his fear. Something was going on here. There was some horrible error if the men in this room had to involve a lowly lieutenant colonel. Something was terribly wrong.

"Gentlemen, with all due respect, I believe you have involved the wrong person here. I swear I will never divulge anything I've heard, but I—"

"Hold your horses, Colonel." Dealey wasn't smiling; his steel core was showing. "This isn't like the last century. It's no Watergate or Contragate. The issues involved here are of the very highest security. There are fewer than two dozen people outside this room who are even aware of the issues. The President is fully involved and will, as your commander-in-chief, answer any questions or problems you may have about what is being discussed."

But what is being discussed? I'm here and I have no idea what's going on. Do I really want to know?

"Sir, I'm intrigued, but—"

Professor Johnson cleared his throat. "Colonel, excuse me. What do you know about the theory of time travel?"

Jamie could only stare at the professor. He half expected the paneling on the walls to turn to rubber pads. *Time travel? Three charred corpses who weren't? Indians? And George Armstrong Custer? Where am I? Maybe I have fallen down the rabbit hole.*

"Uh, Einstein theorized that it was possible. H. G. Wells wrote the best book about it." A light bulb went on. "You're not seriously suggesting that ... No! Time travel?" Jamie's jaw hung slackly.

"I watched them go, even helped them," said the professor blandly.

"And I arrived right after they left," concurred the FBI chief.

"And the President believes them," added the general.

Jamie scanned the faces in the room. They weren't kidding. Jamie tried hard to focus. There was a reason for all this and suddenly he knew what it was.

"And you want me to go after them. Is that it?" Even as he said it, Jamie knew it was too far-fetched. There was no logical reason to go after someone who no longer existed. Justice had been served. Three corpses prominently displayed to the nation. *See what happens when you commit murder?* No, it had to be something else.

The professor was eyeing him as he would a prize student who just solved a complex equation. "Yes, Colonel. That is exactly what we want you to do."

Jamie was dumbfounded. "But, why? As far as anybody knows, the case is closed. There's no reason ... or ... there is something else."

Jordan Phillips leaned forward. "Are you familiar with the Native American Nation, Colonel?"

"Sure. A bunch of wackos who believe they should have a sovereign territory carved out of the United States. That's what led to the assassinations."

"Have you read any of their literature?" asked the FBI chief.

"No. Why? Should I?"

"You can start with this." Phillips thrust a thick packet of papers across the desk. "As you read, you should be aware that the articles, and there are a number of them, written by one Black Feather, are most relevant. Besides being the best researched and most persuasive, our friend Black Feather is more commonly known as Lincoln Long Trail."

"Oh," sighed Jamie. "Maybe the four of you aren't as crazy as I thought."

3:40 p.m.

Jamie rubbed his bleary eyes. The other four had disappeared for lunch and other appointments, leaving him to survive on a ham sandwich and a pot of coffee. Neither the documents nor the reader were allowed out of the room.

Johnson and Phillips were the only ones to return for the afternoon session. They were pleased with Jamie's summation of the Native American Nation position. He obviously understood the situation.

"Okay, I understand the problem," Jamie concluded. "Where do we go from here?"

"Ready to study some more files?" asked Jordan Phillips.

Jamie nodded. "Yes, sir. I guess so. What's next?"

Phillips slid over a slimmer packet. "Shouldn't be as difficult as the last batch, Colonel. Why don't you take this one home with you? Spend the evening with it. See if it fits. We'll have an early meeting tomorrow."

Jamie felt relieved. Even his sparse quarters had more amenities than the Black Room. With a deep sigh, he accepted the folder. Stenciled on the cover were the words:

MAJOR MATTHEW O'SHAUNESSEY - 1831 to ??

TEN

Tuesday, August 3, 2021.

Jamie faced the full panel from the previous day. "Okay, let me get this straight." A late night and three cups of morning coffee made him jittery. "We've got three people from the twenty-first century running around in the nineteenth century, apparently bent on changing history as we know it."

"We *believe* they are there and doing what you say," commented Johnson. "We will not be certain until there is some alteration of history of a significant nature."

"How will you know that?" asked Jamie.

"Oh, some data in some history book will be slightly at variance with what we know. There are people tracking it—as best we can."

"Professor, I may be a little slow, but what happens if there is a dramatic change of some kind?" asked Jordan Phillips. "Like, say someone of historical note dies and *we* know that person didn't die at that time."

"Ah, but we wouldn't know that, Mr. Phillips. You see, we would know only what was reported to us in the history we would have. It *would* be an altered history, but *we* would not realize it."

Now it was Jamie's turn to scratch his head. "So, if there is a change, how the hell will we know it is different?"

"We won't." The professor sat back, smiled, and folded his arms, letting his pronouncement hang in the air.

"But, you just said—"

"That we have people tracking it? Yes, I did. It's possible, not probable, that we may catch some small thing. We've made photocopies of relevant documents from the era on the off chance we may find a difference in the original. As I say, since we do not know what we're looking for, the chances are slim."

General Oglethorpe had added little to the conversations. His job was to brief the President. He was feeling out of his depth. *How the hell do I tell the President that history may change and we won't even know it has changed?* "The boss'll look at me like I've misplaced a few marbles," he muttered.

"Say what?" asked Johnson.

"What? Oh, nothing, nothing. Just thinking out loud. So you're saying that they're already changing things and we can't do a thing to stop 'em?" Oglethorpe asked.

"Precisely, General. We are helpless until our player gets into the game." Johnson leaned forward, intently surveying his, as he considered them, new students. "Practically speaking, we have all the time in the world to place our man in the game. We can drop him in ahead of our friends and maybe he could cut them off at the pass. We could wait for weeks—years—before inserting him. However, in the meantime, real time is passing." He consulted his watch. "I make it eighteen days already. Therefore, changes, albeit minor, have occurred. Every day that passes will result in more changes."

"*If* they got there and *if* they're alive and *if* they're really about to alter ... Jesus!" Jamie was getting a headache.

"Exactly," agreed the professor. "We currently have an uncontrolled experiment. What we need is a control—a check."

"Me." It was a flat statement. Jamie was a white rat. He was the trained, intelligent white rat in the maze. An image came to him. He was running around in circles, whiskers twitching, tail dragging and every time he looked up he could see monstrous eyes critically analyzing his every move. It was an uncomfortable feeling.

The professor beamed at him. The feeling of being a bright pupil was overshadowed by the image of being an intelligent rat.

"Great, Professor," Jamie said. "Only one problem. How the hell do you know what I'm doing?"

"Simple, Colonel. You're going to tell us. "

Jordan Phillips was reminded of how infuriating this man could be. He left it for someone else to ask the question they were all thinking.

"How?" asked the general.

"Newspaper. Nothing to it," replied Johnson.

"Newspaper," repeated Jamie. "Am I supposed to get a job and write a column?"

"Oh, come now, you can be more creative than that." Johnson was very self-satisfied.

Cocky bastard, thought Jamie. "Okay, I give up, Professor. Just how do I communicate?"

"Personals. All you have to do is slip in an innocuous note to Uncle Demetrius occasionally."

"You're assuming they had personals in those days?" Jamie asked.

Johnson was not to be put off. "If they didn't, you'll invent them." He actually chuckled a little.

"Okay, that solves one problem," Jamie continued. "What about this Matthew O'Shaunessey? The guy disappeared during the Civil War and—"

"Probably killed at Gettysburg," interjected Oglethorpe. Staffers in St. Louis had spent days poring over ancient files in the military personnel history facility to locate a possible, and plausible, individual for Jamie to replace.

"Right. I understand that. But, what am I supposed to do? Do I just wander in and say I want to pick up where I left off twelve years ago?"

Oglethorpe was ready for this. "We have a plan for that, Colonel. If you accept the assignment, you will be fully briefed before you leave."

Jamie nodded, content for the moment. "But that brings up another point. What do I do for money? It was a hell of a lot cheaper then, but food, lodging, transportation still cost money."

"If you go, you'll be well provided for. In fact, you'll be quite wealthy." Oglethorpe opened a folder. "The President has agreed to fund you as follows: all retirement and pension pay accrued plus the amount you would have accrued had you completed your current enlistment. As a bonus, you will receive an amount equal to five years pay at your current rate—no taxes or other withholding."

Jamie whistled. He wasn't precisely sure what his retirement package was worth, but when he added the probable figure to five years pay…. "Whew," he said. "I'll be one rich major."

"Of course," continued the general, "it will all be in gold."

"Naturally." *Jamie, you just won the lottery,* he thought.

Johnson put a small hole in the balloon. "It's only fair, Colonel, when you consider that it's a one way trip."

Even that thought was not enough to dampen the warm glow Jamie was experiencing. Another thought came to him. *My God, think of the hunting and fishing in an unspoiled—well, relatively speaking—western U. S. Unfished rivers and lakes teeming with fat, dumb fish. Deer and elk in abundance. And—unbelievably—buffalo, antelope, bears….*

"Did you hear me, Colonel?"

Jamie blinked. "What, sir? Oh, sorry, General. I guess I was dreaming."

"Instant wealth will do that, I suppose," said Oglethorpe. "What I said was, the President is anxious for an answer. What should I tell him?"

The combination of serving his country, unbridled adventure and unlimited wealth was too much to resist. "Tell him, General, that he just bought himself a white rat." Jamie smiled at the perplexed faces around the table. "Major Matthew O'Shaunessey is about to rise from the dead, gentlemen."

Kimberly simply couldn't concentrate on her work. Her office was too hot, too cold, too humid, too dry. "Bullshit," she swore softly. "You know what's eating you. You've waited long enough. Do it!"

She looked at her watch. Two-thirty. Jamie should be in his office. *Should I call, or just go see him,* she thought.

"Be a big girl. Get off your duff and face this like ... like what you are—a contrite, humble, crumb-begging fool."

With the decision made, she hummed on her way to the elevator. She had scrupulously avoided even setting foot on the floor where his office was located. Now, she could hardly wait for the elevator to arrive.

"Hi, Carol. Is Jamie in?"

"Oh." Carol had trouble concealing her surprise. Jamie hadn't given her a blow-by-blow, but she knew enough to be shocked that Kimberly looked so bright and cheerful. "Actually, no. He took the afternoon off after some hush-hush meeting this morning." She didn't say that he had also looked radiant when he blew through the office—with no explanation.

Kimberly was crestfallen. She was primed, her words rehearsed, and now he wasn't here. "Darn. Do you know where he is?"

"I'm sorry. He didn't say where he was going or when he'd be back."

"Oh. Well, thanks."

"If he calls or comes in, should I say you're looking for him?"

"Um, no, that's okay. I kind of want to surprise him. Thanks anyway."

The bounce was gone from her step as she returned to her office. *Where could he be? Just about anywhere. Maybe I should try his place. No, he wouldn't be there and this is too important to leave on an answering machine. I'll call him right after work,* she promised.

Jamie cast his eyes around the spartan place he had called home. The walls were bare, but there hadn't been much there to start with. The closet was empty, ditto the dresser. His TV, disc player, coffeepot, toaster and other appliances would be picked up later, along with his clothes and most of his other personal gear. He would be taking precious little of his life on his journey. The acquisitions of a lifetime made a pitifully small stack in the center of the room.

"Not a lot to walk away from," he mumbled. "It would have been different if ... hell, forget about her. It wasn't meant to be and besides, you wouldn't be taking this trip if—"

The phone interrupted his monologue. He glanced at his watch. Seventeen-ten. *Ha,* he thought, *this could be the last phone call I'll ever get.*

"Partridge here."

"Jamie. Thank goodness I got you before you left. I want you to stop by 1600 Pennsylvania on your way to Andrews. There's someone here who wants to wish you bon voyage."

"Right, General. I'm on my way out the door."

"You're cleared at the north gate."

"Yes, sir."

Not bad, ace. Win the lottery and meet the President. All in the same day. You are one lucky dog.

As he bounded down the stairs, Jamie wasn't sure if it was his phone ringing or another apartment. "Bye, bye phones! Bye, bye faxes! Bye, bye all the noisy inconveniences of life. I'm on my way to a quieter world," he shouted.

But within, a smaller, quieter voice said, Bye, bye Kimberly.

"Rats," Kimberly snorted. "I get myself all worked up and then you don't even have the decency to be home." She almost slammed the phone down.

"Who you talkin' to mom?"

"Oh, nobody dear. Just myself." *Just myself*, she thought. *I'll try later. He's got to come home sometime.* Another thought crossed her mind. *Maybe he has a date. Maybe he's already seeing someone else. No. Well, maybe.* It was not a comfortable thought, she realized.

The warm glow from his meeting at the White House lasted long into the flight to the west coast. The President was taller than Jamie imagined, and very personable. He and the first lady entertained him in their private quarters. They were obviously excited for him. The President was inquisitive about details of the planning and boomed his famous full-throated laugh when he heard the details of communications and the plan to dump Matthew O'Shaunessey right into the middle of the action.

When Jamie left, the President revealed another aspect as he shook hands warmly. "God, how I envy you."

Jamie reflected on how many people envied the President, and yet he had to agree. *Given the choice, I'll take my trip to the past over his job any day.*

Sleep came to Jamie over Nebraska.

Thursday, August 4. Stockton.

"So this is it."

Johnson glowed as he showed off his toy to his next passenger. "As you say, this is it. What do you think?"

"It isn't very big," replied Jamie.

"Climb in. I'm sure you'll find the space ample."

Jamie gingerly stepped through the hatch into the transparent bubble. "I won't break anything, will I?"

"There's nothing to break. The chip controlling your journey is imbedded in the material directly below you. The sensors controlling landing are in the larger black wafer to the right."

Jamie located the two items, the larger sensor package no larger than a 50-cent piece. The control chip was more like a dime and bright gold. "Geez, and that's all that'll be left?" "Precisely. Everything else vaporizes." Jamie squirmed around so he faced the hatch. "How do I ride in here?" "Just the way you are. Your gear, and your gold, will be packaged and provide a seat, of sorts. You won't be there long," chuckled the professor.

Jamie had another worry. "How come I don't get crushed when this thing does whatever it does?"

"Well, it's rather complicated, but when you are ready, you will be operating in a magnetic field. There are certain properties common to—"

Jamie held up a hand. "Okay. You've already lost me. I believe you." He hunched forward and stepped out into the pod bay, shaking his head.

"Isn't there a track, or something for this thing to ride on?"

"Magnetics, Colonel. Remember?"

Jamie stood, seemingly lost in thought.

"Having second thoughts, Colonel?"

He exhaled slowly. "No. Well, maybe. There is the fear of the unknown. Then there's one thing that would change all this – end it right here." He paused, then shook his head. "But that door's closed. She would have contacted me if…. So, I guess there's really nothing holding me back, but what about you, Professor? You know my mission. I can understand that you're not attached to the Teagues, but you know I have to stop Long Trail, too."

Colonel, I may look like I'm in charge, but we all know who pays the bills. A certain very powerful man you met the other evening is somewhat perturbed with my recent activities. I, too, have my orders. Besides, from a purely scientific point of view, we may never know what happened. I made no arrangements with Lincoln to send back information. Remember, Colonel, a military man follows orders; a scientist explores options. *All* the options."

"Well, if it isn't Major O'Shaunessey. How's it going?" Jordan Phillips stepped through the door with a wide smile. "I have a delivery for you."

Jamie had to think for a moment. It was going to take some time to get used to a new name and identity. "It's going fine. Between history lessons, a physical, and a tour of this place, I haven't stopped since my plane hit the ground."

"Sounds like a busy couple of days. When do you fly?" Jamie looked to Johnson, who, as usual, had an answer. "Oh, I imagine he'll be ready by Saturday. We're still waiting for his uniform, clothes, and papers to be completed."

"Well, you can scratch one thing off the list," replied Phillips. He set a large briefcase cuffed to his left wrist on a workbench and fumbled for the key in his pocket. "Ah, here we go."

Jamie felt his heart hammer his ribs when Phillips opened the case to reveal gold ingots. Ten gleaming, shiny ingots.

"Can I *touch* one?" Jamie asked.

"It's your gold. You can shove it up your nose and whistle Dixie, if you want," snorted Phillips. "You'll notice the stamp on each bar. Shows it was minted in a private mint in Denver. Very authentic."

The metal was incredibly heavy. It warmed in his hands as he rotated it. "What am I going to do with this much gold?"

"Oh, I'd deposit it in the bank—several banks would be better, since bank failures were not uncommon in those days. Remember, gold was a common medium in 1875, although amounts this large were unusual. However, you are half owner of a gold mine if I remember correctly. I wouldn't worry. Just don't let anyone see all of it at once."

"You're a pretty expensive courier," commented the professor.

Jordan Phillips smiled. "Your little toy is still off limits to 99.9% of the population, Professor. We can't have just anybody wandering in here. Besides, I wanted to be here for the, what do you call it? Lift-off?"

"Actually, we call it a shoot, same as the low-earth orbit stuff NASA fires off the roof."

Phillips nodded. "There's another reason, too. I've got another case full of the dope on Long Trail and the Teagues. I'm afraid Major O'Shaunessey is in for a bit of a briefing session."

Jamie groaned and gingerly replaced the gold bar in the case. "See you later, you beautiful little creatures."

Jordan Phillips snapped the case shut and they headed for the briefing room. By the time they were finished, Matthew O'Shaunessey was more than ready to depart. His mission was clear: Stop any attempt to change history, but, most important to the FBI director, was the last sentence he uttered. "Get that damned Indian that killed my agent."

3 p.m., Washington D. C.

"I'm sorry, the number you have reached has been disconnected or is temporarily out of service." "That tears it," Kimberly croaked. "He's not at home; he's not at work. He doesn't even live here anymore."

Fifteen minutes later, Darrin Dealey ushered Kimberly into his office. "What's so urgent, Miss Caldwell?"

"I'm sorry, sir. It's nothing to do with work, but I had to see you so I—well, I'm sorry."

"So what's so earth shattering?" Dealey was afraid he already knew.

"I've changed my mind." Kimberly rushed on, struggling to keep her voice calm, her tears at bay. "I was wrong the other night. I don't care what you and that FBI man said. I can't believe Jamie Partridge has done anything wrong. I want him. I love him and I don't care, but he's gone and you know where he is. I want to see him."

"I'm afraid that's not possible at this—"

"It is possible. I know it is. It has to be. Please, Mr. Dealey. Let me see him, talk to him."

"As I was saying, I'm afraid that's just not possible right now. Maybe in a few weeks."

"You have him, don't you? In prison somewhere? Where?"

"Miss Caldwell, please. It's not like you think—believe me."

Believe you? How can I believe you? You're the man who has all the answers. There's nothing you don't know. You knew all about us, didn't you? Knew we were having problems, or rather I was. You knew all about that and you know all about this.

A new thought burned into her. "My God! You've executed him, haven't you?"

"No, no, no. He's alive and well. He's involved in something beyond even my knowledge. What he's doing right now may very well change history. It's that big." *Or*, he thought, *keep history as we know it.* "Look, let me do this. I really can't explain what is going on, however, I'm willing to try to help you. Please, I'm not trying to put you off, but it will require some time. Will you give me until Monday to prove that I'm on your side?"

"He is alive? He's all right?"

Dealey smiled. "Very much alive and I'm certain he's all right." And, he didn't say, quite wealthy. "Until Monday? If I get an answer sooner I'll call you."

Kimberly allowed herself to be ushered out of the office, only half-convinced. There were other avenues and she was not going to pass the time until Monday just sitting on her backside.

"We'll see about your truthing, Mr. Director," she muttered to the closed door. As she turned away, she remembered the widespread belief that Darrin Dealey could read minds. She had a cold premonition he had just read hers.

Dealey drummed his fingers on his desk and ran over the options in his mind. He decided the issue would not die a natural death. He needed help. He made the call on the private—very private—line. It only went to one place.

"George, we may have a problem." He briefly explained the situation. The voice at the other end was calm, reassuring. Before he hung up, Dealey felt relieved. Now it was out of his hands. He was sure the White House would know what to do.

Saturday, August 7. Stockton.

Jamie—no, Matt, the resurrected Civil War officer—took a deep breath. He was ready to embark on the greatest adventure in the history of man. He had tried to think of something to say, words that would go down in history, but all he could muster as he walked toward the pod in the ready bay was, "Jesus, what's this underwear made of? It itches like hell."

"Well," answered Jordan Phillips, "you won't be finding any soft polyester where you're going, but maybe you can rustle up something in silk."

Matt shuffled his rough boots and contemplated his reflection in the windows of the control room. He definitely looked like a hick from the sticks. The homespun coveralls were at least two inches too short, exposing his bare white ankles above the homemade shoes. The red flannel union suit was dirty and ragged with age, and a two-day stubble of beard gave him a faintly ferocious appearance. *I look like I just fell off the pumpkin wagon. People dressed like this don't make historic speeches, and besides, the world will never know about this anyway.*

It was time. There was nothing left to do. He stepped forward to shake hands.

"Bye, General. Tell the President the cavalry's on the way."

To Jordan Phillips he simply nodded his head, then Professor Johnson was ushering him into the pod.

"Okay. You're checked out on the same coordinates Long Trail used. You will arrive within a week, one way or the other, and will be approximately twenty miles from the capital. Good luck."

Matt saw it again. Johnson had the same look the President had. *He envies me, too.* "Roger, Uncle Demetrius. Just shoot this thing straight and fast and I'll be in touch." *I hope,* was left unsaid.

Johnson stepped back to allow the robotic arm to place and seal the hatch cover. In the pod, Matt sat on all his worldly belongings, including a small ransom in gold, and tried to relax while the heat seal was stitched. Everything was automatic now. The computer ran the program. Seal, check systems, slide the pod into the magnetic zone and FIRE!

There was no feeling, no sensation of acceleration or speed. Intensely bright light forced Matt to close his eyes and throw his hands over his face. A scream started deep in his throat, his body convulsed into a tight ball.

He was still screaming when he fell off his supplies and smelled grass. With an effort he uncoiled his body while the scream diminished to a gasping low wail. It took all his willpower to force his hands away from his face and open his eyes.

Dirt. Dark, damp dirt and green grass. His nose was pushed into a clump of grass and it smelled unbelievably rich and sweet.

He cautiously raised his head. Just beyond the clump of grass was a significant steaming pile of road apples. Ugh.

His senses were returning. He was alive. There was a warm sun above. He'd made it! At least it appeared he'd made it.

He raised himself slowly to hands and knees. His world expanded to take in trees, fences and, thirty yards away, a gray horse. The horse was rolling its eyes and tossing its head. Matt tried to laugh. The sound was a low moaning. *Scared the shit outta you, I'll bet.*

He flexed his muscles and shook his head to try to clear his thoughts. With great effort, he managed to stand. *Something wrong with my balance, feel drunk. Stomach doesn't feel so good either.*

He tried to take a step, but tripped over an obstacle he couldn't see. His vision, so clear a moment before, clouded and blurred.

"What you doin', Mister?"

Matt swiveled slowly at the sound. He cocked his head and tried to focus on the source. A man, large, with a rifle. *He's big, getting bigger, much bigger.* Matt seemed to be shrinking into himself. *Helpless. Why do I feel so helpless?*

Matt tried to smile a greeting. It wasn't working. *Why am I crying? What's wrong? Maybe if I say something.*

Matt opened his mouth to speak. A plaintive cry escaped. It turned into a wail, then stopped. He toppled onto his supplies. His vision faded, his movements ceased and there was only the comfort of blessed blackness.

Monday, August 9, 2021. Washington.

The meeting was short, if not sweet.

"Miss Caldwell, let me introduce General Oglethorpe, special assistant to the President."

"Pleasure to meet you, Miss Caldwell. Mr. Dealey has explained your problem to me. Please be seated."

Kimberly nodded and took the chair she was offered.

"Miss Caldwell, I first want to assure you that Colonel Partridge is alive. Further, he is in no trouble with the government, quite the opposite. He is on a special mission of the highest importance." The general gave her his best political smile.

"I see, General. And when will the colonel be returning?"

"I really can't say. There is a strong possibility he may *not* return. I want to assure you he volunteered for this."

And that's my fault, isn't it? she thought. *But you, Mister Dealey, lied to me, didn't you? Jamie was never under any investigation, but you needed him for this mission and needed me out of the way. Right?*

"General, I need to get a message to him."

"Very honestly, Miss Caldwell, that is not possible, however if you wish to give it to me—"

"No, I don't think so." Kimberly was fed up. There was something she didn't know and she didn't like it. She stood up to go.

"One more thing," the general rose with her. "I sense that you may not believe us. Possibly this will change your mind."

He handed her an envelope. The Seal of the President of the United States was embossed in gold in the upper right corner. It wasn't sealed. She unfolded the single sheet of paper and read the brief note from the President. It did put a new light on the matter.

"Jamie met the President? Talked with him?"

Both men nodded.

Kimberly thoughtfully refolded the note. "Thank you, gentlemen. This changes things."

Yep, this changes things. How do I get an appointment with the President? she wondered.

"Think she bought it?" asked Oglethorpe.

"I hope so. For her sake, I hope so," answered the DIA chief.

NEW
BEGINNINGS

ONE

Date unknown - Somewhere in Wyoming Territory.

Her lusty scream was primal. Pure terror. Ruth had no choice. The horror overwhelmed her, forcing her to shriek. Her muscles convulsed, knotting her body into a fetal position. Her balled fists were clamped over her ears. Behind her sealed eyelids, bright spots danced in the black void. The light had been so bright and there was pain there, but her mind blocked the pain—accepting only the terror.

The screams slowly subsided to soft wails, then to coughing and choking as icy water sluiced down her throat. She gagged and expelled the offending fluid.

Feeling slowly returned to her numbed muscles. Cold. Wet. She shivered, then began to thrash on the ground. She opened her eyes, but the dancing spots remained and she found it difficult to focus. Tall grass waved above her, blown and flattened by the wind pushing a thunderstorm, drenching the earth. Lightning blazed above, forcing her to screw her eyes shut again. The crash of thunder assaulted her ears.

She moaned with new fear and rolled onto her stomach before pushing herself up to hands and knees. Dizzy and nauseous, she staggered to her feet and tried to focus her eyes. Her vision was limited to only a few yards. The sea of grass disappeared into sheets of wind-blown water. Overcome with nausea, she slumped back to the ground.

"Linc, help me," she moaned. "You didn't tell me it would be like this. Linc—please—Linc." Her voice faded to a whisper and she curled her body against the cold and wet. *I will die here. I will die here.*

Conscious thought faded. Cold blackness settled over her. Her body twitched for a while before all movement ceased.

"Yes, the hunt was good, but there are not so many buffalo this year," commented Standing Elk. "Some of our people will die this winter."

"Some die every winter," Crow in the Tree reminded him. "I have seen many more suns than you. It has always been the same."

The two Crow warriors rode easily, followed by three younger men. While they spoke softly, they never relaxed their senses. They had traveled far into Lakota territory, following the dwindling herds of buffalo. They were in enemy country and would not be safe again for many days. The thunderstorm which had rolled over them was now east and north, above the line of trees marking the meandering course of the Platte River. Steam rose from the flanks of their horses and the low sun in the west sparkled in water droplets sprinkling from waving grasses. Soon, they would reach a bend in the river where they and their families would stop for the night. One more day would find them at Fort Laramie. There, on neutral ground, they would spend a week or more at the fort and adjoining trading post. It would be a time for trading and renewing acquaintances with others—Cheyenne, Arapaho, and Lakota. The stacks of buffalo, deer and antelope hides they were bringing would be exchanged for knives, blankets, beads, pots, mirrors and, most importantly, rifles and ammunition.

Crow in the Tree swiveled on his horse. He could see for many miles across the rolling prairie and the only group in sight were the people of the village, following a mile behind. Since they passed this way a year ago, four babies had been born. One baby was weak and died before one moon passed, and three ancients died during the dark months of snow and wind. This summer, two young men died, trampled by countless hooves when the buffalo they were chasing wheeled and trapped them amidst the herd. When their horses stumbled, there was no escape. *So, we are two fewer than last year. Forty-four to face the winter.*

"The buffalo are fewer and our family is—what is it, Standing Elk?"

Standing Elk had reined in his horse. He held his hand up for silence and concentrated. After a moment, he relaxed. "I thought I heard something. Now I don't."

Then they both heard it. A thin cry, carried on the breeze. Again it stopped, then started, barely louder than the rustle of the grasses.

Standing Elk pulled an arrow from his quiver and nocked it in his bow. Crow in the Tree changed the grip on his lance, ready to throw or thrust it at a quarry. The three warriors following them noticed their attention and also made ready to attack or defend themselves.

"It came from there, toward the sun," said Standing Elk. He motioned to the other three to come even and form a line. They started forward slowly, their eyes probing the shadows cast by the low hills while their ears and noses sampled the sounds and smells carried on the breeze.

The sounds were not repeated, and Standing Elk signaled the others to return to the trail. As he angled back toward their original course, the wail came again, stronger. It was familiar to him. Babies made sounds similar to this.

Slightly ahead, he spotted a depression in the grass and warily approached until he gazed down at a woman lying on her back. She was wearing the clothes common to women in the wagon trains—calico dress, bonnet and high-topped button shoes. Next to her was a cloth bag, but he did not see a baby. *The woman is dead. The baby must be close.*

"Here," he called to the others. "Here is a dead woman. Be careful, the baby must be near."

Standing Elk's horse shied and sidestepped away as the "dead" woman jerked her arms and legs. Her face screwed up into a pout and rolled from side to side. A wail, just like an infant, issued from her mouth.

Standing Elk controlled his horse as the others rode up and formed a circle. He noticed that the woman-child was young and attractive. Her face was burned to a copper color—matching his own. When she relaxed her face it was pleasant to look upon.

The plaintive sound stopped and her body lay still for several heartbeats. Standing Elk slid off his pony and knelt by her side. As he reached to touch her, the contractions and crying started again. He jumped back, watching her closely.

Crow in the Tree dismounted and knelt by her head. "She is searching for her mother's teat," he pronounced.

He curled his index finger and rubbed it across her lips. The twitching and crying stopped. The lips beneath his finger opened. She lifted her head slightly to grasp the finger with her lips. He let her suck on the knuckle for a moment, then pulled his hand away. Without opening her eyes, she twisted her head from side to side, searching for the finger. When he offered it again, she repeated the sucking motion, but stopped when she received no nourishment. Her twitching and crying were stronger this time.

Standing Elk turned to his son, one of the three younger riders. "White Horn, find your mother and bring her. Bring them all. We will camp here tonight."

White Horn turned and fled the strange place like the wind.

Standing Elk noticed the cloth bag again and bent to open it. The woman-child had few belongings. Clothes, dried fruits and meat, a pistol, but only five bullets, and a hide bundle tied with rawhide. In the hide were a number of coins and many strange objects. He fingered them and tried to divine their meaning.

Crow in the Tree had been watching him. "Medicine bag. I believe this woman has strong medicine. She has been delivered to us as a sign."

Standing Elk was not convinced. "A sign? Of what? Is this good medicine, or bad?"

"I do not know." He contemplated the fussy woman-child, now still and barely breathing. "Maybe she can tell us—before she dies."

Standing Elk tied the bundle and tossed it aside. It would probably be best to leave this magic where he found it. It might bring white disease among them—or worse.

Little Doe knelt and ground scraps of meat, mixed with fat and mashed berries, until it formed a soft mass. Her husband and son ignored her while they watched Crow in the Tree dust the unconscious woman's face with magic powder applied with a sacred buffalo tail. All the while, he repeated a soft incantation to the Great Spirit to bless his efforts to save this poor creature.

When the mixed meat and berries were soft, Little Doe added water, and then dipped a soft piece of buffalo hide in the mush. The woman had scarcely moved since they placed her between two buffalo robes. She was cold and her skin was losing color. Little Doe dripped some food on the cold lips. It dribbled down her cheek. The lips didn't move.

Gently, she parted the lips and pushed the hide from side to side against the woman's front teeth. At first, nothing happened, but then the teeth parted slightly and her tongue slowly cleaned the food from her teeth and lips. Little Doe dipped the skin and repeated the process. This time the reaction was stronger.

"Leave us, my husband. I will tend her."

Standing Elk, White Horn and Crow in the Tree withdrew to the central fire.

"She is alive," Standing Elk announced. There followed a long session as men of the tribe asked questions. Standing Elk and Crow in the Tree had no answers.

"We will take her with us," Standing Elk told them. "If she lives, it is the will of the Gods."

"And my medicine," inserted Crow in the Tree.

"And if she dies?"

Crow in the Tree shrugged his shoulders. "The will of the Gods." Credit was okay, but to be blamed for a death was not a good thing for a powerful medicine man like Crow in the Tree. "My medicine is strong. I believe she will live because I believe she has been sent to us."

"We will see," replied Standing Elk. This woman-child troubled him.

He was more troubled when he returned to his bed.

"She is not white. She is one of us," Little Doe reported.

"How do you know this?" he blurted before thinking.

Little Doe rolled her eyes at him and shook her head. "Come see," she invited.

She bent and pulled back the buffalo robe. In the dim light he found the naked woman exciting. Her body had not thickened from age and childbirth. Her limbs were long and tapered. And, there was no question, she was copper colored from head to foot. Her long, straight, black hair had been coiled in the bonnet. Now it gleamed.

She shivered and Little Doe replaced the robe. She had seen the light in her husband's eyes and it worried her. She had been his only wife for sixteen summers. She suddenly realized she liked it that way. If this woman survived, then what? It was a disturbing question.

She put the question away for tomorrow. Standing Elk had been aroused by the sight. She smiled as they slid between their sleeping robes. *Tomorrow will be time enough to decide. It will not be difficult to see that she dies—if I want.*

Images formed slowly and they had no meaning.

It feels like Saturday. It certainly isn't a school day 'cause mom hasn't bugged me. Maybe it's vacation. Charlie can take me to the river. Maybe we'll swim for awhile. I want to swim in the river, lie in the shade in the afternoon. Maybe Linc will be there. Now why did I think of Linc? He never comes to the river. He doesn't even live near here. Oh, well, he's cute. Maybe he'll come. If I go back to sleep, maybe Linc will be there when I wake up.

Little Doe studied the woman-child's face. She was getting stronger. Her survival was no longer a question. Crow in the Tree was strutting through the camp, proclaiming his healing power to all who would listen.

"Hmph!" snorted Little Doe. "I saved her." *I didn't have to, but I did.* "Take bows, Holy Man. Next time you may fail."

Ruth stirred, rolled her head and opened her eyes for the first time since she collapsed on the prairie. Blurry images pulsed behind an army of dancing white dots. She blinked several times, then shook her head. "Ow," she groaned. The movement was immediately rewarded with a splitting pain behind her eyes and a ringing in her ears.

"Ow?" repeated Little Doe.

"It hurts, Mommy."

"Iturtsmame?" This was a new word. *Maybe the almighty medicine man understands.* Little Doe went to the entrance hole in the tipi.

"White Horn! Find your father and Crow in the Tree. Tell them to come now."

White Horn jumped up from where he was working on a new bow. His father and the medicine man had returned from the trading post tonight in good spirits—in fact they smelled of good spirits—and went directly to the gambling game in Horse Smells Bad's tipi. They were probably still there.

When Ruth opened her eyes again, there were four faces peering intently at her. She blinked several times, but white spots still danced in her vision and the faces were difficult to see in the light from the fire. The woman reached out and stroked Ruth's forehead.

"Hi," said Ruth. "Who are you?"

The woman looked puzzled and turned to an older man who reminded Ruth of her grandfather. His face was seamed and his long, gray hair hung in greasy braids. A feather dangled from his hair and there was a necklace with three large claws on his bare chest.

"She speaks the white man's language," Crow in the Tree pronounced.

Ruth screwed up her face and tried to concentrate. She didn't understand what was said. She realized there was something she should remember, but it floated away. Her eyes closed. She went back to sleep.

The next time she awakened, she was alone in the tipi. It was a warm day and the sides of the tipi were rolled up. Her vision was better and she felt stronger. She raised her head and looked out into the village. Most of the other tipis also had the sides rolled up and she could see people sitting in the shade of their homes and walking through the village.

My God! I made it! Her mind raced as her memory flooded back. Now she remembered everything from the last minutes in the SSLA. Linc giving final instructions, telling her that she and Charlie would land near each other, but not necessarily at the same time. "Stay close to where you land. Find shelter and wait for each other," he had said. "It could be a day, maybe a week before you are together."

"I'm scared, Linc. I—I don't want to leave you. Please—"

"Be brave, Raven. I will join you later. Everything will be all right. You and Charlie have work to do and I have to go to Washington first, but I will come to you. Now, close your eyes."

Then he had kissed her and sealed the capsule.

What happened? she thought. *There was noise. A rushing noise and light—bright, painful. Screaming. Rain. There was rain and thunder. Pain. Sick. Then—then, black. Black until now and—Jesus—how long? Where am I?*

"Charlie!"

Her scream roused half the camp. Little Doe and White Horn rushed in under the sides of the tipi while others crowded around.

"Go get your father," Little Doe ordered. "Have him bring someone who speaks her language," she yelled after the fleeing boy.

Ruth raised herself on her elbows and gazed fearfully at the people forming a wall around the tipi.

"Who are you?" she asked Little Doe. "I feel very sick." She was answered with a blank stare. She probably doesn't understand English, Raven realized.

"*Nituwe he? Lila makujelo.*" Still no response. She tried one more time. Pointing weakly to an unstrung bow leaning against the hide wall. "*He taku he?*" No response from the woman.

Raven felt chilled. *They don't speak Lakota! This is another tribe. I am among enemies. They'll kill me.* Then she was reassured by the obvious. *If they wanted me dead—I'd be dead.*

Her attention was drawn to a tall, dignified man who pushed through the throng surrounding the tipi. Standing Elk ducked under the hide wall, followed by another man—a white man. She vaguely remembered Standing Elk as one she had glimpsed before. His companion was dressed almost like men in the village, but he had a salt-and-pepper beard and blue eyes—distinctly different from anyone else she could see.

She focused on the blue eyes as he bent over her.

"Howdy, ma'am. You speaky English?"

Speaky? Who is this clown? "Yes, of course."

Blue Eyes said something to the others in a language she didn't understand, then knelt beside her. He turned an unlovely face to her and gave an impersonation of a smile. His fetid breath carried the smell of rotted teeth as he exhaled heavily. Raven almost fainted.

"Well, Missee, Elk here says you bin real sick like."

It was difficult to concentrate. Her head ached and her arms were cramping from the effort to hold herself up, but she replied, "Who are you?"

Another blast of stinking air accompanied his laugh. "Me? I'd think you'd a know'd me. Ever'body knows Pinky Fergusson, mountain man. Even got stories 'bout me in dime novels. Ain't ya ever read none? Then agin, mebbe ya don't read—huh?"

Raven coughed and laid back down to escape the awful stench escaping from behind blackened teeth. "No, I'm sorry. I haven't heard of you and, yes, I do read." She fell back on the story she, Linc and Charlie had agreed on. "I am Lakota, from the Oglala *oyate*, I believe. My parents were killed when I was small and my brother and I were raised by missionaries in the east. They taught me to read, write and speak English."

"Well, ya talk like ya was edicated purty good, fer a redskin."

Standing Elk had waited patiently while the trapper talked with his "guest." Now he prodded the mountain man.

Fergusson turned and told him what he'd found out.

Raven had time to collect her thoughts. They weren't very reassuring. *Something happened. Something Linc didn't know about, or didn't anticipate. I'm sick—real sick. How long? What about Linc? Charlie? Is it this way for all of us, or just me? Where's my pack? Jesus.*

She sat straight up, almost knocking her head against the mountain man. "Where is it?" she asked. "I had a pack with—with some clothes and things. Ask him where it is."

Pinky Fergusson didn't hear a word she said. He was transfixed by the sight of her bare breasts. She hadn't even noticed that the robe covering her had fallen away when she sat up.

"Whew. Ain't you a purty one," he croaked.

Ruth saw where he was staring and inwardly cringed. The lust in his eyes sickened her, but she was too agitated to respond. She grabbed the buffalo robe and covered her nakedness.

"Damn you! Ask him. Where's my pack?"

"Eh? What pack?" asked the bewildered trapper. He slowly refocused his attention, but didn't forget the luscious spectacle he'd witnessed. "Wha' ya talkin' 'bout?"

"I had a pack with me. It's got—it's everything I own. Ask him if he has it. Please?"

Pinky managed to translate the request.

"Yep. Elk says they was a pack. Says he left it where they come acrost you."

Where they found me? Then I'm not there. I'm—

"Where? Where'd they find me? Did they find a man there, too? Why'd they leave the pack?" Her mind raced, the words tumbled out too fast for her slow-witted interpreter.

"Whoa, Missy. Ya better slow down. You're not makin' no sense. Mebbe the fever's still on ya." Fergusson smiled. It was supposed to be reassuring. To Raven, it was the evil leer of an ogre.

With an effort, she forced herself to remain calm. "Where they found me, is it far from here?"

Fergusson questioned Standing Elk who answered with many hand motions.

"Nope. Don't appear it's far. Mebbe a day trip. Says they come acrost you on the prairie near the Platte. Was that where you was?"

"Yes, I think so. I—I've been sick. I don't remember much. My brother was with me. He may be sick, like me."

Fergusson shrank away. "What you got? The cholera?"

"No, nothing like that. It's—it's a family disease." She struggled to think clearly and invent a plausible story. "My brother suffers from the same disease. I have to look for him. He may be dying out there. Will you help me?" The thought of traveling out onto the empty plains with this loathsome creature frightened her, but she had to try to find Charlie and her pack.

"Waal, I don't rightly know, Missee. Sounds more like a job fer the soldier boys over to the fort."

"Fort? What fort?"

"Why Laramie, of course. You sure you're not touched in the head?"

"No, I just didn't realize. Where's the fort?"

"Jest over the rise. Mebbe a quarter mile."

Raven needed time to think. She was exhausted. Just the effort of sitting up had drained what little strength she had. There were so many questions. So many....

She passed out.

"She sleeps," announced Little Doe. "She is still not well."

"What did she want?" Standing Elk asked Fergusson.

"Says she has a brother. He may be near where she was. She wants to look for him, and for the pack she had."

"Hmph!" replied Standing Elk. "She is not Crow. Who are her people?"

"Oglala, she says."

"One sick Lakota is enough in our camp. Her brother must be dead. Her medicine bag is worthless." Standing Elk led the mountain man out of the tipi. Even with the sides up, the man left a powerful odor.

Fergusson returned to the trading post, weighing his options. Before sunset he'd made a decision. The Lakota squaw was a stranger—an attractive stranger. If he could locate her brother and bring him in, he was sure she'd be grateful. No sense bothering the army with such a trivial matter. Better to keep it to himself.

Mounted on a broken-down mule and leading another, he left Fort Laramie early the next morning. He crossed the bridge over the Laramie River, paid his toll and then headed south for the Platte Road and the boundless prairie. First, he'd find the brother. Then, he'd take his reward. He smiled and scratched his crotch as he faced the vast sea of grass and set out for the place Standing Elk had described.

Raven awoke from a deep sleep. There was a moment when she felt comfortable, warm and secure. Then she was fully awake and suddenly depressed and confused. The tipi was empty, but she could hear sounds in the camp. She closed her eyes and tried to organize her jumbled thoughts.

Okay, I'm at Fort Laramie. I'm sick. How long? How many days? Who are these people? If Charlie's dead, what then? What'll happen to me? Without the magic tricks and Charlie to convince the people we have magic to overcome the white man, what then? I'll be nothing more than a squaw, that's what. Nothing will change. I'll be trapped here, or maybe traded to another tribe. I could go to the army—throw myself on their mercy. Then what?

"Oh, Linc," she groaned. "Linc, help me. Please be alive. Come to me, Linc. I need you."

No, damn it! You're Raven, Lakota Medicine Woman. Nobody's going to rescue you. Pull yourself together. Think!

She sat up, but almost collapsed as the blood drained from her head. For a moment she felt desperately sick. As her head cleared, she felt the breeze on her bare back and was then assailed with the smell of her body. Dried sweat, and worse, choked her. "God, I need a bath," she mumbled.

She pushed the thought aside and studied her surroundings. Sleeping robes were piled around the perimeter of the tipi. A fire circle, baskets and cooking implements filled the center. Nearby, she spotted her clothes, rumpled and carelessly piled against the hide wall. She fumbled for the clothes, struggling to dress.

It was a slow process. She was weak and dizzy, but gaining strength every moment. When she stepped out of the tipi, two scrawny dogs stopped wrestling for a moment to growl at her. She ignored them and looked around.

"What the hell am I doing here?" she wondered aloud.

She stumbled on through the camp. A few old people and some children watched her passing, but did not seem interested in her. Ahead, the tipis parted at the edge of the village. Across the plain she could see buildings. It didn't look like a fort. There were large buildings—some two stories. They floated in a haze of wood-smoke and dust. People moved on the plain in wagons, on horses and on foot. In the distance there were other Indian camps, and one made up of wagons drawn in a circle.

This is it. It's real. I made it this far, but now what?

A bugle call sounded faintly in the distance. *The army. If I go to them ... tell them about Charlie ... ask them to look for him ... maybe it's not too late ... got to find him—and the pack.*

By the time Raven realized she wasn't alone, it was too late. Pain exploded across her back. She lurched forward and fell to her hands and knees. When she swiveled her head, she saw a large squaw with a stout piece of firewood held like a baseball bat. The woman scowled fiercely and yelled at her. She pointed back toward the village with the stick, and then kicked Raven in the side.

Raven rolled on the ground and sized up her adversary. *Don't be stupid. You're sick, weak and unarmed. Even this fatso could beat the hell out of you.*

Meekly, Raven got to her feet and retraced her steps to the tipi. An old man, face deeply lined from years of sun and wind, joined the squaw, herding her along. They cackled and scolded her as they went.

Raven entered the tipi on rubbery legs. The strength she had felt was completely gone. All she wanted to do was rest, but her captors had other ideas.

The woman pointed and screeched at her. Raven finally understood her hand motions. The squaw was ordering her to undress. She wearily obeyed, slowly removing her dress and shoes. The woman scooped up the clothes and continued to point until Ruth stood naked before them. She wanted to spit in the eyes of the old man and extinguish the lusty sparks she could see there, but the woman put out his fire with a sharp smack of her stick. They left in a heated argument, the woman clutching the last of Raven's possessions.

Weak, naked, shivering and tired, Raven collapsed on the buffalo robes, wrapped herself among them, and fell into a fitful sleep.

TWO

Wednesday, August 18, 1875. Near Skinner's Hollow, Virginia.

"Goodness, Isaac, whatcha got there?"

"Dunno fer sure. Found 'im by th' barn. Don't seem like he's in good shape." Isaac was awkwardly carrying a limp young man in his arms.

"Well, tarnation. Bring the boy in." Abigail Fortner made soft clucking sounds as she followed her husband to the bedroom. It wasn't a real bedroom, but a section of the cabin partitioned by a blanket. Isaac laid the body on their simple bed. The young man's legs hung over the end, but he was unconscious and barely breathing and, therefore, Isaac didn't think he'd notice.

"My, ain't he a strange lookin' one," Abigail noted.

"Sure ain't no nigra." She studied him for a moment. "Injun, ya reckon?"

"Ma, ain't been no injuns 'round here fer years. Mebbe he's—well, hell, how do I know."

"Ain't no never mind nohow. Y'all git back. Let me see what I c'n do."

As Isaac turned to go, the body on the bed quivered and uttered a plaintive little cry. Abigail cocked her head. The sound was familiar, though her childbearing years were long gone. "Why he sounds jes' like a new-born."

"Mebbe he's sick in the head," suggested Isaac.

Abigail had other ideas. "Run t' th' barn 'n' fetch me some milk. Scoot now." She bent over the form on the bed and started to make a comfortable nest.

The pack was lying in the shadows. Isaac stumbled over it and almost fell. When he returned to the house, he handed the pail of milk to Abigail, settled himself into one of the rickety chairs at the table, upended the pack, and buried himself in examining the contents. Abigail paid no attention as she hustled back behind the blanket.

The few clothes, revolver, ammunition, and dried fruits and meats in the pack were not unusual, but Isaac whistled softly when the leather pouch divulged almost $100 in coins and bills. "More 'n' enough fer a man fer a year," he mumbled. Most years, Isaac's vegetable and tobacco production did not yield much more. He eyed the blanketed alcove speculatively. Questions buzzed in his mind. *Be simple if'n th' boy were to die,* he thought.

Linc associated foggy images of San Francisco with the misty view of his new surroundings. Sounds came softly—muted through the fog—voices, disembodied, and speaking a strange dialect he could not quite comprehend. He snuggled deeper into his warm bed. *Later. I'll get up later. Then it'll be time to do ... do ... What? Something important. Later.*

Two weeks passed before Linc had the strength to stumble through the door and prop himself against one of the poles holding a flimsy overhang above the porch. When he caught his breath and his racing heart had slowed, he gazed with new wonder at his surroundings.

The morning was bright and brisk. Wisps of steam rose from grasses warming in the sun and mixed with wood-smoke hanging in the still air. There were cleared fields surrounded by thick forests, cloaked in greens, flecked with dazzling reds and fiery yellows, early harbingers of the coming winter. The Shenendoah Valley. Snatches of *Dixie* ran through Linc's mind, only there were no cotton fields here and no darkies toiling in the sun. The house, barn and sagging outbuildings were weathered, patched with rusty tin. This was a poor tobacco farm where only the chickens strutted and looked upon his intrusion with haughty pride.

The last few days Linc had finally been able to concentrate and learn what had happened. He now knew the flight through time had almost killed him. Had it been the same with Ruth and Charlie? Were they alive? What would he find when he reached the Dakotas? His thoughts led him back to Stockton and Ruth. So warm, yielding—and terrified. But he had all the answers and a grand plan. Now, he feared, he had killed her.

He shook his head. There was no sense in pursuing this line. A Lakota medicine woman named Raven would be waiting for Black Feather next spring, or....

At least there had been no problems with Isaac and Abigail. They had accepted his explanation of his life. Born in the Ohio Valley as a half-breed, raised and educated by missionaries when his parents died, and now on his way to Washington, D.C.—no, not D.C. Here it was called Washington City and generally spoken with a slight sneer. Abigail and Isaac had lost both their sons in the war. This was Confederate territory and Yankees were devils incarnate—the source of all sin and trouble.

He had been vague about his business in Washington, only that it had to do with his people. Now it was time to plan his actions.

"What'cha starin'at, Black Feather?"

Abigail's voice startled him. He'd nearly fallen asleep while leaning against the post.

"Oh! Nothing, really. The sun feels good. Makes me restless, but I can't seem to get the energy to move."

"Well, y'all oughta jest go back 'n lie down a bit. You're none too strong yet. They'll be time enough fer doin' chores 'n sech. Go lie down now, y'hear?"

"Yes'm. I guess I will."

He staggered back to the pallet they'd arranged near the stove and slipped almost immediately to sleep.

Tuesday, September 8, 1875.

"Y'sure y'all got to go? Ain't a great day fer travelin', Boy." Isaac watched critically as Black Feather packed his few belongings. Abigail hovered over the stove, preparing corn dodgers for him to eat on the way.

Black Feather Lincoln. That was the name he had given them. They weren't too happy about the Lincoln part until he explained it had been his father's last name; but his father was not related to the late President.

"Yes, sir, I have to go, but I surely do appreciate all you've done for me. I want you to take this."

He dropped a shiny ten-dollar gold piece into Isaac's hand. Isaac palmed the coin with a nod of his head. "Thank'ee, though it warn't necessary. When y'all get t' Skinner's Hollow, jest look up Tinker Martin over t' th' livery. He'll fix ya up with a good horse fer a fair price."

Abigail fussed over him like a mother hen. "Y'all come back when you're done up to Washington City, y' hear?"

"Yes'm. Thanks for your kindness."

Black Feather Lincoln stepped out strongly, following the ridge between the wheel ruts that led to the road to Skinner's Hollow and Washington City.

The trip to Washington lasted four uneventful days. Wherever he passed, he did create a minor stir, however, that was summed up by the owner of a roadside inn on the second day. When Black Feather asked for food, the owner surveyed him critically, hesitated, then finally asked, "Boy, you sure ain't white but you sure don't look like a nigra either. Jes what is you, boy?" The owner was not impressed by "Lakota warrior," and Black Feather found himself at the back door waiting for his food.

When he arrived in Washington City, he was surprised at how small it was. The broad, muddy avenues were framed with row houses, "temporary" office buildings left over from the Civil War, but now bulging with bureaucrats tenaciously clinging to jobs of dubious worth. *And this is just the beginning,* he thought. The magnificent monuments to Lincoln and Jefferson did not exist in the overgrown fields where they would later sit. Even the Washington Monument was only a truncated stone tower surrounded with wooden scaffolding. Black Feather's initial reaction to the capital city was disappointment.

Carriages, drays and delivery wagons moved in stately procession past sidewalks, where the pace was slower. Crowds of strollers, mostly Negros, moved aimlessly for the most part. When necessary, the Negros placidly shuffled into the street to allow faster-paced white men in suits and top hats to pass.

"Watch it, Boy. Get out in the street where you belong."

Black Feather was startled and jumped to the side to avoid a collision with a portly, heavily jowled and bearded white man in a dark suit and vest. A quick retort leaped to his tongue, but he stifled his acid reply. His place in the social order was well established. He resented eating "round back with the nigras" and bedding in lice infested stalls or cramped attic rooms, but "civil rights" were the jealously guarded privilege of the chosen race. He did not belong.

When we have a Lakota Nation, it will be different. Maybe we can teach equality. The thought brought a smile to his face.

"What y'all smilin' at, Mister?"

He turned to find a skinny Negro girl, barefoot and wearing a frayed cotton dress, looking intently at him. "Y'all new here?"

"Um, yes, I guess so."

"Then y'all be needin' a place t' stay. My mammy's got a nice room y'all c'n rent. Wanna see it?"

"Not right now, but thank you."

The girl cocked her head and looked quizzical. "Y'all sure 'nuf sound funny. Where y'all from?"

"Dakota Territory. Listen, I gotta get goin'."

"Name's Melissa. Y'all rent my mammy's room 'n' ya git me with it. Quarter a day. Ya ain't gonna git better 'n that."

Black Feather almost ran when he realized the extent of the offer. *Jeez, she can't be more than eleven or twelve. What kind of town is this?*

The place he found was not much, but it included breakfast and dinner for fifty cents a day, and he had it to himself. It was a lean-to behind a shanty in a narrow alley.

Accommodations were somewhat better at the Hopkins Arms Hotel on 16th St. between K and L. Matthew O'Shaunessey, part owner of a Colorado gold mine and only recently recovered from amnesia suffered at Gettysburg, stepped onto the second floor balcony and gazed around at a town he had been intimately acquainted with, but now barely recognized. Instead of massive government buildings of stone, steel and sheets of glass, his vista included clapboard houses, wooden and brick office buildings, dirt streets with wooden walkways, and garden plots tucked in the mozaic. To his right, only two blocks away, was an open field with a few trees, grandly named Lafayette Park. Just behind the park a few lights shone in the early evening gloom at the White House.

Matt smiled. *If I play my cards right, I might even be able to get myself invited to the White House...again. I'll be the only man in history to be invited to the White House in the twenty-first century and the nineteenth century.*

With pleasant thoughts, Matt went into his room, got ready for bed, slipped between the sheets and planned his actions for tomorrow. He had a meeting with a Major Mason at the personnel office of the War Department. He was confident, but a number of things could go wrong.

His last thought before sleeping was, *I wonder what Black Feather is doing tonight?*

A sergeant showed Matt to Major Mason's cramped office on the third floor of a nondescript brick building. The office reeked of stale cigar smoke mingled with the pervading odor of unwashed clothes and bodies that Matt was becoming accustomed to. A thin layer of coal dust from the overhead heating duct clung to the walls and ceiling and filtered what little light came through the one small window.

Matt shook hands with the major, who barely fit behind his tiny desk. He was overweight and balding with a heavy mustache and side-whiskers that were going gray. A fat cigar, unlit, was clamped between yellowed teeth. They quickly dispensed with pleasantries and Matt spent twenty minutes explaining his existence to the major.

"Let me see if I have this straight, Mr. O'Shaunessey," Major Mason said as he leaned back in his swivel chair and stroked his side-whiskers absently. "You say you were injured at Gettysburg on July 3, 1863. Where, exactly, did you say this injury occurred?"

"I didn't say, sir, but it was with Colonel Bowes outfit, under General Buford, on Seminary Ridge. I'd just been assigned to his unit a week before."

"I see. And just what was the nature of your injury?"

"I'm not sure, sir. The folks who took me in said they found me bloody and unconscious about ten miles from the battlefield. I don't know what happened or how I got there. In fact, sir, I didn't remember a thing."

"And these folks—what were there names again?"

"Hasty, sir. Hiram and Jessica Hasty."

"Yes, Hasty. You say they're dead now?"

"Yes, sir. Mr. Hasty got the consumption 'bout six months ago and dear Jessica—she was like my own dear, sainted mother—just got real sick and passed on a month ago. I buried her next to Hiram and burned their place to the ground, like she asked me to do."

"They didn't have any kin?"

"No, sir. Nary a soul, and they weren't what you'd call sociable people. They had their little place up there in Delaware Gap and I don't ever remember them even entertaining anybody."

"Oh, come now. They must have had some contact with neighbors. How about food? Where'd they get their supplies?"

Matt furrowed his brow as if deep in thought. "You know, sir, I don't rightly know. Hiram used to go somewhere, maybe once a year, but after he died, Jessica never left the place."

"What about you? You just sit on your hands for twelve years?"

"No, sir! I worked hard. They told me I was their son and explained that I was a little touched in the head and it was better if I wasn't 'round people."

"And you never questioned that?"

"Well, sometimes, I guess, but I didn't have any reason to doubt 'em."

"But now, all of a sudden, you know who you are, right?"

"No, sir. Like I told you, I'm still a little confused. You see it wasn't until just the day before she died that Jessica told me to go up the hill behind the cabin to the rock cave where we stored supplies. Way back in a corner there was a pile of rocks. That's where she told me to look and to bring her everything I found there."

"Just what did you find?"

"That pack." Matt pointed to a large deer hide bundle on the chair next to him. "It's all I've got in the world."

Matt untied the drawstring and began to remove articles. "This here's my uniform." The material was old, musty and ragged, but obviously a Union officer's uniform. The blouse and jacket were splotched with rusty stains. "I guess I was a little bloody, sir."

There were also boots, worn and cracked; a rusty pistol in a dried holster slung on a belt, peeling with age; and a packet of letters that Matt stacked neatly on the desk.

"The letters are what told the story, sir. You're welcome to read 'em. They're all from my brother. He's the only family I had."

Mason cleared his throat and spoke with new respect. "Have you contacted your brother, Mr. O'Shaunessey?"

"My brother's dead, sir. I wrote to him, but the letter came back. This came with it."

Matt produced the letter written on newer paper than the ones he'd shown from his brother, to Mr. Timothy O'Shaunessey. A second letter, from the law firm of Jeremy Steele, Esq., Leadville, Colorado, contained the information about the cave-in at the Lucky Irish Mine on August 10, 1863. The letter concluded:

> "I am grieved to report the death of your brother. You also must be informed that, since there was no contact with any relation for seven years, the property has passed to other hands. The mine further collapsed before said transfer and has never been reopened."

"Well, Mr. O'Shaunessey, or possibly I should call you Major O'Shaunessey, I believe I shall have to take this up with the colonel. We'll have to check the records, of course—"

"I understand, sir. I must admit, I would find this hard to believe myself, and it's happened to me. There is one more thing."

Matt produced two shiny bars from the bottom of the sack. "These were there also. They were minted in Denver. I guess I brought them with me when I came east."

Mason sucked in his breath. Majors in the army were not generally allowed in the same room with gold ingots. "Whew! Are those real?"

"Yes, sir. At least according to the assayist, they are."

Mason shook his head. "It's almost like you've traveled through time and missed so much, but arrived so rich."

"Yes. It is rather like that, now that you mention it."

Mason heaved himself to his feet and extended a pudgy hand across the littered desk. "Mind if I keep this stuff? Not the gold, of course," he hastened to add.

"No, sir. No problem." Matt picked up the ingots. "I'll be at the Hopkin's Arms, if you need me."

Matt smiled and whistled tuneless airs as he left the building. The two gold bars were only a fraction of the wealth he had brought with him, but it was certainly enough to make an impression.

Lunch at the Willard Hotel, he decided, would be a fabulous way to celebrate his achievement with the major. He'd heard the President occasionally dropped by. Maybe he could rub elbows with the President of the United States and share war stories.

The Bureau of Indian Affairs was located in a "temporary" wooden building which had obviously been converted from use as a barracks ten years earlier. The clerk who greeted Black Feather barely resisted sneering. Small and officious, he looked uncomfortable in his boiled shirt and stiff collar. He peered over the top of his spectacles and asked, "You want to see who?"

"I would like to speak with the Director of Indian Affairs," replied Black Feather evenly.

"Do you have an appointment, Mr....?"

"Black Feather. No, I do not, but it is quite important that I see the director."

"Impossible without an appointment. Sorry."

"Then may I please make an appointment?"

"Why don't you just leave a note? I'll see that the director gets it."

Stay calm. He's just doing his job. "I prefer to speak directly with the director. When would that be possible?"

"I'm sure I don't know. He's a busy man. Very busy." The tone implied that he would always be too busy to meet an Indian. "Maybe you could check back tomorrow."

Black Feather considered his options. Then he nodded agreement. "I'll do that. In the meantime, please mention to him that Black Feather, an emissary of the Lakota people, is in town for a short while with information concerning a massive uprising planned by a coalition of tribes in the Dakota Territory. I believe this uprising can be averted and many lives saved if action is taken immediately. It is urgent that we talk as soon as possible." He politely tipped his hat to the rude clerk. *Put that in your pipe and smoke it, you ignorant son-of-a-bitch,* he thought. Black Feather left the office with a smile.

Matt approached the Willard Hotel on a wooden walkway crowded with lunchtime crowds. His head was bowed, his thoughts far from the crowd. *Some things don't change, like government bureaucrats covering their asses and crawling with all intentional speed toward mediocrity. So, how much longer? You know the records will check out. They won't even bother to check your story about a family that took you in. So? A few weeks? A month? Meantime, where the hell is Long Trail, or Black Feather. The town isn't all that damn big, but I haven't heard a thing about an Indian stirring the pot. Maybe he's dead? Did the same thing happen to him that happened to me?*

Lost in this train of thought, Matt didn't notice the smartly dressed, copper-skinned, braided Indian who stepped off the walkway to let Matt pass.

After lunch, Matt walked to the office of the *Washington Post* and, after some discussion with a helpful clerk, placed a small article for the next issue.

Monday, October 4, 2021. Berkeley, California.

Demetrius Johnson tried hard to remain calm. He failed. His hands shook. He closed his eyes and concentrated, then opened them and read the message again.

> *"Dear Uncle Demetrius. Guess what I just invented? The trip almost killed me. I do not recommend sending others by the same route. Still searching for our lost cousins.*
> *Matt."*

Johnson's eyes flew to the top of the page. *"Washington Post, October 2, 1875."*

The note was in a section by itself, headed: *"Personals."*

THREE

Dates unknown. Near Fort Laramie, Wyoming Territory.

Think! What would Linc do? What about Charlie? You've got to do something, or Raven, the almost great Lakota Medicine Woman, is going to be vulture bait. There's got to be a way out!

Three days had passed since the hag and her lusty old man had taken Raven's clothes. Little Doe had substituted an old deerskin dress, so she had a measure of modesty when she left the tipi. The seams were splitting and it smelled like rotting carrion, but it was the only covering Raven was allowed, and it was only allowed when she went to relieve herself. Someone always accompanied her on these short trips, and there was a man just outside the tipi in case she tried to escape.

I'm stronger now. Sooner or later I'll have to knock someone on the head and run for it. Run where? The fort? It's my best chance, but what if they don't believe me? What if....

The flap on the tipi flew back. Late afternoon sunlight streamed in. Raven blinked in the strong light.

"Waal, glad to see you're still here. I'll bet you was just waitin' fer ol' Pinky Fergusson, wasn't ya?"

"Who?"

"Mebbe ya don't remember. I was here th' other day. We talked some 'n' ya tole me 'bout your brother. Remember?"

She remembered. The stinking mountain man with rotting teeth. "Yes, I remember you. Can you help me? I need to get to the fort."

"Yep. I'm a gonna help ya. Already have. Here. Git dressed."

He tossed her the rotting deerskin dress. She pulled it over her head and managed to twist it down around her body while staying under her blanket.

"You"re right proper, fer a squaw." His pronouncement seemed to amuse him and he gave out with a cackling laugh. "You'll be pleased to know that me 'n Standing Elk's made a deal."

Raven noticed Standing Elk, her savior, for the first time. He stood silently just inside the flap.

"What kind of deal?" she asked.

"Straight up trade," Fergusson replied. "I come into a little property recently 'n Standing Elk traded you to me." The mountain man smiled broadly and nodded to Standing Elk who nodded back.

I'm going to faint. There's no way I can go...

"Turn around," Fergusson commanded.

Raven saw a length of twisted rawhide in his hands. "Why? What are—"

She screamed as he whipped out a hand, caught her left arm and used it to spin her around. He forced the arm high behind her back and twisted it. She tried to break away, but the scrawny man was very strong. He managed to capture her other wrist and wrap the rawhide tightly around them. Raven looked to Standing Elk, hoping he would help. The Indian scowled, but remained motionless.

"You bastard," she hissed at Fergusson. "I'll come with you. You don't have to do this."

"Waal, this'll make sure now, won't it," he answered.

He pushed her ahead of him, out of the tipi. Another, longer thong was looped around her neck before he mounted a decrepit mule and led her out of the camp. Hardly anyone seemed to notice her passing.

The next hour was pure torture. The shadows lengthened as the sun lowered in the west. The rawhide chafed her wrists and neck; stony ground gouged her bare feet. They were headed south, away from the fort and away from the other camps. At one point in the dusky twilight Raven saw a line of horsemen going north, toward Fort Laramie. They were silhouetted against the setting sun, but a long way off—too far to hear her, too far to help. Raven plodded along behind the bony man on his bony mule, too numb to think or plan.

"Hold it, Girl. You jest stay put while I git a light."

They'd stopped at the base of a low bluff. In the dim twilight, Raven made out the shape of a shelter—skins stretched over poles—set in the side of the hill. Fergusson disappeared inside and soon there was the soft glow of a lantern between the edges of the skins. He threw back one of the skins and pulled on her lead rope.

"Got a surprise fer ya. Come on in."

The interior was a stinking mess. Piles of buffalo robes and other animal pelts littered the floor. The shelter was dug part way into the slope and supported with large, squared timbers. Fire-blackened cooking utensils, lanterns, animal traps and other odds and ends hung from the rafters. Raven didn't see anything surprising.

"So, what's the surprise?" she asked.

He pointed. "In the corner. Over there. Know him?"

She moved forward cautiously. There was a body lying wrapped in a buffalo robe. Only the head was visible, but there was no doubt.

"Oh, my God! Charlie! Charlie!" She stumbled to where he lay and knelt beside him. He was emaciated and barely breathing. Her huge, hulking brother had been reduced to a veritable skeleton.

She spun towards Fergusson. "He needs a doctor! We have to get him to the fort. He must live. It's very important!"

Her pleas fell on deaf ears. Fergusson just stood there and smiled at her, but there was no mirth in his eyes. He jerked on her lead rope, pulling her off balance onto her face on the floor. He casually strolled to her and hooked a boot under her stomach and rolled her on her back, then squatted beside her.

"Now this here's the way it's gonna be. The onliest doctorin' he's gonna git is from you. He lives, fine. He dies, so be it." He reached down and roughly grabbed the rope around her neck and easily pulled her into a sitting position, her face inches from his. "You're kinda high falutin', fer a squaw, but I figger you'll come around. You're mine now—you and him.

You do what I say, or I'll kill the both of you. You understand?"

Raven nodded. She wanted to vomit, to scream. She wanted to kill, but she nodded her head in agreement.

"Good," he snapped. "Now you 'n' me got a little business to attend to afore you start doctorin' your brother."

Oh, dear God, let this be over. Let me die now. She watched the filthy wretch walk to the corner and retrieve an iron loop. The loop was attached to a rusty chain that clanked on the ground as he walked toward her. It was an iron collar, hinged, with an old padlock attached. Fergusson lifted the rawhide tether off of her neck and replaced it with the iron collar, then pulled her wrists up behind her, and cut the thong binding them.

"Git yer dress off." His words were raspy, his breathing rapid.

Raven stood up, massaging her chafed wrists. The chain hung like a massive weight, threatening to pull her back to the floor.

Smack! The stinging blow to her cheek was followed by another. "Strip, you goddamned squaw. Move."

Raven closed her eyes and reached down for the hem of the dress. She turned her back to her captor and slowly pulled the dress over her head and let it slide down the chain to the floor. She caught a glimpse of Fergusson in his long-john underwear when he pulled her around. Blessed blackness came with the touch of his gnarled hands.

When Raven regained consciousness, Fergusson had satisfied his lust with her. He showed her the keg of water outside the shelter and the stores of food scattered along the back wall. "I got some business to tend to. Be back later, so don't git no ideas 'bout doin' anything cept tendin' yer kin 'n learnin' to treat me better." He disappeared into the black night.

Two days passed. Two long days and two longer nights. Raven spent most of her time trying to force water and bits of meat she chewed and mixed with water into Charlie's mouth. He hung on the edge of death and she was losing hope that she could save him. She sat with his head in her lap, stroking his hair and rocking him gently. She realized he was in a coma, the last sleep before death. *You can't die Charlie. You can't. I need you.*

Charlie had a collar also, although Raven couldn't see why it was necessary. She had tugged on her chain until it was taut. She found that it was anchored near the ceiling to one of the massive upright supports with a rusty, but strong, U-bolt. If she stretched the chain to its limit, she could just get outside the shelter a few steps to the woodpile. When she surveyed her world, it was a bleak picture. A shallow draw curved away and cut off her vision in both directions. Dried grasses on the banks rustled in a chill wind. There were no trees, no signs of neighbors, not even animals. Nothing.

Yesterday, she had initially felt some hope that she could salvage the situation. She searched the interior for a weapon—knife, gun, club—something to give herself an advantage when Fergusson returned. She considered the animal traps. Most were for small game, although there were two larger traps with wicked looking metal jaws, but she couldn't pry the jaws apart. She finally settled on an iron skillet which she hid under a buffalo robe near where she slept. If Fergusson forced her down again near the frying pan, she would use it to beat him unconscious.

As the day wore on, Raven began to lose hope. Charlie didn't stir and she could only force small dribbles of food into his mouth. By late afternoon, Fergusson had still not returned and her thoughts turned to what would happen if he abandoned them here. Food and water would run out, probably in less than a week. They would starve to death and their carcasses would feed the wolves and vultures. *How long does it take to starve to death? What does it feel like? Is there a lot of pain? Stop it! There must be a way.*

As she thought, she paced the interior of the shelter, dragging the clanking chain behind. She examined the post and the bolt. *Cut the post? Burn through it? Cut the bolt? How?*

Then she noticed a piece of cracked mirror nailed to one side of a post. She pried it loose. It could be a weapon with its sharp, jagged edges. She imagined plunging it into Fergusson's back, or, even better, his crotch.

The image in the mirror was strange to her. The confident young woman with long, shiny black hair, smiling eyes, and straight, white teeth was gone. That person had been replaced. Greasy, matted hair framed a dirty, swollen face. Her eyes peered from sunken sockets, darkened by smoke and dirt. Even the teeth behind her swollen lips had lost their bright, white luster.

She shuddered and slumped to the ground. The mirror was the answer. She had a deadly weapon. She idly turned the mirror over and over in her hand while examining her bare arms. *What if...? If I fail, then what? Wait to die? No. Charlie first. It won't take long for him to bleed to death. ...As soon as I'm certain he's gone, ...two quick moves. ...It won't really hurt.*

She concentrated on the throbbing pulse in her wrists, intricately planning the precise incisions. She almost missed the slight motion from under the buffalo robe. Charlie had moved!

The next morning she pawed through a stack of buffalo hides seeking a clean one to keep her warm. There was a thin sheet of ice on the water in the barrel and gray clouds scudded on a fitful wind, a portent of icy blasts to come in the months ahead. Deep in a pile of buffalo robes her hands found a canvas fabric.

The packs! They were both there. She was saved! They had pistols, ammunition, money, clothes, more food!

It was all *gone*. He'd taken what they needed most—guns and money. *He only left the clothes and a bunch of useless magic tricks.* She remembered his words, 'I come into a little property recently.' She realized what property purchased her from Standing Elk. *The son-of-a-bitch bought me with my own money. Damn!*

Raven cried herself to sleep. Her last hope was gone.

The sharp pain in her side brought her instantly awake.

"Git up, you worthless squaw!" Fergusson punctuated his command with another kick.

Only half-awake, Raven instinctively crawled away from the sound of his voice. When she looked up, she could see him leering down at her, his breath heavy with liquor.

"Git yer clothes off." He stepped away from her, beyond the reach of her chain, and began removing his clothes. He made sure his pistol and knife were well out of her reach.

Raven crouched, ready to fight him. He cackled as he staggered toward her in his long-johns. He circled her warily, then faked a lunge at her. "Ow! Jesus Christ! What the—"

Fergusson hopped around on one foot, his other foot firmly grasped in both hands. He winced and gingerly stepped down on his injured foot and pulled up a buffalo robe. "What the hell? What's this fry pan doin' here?" He hefted the pan and glared at her. "Oh, I see. You planned to mebbe crown me? You bitch!" he roared.

Cold fear stabbed Raven. Her breathing was harsh, uneven.

Fergusson flung the offending skillet to the far end of the shelter, lunged forward and yanked Raven's chain up from the floor. One sharp jerk on the chain and she was ripped forward, landing face down at his feet. He flailed at her with his fists, and his good foot, as she tried to curl her body into as small a target as possible. She was dimly aware of the unbroken string of curses that accompanied the blows.

Dazed, sore, and broken in spirit, she offered no resistance when he tore off her dress and spread her legs. He hadn't found the mirror. Soon she would end this nightmare. *Charlie first, then....*

Raven sucked in sharply. *Charlie! His eyes are open. He's watching. Oh God, please. let him live. Let me live. Give us revenge!*

When Raven awoke, Fergusson was gone. What was left of her dress would no longer cover her nakedness. She crawled painfully to Charlie's side, searching his face for signs of improvement. Yes, he was breathing, and his face had more color than previous days. Maybe he was getting better. She pulled a buffalo robe over herself and devoted her day to tending her brother.

She briefly considered taking Charlie's clothes to cover her nakedness, but decided he needed the extra warmth the clothes provided. She didn't want Fergusson to know she had discovered her pack, so she turned to the piles of hides and used the mirror to cut a slit in a deer hide large enough to slip over her head. She used thin strips cut from another pelt and inserted them into small holes she gouged to lace the sides together.

Over the next two weeks Charlie continued to improve, but very slowly. Raven fed him, cleaned him, alternately cooing and swearing at him. "You're just like a baby," she often told him. *Maybe that's it*, she reflected. *It was the same with me. It must have been. We arrived here as helpless as newborn infants. Maybe we were, like, born again. It's probably something they didn't realize. And if it happened to us… What about Linc? Did someone find him? Nurse him? Is he alive?* The thoughts rattled in her mind. She wanted to talk to Charlie about all this, but he still had not spoken and gave no indication he understood her words. She often thought that he might have suffered brain damage as a result of his near starvation. If that was true, he would be little or no help to her if they ever escaped. The only time a glimmer of understanding appeared in his eyes were the times when Fergusson was present. Raven could see Charlie's eyes harden. His stare was intense. His eyes never left the mountain man when he was in the shelter.

Fergusson was gone more than he was there. When he did appear, he brought supplies, occasionally fresh meat and animal skins and dragged the water barrel off behind his bony mule to fill it up. When he slept in the shelter, it was always at the far end, well removed from Raven, although she gave him no trouble and he found her compliant to his demands.

Raven cooked for Fergusson, spoke to him when necessary and meekly allowed his infrequent violations of her body. Until Charlie was stronger and they could plan together an escape from the monster, she had to force a willing compliance. When his bony body was pressed against her, she distracted herself by planning the hours of torture he would endure before dying at her hands. She also consoled herself with the thought that he would probably be gone the next morning. That was his pattern—take her, then leave for a day or two.

"Charlie, do you understand me?" Raven held her brother's head between her hands and concentrated on his eyes. He was stronger, able to sit up and move around, but still hadn't spoken.

Charlie nodded, his head trapped between her hands. Her heart jumped. They were making progress.

"Do you know who I am?" she asked.

"Sure, you're Ruth, my sister," he mumbled.

Raven blinked back tears. Her brother was coming back to her.

"Wha' happened? Where's this place?" His face showed the intense concentration required to form the words.

"It's a long story. You almost died, but you're going to be all right. Just rest a little."

"Wanna beer," Charlie said, then closed his eyes and slept.

Raven lowered his head and smiled. *Good luck, brother mine. We have lots to do before you'll even have a chance to find a beer.*

From that point, Charlie's recovery accelerated. When Fergusson returned two days later, Charlie was clearly stronger and his first words alerted the mountain man to a new danger.

"You're the fuckin' cocksucker who's been fuckin' my sister. I'm gonna fuckin' cut off your balls and shove 'em in your cocksuckin' mouth, asshole."

Raven's heart sank. They hadn't planned an assault on Fergusson yet. Charlie was still too weak to be of any help. The effort of his outburst had caused him to sink back on his bed.

Fergusson reflexively stepped away from the enraged Indian and slipped his right hand to the butt of his pistol.

"Waal, now. Seems you've got a burr in yer saddle. Yer purty God-damned ungrateful, considerin' I saved yer worthless fuckin' life." Fergusson squinted at Charlie, curling his lip in a disdainful sneer. "You ain't no more worth to me than a stinkin' polecat, 'n about as unpleasant." He fingered the pistol, then withdrew it from his holster.

"What are you doing?" cried Raven.

Fergusson waved the pistol at her. "You jest git back 'n don't give me no trouble."

Raven stood her ground. "You can't kill him. I won't let you."

"You git back 'n shut yer trap or I'll shoot the both of you."

"Please," begged Raven, "don't do it. I, we'll do whatever you want. Charlie won't be any trouble. I'll see to it."

"He ain't gonna be no trouble, that's fer sure. Now git back, bitch."

Charlie heaved himself to his knees and tried to stumble to his feet. Fergusson turned and fired. Charlie tumbled back onto the floor, then started to rise again, his eyes boring into Fergusson. Two more quick shots, directly in the chest, seemed to have no effect on the enraged Indian. Fergusson backed slowly away and took careful aim at Charley's head, cocked the hammer and squeezed the trigger.

Raven's muscles finally responded to the urgent messages from her brain to do something. Fergusson had taken a wide stance between her and Charlie. His back was to her and he was straddling the chain on the floor leading from the post to her collar. Raven grabbed the chain with both hands and pulled sharply as she threw herself backward. As if it had a life of its own, the chain snapped off the floor and slammed into Fergusson's crotch. His cry of pain was drowned out by the crack of the pistol. Raven glimpsed Charlie as his head jerked back and he crashed against the wall, but there was no time to think.

She was pulled sharply forward as Fergusson's body slumped to the floor. She used the momentum to throw herself on his back and whip the chain around his neck then lunge away from him, and pull the chain taut. Fergusson thrashed wildly on the floor, vainly trying to free himself from the strangling iron links. Raven strained with her whole body, willing the life out of the scrawny body.

Fergusson's neck snapped with a sound like a dry twig breaking. His body went limp, eyes and tongue protruding, bowels emptied, fists clenched in his final, futile fight.

For long moments, Raven continued to throw her weight against the chain. When she finally realized he was dead, she fell on her side, totally exhausted. She couldn't bear to look at Charlie. She had been too slow. It was too late for Charlie Talks Too Much.

She might have stayed that way all night, but she became instantly alert when she heard a groan. With a gasp, she desperately pulled on the chain before Fergusson could escape. Then she saw that it was Charlie, not Fergusson, who had groaned. His head and the wall behind him were bathed in bright red blood, but he was moving! He wasn't dead—yet.

In her rush to get to Charlie, she forgot about the chain around Fergusson's neck until his dead weight pulled her up short and almost broke her neck. She quickly untangled the chain from the body and knelt by Charlie. As she wiped away the blood, she could see that the bullet had hit to one side and carved a deep furrow in Charlie's scalp. She frantically wrapped a piece of torn blanket around his head and cinched it tight. The bleeding slowed and then stopped. Charlie opened his eyes briefly, then fell asleep. Raven collapsed beside him, exhausted.

When Raven awoke the sun was shining through the cracks between the skins hanging on the east wall. She was cold and stiff. Every muscle in her body protested when she moved. Charlie was breathing softly. She forced herself to look at Fergusson. He appeared very dead, very stiff. She almost gagged from the smell. It was all she could do to stagger to her feet and stumble the few steps to his side. *How the hell do I move this stinking piece of garbage.* She settled on dragging him, feet first, to the woodpile. She almost vomited when she knelt beside him and went through his pockets. *He must have keys. He's got to have some keys! Aha!*

She dragged the ring of keys from his pants pocket. The second key released the padlock on her collar. She opened the collar with a contented sigh and let it slide to the ground. She released Charlie, built a fire, and heated water to clean Charlie's wound. He regained consciousness before she finished.

"How'd we do?" he croaked.

"Real well, real well. He's dead," she replied.

"Dead? How?"

"I broke his neck."

Charlie looked at her with new respect. "Glad you're not mad at me. A bulletproof shirt wouldn't help much against you."

"Oh, that's okay. You've got a bulletproof head, too."

Charlie rubbed the tender flesh on his head. "Not quite. I'm thirsty. Get me a beer."

Raven started to giggle, then laugh hysterically. She couldn't stop. Between bursts of laughter, she managed to gasp, "Get your own damned booze, Injun. I'm busy."

A week passed before they were ready to leave their former prison. A thorough search of Fergusson's corpse and the contents of the shelter had turned up a number of useful items: a pistol, a rifle, two good knives and some ammunition—along with cooking utensils and food—guaranteeing their immediate survival. The old mule, three dollars and sixty-eight cents in change, and some marketable hides would get them on their way. Charlie had located the most valuable item buried deep under a pile of hides—a small pouch filled with gold dust.

Raven found the creek where Fergusson had filled the water barrel. She scrubbed her body until it was pink and tender to the touch, but still felt filthy. Clean clothes from her pack refreshed her spirit and she spent two days fashioning rough shoes from buffalo hide. "Not very fashionable," she observed to Charlie, "but serviceable. I'll get new shoes at the fort."

They spent long hours planning. First, to Fort Laramie for supplies and information. Then they would start their pilgrimage through the villages of the Lakota and Cheyenne tribes, starting with the Oglala at the Red Cloud Agency at Fort Robinson in Nebraska.

As they trudged to the east, a black cloud of smoke rose high behind them on a cold north wind. Kerosene, liberally poured over a rotting corpse and dashed on the structure and its contents before starting the fire, was reducing Pinky Fergusson and all that marked his life to an insignificant pile of char and ash.

Winter was coming to the Great Plains. Two lonely figures, leading a broken down mule, wrapped themselves in buffalo robes and set out on their delayed quest. They had a message to spread, tribal leaders to convince—and they had to pave the way for the Messiah, Wiyaka *Sapa*, the man the whites called Black Feather.

If he comes, mused Raven to herself.

"No, when he comes," she announced to the barren plains.

FOUR

Fort Laramie, a sprawl of buildings surrounding an impressive parade ground, lay nestled in a horseshoe bend of the Laramie River. All the trees along the river had been sacrificed for construction and firewood, giving the river and buildings a stark appearance. A large American flag topped the flagpole at one end of the parade ground and it was the first sight Raven and Charlie had of the post as they came down from the low hills to the south.

"Whew," breathed Charlie, "lots of blue coats in that ant hill. Hope they're feelin' friendly today."

Raven nodded agreement. There was lots of activity, mostly centered on the parade ground. As she watched, a bugle call stirred the ants into action. The formation dissipated and many of the soldiers disappeared into buildings. "Must have been some kind of muster, or something. Let's go."

As they neared the river, they passed through several scattered family groups huddled near tipis. The tribe who had discovered her were, blessedly, not there. The few Indians in the camps appeared meek and docile—and poor. Horses were the common measure of wealth among the peoples of the plains and these groups had only a few near their camps. Across the river and east of the post were several covered wagons, probably families who had been delayed on the trail and had decided to winter here, or possibly families who had "seen the elephant" and decided to return to the country they had left the previous spring. Although the great years of wagon trains were already history, there were still families too poor to afford to take the train west.

Even though wagon trains no longer rolled into Fort Laramie, there was plenty of civilian traffic. Men on foot, horseback and in wagons arrived daily from the south and disappeared to the north. Cheyenne was the gateway to the new gold fields in the Black Hills and the main road to the fields passed through the fort. Pack trains passed through carrying supplies to the miners and bringing gold back. The rape of *Paha Sapa*, the holy Black Hills, was on.

Raven and Charlie decided not to face the sentry on the footbridge across the river, but led the mule through the shallow stream and onto the post.

"What now?" asked Charlie.

"See if we can find a place to stay."

"Yeah, I'm sure they have an Indian motel around here somewhere," sneered Charlie.

"Hey, what you doin' here? Git back 'crost the crick where you belong. Tradin's all done fer the day." The speaker was a slender soldier with a pocked face who was fastening his suspenders as he emerged from the nearest building—the latrine. The chevrons on his sleeve identified him as a corporal. "G'wan, git." He punctuated his order with a wave of his hand as he turned away.

"Excuse me, Corporal, but my brother is ill and we need a place to stay. Could you help us?"

The look of shock on the soldier's face was comical. "I never heared a squaw talk English so good. You must be purty edicated."

Raven stifled a sharp retort. "We were raised in the east by missionaries. Can you help us?"

Recovering from his shock, the corporal took time to appraise her more closely. Raven didn't like what she saw in his eyes. "Mebbe. Yeah, 'n mebbe you'll remember t'was Corporal Judd what helped you, huh?"

Raven continued evenly. "Certainly, Corporal. I'd be most appreciative."

"Yeah, well, okay then. Come with me. You need to see the sergeant of the guard. Mebbe he kin fix you up."

The sergeant was half potted and in no mood to be bothered with a couple of pesky Indians. He ordered Corporal Judd to "show our distinguished guests to the stables." They would be allowed the use of a stall in return for helping with stable duties. Their first duty was to clean the stall they would occupy.

Raven wanted to leave the post as soon as possible, and Charlie was in a foul mood. He desperately wanted beer, but was finding it difficult to obtain. When he did get four bottles, he got drunk and combative. Luckily, he passed out before anyone noticed and spent the next day recovering in the dim solitude of the horse stall. He might have gotten drunk again and caused serious or fatal damage, but he purchased some bread from the sutler and got deathly ill after eating it.

Raven watched him helplessly retching and shook her head. "You are one dumb Indian."

"Whaddaya mean?" he croaked.

"You see where the bakery is, over by the river?"

"Yeah, so what?"

"Did you happen to notice that the latrines are *upriver* from the bakery?" She left him in his misery to sort out the reason for his illness and put her efforts toward locating and purchasing horses and supplies for their trip. Her biggest disappointment was that she was unable to purchase ammunition for their weapons. There was talk of war and she was the enemy. The refusals were polite, but firm. No ammo for redskins.

Corporal Judd supplied the answer. He was pressing for the return favor he felt he was due. When he accosted Raven, for the third time in two days, she warmed to his attention. "Why don't you come see me after supper tonight?" she cooed. "I'll be extra nice to you if you can get me some bullets for our guns." She smiled sweetly and touched his arm lightly.

Judd turned a bright crimson and stammered, "Su—sure. They's usually some extry stuff lyin' 'round." He regained his composure and remembered he was the boss. "Now you make sure you're there 'n all gussied up proper 'n make sure your brother, or whoever he is, ain't 'round. He gits uppity 'n he's lible to git hurt. You understand?"

"Certainly. Don't worry. It'll be just the two of us." She put an extra sway in her hips as she sauntered away.

Raven had a lantern dimly glowing in the stall when the corporal arrived. Charlie was nowhere to be seen.

"I got what ya asked fer." He dangled a canvas bag that clinked when he shook it. "Now," he licked his lips in anticipation, "it's your turn."

Without a word, Raven slowly unbuttoned her blouse. She made sure he clearly saw that she wasn't wearing anything under it. His eyes bulged and he groped to unbutton his fly.

Nobody heard the dull clang of the shovel that felled Corporal Judd. It was a measure of how weak Charlie was that the blow didn't kill the soldier. He wound up for a second blow.

"Enough," hissed Raven. "He can't stop us now. There's been enough killing. Let's go!" She buttoned her blouse and grabbed the bag of ammunition. Charlie had the horses and mule ready at the corral. The last person to see the two was the guard at the new steel bridge over the Platte River two miles to the east. Raven and Charlie paid their toll and melted into the night, heading east. Once again, they became hunted fugitives.

They followed the wide trail along to the Platte for several miles before angling north across the rolling hills stretching from Wyoming into Nebraska.

It was unseasonably warm the day they arrived on the pine-covered, rocky cliffs overlooking the White River and Fort Robinson. Raven paused on the rocks and absorbed the sight. It was very different from the Nebraska State Park she had seen in the twenty-first century. The buildings, some of impressive stone, that marked Fort Robinson as she remembered it, had not been built yet. Gone, too, were the manicured lawns, stately trees, picnic and campsites. A rag-tag collection of temporary buildings, out of place in a peaceful valley, housed the soldiers who guarded the Oglalas under the leadership of Red Cloud. In time to come, the fort would be the site of the death of the great Lakota leader Crazy Horse and a detention camp for German prisoners of war during World War II. *Ah, you have a sordid history, Fort Robinson. You exist to hold and enslave. We must succeed! You must not be allowed to continue. When this is our land, you will be destroyed.* She urged her horse ahead. They would bypass the few military buildings in the valley and head directly for the large Lakota camp they could see by the river in the distance.

Raven swallowed hard when she saw him face to face. He looked just like every picture she had ever seen: Red Cloud, Oglala war chief, the man who bedeviled the whites and made them abandon the Bozeman Trail, then burned their hated forts. Red Cloud, who still wielded great power and was respected even in the capital of the enemy. Red Cloud, the man who had met Presidents. Now he stood before her, the leader of her *oyate*, General of the Oglala.

They dismounted their horses and faced the Lakota leaders. Raven wiped her sweaty palms nervously on her dress. It was difficult to express herself in the Lakota language, even after years of study. It was different to try to use the language on a daily basis and fully express her thoughts and feelings, but the twenty men seated before her did not speak English fluently, and it was critical that she impress them, so she fell back on the lie that was becoming truth.

"I'm sorry," she explained in Lakota. "Since I was raised by missionaries in the east for most of my life, my Lakota is not perfect."

Twenty pairs of dark, expressionless eyes bored into her.

She stumbled on, struggling to remember the message she had memorized. "I am but a poor vessel, sent to show a portion of the medicine possessed by Black Feather, the man who can save our people. My brother, Man-Who-Turns-Bullets, also has a small part of the great powers Black Feather holds. Later, he will cast aside any doubts you may have. Our medicine is small. Black Feather makes great medicine."

Raven spoke directly to Red Cloud. The fate of the whole mission might rest on her ability to convince him to actively support the plan. The rest of the Oglala chiefs and warriors in the tipi would follow his lead. The two shamans would almost certainly be jealous and argue against any medicine she produced. It would be up to Charlie to convince them.

Red Cloud still showed no emotion. His broad face remained placid and closed. He did nod slightly, a sign to continue.

Smile. Don't let them think you're scared to death. The show must go on.

"I'm sure you have wondered how the white men produce what they call *coins*, " she began. "You see these?" She held up five common three-cent pieces for them to inspect. "The whites have special machines to make them, but the machines are not needed if you know a secret." She wrapped the five coins in a handkerchief and handed them to the nearest man to her right. "Hold these, I'll want them back later," she said. He held the handkerchief gingerly, as if afraid it was going to disappear.

"This pipe is the secret," Raven continued. She held up a familiar length of hollow reed for their inspection. "You see, there is nothing in it." She swept the reed around quickly for their inspection.

"Now, watch closely." The reed was held vertically, in front of her body so they could not see the interior. "Abracadabra, don't screw it up," she intoned softly while waving her free hand above the reed. With their eyes diverted, the hand holding the reed worked the magic. By the time she placed her free hand below the open end, the coins, five in all, tumbled obediently into her upturned palm. Without a word, she swept her hand around close to the startled faces before her while replacing the magical reed with an ordinary one behind her back. The tribal leaders were so engrossed with the shining coins in her hand that they did not notice the switch.

"It's easy," she told her audience. "Who wants to try?" She offered the reed to each man seated before her. Some were tempted, but there were no takers. She closed her fist and pocketed the five coins.

She noticed that some of the men were glancing at Charlie instead of concentrating on what she was doing. She could see in the corner of her eye that Charlie was fidgeting. He looked nervous. She didn't blame him. His turn was coming.

Raven dragged herself back to the show. "There are still five more coins here," she said, indicating the handkerchief still tentatively held by her dupe. "Will you please untie the cloth and show us the coins?"

The man did as he was asked and held up the five coins.

"Thank you," said Raven. "Now, put them back and tie up the cloth and give it to me."

He eagerly handed the package back to her, glad to be rid of it. She smoothly pulled the switch as she passed the bundle from one hand to the other and then offered it to Red Cloud.

"As a great leader, chief of a mighty nation, I want you to have the coins as a present."

Dubiously, Red Cloud took the package and opened it. His eyes went wide and bored into her as he rolled five hazelnuts from the handkerchief into his hand. Then he swung his eyes to the man who last had the coins. "What have you done with my money?" he asked.

The look on the man's face was classic. His jaw sagged and his eyes bugged out. A murmur went up around the circle. Surely this was great magic, but useless. Better to turn nuts into money than the other way around.

Raven knew it was time to make the big play. "Come, let us go outside and I will show you even greater magic."

Raven watched the two medicine men in the group closely. Even they seemed to be impressed with what they had seen, but this was the acid test to gain their support. Charlie walked fifteen paces toward the open end of the camp. As he walked, he chanted a meaningless sing-song calling up the spirits to protect him from harm. The words *"wiyaka sapa"* were repeated again and again. It was important for these people to know that he was calling on the great power of Black Feather for the coming test. When *Wiyaka Sapa* came and walked among them, he would be a legend already.

Raven asked one of the medicine men for the pistol she had asked him to bring to the meeting. It was an ancient, rusted single shot pistol with a big barrel.

Charlie opened his buffalo robe and raised his arms toward the sky as his chant picked up volume and speed. Raven braced the pistol with both hands and took careful aim. Her palms were sweaty, the pistol heavy in her hands. She moved three steps closer to Charlie. *Don't miss. The center of the chest.* "Oh Holy Shit, I'm going to shoot my brother," she mumbled. She gulped and squeezed the trigger. The old pistol roared and bucked painfully in her grasp.

The effect on Charlie was less spectacular. He grunted and backed up two paces.

He raised his arms over his head and started to chant again of the great power of *Wiyaka Sapa*. All around there was a great silence, warriors shocked by this incomprehensible deed. The silence was broken by an excited babbling from all the gathered warriors. A few, braver than most, reached out and tentatively touched Charlie. Surely this was great medicine!

Both had demonstrated great power and they were invited to stay with Red Cloud as honored guests. When they left, Red Cloud gave them a precious gift. He included them in his *tiyospaye*; his extended family. Nothing is more important among the Lakota than kinship. Raven and Charlie arrived with no family, but left as Oglala *oyate*, in the *tiyospaye* of the great Red Cloud.

On the third morning, they left with an escort of two warriors to travel north to the agency housing Spotted Tail and his Brule band. Their escort spread the word of the powers of *Hecala Win* and their message was greeted with anticipation. Charlie added a few new twists to his act and the Brule on the reservation were convinced that a mighty new medicine had come to the Lakota. There were no fences around the reservations and, as Indians came and went from reservation lands, the visitors took the message abroad to their own villages. So the word spread among the *tiyospaye* of the Lakota.

Raven and Charlie followed the White River north into western South Dakota, then cut east and followed a tributary of the White which they called *Cankpe Opi*, better known to whites as Wounded Knee Creek.

Late one blustery afternoon they paused in a pleasant little bowl-shaped valley surrounded by grassy hills lightly covered with pine trees. Raven dismounted and knelt in the grass, caressing it with her hands. "If we are successful, this valley will never taste the blood of the Lakota. There will be no massacre here." Charlie knelt beside her and offered his own prayers in this valley which would come to represent all that the Lakota dreaded and feared.

The next afternoon Raven called to her brother, "Charlie, stop!"

"What now?" he snapped. He had been moody and withdrawn all day, barely speaking to her.

"Don't you know where we are?" she asked.

Charlie looked around with no real interest. "Yeah, somewhere on the res, only there ain't no res yet. What's the big deal?"

"We're home, Charlie," she whispered. "We're home."

She slipped from her horse and walked a short distance through the grass, then pretended to climb three steps, raised her right hand and knocked three times on an imaginary door. "*Ani*, are you home? *Ani*, it's me, your daughter come to visit." She listened intently, then turned away. "Mother isn't here, Charlie. She won't be here for another hundred years."

Charlie stood to one side, hands on his hips, staring at a bare patch of ground.

"Charlie, what're you looking at?"

He muttered something she couldn't hear, the words caught by the breeze.

"What? Speak up."

"I loved that old truck."

Then she remembered. Charlie's first car, a used Chevy pick-up, red with gray primer spots, the rear window long since bashed out. When she last saw it, it was one of five cars and trucks slowly rusting and returning to mother earth.

They camped there that night. Charlie mellowed, then became melancholy, dredging up old dreams, remembering the days when he believed he would become a leader among his people. He remembered the days before liquor, rejection, disappointment.

"You have another chance, big brother," soothed Raven. "You will be remembered as the man who saved the people. They will sing songs about you."

"Bullshit! *Wiyaka Sapa*, the Lakota Prophet is the man they'll remember, and *Hecala Win*, Raven Woman with magic hands. I'm nobody!" He angrily rolled himself in his blanket and turned his back to his sister, ending the conversation.

Raven sat at the fire for a time, her thoughts wandering. *How do I help you, brother? Will he come? When? Are we fools, or saviors? Or, neither? Tukanhila give me strength. Give me answers. Before we go further, we must visit Paha Sapa. I need a vision. I need Wiyaka Sapa. Where are you Linc?*

The next morning Charlie was still in a foul mood but ready to accept his role in this life. In Lakota culture, men were the hunters, providers and defenders. Women owned the tipi and its contents and were responsible for all the work in camp. Charlie was becoming a model Lakota male. He refused to lift a finger to help Raven pack.

As they turned to leave, Raven took one last look. "Charlie, you remember the tire swing on the old cottonwood tree?"

He grunted a reply.

"The tree hasn't even sprouted yet." She nudged her horse with her knees. "Bye, Mom," she whispered.

They topped a hill to the west and spied *Paha Sapa*, the sacred Black Hills, a dark saw-toothed range under a leaden gray sky.

There's a storm coming, thought Raven then turned resolutely forward. The Black Hills were old friends and she was anxious to make their reacquaintance.

FIVE

Thursday, November 4, 1875. Washington City.

Matt absently stirred sugar into a second cup of coffee and concentrated on the short article in the newspaper. His dinner of fried beef, fried potatoes, and limp vegetables rumbled in his stomach. *So, it's started,* he mused. *Portent to disaster.*

The article reported the results of a meeting held by President Grant to review government policy regarding the Black Hills and the miners who were streaming, illegally, into the very heart of the Great Sioux Reservation. The President had met the previous day with several men: Lieutenant General Phillip Sheridan, Commander of the Military Division of Missouri; General George Crook, Commander of the Department of the Platte; General William Belknap, Secretary of War; and Zachariah Chandler, new Secretary of the Interior. The upshot of the article was that miners would no longer be turned back from the Black Hills or be forcibly rejected.

Matt pondered the results of this subtle shift in government policy. *It's pretty obvious that this gathering of hawks is inviting the Sioux to react to increased incursions into their sacred land. So, the Indians attack the trespassers, the government cries foul deed, the people clamor for retribution, and—hot damn!—an excuse for war. Send in the troops, crush the hostiles, open the land for settlement. Neat. No declaration of war and no consultation with a possibly balky Congress—whose members might bring up the messy issue of the 1868 treaty guaranteeing the land forever to the Sioux and Cheyenne.*

Matt smiled. "Tricky Dick would be proud."

His mood shifted abruptly. *It's a shitty deal, we know that now, but my job is still the same. Just see that it happens. Take out the opposition who want to change history. Then again, maybe they didn't make it. Maybe I'm chasing ghosts who never were.*

Tuesday, December 7, 1875. Washington City.

Crisp, clear autumn had become gray, wet, cold winter and Black Feather's mood shifted from frustration to boredom and occasional anger. The city of Washington held no luster, and little hope. He was mired in the bureaucratic mess called government. His attempts to reach key personnel in the War Department and Department of the Interior were universally rebuffed; occasionally politely, but generally curt, rude subordinates handled the rejections with pleasure.

The meeting today was his last chance. Colonel Simon Farrington, a liaison officer for the Army Department, had reluctantly agreed to meet the Lakota emissary and include a representative from the Bureau of Indian Affairs. Black Feather presented himself to an enlisted man in a small ante-room in the now familiar War Department. He'd taken pains with his appearance today: stiffly starched white collar, freshly boiled white shirt set off with a conservative cravat and dark waistcoat, striped trousers, and polished black boots. His hair was neatly braided, squeaky clean.

"Colonel Farrington will see you now," announced the aide. He held the door and closed it softly behind Black Feather.

The colonel's office was a step up from most Black Feather had seen. Dark paneling, a heavy oak desk with matching side chairs and shiny spittoons, all sitting on dark carpet covering polished oak floors. The colonel was a caricature of what a staff officer with too many years of riding a desk chair should look like. Graying hair, receding at the temples, curved down to substantial mutton-chops framing a round, florid face. The round head was perched on rounded shoulders above an ample gut hanging over short, fat legs. He chose to stand directly in front of a large American flag, stretched on the wall, where the gray light from the one window would hit full on his elaborately trimmed uniform. The entire effect made Black Feather think of a toy soldier in *The Nutcracker*.

The second man was obviously a diplomat. His spare frame, elaborate frock coat, and striped pants perfectly suited his erect posture, stiffly held even when seated, as he was now in a side chair. He had a fringe of clipped white hair on his otherwise bald pate and a neat moustache sandwiched between thin lips and a bony nose. Bright blue eyes studied Black Feather, but gave no light to the soul lurking behind them.

"Ahem, yes, Mr. Blackbird, I believe." The colonel stepped away from the flag as he spoke and tentatively extended a pudgy hand, as if this wild creature might snatch it away if he weren't careful.

Black Feather briefly clasped the hand. "Black Feather, Sir," he said softly. "In my language it is *Wiyaka Sapa*, but I also have a Christian name, if that would be easier. You can call me Lincoln."

"Lincoln? As in Abraham?"

"Yes, sir. I was adopted some years ago by a white family who educated me and greatly admired the late President. They graced me with the name."

"Ahem, well yes, Lincoln it will be. I would like you to meet Mr. Thaddeus Bright, Department of Indian Affairs."

Black Feather took the bony hand, surprised at the strength of the grip. The man might look like a striped-pant sissy, but he was a physically powerful man.

"Ahem, please be seated, Lincoln. Cigars, gentlemen?"

Black Feather and Thaddeus Bright refused, but waited while the colonel prepared and lighted a fat stogie. Cigar smoke and sweaty bodies were two aspects of nineteenth century civilization that Black Feather could barely tolerate.

As he watched the lighting ceremony, Black Feather wondered if the colonel was aware that less than two years previously a United States general had gone to a peace conference with Modoc Indians in California without a pistol, but carrying a box of cigars. An hour later, General E. R. S. Canby was dead, assassinated by the Modoc leader, Captain Jack.

"You know, those things can kill you," commented Black Feather.

Farrington regarded him coolly as he sucked deeply on the cigar. "Do tell. So what is it we can do for you?" If the colonel understood the significance of the statement, he didn't show it.

"I'm certain you've heard why I'm here, Colonel, so I'll be brief. It is my intention to start serious negotiations between my people and the government of the United States of America to draft a treaty—binding and fair between us."

"I see. You want to negotiate a treaty for the Sioux Indians with the United States. I find this quite remarkable, considering we already have an adequate treaty. Why should we want another?"

"Unfortunately, sir, the existing treaties—there are several—are totally inadequate, unjust, already broken, and doomed to utter failure. The treaty I propose would bind what you call the Sioux, along with other peoples of the Great Plains, who will be united in sovereign territory as a new nation, the United Lakota Nation. The territorial extent of the new nation will be as defined in the Fort Laramie Treaty of 1868."

"A sovereign nation?" interjected Bright. "I had no idea such a nation existed. Where, exactly, is the seat of government and who are the elected leaders of this nation?"

"The nation will be formed, Mr. Bright, based on a constitution patterned after your own. Selection of the capital city and election of leaders will follow. Assistance for the constitution and formation of government would be provided by the United States. It will require time to unify the people, educate them, and alter the traditional ways of governing, but it can be done. The treaty will provide the time and assistance."

"What an intriguing notion, Lincoln. Imagine, a united people formed from individual tribes who speak different languages, worship different gods, and frequently war on each other." Bright let the irony drip heavily onto each word as he ticked off these points.

Black Feather struggled to suppress his emotions. "It has been done before. Witness your own nation, immigrants all, from many language and ethnic groups. Unfortunately, your government has relentlessly destroyed organized government of native peoples.

"Even before the founding of the United States, the French and English colonists tore apart the Iroquois League. This was once a stable, powerful confederation of five tribes that controlled most of the northeastern part of this country, but they were led to ruin by whites."

"Ahem, I think you have it wrong, Lincoln." Farrington said. "The Iroquois destroyed themselves when they chose sides between the French and the British. Besides, they had no real towns, or farming or manufacturing as a civilized society must."

"But the Cherokee did, Colonel. Even your own leaders called them 'the civilized tribes,' and you made treaties with them and the Creeks and Choctaws, guaranteeing their lands forever. Andrew Jackson made that treaty and, four years later, Andrew Jackson abolished that treaty before sending those nations into exile. In fact, sir, your government has a perfect record when it comes to establishing and abolishing treaties. I'm afraid, nay certain the record will be kept intact now that all land east of the Mississippi has been cleared of the native people who lived upon it for countless generations. Now it is the turn of the Lakota, Cheyenne, Arapaho, Pawnee, and many others to be systematically destroyed in your quest for Manifest Destiny. I offer an opportunity to reverse this shameful trend and to end the genocide of Indians in America."

"The what? What's *genocide*? " asked Bright.

"It is the organized slaughter of one people by another, sir."

"Preposterous!" exclaimed Bright. "In the first place, there is no plan to slaughter Indians, quite the contrary. We bring civilization, education, medicine, enlightenment, a better way of life."

You pompous ass, thought Black Feather. *If you only knew the results of this thinking. If you only knew the hardship, anger, resentment, physical and mental pain this government has imposed on my people you might think differently. And the deaths. The slaughter of whole cultures. Then again, maybe it would make no difference at all to you. "*You also bring disease, alcohol abuse, no understanding of our ways, and death. Your President vacillates between your department, the army, and the churches as to which method will best subjugate and enslave our people. What I mean is, it isn't all brightness and light, sir."

Bright waved a hand as if swatting a pesky fly. "Minor problems, of no real import. In the long run, the Indian will be better for our enlightened concern."

"I believe the problems are substantial, Mr. Bright. President Grant is currently fighting for his political life, in large part because of gross improprieties in the current reservation system and your bureau."

He was referring to congressional hearings arising from scandals exposed in the contracting and delivery of allotments guaranteed to reservation Indians. The hearings had led, in part, to the resignation of Columbus Delano as secretary of the interior in October. His replacement, Zachariah Chandler, was a strong supporter of returning control of Indian affairs to the military. Now there were rumors that a new round of investigations might soon be launched. Democratic senators were asking hard questions of the Republican administration, touching even President Grant's family.

Thaddeus Bright, a Republican appointee, flushed crimson and seemed about to explode when the colonel smoothly stepped in.

"Ahem, Lincoln, that may all be much political ado over nothing. We shouldn't judge until all the facts are in. It remains true that the President, and, for that matter, the top generals who decide policy for the army, remain national heroes. Fine, upstanding men."

"That is only another reason it makes intelligent dialogue between us so difficult, Colonel. You see, some of your national heroes are, to the people of my nation, war criminals."

A heavy silence, broken only by the rhythmic ticking of the wall clock, hung in the room.

Now you've done it, thought Black Feather. *How can I ever get these pig-headed, ignorant, political baboons to negotiate as equals? When they look at an Indian, they see only an impediment to 'civilization.' We're not quite human.*

Black Feather decided he had nothing left to lose, so he took the last gambit left. "Even as we sit here, gentlemen, orders have been issued to Generals Terry, Crook and Gibbon to wage a winter campaign against northern Cheyenne and Lakotas who are considered hostile because they are living peacefully in winter communities on land that has been theirs for countless generations. A three-pronged attack by your army into the heart of land guaranteed to us by treaty, and which certainly should be ours by right of ownership and occupation, is being planned, and will be executed because your own Constitution denies us the basic right of property ownership you take for granted. The Fourteenth Amendment, freeing the slaves and making them eligible for citizenship in the United States, left only one disenfranchised people in this land—and they are the people who were here when you came. Do not talk to me of benevolent enlightenment, Mr. Bright."

Colonel Farrington had gone pasty-white. He definitely appeared unwell.

Black Feather bored into him. "Yes, Colonel. We know the plan. Great tragedy lies ahead unless we work to avert it now. How many more fatherless children and grieving widows must there be—on both sides—before we will learn? I hold forth an olive branch of peace, an opportunity for equals to negotiate in good faith and avert disaster. Is there nobody who will take hold of the chance?"

Farrington had regained his composure. When he spoke, it was with cold reserve. "I'm quite certain you are misinformed concerning the movements and motives of the United States Army. It would be utter folly to pursue this, or to speak of it again. I believe our time is up."

The colonel rose, but did not offer his hand. He clasped them firmly behind his ample girth. The interview was over.

As Black Feather stood, Thaddeus Bright asked, "And when this United Lakota Nation of yours is formed, I suppose you will be the first President?"

"No, sir," replied Black Feather coolly. "I plan to be part of the Interior Department. I will head the Bureau of White Affairs for the nation. Perhaps we'll establish reservations where the whites can be benevolently brought to understand how they must live within our borders."

He strode from the room, sick at what he had done. There was no chance to peacefully institute the plan. Now it would have to be done quite differently.

Farrington rocked back in his chair. "Well, what do you make of him?"

Bright folded his hands piously and contemplated them. "What he said about the army plan, true or no?"

"Of course not! It's been made quite clear to the few roaming bands not on the reservations that there will be no problem if they report to their reservations by January 31. Besides, how could he know what the army plans? Even I don't know these things. There's no way he could know."

"Then, you don't know that it isn't true?"

"It can't be! Forget it. What about him? What do we do?"

"Maybe," mused Bright, "he should meet Zachariah."

"Chandler? The secretary himself? Better he get a bullet between the eyes some dark night in an alley. What earthly good does it do to let him live, let alone meet the secretary?"

"Humor me, Colonel. It might be quite interesting to watch the sparks fly. I'll try to arrange to have you present for the festivities, then you can engage the services of an assassin, if you wish. What was that word he used? Genocide? Preposterous! No such word, I'm sure."

Matt felt like a tourist who had missed the last bus out of town. Between occasional trips to the War Department to see if there was any decision on his request to join the army, he visited the hallowed halls of Congress and listened to boring dialogues between self-important senators and representatives. There was no mention of an Indian prophet stirring the bureaucratic pot with dire predictions of disaster. In fact, there was no mention of war with the Indians in Congress, but there were articles in the newspapers referring to the upcoming campaign. One, in mid-November, quoted from a report by an inspector from the Bureau of Indian Affairs. Referring to the Sioux and Cheyenne in his official report, Edwin Watkins had said:

"The true policy, in my judgement, is to send troops against them in the winter, the sooner the better, and whip them into subjection. They richly merit the punishment for their incessant warfare on friendly tribes, their continuous thieving, and their numerous murders of white settlers...."

The article continued in the same vein, obviously intended to inflame feelings and justify later actions. Matt read this and other articles leaked to the press, knowing that the President was pulling the strings.

In late November, Matt placed an article of his own in the paper. Under "Personals" to Uncle Demetrius he wrote:

"Still no sign of our cousin. I'm joining the army and heading west. Will advise when I leave this place."

Matt spent most of his time prowling the city and surrounding countryside, vainly searching for one man who would stand out in the crowd. He was beginning to believe Lincoln Long Trail had not survived the passage to the past. Matt was tired. He was tired of the shabby, unfinished, temporary look of the city, and tired of the daily assault on his senses from the evidence of grinding poverty. He was tired of seeing the second-class status of former slaves, now free, but huddled in their shanty towns with little hope and no jobs or money, and tired of Civil War veterans, many missing limbs, who hobbled or crouched on corners begging pennies. Most of all, he was tired of his fruitless search.

At night, sometimes too tired to sleep, he realized how lonely he was. He was a man with no past and an uncertain future with no friends. He longed for intelligent conversation with life-long friends, or an afternoon at a ball game, a friendly drink in a bar. Visions of evenings with Kimberly and Randy crowded his thoughts. He imagined long conversations with her and the days the three of them might have spent together. He longed for her caresses, her scent and soft skin, the tender moments they might have spent together.

"I'm wealthy beyond my wildest dreams and unhappier than I've ever been," he whispered to his empty room. He rolled over and tried to shut out the loneliness. "Tomorrow's another day and Jamie is a fading memory. Go to sleep, stupid."

SIX

Saturday, December 11, 1875. The White House.

The pile of steaming horse dung was lurking in the shadows. "Shit," exclaimed Matt as he planted his left boot, brand new and shiny, directly into the warm mass. He left the sweeping drive in front of the White House and found a clump of grass to wipe the boot clean.

Matt was surprised and excited when he was informed only three days ago that his story had been accepted and he was restored to the rank of first lieutenant and assigned, as he had requested, to the Seventh Cavalry, stationed at Fort Abraham Lincoln, Dakota Territory. The restoration of military rank was accompanied by a gilt-bordered invitation to a reception at the White House, one of several the President was hosting for the holiday season. When he asked why he had been so chosen, he was told, "You'll find out, Lieutenant. Just be there."

Matt passed the carriages waiting to discharge gentlemen and ladies in all their finery and presented his invitation to the sentry on the portico. He chuckled when he thought of the vast changes in security and access to the residence at 1600 Pennsylvania since the last time he had been here. *No alarm systems, no rocket launchers on the roof, no bulletproof glass in the windows, no swimming pool in the basement. Why, I could walk in here and shoot the President and walk away, scot-free.*

The interior was also amazingly different from the White House of the twenty-first century. Smaller, with dark walls and carpets. Ornate, heavy, dark furniture sat in brooding shadows where the gaslight was dim. The feeling was rich, but somehow sinister. Matt felt very out of place, but he strode forward confidently to join the receiving line entering the East Room. Most of the men were dressed in their finest dark-striped suits and accompanied by elaborately gowned women who alleviated some of the gloom with their bright colors and beaming smiles.

Some things don't change. An invitation to a party at the White House is a universal opportunity for a woman to buy a new dress, and only the very finest will do. Thank God I'm not married! The thought momentarily awakened a vision of Kimberly Caldwell. *God, she'd make these women look like cows.*

His reverie was broken as he found himself face-to-face with Ulysses S. Grant, sixteenth President of the United States of America. He heard his name announced by an aide, but it was as if in a dream.

"First Lieutenant Matthew O'Shaunessey, Seventh Cavalry."

Mechanically, Matt extended his hand as he studied the seamed face, thick beard and merry eyes of the President. "Aha! I've been quite anxious to meet you, Lieutenant. I must have a quiet chat with you later."

"I'm honored, Mr. President, but I am also somewhat mystified as to why you should want to meet me."

"Why you must realize the stir you've caused in official Washington, Lieutenant."

"No, sir. I'm afraid I was unaware of any stir."

"Well, Lieutenant, they're calling you 'Lazarus' over at the War Department. I must say I've never heard of anything so amazing in all my years. To think that a man could survive Gettysburg and not even know who he is for twelve years. I would say that is as stunning as if someone got lost in time and reappeared in a different era."

Matt smiled. "Well, put that way, I guess it is a bit of a miracle, Mr. President."

The President passed Matt to his wife, Julia, who gazed up at him with her slightly crossed eyes, smiled and shook his hand warmly. Then he was free of the line and wandered toward a long table groaning under the weight of hors d'oeuvres and punch bowls. The table was attended by white-liveried Negroes who bowed and served the guests.

Matt sipped his punch and surveyed the growing crowd. Among the suits there was a sprinkling of uniforms, most heavy with gold braid. This was territory not usually open to a lowly lieutenant. These were staff officers, not the fighting generals. Sherman, Sheridan, Crook, Terry and Gibbon were in their respective western headquarters preparing for the winter campaign to subjugate the remaining Sioux and Cheyenne, whom the President deemed hostile.

Also notably absent from this, or any party thrown by the President, was Lieutenant Colonel George Armstrong Custer who was on leave with his wife in New York, but had visited the capitol briefly during his leave. Matt knew he would meet Custer, his new boss, soon enough.

Matt froze, and his attention focused on one guest, a man patently out of place. Copper skin, long black braids, a face burned into Matt's memory. *So, Lincoln Long Trail, you made it. But what the hell are you doing here?*

Long Trail was deep in conversation with a short, fat colonel who was leading him to one of the striped-pants set. As Matt watched he could see the introduction and hand shake. He struggled to place a name with the third party. He had been extensively briefed on the major people he might encounter and the face rang a bell in his mind. Then it clicked. *Of course, Zachariah Chandler, the newly appointed Secretary of the Interior. The man in charge of Indian affairs.* Matt sidled through the crowd to be able to overhear the conversation.

"… opportunity for lasting peace, perhaps our last chance," concluded Black Feather.

"But, my dear fellow," said Chandler, "peace will be assured as soon as the hostile tribes report to the reservations, as they have been ordered to do. I'm certain our government will …"

"In the middle of winter?" exploded Black Feather. "The hostile tribes, as you call them, are peacefully camped in winter quarters and yet they have been ordered to move many miles in the dead of frozen winter with old men and women, babies and sick people at a time when even conditioned military men are usually confined to their posts; and now those military men are being ordered to attack the winter camps."

"My dear man, I think you overstate the difficulties."

"Mister Secretary, you're from Michigan, so I would expect you to understand the difficulties of winter travel more than most."

Chandler bit his lip, peeved at the effrontery of this obviously educated savage. Of course the army was going to attack. It was the only way to impress these last few savages to adapt. It was for their own good. "Well, if it is as you say, I'm sure the presence of our army will convince these people to move by the deadline, yes?"

Black Feather struggled to control his emotions. When he spoke, it was with calm authority.

"Mister Secretary, let me ask you a question, and I ask for your serious consideration. If my country sent an army against your country, and your country had no standing army of your own, but you did have a wife and family and you were living on land that your family had owned for hundreds of years, what would you do?"

Chandler started to respond, but Black Feather held up his hand. "Please, I'm not through yet. Suppose further that your country and mine had a treaty, binding on both parties, duly ratified, that guaranteed your land and your freedom. Sir, would you be mad enough to fight to save your family and your land?"

Mesmerized, Matt tore his eyes from Black Feather's face. A small crowd was forming around the debate. Chandler seemed momentarily stumped, but quickly recovered and switched gears.

"Ah, what you propose is difficult to respond to, but I understand that you would replace all this with a new treaty, a new nation?"

"Yes, but a treaty unlike any ever agreed to between our peoples."

"Oh? How so?"

"This time the treaty would be *written* in both languages, so all parties could fully understand the terms. This time my people would have their own attorneys present. This time my people would be involved in setting the issues to be discussed. This time—"

"Whoa! Hold it!" Chandler had his hand in the air, waving for attention. "You've convinced me. I believe we should have more meetings, discuss the issues, formulate plans. You'll find I'm sensitive to the potential problems."

"I'm at your disposal, Mister Secretary. When shall we meet?"

"Well, not so fast, young man. I'll appoint a committee to study the—"

"Not good enough," Black Feather snapped. "Time is our common enemy. We must act quickly." He glanced around at the small crowd they had attracted. His eyes locked with Matt for a moment. "I'm sure these people will be interested in a swift resolution to this problem."

Matt found himself drawn to the intense, intelligent young graduate student. *He locked the Secretary of the Interior in knots. If he's successful, he just might change history.* It was an unsettling thought.

In another corner of the room, Grant partied with his military guests, unaware of the possible disruption to his carefully conceived plans to open new territory to his land-hungry constituency.

Matt slipped away from the reception as soon as he could and withdrew to the shadows where he could observe the guests as they left. Before long his quarry emerged and set off at a fast pace to the southeast along Pennsylvania Avenue. Matt followed, staying a block behind on the opposite side of the street as they left the central area of the capitol. Black Feather was heading into progressively poorer areas with fewer buildings and street lights. Several twists and turns took them off the major streets and into the muddy lanes lined with shanties and hovels populated by Negroes. There were no other pedestrians and Matt lagged further behind to escape detection. Eventually he lost sight of Black Feather and retreated to safer territory. *Of course,* Matt thought. *I've been looking in the wrong places. You're poor and a minority. It makes sense that you wouldn't be living in a hotel or major boarding house. You've holed up in the only place available to you.*

Matt returned to his hotel and took off his new uniform. A plan was developing, but it would take time, time he might not have, now that he was commissioned and due to be sent west.

Friday, January 7, 1876.

Black Feather was thoroughly discouraged. Almost a month had passed since his meeting with Secretary Chandler at the White House. The formation of a committee had taken ten days. Then the first meetings were delayed until after the holidays. This, finally, was the first week of actual dialogue.

The five members of the committee were all minor functionaries from the Department of the Interior and the Indian Commissioner's Office. "A collection of flunkies to handle this minor problem we seem to have," is the way Secretary Chandler had described the committee to J. Q. Smith, his Indian Commissioner.

The meetings this week were sporadic, short, and little of substance had been discussed. Due to schedule conflicts, it was difficult to gather all five members at one time and one or another seemed to have pressing business elsewhere just about the time any serious discussion started.

The committee members insisted on progressing from "preliminary findings" to boring into Black Feather to assess his background and training, an area he necessarily kept as vague as possible. It quickly became obvious that the committee members were little more than glorified clerks, with little understanding of the problems facing the Indians they were supposedly responsible for.

One member, replying to a question from Black Feather regarding how the Indians were supposed to live on the reservations, replied, "I'm certain the government will purchase excess crops raised by the Indians for a fair price."

"What excesses, sir," asked Black Feather, "are you referring to?"

The man looked exasperated as he tried to explain this simple concept. "Excesses are the amounts over and above those required for subsistence. This is how farmers make the money to purchase the other products they need."

"You assume, of course that Indians want to be farmers?"

"Well, naturally, they will have to make some adjustments, but the treaties specifically authorize supplying mules, plows, seeds, everything they need to start successful farms."

"And land? What about the land, sir? You must realize that the lands set aside for reservations are the very lands your own farmers have found so useless that they, with all their experience, haven't even tried to farm, and yet your government expects Indians to be successful on this same land."

And so it went. Serious discussion sidetracked into meaningless alleys with no understanding between the parties.

This morning Black Feather believed he had made a breakthrough when he presented his brief on how a Lakota nation could be formed. The document outlined the formation of government patterned after the United States with three arms—executive, legislative and judicial—backed by a constitution guaranteeing basic rights and binding the nation to the United States as an ally for all time. Instead of mules and plows, the United States would provide the Lakota Nation with advisors, loans and trade agreements. Colleges and universities would be founded to teach Indians more than farming. Time would be given for the people to make the adjustments, time for the older generation to abandon the hunt and nomadic lifestyle they craved and a younger generation to embrace the new concepts and step into the roles they would occupy as the new leaders.

Two of the committee members seemed especially intrigued with the idea and asked probing questions about implementation of the plan, but the inevitable stonewalling soon started and the discussion turned up another blind alley.

"Obviously the plan has some merit, however, it is far beyond the capacity of this committee to act on the proposal," intoned one member.

"Certainly," spoke another member, "this should be referred to Secretary Chandler. I imagine he can eventually see that Congress reviews it. In a year or two it—"

"We don't have a year or two," fumed Black Feather. "At most we have six months."

"Oh, why is that?" asked the first member.

Now you've done it. What do you tell them? The truth? Part of the truth? A big lie?

Black Feather got up from his chair and paced the room, earnestly searching the five faces, seeking the key to unlock their minds. "I say six months because by June it will be too late for this plan, or any rational plan for future relations between our people, to succeed. Your country is preparing to go to war with my people again, only this time I fear it will be different. The war you bring will not provide peace. How many men must die? How many more widows, on both sides, must there be?"

He realized he wasn't quite reaching them. He stopped pacing and leaned over the table. "Unless we make some progress toward peace, I foresee disaster this spring. Possibly earlier, but certainly by the end of June, there will be a major confrontation between your army and my people. Hundreds may die because this time we are fighting for our lands, our lives and our culture. My people will not meekly surrender at the end of January as they have been ordered to do. They will not give away any more land without a fight. Will you help me stop the bloodshed before it starts?"

His pronouncement was met with silence. Only the steady ticking of the clock on the wall broke the silence and underscored that Black Feather's worst enemy, time, was slipping away.

"You sound almost like a prophet, Isaiah or Job, delivering God's messages," commented one member.

"Maybe I'm more like John the Baptist, only I don't announce the coming of a Messiah, but a day of doom. I know I am right, but only time will convince the world. That is why I beg you to consider this proposal and move forward now. The tragedy I see in the future is avoidable. You have the key."

The rest of the afternoon was spent in more haggling, more side issues, more misunderstanding. By the time the meeting ended, it was dusk. Swirling snow blew in Black Feather's face as he pushed through the door to the street.

The sound of the first shot was muffled through the blowing snowflakes. The bullet ricocheted off a brick only inches from Black Feather's face. He was pelted with fragments from the brick and instinctively tried to pull his head down between his shoulders. He also tried to run, but slipped on the snow and ice at the top of the steps. It probably saved his life. As he fell, another round chipped the bricks behind him. He scrambled on his hands and knees. The papers he was carrying broke free and danced in the wind as he slid down the stone stairs to the street. The fall jarred him and left him momentarily stunned. He raised his head slowly and spotted a shadowy figure in an alley across the street. The dim, heavily cloaked figure had a pistol extended at arm's length. The pistol moved, centering on him.

My God! They're trying to assassinate me! Black Feather bunched his muscles and pushed himself awkwardly to his feet and ran blindly down the deserted street, fearing for the next shot. Behind him, the door to the building he had just left opened. Two men in deep conversation huddled against the snowy blast and didn't see him disappearing into the storm. By the time they saw the scattered papers in the street, Black Feather had disappeared and his assailant had turned and melted into the shadows. The men saw the papers and stooped to gather them up. A quick glance and they recognized them as papers relating to the hearings they were attending.

"Wonder why Black Feather abandoned his stuff?"

The second man shrugged. "Who knows. Hard to tell what goes through a savage mind."

"Oh well, I'll just keep 'em and give 'em back to him Monday."

Black Feather tried to think as he sprinted through the deepening gloom. *What'd I do to get them so upset? How many men are looking for me? Do they know where I live? Who can I turn to? Where do I go? Shit, injun! You'd better get the hell out of Dodge.*

He ran until he was completely out of breath, then slumped against a recessed entry to a building, his lungs burning, his mind in turmoil. He'd obviously worn out his welcome in Washington and accomplished exactly nothing. There would be no new orders to the troops to stay in their forts. There would be no discussions with congressional committees. There would be no Lakota nation.

"Gotta get money, clothes, a horse," he mumbled. "Gotta take a chance on my place, but carefully."

It was after midnight when he sneaked into his lean-to like a thief in the night. It took only moments to bundle his belongings into his valise and slip out into the inky blackness. The next morning an irate citizen reported the theft of his favorite riding horse along with saddle and tack. It was impossible to tell where the thief had gone. All tracks had disappeared in the falling snow.

Matt stomped the caked snow off of his boots and shook it off his cloak. He closed the door to his room before taking the cloak off and unbuckling his gunbelt. Although army officers were entitled to wear sidearms, it was unusual to see in the confines of Washington. He didn't want any nosy witnesses asking stupid questions.

Mostly, he was disgusted with himself. Almost a month of careful stalking had failed to lead him to Black Feather's hideout. Days passed when he never sighted the Indian, and when he did there was no pattern. Finally, this week, he had established a pattern. Apparently the meetings discussed at the White House had commenced. Black Feather started coming and going from the same building every day. Today had been perfect, but...

How could I miss? Now the son-of-a-bitch will be on his guard. I'll never have it so easy again. Next week I'll have to start all over. And what about orders? They granted me leave time to get my life together, but sooner or later I've got to report to the Seventh Cavalry. Christ, I don't have all the time in the world to get this done.

There was another nagging thought. *Do I really want him dead? Is it really necessary, just to preserve history as we know it? Maybe there's another way. No. We discussed that. There's really no other way. They all have to die.*

He cradled his revolver, then slipped it into the holster and stuffed it under the bed. Tomorrow he would start the hunt again.

Tuesday morning, January 11, 1875.

For the second day in a row the committee members met, but Black Feather again failed to appear.

"What do you think could have happened to him?" asked one member.

A second member shrugged. "Who knows how that savage thinks. What do we really know about him? He never even told us where he was staying, or where he was educated, or what he did before he came to Washington. Maybe he realized how hopeless it was and just gave up. At least now we can go back to important work. If he shows again, we'll see what happens."

"I don't think that's the answer," said the first member. "He wouldn't just drop his papers in the street and take off. I think I'll show these papers to my father. Maybe he'll have some ideas."

His father was a prominent clergyman, one of a number of ministers from different denominations who had consistently pressured the President to continue his peace policy with the Indians.

"Ha, good luck. Your father and all his friends aren't likely to make Grant blink."

"Well, it seems the least I can do. After all, the man did know the Bible. He can't be all bad."

Monday, January 17, 2022. Stockton, California.

Demetrius Johnson was in a foul mood. Nothing seemed to be going right, least of all anything to do with Project T. There seemed to be no changes occurring in the historical pattern his researchers were tracking so diligently. Even the Director of the FBI had stopped calling to ask for updates. Now there were new concerns that the billions of dollars spent on the project in deepest secrecy might be exposed, and further concerns that future funding might be curtailed, or even eliminated.

A short personal in December had raised hopes, when Matt sent a message that he had spotted his cousin but "was not able to give him your message." What did that mean? The only "message" Matt was supposed to deliver was a bullet. Now, over a month later, nothing.

The telefax buzzed, interrupting his gloomy thoughts. Johnson angrily punched the receive button and the screen lit. The message scrolled slowly from bottom to top.

Dear Uncle Demetrius,

Saw our cousin last week and tried to deliver your message. I don't think he understood and he has been avoiding me ever since. I have orders to Ft. A. L. I will look for more relatives when I get there.

Matt

Johnson punched "SAVE," then dialed another number and punched "SEND." He was a little less gloomy. The game was continuing and he was sure the President wouldn't pull his funding as long as it continued. "Read it and fund me, Mr. President."

Damned shame about Linc, he brooded. Then he brightened. "The game's not over quite yet."

SEVEN

Winter, 1875-76. Dakota and Montana Territories.

The trip into the Black Hills was both exhilarating and terrifying. Raven and Charlie followed the old trails, ancient beyond years, but also crossed new trails, deep in mud, hacked out of the virgin wilderness. Where possible, they avoided the white man's pack trails and skirted the few white miner's camps they encountered. Raven dreaded the thought that a miner out hunting for game might spot them and rudely end their quest, or worse, that Charlie might kill again. He was jumpy, always nervous, and his rifle was an extension of his attitude.

For Raven there was the thrill of seeing familiar but subtly different places she remembered from her childhood when she and Charlie camped with their parents along the crystal creeks flowing out of the pine and aspen forests. She remembered the rich smell of wet earth after a late afternoon thunderstorm. The crackling lightning and booming thunder terrified her as a little girl. There were also the more pleasant memories. The sounds of birds in the trees, or the breeze through the pine, spruce and aspen. Sunlight on rocks, or sparkling in the musical water of a swift creek. But now there was the new reality, nowhere more evident than in the hills overlooking the new village of Deadwood.

Raven searched for familiar sites, but this was not the slick Deadwood of the twenty-first century. There were no brick and stone buildings, no casinos and gift shops crowding the main streets—sucking up tourists dollars. The Deadwood she saw was raw—composed of tents and wood frame buildings, still oozing sap into the muddy, torn-up gulch. The wind carried the scents of wood smoke, roasting meat, and fresh pine. The slopes above town were already almost denuded of trees and the sound of axes in the woods beat a tattoo, painful to hear. They passed on quickly, searching for a private place where they could commune in peace with Mother Earth.

A blizzard, marching down from the Canadian north, drove them to shelter in a cave, far removed from any sign of man. For three days the storm raged and the temperature plunged below zero. While Charlie huddled over the fire they kept going night and day, Raven ventured out to a sheltered ledge in the lee of the peak and wrapped herself tightly in her buffalo robe for hours at a time. The vision she sought eluded her, although she felt close to her ancestors. She felt more fully the strength the Lakota people drew from the land. She ate little, but felt stronger when the storm had passed. It was time for them to carry on. The month the Lakota called "The Moon of Frost in the Lodges" was approaching. She knew they would never survive the winter unless they had shelter when the worst storms arrived.

Life became a cycle keyed to the weather. They would move in with a *tiyospaye*, deliver their message, and then wait until the clear days between storms when they would be guided to the next village and repeat their performance. They found the villages, usually thirty to forty lodges, tucked in bends of rivers and streams with magical names—Powder, Rosebud, Tongue and Big Horn. As the weeks passed, they heard no word of *Wiyaka Sapa*. Raven began to believe he might have died and her heart and will flagged in the dark hours of the night.

They faced their greatest challenge in late December. They were escorted into a village on the Powder River, a hundred miles from the nearest military post at Fort Abraham Lincoln. It was the biggest village they'd seen since leaving Red Cloud's Agency. It was the *tiyospaye* of *Tatanka Yotanka*, the great and influential medicine man of the Hunkpapa Lakotas. Sitting Bull would be key to the success or failure of the mission and Raven found herself as nervous as she had been at the first presentation to Red Cloud.

The story she told was already familiar to her listeners, but she embellished it and spoke more forcefully than usual. Sitting Bull himself was an eloquent speaker and she sensed he appreciated her skill as she wove the story of the prophet to come, performed the coin trick and added a trick she had not used previously.

At one point she stumbled badly and lost her concentration. A movement against the wall of the large tipi distracted her. The woman sitting next to Charlie got up and moved to a new place. Ruth groaned inwardly. Charlie was probably making a play for her. He was becoming more unmanageable every day. He was still thin, almost gaunt, a shadow of the big brother she had known. His once garrulous nature had never fully returned after his ordeal on the prairie, and recently he spoke only rarely and when he did, he was surly, even rude. The most disturbing problem now was memory lapses. They had a heated argument this morning over the name of his first girlfriend. Raven was positive her name was Angel Standing Bear, but Charlie swore that wasn't her name, but couldn't remember what it was.

A doctor might help, she thought. *But no, there aren't any CAT scans or arthroscopic surgery or any medicine to help Charlie.* She dragged herself back to the show.

She began to worry anew when she announced the dramatic conclusion. The medicine man carrying the pistol they would use had sneered openly several times. He was obviously a skeptic and, possibly dangerously jealous.

Everyone eagerly jumped to their feet and pushed toward the one exit. Outside, they fanned out to leave room for the spectacle they had heard about. The only one who was not excited was Charlie. He was getting tired of being used as a living target. His chest and back ached from the deep bruises left from previous shows and he was beginning to think, irrationally, that one day the shots might not be aimed at his torso.

He shuffled through the snow, all the time calling on *Wiyaka Sapa* to protect him. Raven asked the smirking shaman for the pistol. She suspected he'd probably packed a special round with extra black powder. She speculatively handled the pistol as if weighing it. "This feels a little heavy," she commented.

The medicine man shrugged. "It is regular white man's gun. Nothing special."

Raven had an idea Charlie would really feel this one. She noticed that Sitting Bull was watching her speculatively. *Aha, so you're in on this.* The thought gave her an idea.

"Perhaps the great *Tatanka Yotanka* would like to test the power of *Wiyaka Sapa*. She extended the pistol to him. Clearly, this was new to him. He did not expect to participate, and possibly prove the power of the new prophet. He gravely nodded his head and accepted the weapon.

"Aim for the heart. If he is a false warrior, he will die," said Raven as she stepped away and crossed her fingers behind her back.

Charlie opened his buffalo robe and raised his arms toward the sky as his chant picked up volume and speed. The heavy cotton shirt he was wearing showed the ravages of multiple shots at close range. The holes were beginning to run together into tatters. He stumbled and his eyes opened wide when he saw that Sitting Bull was pointing the gun at him. He looked wildly at his sister, but saw only a warning in her eyes. Trust me, the look said. Charlie felt like he might faint. He realized he didn't want to die. He was not a fool, nor did he want to be a martyr. Before he could act, the drama was played out.

Sitting Bull braced the pistol with both hands and took careful aim. When he squeezed the trigger, the pistol roared. Flame erupted a foot or more from the muzzle.

Charlie grunted, stumbled, almost losing his balance, then slowly sank to his knees on the frozen ground. The medicine man almost broke into a grin, certain his medicine had prevailed. Charlie fell to his hands and knees, searching the ground for the flattened bullet that would prove his power. He was also catching his breath. The impact had stunned him more than usual.

"Aha!" Charlie plucked the misshapen piece of lead off the ground and held it above his head as he started to chant again of the great power of *Wiyaka Sapa*. It was the medicine man who now looked stunned. Charlie rose and walked straight to the man, took his hand, turned it palm up and dropped the bullet in his palm. It was a long moment before the man could tear his eyes from Charlie to look at what was left of his medicine. The silence was absolute.

The acceptance of *Wiyaka Sapa* in the Hunkpapa camp started with the trilling of one tongue among the gathered warriors. The sound swelled as over a hundred tongues took up the ancient call. Raven felt the hairs on her neck move with the din. Charlie stood with a beatific smile on his face, then wrapped his robe securely against the cold and started a slow, shuffling dance within the circle of converted Lakotas. A drummer rushed into the circle and was joined by others. A deep, booming heartbeat, the soul of a Lakota warrior, reverberated from the taut, buffalo hide drumheads. There was a new dance on the Great Plains. The *oyate* of the Lakota—Oglala, Hunkpapa, Miniconjou, Sicangu, and more—called on a new prophet. They waited for the man who would show them the way. *Wiyaka Sapa* was the name on every lip.

Later, when they were alone in their private lodge, Charlie returned to his usual foul mood. Raven was tired and willing to leave him alone, but he wanted to talk.

"I'm cold. Shit, I've never been as cold as this winter. Why don't you build a bigger fire?"

"If you want a bigger fire, build it yourself. I'm tired."

"Wouldn't do for me to do woman's work," Charlie retorted. "That's the only thing good about this place—women got their place and men got their place. Ain't my place to do fires, cookin' or anything else I don't wanna do."

"Yeah, Charlie, you're getting real good at not doing what you don't want. We probably should've dragged that old beat-up sofa of yours along so you'd have a proper place to do nothing."

Charlie looked confused for a moment. "What sofa?"

"Oh Jesus, Charlie. You mean you don't remember that ancient relic in your shack? You spent half your life on that damn thing."

Charlie sat silently, staring into the flames. "Put some wood on the fire. I'm cold."

Raven felt a chill now. She studied him closely. "Charlie—look at me. Look at me!"

He swiveled his head up and met her eyes.

"Are you seriously telling me you don't remember your sofa?"

Charlie let his head drop until he was gazing at the fire again. "Don't know what the hell you're talkin' 'bout. Just shut up and put some damned wood on this fire!"

Raven lay awake long after Charlie had rolled over and started snoring peacefully.

Something is wrong. Really wrong. Charlie's losing it. His mind's going and there isn't a damn thing I can do about it. Oh Linc, Linc, I need you. Please hurry or I may be next. Tell me what to do. Make me believe the dream. Hold me, love me, love me, love me.

The days in the Hunkpapa winter camp followed the cycle Raven and Charlie had established in every camp they had visited. Once the people believed in the magic, Raven delivered the message of the prophet to come, a man with great powers who would confound their enemies. If she sensed she was losing her audience, she pulled out another trick or two to remind them of her power. She remained aloof from the politics, content to let the men decide the issues. They always decided as she wanted. Men in the nineteenth century were no different from men in the twenty-first century. As long as it seemed the men in power controlled the fate of the people, they were content. The only woman who had held the office of President of the United States had said as much when discussing the great achievements of the Congress she had so elegantly controlled without seeming to do a thing.

Like an electric shock, the name *Wiyaka Sapa* raced through the camp. The afternoon was waning into an early, bitingly cold evening when Raven heard the words. She stumbled through the snow to grasp the messenger's arm and ask him to repeat his news.

"It is true!" he replied. "It is as you have said! He's coming! Little Antelope has heard his message! He brings great news!"

The man tore from her grasp and raced to spread the tidings. Raven stood, buffalo robe tightly clutched against the cold, and tried to keep from fainting. She had almost given up. Linc, now known far and wide as the prophet Black Feather, nearly died in her soul, but now he was alive. She heard the muted noise of excited people, saw them stirring in the cold winter afternoon, and then they blurred as tears filled her eyes. She staggered to her tipi and collapsed in the warm, familiar interior and sobbed where none could see her. She finally admitted the truth to herself. *I thought he was dead. I never believed I'd see him again. But now you're here. Now—now we can—What?*

New plans would wait until tomorrow. *Hecala Win*, an exhausted messenger, fell asleep.

"Hey. Is this any way to greet a returning warrior?"

Raven came awake slowly, trying to focus on the familiar face in the flickering firelight. She reached up tentatively and stroked his face and hair, then gripped him tightly and buried her face in the curve of his neck, too overcome to speak.

Black Feather clutched Raven and slid down to lie next to her. The moment was all he had wished for. There was so much to tell, so much to find out, but that could wait. Without loosening her embrace, he slipped out of his clothes and under the buffalo robe. The coming together was passionate, almost desperate. Then, again, slowly and tenderly. "You are my woman through all time. We will never be apart again," he whispered in her ear. She had not spoken a word and now she only buried her face deeper against his neck and gently stroked his back, gaining strength from her man.

"Ouch! Why do you always wear that damned arrowhead!" A thin line of blood welled from her left breast where the stone had pricked her skin.

Black Feather was startled, then he started to laugh. When he could control his mirth, he stroked her hair and assumed a serious attitude. "Is this the way a Lakota woman greets her man? After he has traveled over a hundred and fifty years to be with her? First she seduces him and then complains because he wears a symbol of the power of his people? Is she so fragile that this small stinger pricks her skin and she finally—finally—speaks only to rebuke him?"

Raven started to respond, but he silenced her with a kiss.

"The arrowhead I wear," he continued more seriously, "was taken by one of my great-great grandfathers from a Lakota warrior who died in Washington, D.C. It has been passed from father to son. At least, that's the story. Who knows if it is true?"

Raven studied his face and found it honest and handsome, open and loving. This was her man, through all time. She grasped the arrowhead and swiftly sliced his chest. "Now the stinger has pricked both of us. If you mix your blood with mine—"

"I take you, Raven, to be my wife," he intoned gravely as he smeared the blood of their bodies.

Later, Black Feather sat in the lodge with Raven and Charlie and told them about his time in Washington and his trip west.

"I stole a horse that night and headed west. I rode that horse hard, all the way to St. Louis. I used just about the last of my money for a train ticket to Cheyenne, and then stole another horse and headed to Fort Robinson.

"It was when I got to Fort Robinson that I learned the two of you were alive. Red Cloud greeted me like a long-lost brother. He sang the praises of *Hecala Win* and her brother. It was the same when I reached Spotted Tail. I've been escorted from camp to camp like a conquering hero."

"What's the big deal?" asked Charlie. "You said yourself you didn't change nothing in Washington. Custer's still comin' to the Little Big Horn." Charlie stared moodily into the fire.

Black Feather looked quizzically at Raven who warned him with her eyes. *Later, I'll tell you later.*

"I don't know," Black Feather answered. "There was a moment, the last day we met, where I thought maybe, just maybe, I was getting through to one or two of the committee members."

"Yeah, just before they tried to snuff you."

"Maybe," Raven suggested, "it wasn't the committee. Maybe it was the army, or the President."

"I've thought about that and you might be right about the army, but I doubt Grant had anything to do with it. I only met him once at the reception and just for a moment, when I was introduced to him. I don't think he knows I'm alive."

Raven shifted her position closer to Black Feather. "There is one other possibility," she said. "Someone may have been sent after all of us—from the future."

Charlie's head snapped up. "You're nuts. Who'd do somethin' like that?"

"Why not, Charlie? You're wanted for two murders. I'm implicated in both of those and Linc stole from the museum in Sacramento. There are some people who might be pretty mad about all that. They could have sent like a bounty hunter to get us."

"Shit, I didn't kill nobody 'n besides, how'd they know where to look?"

Black Feather looked thoughtful. "The computer would tell them where to look. The coordinates and shot timing would give them where and when, but—no, that's pretty far-fetched. They'd need more of a reason to do that, besides, nobody's tried to kill you. No, I don't think that's it. It probably is the army. We should be all right now."

Raven wasn't so sure, but she was too happy to argue. Charlie, however, seemed spoiling for a fight.

"Well, at least someone else's gettin' shot at. I'm gettin' sick and tired of being a target. It's all bullshit anyway. Nobody cares what we say."

"That's not true, Charlie," snapped Raven. "Maybe if you'd open your ears and shut your mouth, you'd hear what the people are saying."

Black Feather sat quietly, embarrassed by the exchange between brother and sister.

"Yeah, I've heard what they say. *Wiyaka Sapa* this 'n *Wiyaka Sapa* that. He's gonna save us all from—whatever. The two of you got some grand plan 'bout somethin' that's never gonna happen. Maybe you don't need me." He rose abruptly and stalked out of the lodge.

"What the hell's going on?" Black Feather asked immediately.

Raven sighed. "It's strange, strange and sad. Charlie's losing his memory. First it was little things, but now he's getting to the point that he denies he ever lived in the future. You heard him say he didn't kill anybody?"

"Yeah, but I thought he was just, I don't know, making a joke."

"It's no joke. He really can't remember and it gets worse every day. Then, too, he's jealous."

"Jealous? Of who?"

"Us. He had me to himself, but now you're here. He wants a woman of his own, but the only ones he's attracted to are already married. He's been a real pain in the ass."

Black Feather digested the information, seeking answers. None came to mind. Charlie was important, but, at this stage, he'd proved his power and it was more important now to keep him out of trouble with the people.

The next morning was clear and cold. It was time to move to the next village. Two warriors rode ahead to lead the way. Raven and Black Feather rode together and a disconsolate Charlie followed far to the rear leading the packhorse and travois. Time was passing. Armies were massing for their winter assault to punish the "hostiles".

A GOOD PLACE TO DIE

Orders and Incidents

Tuesday, November 9, 1875. General Phillip Sheridan to General Alfred Terry; Commander, Department of Dakota.

> "...the President decided *(at the November 3 meeting)* that the orders heretofore issued forbidding the occupation of the Black Hills country by miners should not be rescinded, still no fixed resistance should be made to the miners going in.... Will you therefore quietly cause the troops in your Department to assume such attitude as will meet the views of the President in this respect."

Friday, December 3, 1875. Secretary of the Interior, Zachariah Taylor to Secretary of War, William Belknap.

"... I have the honor to inform you that I have this day directed the Commissioner of Indian Affairs to notify said Indians (*hostile Sioux*) that they must remove to a reservation before the 31st of January next; that if they neglect or refuse so to move, they will be reported to the War Department as hostile Indians and that a military force will be sent to compel them to obey the orders of the Indian Office.... I have the honor to request that the proper military officer be directed to compel their removal...."

Monday, January 3, 1876. Sheridan to General William Sherman.

Sheridan reports both of his departments, Dakota and Platte, are ready to move against the Sioux and that "directions to that effect be communicated to me as speedily as possible, so that the enemy may be taken at the greatest possible disadvantage."

Tuesday, January 18, 1876.

Representative William Steele, Wyoming Territory, introduces a bill in Congress to open all unceded Sioux lands in Wyoming to "exploration and settlement."

Thursday, January 20, 1876. Department of the Army to First Lieutenant Matthew O'Shaunessey, Seventh Cavalry.

"You are directed to present yourself for duty to the Acting Commanding Officer, Fort Abraham Lincoln, Dakota Territory."

Monday, January 31, 1876.

The deadline for hostile Indians to report to reservations passes. No Indians report to any agency.

Tuesday, February 1, 1876. Zachariah Chandler to William Belknap.

Chandler forwarded a recommendation from J. Q. Smith, Indian Commissioner, to begin hostilities and comments that "said Indians are hereby turned over to the War Department for such action on the part of the Army as you deem proper under the circumstances."

ONE

Sunday, February 13, 1876. Chicago, Illinois.

Matt relaxed in an overstuffed chair in the Railroad Hotel and scanned the day's papers. The Chicago *Tribune* was reporting an interview with George Custer, who was on his way to St. Paul to report to General Terry. When asked about the scope of possible upcoming action against the Sioux, Custer had replied, *"I can't tell where the field of operations will be. Probably they will cover a large territory. However, I don't think that an Indian war, no matter how serious, will prevent people from rushing to the Black Hills."*

Matt smiled. Custer had just put his foot firmly in his mouth.

There were two things Matt noticed as he moved west from Washington on the railroad. One was that the eastern newspapers were filled with editorials urging President Grant to continue his peace policy toward the Indians in the face of mounting speculation that he was abandoning that policy. A number of church leaders led this attack and they seemed to be getting stronger in their denunciations. The papers further west were increasingly shrill in their call to end the "Indian menace". Where the menace was real, a policy of peace was unacceptable.

The other thing he had observed were the large number of men and families heading west, even in the dead of winter. There was a feeling that new lands would soon be available, and these prospective miners and settlers planned to be in on the ground floor.

Matt had just missed seeing Custer and now it looked like he would be trapped in Chicago for at least a day as a blizzard was blowing across the plains, halting train traffic. He felt better, now that he was on the move with orders and a firm destination. He was anxious to see the unspoiled west he had only dreamed of before.

One cloud remained. What had happened to Black Feather? Whatever he was attempting to do in Washington seemed to have ended after Matt fired at him. There had been no sign of him the next week and it looked as if he might have fled the city. Or, maybe he was wounded and holed up somewhere. Matt had a feeling they would meet again.

February, 1876. Little Powder River, Montana Territory.

Black Feather stared into the twisting shadows playing across the lodge poles and hide covering. The fire gave light and some warmth, but icy winter gripped the camp. The January 31 deadline for roving bands to report to their reservation agencies had come and gone. He knew that there had been no surrenders. By now General Sheridan had issued orders to his department commanders to prepare for action against the hostile Sioux and Cheyenne in their winter camps.

Black Feather was wrapped in brooding thoughts. Would the agency Indians follow the plan Raven had laid out? When can we move again? What about Charlie?

Raven stirred in the buffalo robe, brushing her body against his. He swiveled his head and found her eyes open, searching his face.

"What you thinking about, Tonto?" she teased.

"Mmmm, I was just wondering if all women are as pesky as you are, or if they're all as good as you in bed."

She smiled and moved her hands, gently stroking him. "Well, I don't know about all women, but I do know I'd better not catch you experimenting, or"—she stopped stroking and not too gently gripped him where it would hurt the most—"I'll arrange for a sudden termination of your experiments."

Black Feather jumped a little and smiled at her. "Not to worry, Pocahontas. I'm one contented warrior."

Raven stopped smiling and slid her hand up on his chest, fingering his arrowhead. "Tell me again about the messages. Tell me why they're important."

"You know why, don't you?"

"Sometimes I forget. Humor me."

"Sure, no problem. It was important for you to tell the reservation groups under Red Cloud and Spotted Tail to do two things. First, make sure large groups leave the reservation this spring to hunt, and second, to refuse to help the U.S. Army when they ask for scouts to help on their campaign. Right?"

"Yes, but isn't that what they were going to do anyway, even if I didn't tell them?"

"Yes, but your *vision* of the army coming to ask for scouts when you couldn't possibly know that would happen, will convince them of your power. When I meet Crazy Horse and give him my prophecy it will cement their trust in us and make it possible for them to follow the plan later." He shifted slightly and looked into her troubled eyes. "Tell me something. Are you having trouble remembering things?" he asked softly.

Raven sighed. "Yes, sometimes. Not like Charlie, but sometimes I can't recall things from the other time. I forget names, places, things get fuzzy. I feel it's slipping away."

Black Feather was silent for a long time. "It's happening to me, too," he confessed. "I think of Lincoln Long Trail and he seems like another person. I don't remember equations that were second nature to me, or classes I took, or people I knew. Maybe, after a while, there won't be any *then*, only *now*. No Linc, only *Wiyaka Sapa*."

Raven felt a chill. *If it's happening to you, we're all in trouble.* "We'll be OK. I'm sure of it, only—"

"What?" he prompted.

"Only we came here to change things, but nothing's changing. What good will it do if we convince every damn Indian in a thousand miles to follow your plan if nobody in Washington will take us seriously?"

"Have a little faith. We may just have to improvise, but I feel we have a chance, a good chance, to stop the killing and establish the Lakota Nation."

"I don't know. Maybe I'm just tired. This used to be home. Sure there were problems, but it was home. Now—now I feel like a stranger in a strange land. I'm cold. Always cold. These damn buffalo robes are heavier than sin and not nearly as warm as a simple damned down jacket. You know what I want?"

"What?"

"A hamburger. A simple, old-fashioned hamburger with onions, tomato, sauce—"

"On a sesame seed bun?"

"Oh, quit it. I'm serious. I'm tired of buffalo, buffalo, buffalo. And I want a milkshake. Strawberry, with the seeds in it. Thick and creamy. I want to wear a new dress and wash my hair in a steaming hot shower with lots of soap."

"Hey, stop it. Those things will come again, only next time it could be even better." He rose on one elbow and gazed into her eyes. "We have to have faith. I need you. Without you, I'm lost and I'll never find my way to a home."

"It's funny you mention home. Charlie and I stopped where we used to live, or where we will live in the future—or whatever. We also passed your home. I thought of Amy and ... and ... what was your mother's name?"

"Marie."

"That's right—Marie. Don't know how I could forget that. Anyway, I thought of all of you. It was about the time I began to give up on ever seeing you again. Now you're here. Now I believe again."

Black Feather shook off gloomy thoughts he couldn't express to her. "It's time to move. I have a prophecy to deliver to a man named *Tashunke Witko.*"

"God," she breathed. "I can't believe we're really going to meet Crazy Horse. I get shivers just thinking about it."

Tuesday, February 29, 1876. St. Paul, Minnesota.

George Custer was excited, eager to begin the campaign he had spent the last two weeks planning with General Terry. The coordinated winter campaign envisioned by Grant and Sherman was getting off to a slow start, but Custer relished the role he and the 7th Cavalry would play in subduing the last major group of hostiles on the Great Plains.

There were problems, of course, but Custer had supreme confidence in his ability to solve or rise above them.

His discussions with Terry started badly. Terry had been keeping the campaign secret, but Custer's comments to the press had let the cat out of the bag. Custer had been forced to swallow his pride and inform the newspapers that he knew nothing of a campaign and wouldn't have said anything even if he did.

General Terry had his own share of problems. Custer's Seventh was understrength. He wired Washington asking for three companies of cavalry to be added to Custer's force. He ended the request by observing that the 550 men available to Custer *"is not sufficient for the end in view. For if the Indians who pass the winter in the Yellowstone and Powder River country should be found in one camp they could not be attacked without great risk of defeat."*

The request was denied. Likewise, a request for more officers was denied. Only one officer, Lieutenant Matthew O'Shaunessey, was en route to Fort Abraham Lincoln.

Custer faced these setbacks with renewed energy. Since supplies and reinforcements in the field would be sent largely by steamboat on the Yellowstone River and navigable sections of the Big Horn and Rosebud Rivers, he couldn't take to the field until the ice melted and washed down the Missouri past Fort Abraham Lincoln. There was time to change minds in Washington.

George and Libbie Custer left St. Paul for Abraham Lincoln in high spirits. This campaign would make him more famous than his Washita River winter campaign that subdued the southern Cheyenne, and this time he wouldn't lose part of his command and be vilified for it. This time the Seventh would cover itself in glory.

Wednesday, March 1, 1876. Fort Fetterman, Wyoming Territory.

General George Crook moved to the side of the trail to observe his column as it advanced northwest from Fort Fetterman. A snowstorm the previous day had left drifts sparkling in the morning sunlight. Guidons snapped and crackled in the icy wind. Dry, drifting snow skittered on the frozen surface like a bright fog. Although there's always a risk, the ice on the Platte River supported even the weight of supply wagons following the plodding infantry units and mounted cavalry. Further back, the beef herd and pack train mules lowed and brayed, indignant at having to move on this freezing morning.

Crook had 662 men, and supplies for forty days. Somewhere to the north he hoped to surprise and punish hostile Indians. He would pinch any hostiles back to the east where Custer and his cavalry could trounce them, while Terry and Gibbon guarded the Yellowstone River to the far north, turning any hostiles back between the Custer and Crook forces. Of course it would be different if Custer, Terry and Gibbon were not in the field.

"Beastly cold this morning, sir!" shouted a passing officer.

Crook smiled. "The worse it gets, the better, Captain. Always hunt Indians in bad weather!" He wheeled his horse and headed to the front of the column. One thought disturbed him; he only had a handful of guides and scouts. He would have liked more eyes and ears scouting the country ahead. The more friendly Indians, half-breeds and hunter-trappers he could recruit, the more secure he felt. He didn't feel secure on this trip.

Crazy Horse's winter camp was large, containing lodges of both Oglala Lakota and Cheyenne families, and well positioned on a wide bend of the east fork of the Little Powder River. Herds of horses grazed far and wide along the banks of the river, scratching the snow for brown grass. The village lay on a white blanket of snow, highlighted by the slanting rays of the sun, already plummeting in the late afternoon. The temperature was falling as fast as the sun. Smoke curled from fires in every lodge in the village. Normally, everyone in the camp would have been in a lodge, but now they lined the entrance to the village as Black Feather, Raven and Charlie, facing the setting sun, rode between solid ranks of men, women and children bundled in blankets and heavy buffalo robes. In the eerie silence, the only sound was from the horse's hooves and the occasional yapping of camp dogs sniffing around the visitors.

Crazy Horse and two other chiefs stood apart before the large council lodge in the center of the circle. To one side were the guides who had trotted ahead to announce the coming of *Wiyaka Sapa*.

Black Feather stopped, raising his right hand in peace. Crazy Horse showed his hand in friendship. "We have heard of your coming, *Wiyaka Sapa*, and have prepared a lodge for you. Please join us."

"I thank the great *Tashunke Witko*. We have come far with important messages for your people." Three braves hurried forward to take the horses as Black Feather, Raven and Charlie dismounted. An *akacita*, his face painted with the distinctive black stripe announcing his position of importance in the village, led them to another lodge placed to the left of the council lodge. Black Feather recognized the honor they were being shown by Crazy Horse. Their lodge would be close to the council lodge where meetings would take place.

As the three guests moved toward their lodge, the people in the village retreated to the warmth of their own tipis. There was something comforting just to see the prophet, Raven Woman, and The Man-Who-Turns-Bullets, the name Charlie had earned.

Raven lagged behind, sneaking glances at Crazy Horse, the most famous Lakota warrior ever. She liked what she saw. Although he was heavily cloaked, she sensed that his tall frame was trim. His face, never photographed, was light skinned. He had a sharp nose and black eyes with light, curly hair adorned with only the single feather of a hawk. There was an aura of quiet strength and reserve about him, marking him as a leader.

Crazy Horse and the others who had stood with him retreated to the council lodge.

"Perhaps we should wait to hear what *Wiyaka Sapa* has to say before we continue," said Crazy Horse.

He-Dog, one of Crazy Horse's closest and oldest friends, demurred. "Our minds are already set. I have always stood beside you in a fight, but our lodges have old people who cannot stand before the horse soldiers. It is better that we go to Red Cloud and live on the agency."

"Our people feel the same," added Old Bear, a Cheyenne chief. "We know the soldiers are coming. I am older than you, Crazy Horse. I have counted many coups, but now it is time to give up the old ways, before we are all dead." Old Bear thought for a moment. "However, one day will not make much difference. We will stay and hear what the prophet has to say."

He-Dog nodded agreement. "We will stay also. It will be a good feast." He flashed a wide grin and, for a moment, it was like old times.

The messenger came to Black Feather's lodge the next morning as the sun approached the noon hour. "Crazy Horse will see *Wiyaka Sapa* now. All of you come."

Black Feather rose and stretched. The feasting the previous night had been awesome. He was amazed at how much meat was consumed by men and women at a large feast. It was impolite to take anything away, or to turn down food that was offered. He was still stuffed. "Tell him we are coming."

The council lodge was packed, except for a place of honor to the left of the *catku*, where Crazy Horse was seated. *Akacitapi* occupied most of one side of the lodge. The three guests filled the final space. Crazy Horse took up the sacred pipe and the ceremony began.

Crazy Horse formally welcomed the guests, then asked Raven if she wished to address the council. Black Feather noted how eagerly the men leaned forward to observe the magic they had only heard about.

It was also the first time Black Feather had seen her performance, and he found himself as entranced as the rest. Her movements were polished and she kept up a lively banter to distract the audience from what her hands were doing. Charlie sat next to Black Feather, obviously bored, his eyes focused on a spot on the ground between his legs.

Then it was Black Feather's turn. He took a deep breath, rose and paced the center of the lodge around the fire as he spoke.

"Many soldiers are coming against the Lakota and Cheyenne people this year. They are coming from the rising sun and from the forts along the Holy Road on the Platte River. This time they mean to force all of us to go to reservations and give up more of our land. I have seen a vision. Many times I have seen it, and always it is the same. I see a camp with many lodges. There is snow on the ground. It is early in the morning. Horse soldiers come to the camp and attack. The people in the camp all run into the trees. They have lost the camp and their horses run before soldiers who are stealing the herd, but"—he paused for effect—"they have not lost the battle. If they rally and turn on the horse soldiers, they will drive them away. I hear many voices shouting, Ho-ka-he! *Ho-ka-he*! I see horse soldiers dying and running from the camp and brave warriors stealing back the horses that were driven away. That is what I have seen."

There was a stunned stillness for long moments. Crazy Horse broke the silence. "When will this happen?"

"Soon, but I do not know the day." responded Black Feather.

"Is this the camp in your vision?" asked He-Dog.

"No, I do not believe this is the camp, but it is a camp near here. I believe runners should be sent to warn all camps." Black Feather sat down. It was time for debate. The discussions were long and loud. Some were for attacking the soldiers before they could get close to any camp, others doubted the vision completely. Crazy Horse took no part in the arguments. When the voices in the council lodge died down, Crazy Horse announced his decision.

"I believe *Wiyaka Sapa* has seen a strong vision. *Akacitapi* should go to *Tatanka Yotanka* and the Cheyenne camps to warn them. If there is an attack, the vision was true. If there is no attack, at least we will have been ready. I have spoken."

There was no dissent. Runners were chosen to leave the next morning, but first there was the finale they were all eager to see. Once more Charlie would stand and invoke the power of *Wiyaka Sapa* to save him from a bullet. A lane was cleared in the center of the village and everyone watched the spectacle. Charlie went through the motions, but his heart wasn't in it. He made very little of the retrieving of the spent round, dropped it into Crazy Horse's hand, then disappeared into his lodge. He didn't reappear for the feast that night or dance that followed.

The next morning teams of runners departed under threatening skies to carry the warning of *Wiyaka Sapa*. He-Dog and Old Bear delayed one more day, but nothing Black Feather had said had altered their desire to take their people to safety on the Red Cloud Reservation in Nebraska. They would travel slowly south, counter to the army moving north from Wyoming. They were surrendering. There was nothing to fear from the army.

Black Feather watched them go before retiring to his lodge. For now he had done all he could. Events of the next two weeks would establish him securely as a great prophet, or as nothing. *What will happen is known. I have now told it. There is no more, for now.* There were no more stops to make, no more shows to stage. From now on, he, Raven and Charlie would stay with Crazy Horse and the Oglala. Soon the camp would swell with families now beginning to leave the starving conditions at the Red Cloud and Spotted Tail agencies. Then the greatest coming together of northern plains tribes in a decade would culminate in a great Sun Dance. Still later, there would be an even larger village on a stream the Lakota called *Peji-sla-wakpa*.

The whites called it Little Big Horn.

Orders and Incidents

Wednesday, March 1, 1876. Washington.

General William Belknap, Secretary of War, tenders his resignation to President Grant to avoid impeachment proceedings for graft involving Indian reservation agents.

Thursday, March 2, 1876. South Cheyenne River, Wyoming Territory.

General George Crook has his first brush with hostiles. A party of Lakota steal his herd of cattle during the night. He will be forced to cut short his planned forty day mission.

First Lieutenant Matthew O'Shaunessey reports for duty to Major Marcus Reno, acting commanding officer, at Fort Abraham Lincoln, Dakota Territory. His assignment to the Quartermaster Corps is, he is assured, temporary, until Custer returns to resume command.

Sunday, March 5, 1876. Old Fort Reno, Wyoming Territory.

After shadowing Crook's column all day, a party of Lakota attack after dark, pinning down the camp but inflicting only one injury. The raiders escape unscathed.

Monday, March 7, 1876. Fargo, Dakota Territory.

A special train pulls out of Fargo bound for Bismarck. The special has three engines, two snowplows, and forty men assigned to shovel snow off the tracks. George Custer, his wife, Libbie, his dogs, and a servant occupy a private car at the rear of the train. It is 200 miles to Fort Abraham Lincoln.

Tuesday, March 8, 1876. Colonel John Gibbon to General Alfred Terry.

"… After crossing the Big Horn, my next objective will be any camps of Indians I can hear of in that vicinity.… I would like to know beforehand, if possible, General Crook's probable course.… It ought not to take long to finish up this matter satisfactorily."

TWO

Friday, March 10, 1876. On the Northern Pacific rail line, near Crystal Springs, Dakota Territory.

George Armstrong Custer possessed many qualities, but patience was not among them. He was daring, even impetuous, brave, resourceful, decisive. Now, he was inflamed. He paced the private car like a caged animal, pausing occasionally to clear a small patch of glass to peer into the never-ending white blizzard blanketing the landscape.

"Why can't they move the God-damned train?" he fumed.

Libbie was no help. "Patience, Autie. They're doing the best they can, I'm sure."

The special train had been snowbound for a week in one of the worst blizzards of the nineteenth century. There was no sign they would move soon. Trapped with them on the train were infantry troops and hopeful gold miners. A telegraph had been set up to communicate with Fargo and there was a possibility of relief, at least for the Custer party.

"Well, their best is no help at all! Alfred wants the Seventh on the march by April 5th. How the hell am I supposed to get organized when I'm sitting in the middle of this God-forsaken prairie in a snowstorm?"

He was interrupted by a knock on the door at the end of the carriage. The door opened to admit a half-frozen messenger and a blast of arctic air.

"Sir, I am instructed to inform you that your brother has arrived with sleighs to transport you to Bismarck."

"Tom? Tom's here? You hear that, Libbie? We're rescued at last! Sergeant, bring him here at once! We leave within the hour!"

It would take three days, but Custer was on the move. The train wouldn't move for another week.

Thursday, March 16, 1876. Otter Creek, Montana Territory.

General Crook was understandably upset and discouraged. For over two weeks his column had moved north and west into Montana, battling blizzards and sub-zero temperatures. The column had been spied upon by roving Indians, his beef herd stampeded, and his camp attacked, but his scouts had not located any hostile camps. Short on rations, his men grumbling, he had been forced to turn south the day before and now faced the prospect of returning to Fort Fetterman after no offensive contact.

His eyes were drawn to two horsemen racing across the snowy plain, the horses' hooves casting plumes of snow in their wake. *What's wrong now?* he thought.

"Mister Grouard!" he shouted over his shoulder.

His chief scout, Frank Grouard trotted to his side. "Looks like a couple of our scouts, General."

That's a big part of our problem, thought Crook. *We don't have enough damned scouts.* "See what's got 'em so riled." To his second in command, Colonel Joseph Reynolds, he called, "Halt the column! Tell 'em to keep their eyes open."

Grouard quizzed the Crow scouts for several minutes. "Seems they spotted two bucks leavin' the valley. They was headed east up a creek just a bit south of here. I know that country, General. They was probably headed to a camp on the Powder, 'cross the divide."

"How far to the Powder from here?"

"Mebbe eight hour ride, more or less."

Crook considered his options. Maybe his luck was changing. "Okay, Frank, have 'em check the trail. We'll halt here 'til they get back. Tell 'em two hours, no more."

Grouard issued the instructions and the scouts headed for the horse herd for fresh mounts, then raced away.

Less than two hours later the scouts returned. They confirmed that the trail showed clearly that the two Indians had come and returned on the same trail. There was almost certainly a camp across the divide.

Crook wasted no time. He dispatched half his force under Colonel Reynolds to make a night march to the Powder

River, locate the camp, and attack at dawn. He would lead the balance of the column south and meet up with Reynolds the following day. By five in the afternoon the detached units swung away to the east following the trail through scattered snow flurries in the twilight gloom. Frank Grouard led them, often on foot, as he traced the dim trail.

Friday, March 17, 1876. On the Powder River.

The snow flurries eased about midnight, but the temperature fell well below zero as the tired troops advanced through broken country. Somehow Grouard kept them on the trail, which had grown larger. Surely a large village lay below on the river, and just after sunrise they spotted it, over 100 lodges nestled on the snowy bank against a backdrop of brush and trees.

Reynolds divided his forces for the attack. One battalion would descend to the river and attack the village, charging through and firing pistols. At the same time, another battalion would run off the horses, denying the Indians their transportation. The remaining two battalions would position themselves in the trees above the river to fire from ambush once the Indians were driven from their lodges.

The surprise was total. The troopers raced through the village and fired blindly into each lodge as they passed. The lodges erupted with men, women and children scattering pell-mell into the trees, some naked, but each man carrying his weapons. The rout was total. The horse herd, stampeded up the river, was of no use to the warriors who raced into the woods. In a matter of minutes the village belonged to the army. The Indians were in perfect position for the planned ambush from above. There was only one problem. The units assigned to the ambush had not reached their position.

He-Dog and Old Bear realized as they ran that this must be the attack Black Feather had prophesied. They stopped running and began to exhort the braves to get the women and children to safety and then turn on the attackers. "We have not lost this battle!" He-Dog shouted again and again to those around him. Others took up the cry until over 200 warriors had heard the words and believed. Almost everything they owned was in the village—food, clothing and shelter. The difference between life and death in the middle of the bitter, freezing winter weather was in their sight, but in the hands of the enemy.

Captain Egan, in charge of the forces in the village, was mystified. "How come nobody's shooting at 'em from above? Jesus, if they turn around—" Even as he spoke, his command began to take increasing fire from the trees.

"Dismount! Draw carbines! Take cover and return fire!" he ordered. To one side he saw two men go down. One crawled to safety, the other lay crumpled in the snow, lifeless.

Egan grabbed a passing corporal. "Corporal! Find the colonel. Tell him we are being attacked. We need help! Go!"

"Yes, sir!" The man flew from the village, thankful to be out of range of the enraged Indians.

The battalion assigned to command the bluffs had still not reached their assigned position. Now they were withdrawn and sent into the center of the camp. Colonel Reynolds sent them with orders to burn the village. Grouard tried to argue with him, saying, "Colonel, we could use the blankets and especially the meat!"

Reynolds would have none of it. He meant to punish the savages. Nothing would punish them more than to lose everything they owned.

Over the next hour, more reinforcements poured into the village, but it soon became apparent it was the U. S. Army that was under siege. Carrying four dead and six wounded, the army managed to retreat in the early afternoon, leaving smoking ruins where a peaceful village had been that morning. There were bloody trails in the snow indicating some Indian casualties, but there were no dead Indians lying in the village to show success for the troops.

By nightfall, the strike force hooked up with the main column. Officers and men were exhausted, hungry, freezing and argumentative. The attack had been badly bungled and all they had to show for their efforts were 700 captured horses.

He-Dog and Old Bear joined with the rest of the villagers to sift through the smoking ruins of their lives, salvaging scraps of clothing and hides to cloak themselves against the coming night. One small band of young men rounded up some of the horses the army missed and set off in pursuit of the retreating army units. Revenge kept them warm through the long afternoon chase.

Saturday, March 18, 1876.

Crook's early euphoria evaporated the previous evening. There were no satisfactory answers to his questions. "How large was the village?"

"Over 100 lodges."

"Whose village was it?"

"It may have been Crazy Horse's, but maybe not."

"How many Indians were killed?"

Shrugs, all around. "Maybe none."

The chief scout offered the only possibly helpful information. "We found a wounded squaw in one of the lodges. She said Crazy Horse wasn't there. His camp's somewhere north 'n she said Sitting Bull's up that way, too."

Crook didn't bother to ask what happened to the wounded squaw, the only tangible hostile casualty. He went to bed unhappy. The meat could have kept them in the field for another chance, but it was charred trash now. Of course, there were 700 horses. They could feed the troops for a long time.

"General Crook, sir?" The messenger didn't quite whisper, but he really didn't want to be the one to wake the general and his voice showed his discomfort.

"Yes. What time is it?"

"About four a.m., sir."

"What's so important?"

"Um, sir, I've just been told that the Indians stole their horses back, sir."

When there was no response, the messenger slipped out of the tent and made himself scarce.

Monday, March 20, 1876. Fort Abraham Lincoln.

Custer's arrival the previous week brought new life to the fort. Now that the general had returned, planning could go forward for the long-awaited campaign against the Sioux. Matt caught only glimpses of Custer, coming and going from extended meetings with Major Reno and Captain Benteen in the headquarters building. Finally, Custer had time to greet his newest officer.

Matt entered the office and saluted smartly. Custer idly returned the salute. "At ease, Lieutenant." He continued to study Matt's service record for a moment. "Nice to meet you,

Lieutenant. I heard some interesting things about you when I was in New York. You caused quite a stir in Washington."

"Yes, sir. I guess I did." Custer looked like every picture Matt had ever seen. He was lean, his famous golden curls clipped somewhat shorter than most pictures, his face seamed, but still boyish for a man thirty-seven years old. His movements were quick and precise, his voice strong.

"I see Reno has attached you to the pack train unit for now. That command may change when we take to the trail. You ever fought Indians?"

"No, sir."

"Hmm. Well, I need officers and it isn't likely we'll see much actual fighting anyway. Do what you can for now to shape up the packers. We won't be taking wagons this time, so the pack train will be our supply depot. We'll get together later. I want you to meet my wife. We'd both like to hear more about your experiences."

Almost two months would pass before Custer could have his next meeting with Matt. The next day Custer took the stage from Bismarck headed for Washington. He was under subpoena to testify before another congressional hearing investigating the Grant administration. With the best Indian fighter in the west missing, General Terry was forced to again postpone the abortive winter campaign.

Thursday, March 23, 1876.

Like destitute cousins, He-Dog and Old Bear led their people into Crazy Horse's camp. Lightly clothed, they were suffering from frostbite, or worse. Some were injured, some had died and been left on the trail.

There were no travois behind the horses, no lodges, no food, no cooking implements. Crazy Horse knew what had happened before they spoke. All around, his people moved forward to help. The mass of refugees melted into warm lodges. Fires were stoked, food prepared. Those who had, shared with those who had not. The lodges would be packed until new poles could be cut and new hides sewn for covers.

An hour later, He-Dog and Old Bear met with Crazy Horse, Black Feather, and other leaders.

Old Bear nodded to Black Feather. "It was just like your vision. We were careless. The horse soldiers surprised us and took our camp, even stole our horses."

"They gave us no warning!" said He-Dog. "We never had a chance to tell them we were surrendering! They treated us like dogs!"

Grim and determined, the two leaders faced Crazy Horse and made a new vow. "There will be no surrender. Our people are united with you. We will rest here and then go to the camp of Sitting Bull. When the soldiers come again, they will be the ones to suffer!"

For Black Feather, it was the defining moment of his quest. Any lingering doubts about his abilities had been answered. It was a powerful feeling, but he had no time to enjoy it.

Raven burst into the tipi. "Come quick! Charlie's in trouble!"

Black Feather jumped to his feet and raced after her.

Charlie had been uncommunicative since his last performance. Raven and Black Feather had seen little of him. They heard he was gambling occasionally, but nothing else. Now he strutted at the edge of the camp, his face flushed. He was barefoot in the snow and without a robe to keep him warm. When he spoke, his words were slurred. "Got it all. They got it all, the sneaking, cheating bastards!"

Thank God he's speaking English, thought Black Feather. *At least nobody'll understand him, I hope.* "Charlie, what're you talking about?"

Charlie tried to focus his bleary eyes. "That you, Black Feather? You still whoring with my sister? We was better off without you. You messed everything up. Why don't you go back to—to wherever you come from? Don't need you. Never needed you."

"Charlie, stop it!" snapped Raven. "You're making a fool of yourself. You're sick. Come lie down."

Charlie stopped walking and faced her. There were tears in his eyes. "I—I'm sorry. I wasn't there for you. I couldn't help you. My fault. My fault."

"No, nothing was your fault. You've always been there for me, Charlie. Come on, let's go inside. Please."

He seemed ready to collapse. She started to move toward him to help him, but he suddenly straightened and pointed his finger at a man standing not far from him. "It's his fault! He cheated me out of everything!" He staggered toward the man. "You're a cheat! You hear me? Got even though. Seen your wife recently? Ask her 'bout me. Bet she liked every minute."

The man he was taunting may, or may not, have understood the words, but it was clear he understood the menace and the meaning. His knife was a blur. The first slice ripped Charlie from side to side just below the rib cage. The return swing dug deeper, an inch below the first cut. Blood gushed from both slashes.

Charlie raised his arms and began to chant the familiar words he always used in his act invoking the power of *Wiyaka Sapa* to protect him. He apparently felt no pain. He appeared to be in a state of ecstasy.

The man with the knife backed away, his face a mixture of fear and awe. His eyes told him the man standing before him should be dead, but he still stood and called on *Wiyaka Sapa*. This was a power the man couldn't comprehend. He turned and fled.

It was all so fast. Raven clamped a hand over her mouth to stifle the scream in her throat. Black Feather started to react, but realized it was useless. Part of him was horrified. Part was relieved.

The pain finally penetrated Charlie's alcoholic fog. His hands reached for where the pain was, his eyes following. He tottered, almost fell. When he looked up, his eyes were clear. "He cut me, sis. He cut me bad. Stupid shirt didn't work." He sagged to his knees. "Help me, sis. I'm cold. Never been so cold as this year. Put some wood on the fire, okay? Gonna sleep now."

Raven dimly watched Charlie fall on his face in the snow through blinding tears. She forced her feet to move and knelt beside him, tentatively reaching out to smooth his hair. "It's all right," she sobbed. "You did the best you could. You've always done the best you could." When she looked up across his body, her eyes locked with Black Feather. "He's gone, Linc. Charlie's gone. What are we going to do? We've made a mistake. We can't change a thing. And, if we can't change it, what happens to us? Are we really here?"

The next morning, Black Feather led the horse and travois bearing Charlie's body wrapped in a buffalo robe. Raven rode beside her man, her head high, her eyes dry. Black Feather noted the eyes of the few people they passed as they left the camp. *They have questions. Now they have doubts about my power. Damn! I've got to do something to restore their faith.* Late that afternoon they found the place they were looking for. High on the divide above the Powder River was a rocky promontory with a grove of pines to shield the worst of the north winds of winter. They made camp and Black Feather cut and lashed a number of the smaller pines to make the final resting place for The Man Who Turns Bullets. In the dark of the early evening they gently raised Charlie's frozen body to the scaffold. Raven hung a shield and a single eagle feather from a crosspiece to alert any who passed this way that a warrior lay here.

Black Feather walked to the edge of the rocky bluff and methodically cut Charlie's bulletproof shirt into hundreds of tiny pieces. He tossed the scraps into the air to be borne away on the wind.

"Why'd you do that?" Raven asked from behind him.

"I don't know. Just, well, it was ruined anyway." He turned and looked at her. "I warned him about knives and arrows. I guess he forgot that part, too. We'll go back tomorrow. I have to make them believe again."

Saturday, March 25, Fort Abraham Lincoln.

The Valentine's Dance had been postponed twice. Now Custer was gone again, but the dance would go on without him.

Matt was lucky. With the shortage of officers, he had a room to himself on the bottom floor of the barracks. He took his time and dressed with care. There was at least one attractive, unattached young woman on the post, but many bachelor officers.

Lights from the headquarters building shined through the windows like welcome beacons, casting bright yellow oblongs on the snowy ground. The band was playing a merry song when Matt stepped into the hall. Major Reno and Libbie Custer headed the reception line along with other senior officers and their wives. Mrs. Custer favored Matt with a particularly dazzling smile. He'd heard of her charms and immediately saw how she could captivate men and possibly make other women feel ill-at-ease.

"Lieutenant, how nice to see you. Autie told me so much about you. We must have some time together this evening."

Matt smiled and bowed slightly. "At your service, Mrs. Custer." She was well known for taking junior officers under her wing. Obviously, Matt was her special task this evening.

He got some punch and circulated with the other juniors making small talk while he appraised the crowd. Another part of his mind thought of the women in the room who would be widows before the Fourth of July. There was Libbie Custer, of course, but also Mrs. Yates, Mrs. Calhoun, and Mrs. McIntosh. Their bright ball gowns and flashing smiles would be exchanged for widow's weeds and tears. It wasn't a happy thought.

"Ah, there you are, Lieutenant." Libbie floated up next to him with her radiant smile lighting the way. "Since you're new here, I suppose you might be a little lonely."

"Actually, ma'am, I've been too busy to notice."

She laughed, then asked him all about his miraculous survival. She was knowledgeable and truly interested in putting him at ease. The talk drifted to the hearings in Washington, politics in general, and life in New York. Matt found her an intelligent and witty companion. Finally, she took his arm and steered him across the floor. "I've been monopolizing you, I'm afraid." They approached a knot of officers and a lone young woman. Libbie sailed in smoothly.

"Gentlemen, I think you need some competition." This got a polite chuckle from the men. "Agnes, dear, I want to present Lieutenant Matthew O'Shaunessey. Lieutenant, Miss Agnes Wellington, the most eligible lady at Abraham Lincoln."

Matt smiled and bowed to the obviously embarrassed young woman. *She's young enough to be my daughter*, he thought.

Pleased with her efforts on behalf of Matt, Libbie graciously bowed out. "I'll leave the field of battle now, gentlemen. Good night."

Matt soon made polite apologies and retired to his quarters. His party spirit was pricked by too many thoughts of dead men and their families. He fell into a restless sleep, haunted by little girls, widows and one particularly beautiful woman, but a woman he could never have. As she floated away, he called after her.

THREE

April, 1876. Montana Territory.

Black Feather returned to Crazy Horse's camp with new resolve. In addition to his role as messiah and prophet, he now added teacher.

"I have to believe in the mission," he told Raven. "We will be successful. There will be a Lakota Nation! A nation needs leaders, leaders need education. I told a man in Washington that the treaty would be different this time—it would be in both languages. That leaves a problem. These people don't know how to read or write their own language."

Raven tried hard to stifle a laugh. "Oh, so now you're going to teach reading and writing?"

"Hey, I've been a student all my life. I should know something about teaching by now. Besides, there's so much these people have to learn if they're going to run a government. We'll get help, of course, from Washington when the treaty is signed, but if we can't help ourselves, it won't be much different from the reservation system. There's time. Surely I can teach them something!"

Black Feather's efforts initially seemed to be going well. He taught language and government and Raven led classes for the women in basic hygiene, diet and care of infants. Often there were as many as fifty men crouched around Black Feather when he spoke.

By the third week of April, a change came across the prairie. Days were longer, warmer. Spring arrived in tiny, tenuous steps, as if the land was not sure the icy blasts of winter would end. As the sun stayed longer in the sky, tinges of green appeared in the open meadows. Soon new grass sprouted thickly and was greedily attacked by horses grown weak from poor fodder. Leaves followed. Flowers followed leaves, splashing color amidst deep white blankets of snow in the hollows and on the northern slopes. Insects and birds added motion and song to air that grew softer every day.

With better weather, the camp swelled with new arrivals. The "summer roamers" were leaving the reservations

A Good Place To Die 233

in unusually large numbers this year. The lure of possible war with the horse soldiers, buffalo hunts, and renewed acquaintances with old friends made it easy to leave the miserable conditions at the Red Cloud and Spotted Tail agencies.

Instead of growing larger with the influx, the crowds at Black Feather's school dwindled. Every time the camp moved, more men went hunting, raiding or just riding, for the pleasure it afforded. Besides, they were getting bored with Black Feather's visions of a Lakota Nation and the leaders they would have to become. Only a handful of hard-core holdouts continued to attend the classes on any kind of regular basis. One, named *Kahektabya*, Bringing-up-the-Rear, was destined to never be a warrior or hunter, but he showed a strong aptitude for reasoning, writing and reading. He was nineteen this summer, tall and slender. Whenever he could, he pestered Black Feather with questions, always seeking more knowledge. Whenever Black Feather got discouraged, Bringing-up-the-Rear gave him reason to smile.

Washington.

George Custer chafed at the slow pace of the Clymer Hearings. The Democrats in Congress were in full voice, hot on the heels of scoundrels and scalawags in the Republican administration. Men like Custer, who had observed and reported numerous instances of misappropriations of funds and supplies in the reservation system, paraded to the witness chair and gave damning testimony, but it seemed it would never end. Some Republican newspapers were accusing Custer of initiating the whole scandal to further his own political ambition!

"Preposterous," snarled Custer to any who would listen.

The final straw was a call for his court martial by ex-Secretary of War Belknap on the grounds that he had given false testimony. This amused Custer.

"I've only said what many others have confirmed. I stand by my testimony," he told reporters. He was becoming the darling of the Democratic press. His New York publishers loved it.

He wrote long, passionate letters to Libbie. He lobbied General Terry to get him relieved and returned to his rightful place in the west. He knew that with the coming of summer, the large winter camps of Sioux and Cheyenne would break up into smaller units for the summer season. The task of catching and defeating them would be magnified—might even have to wait another year.

He was also alarmed at a growing movement among eastern interests to pressure President Grant to restore his peace policy with the Indians. Led by a coalition of clergymen, editorials in all the newspapers decried the Crook expedition and urged an end to all army action. One particularly powerful prelate even hinted that he knew of a peace plan he believed could work. Unless action could be taken soon, Custer believed Grant might cave in to public pressure if, for no other reason, than to save his job.

Fort Abraham Lincoln.

Matt's assignment to the pack train company had one pleasant aspect. The sergeant in charge of the mules was Asar Cromwell, commonly known as "Ace," and uncommonly versed with gossip and horse-sense. He treated the mules with a respect he didn't always share for his human associates.

Matt leaned on the corral and watched Ace supervise two recruits as they labored over repairs to saddles and bridles. Ace punctuated his orders with a fluent, ever-changing string of profanity that made Matt smile. Between times, Ace educated his new "Lootenit."

"Like I was sayin', Lootenit, it's actually Colonel Sturgis who's in charge, but he don't get to the fort often. He's usually off recruitin' God-rottin' recruits, such as them." If the recruits took offense, they were smart enough to hide it. "So, with Sturgis gone most times, the general's the boss. He likes t' be called general, y' know. Smart man never calls 'im colonel.

"Now the general, he's gone a bit too. Was gone all winter to New York. Back there makin' a name fer hisself. He's big on that. Course he come back jest to git off t' Washington. Hope he fries some o' them folks what steal more'n they ever send us." Ace paused to spit a wad from the chaw packed in his cheek. "Damn, dirty little spider jest went to tobaccer heaven. Probably pissed 'im off proper.

"So, what was I, oh, yeah, Custer's in Washington, Sturgis is God knows where, so that gits us down to th' major. Now, the way I figger is the major he don't like the general much. No way in hell they'd ever git t' be pals. Same with Benteen. Reno 'n Benteen both got powerful bad feelins toward the general. The major, he, well now don't say nothin', but he hits the bottle pretty hard. Bin known t' say some things that, well, it ain't no place for a lootenit to stick his nose in, if'n y' know what I'm gittin at."

Matt nodded. "Got it. Don't take sides."

Ace nodded approvingly. "You're right smart—fer an officer."

"So I gather you think the general is pretty good?"

"Didn't say that. Nope, didn't say that exactly. See, the general, he's got his good 'n his bad. Like he's a good man in a fight. Stands up tall, speaks his mind, gits things done. Don't think the man sleeps sometimes. He's like a seven day clock—wind him up once, he'll go all week. Ain't natural somehow. Lotsa men call 'im Iron Ass cause he can sit a saddle all day 'n most 'o the night. Cover mebbe sixty miles a day.

"Tell y' th' truth, Lootenit. The general's like Bingo, my lead mule. Contrary. They's times when the general's nice as can be, then there's times when he's meaner 'n a pissed off rattler. He can be real happy, excited like 'n next thing y' know he's quiet, sad like. I seen him when he's real generous, 'n other times he wouldn't give y' water if y' was dyin' in the desert. He drives men hard—animals too. Don't rightly like that part. Then they's times when he's real lazy 'bout things. One thing fer sure though. He gives y' an order, y' better hop to right fast 'n get it done. I've seen him whip a man fer not followin' orders. They say he shot some deserters once. Don't rightly know 'bout that though. Yep, he's contrary."

"Well, I guess he has some good qualities. His wife seems to be a real lady."

Ace nodded enthusiastically. "That she is. That she is. Salt o' the earth, that woman. Tell y' somethin'else, too. Don't ever say nothin' bad 'bout the general she might hear. She'll have yer guts fer garters 'n smile while they's doin' the guttin'."

Matt had to laugh. Libbie Custer was many things—thoughtful, caring, giving and, yes, tough—but not bloodthirsty.

Ace had thoughts on all the officers and most of the non-coms and he kept Matt pleasantly entertained when they had time to talk. His final pronouncement on Custer was, "If'n they's goin' t' be a fight, I'll take my chances with th' general. You can have th' others."

"Right stupid idea, if'n y' ask me, Lootenit."

"We weren't asked, Sergeant. We were ordered."

Ace shook his head, spat a wad, then wandered off to start saddling mules.

Matt faced the twenty recruits Colonel Sturgis had sent to the post. They looked ill-at-ease in their new uniforms. Most were farm boys not long off the ship from several European countries.

"Can any of you men ride a horse well?" Matt asked hopefully.

Two hands were tentatively raised while a half dozen others crowded around someone who could translate the question for them.

Matt sighed. It was going to be a long day. Major Reno had an idea that the new recruits could be taught to ride mules, since horses were in short supply. Every man would be needed when the long-delayed winter campaign got underway.

By early afternoon it was apparent that green recruits riding uncooperative mules wasn't the answer. The corral resembled a three-ring circus with recruits running after bucking mules, or sailing through the air with the greatest of unease as the mules won every contest between man and animal.

Ace swore, cajoled, ranted, then swore some more. Nothing worked. He didn't see the humor when Matt broke out laughing at one point. "Ain't funny, Lootenit! Somebody's gonna git kilt if'n we keep this up!"

Matt agreed. Reno reluctantly called a halt to the experiment.

Saturday, April 29, 1876. Washington.

"Simmer down, George."

"Simmer down? Dammit! Am I supposed to take the loss of my command with good grace and humility?"

General Sherman swiveled his head to follow Custer's pacing form. "The President's under a lot of pressure, George.

These hearings are rocking his administration to the core, and your testimony has been especially damaging."

"But he's acting like I started the whole thing. All I'm doing is telling the truth. I'm under oath, remember."

"Look, give me a day or so to calm him down. I'll excuse you from the rest of the hearings. You can see him Monday and then return to your post."

"You think so? You think he'll change his mind?"

"I'll bet on it. Look, we need you out there, George. Crook didn't exactly cover himself with glory this winter. In fact, the whole winter campaign sort of fizzled, but now he's back and ready to push north. Gibbon's poised on the Yellowstone at the Big Horn River. All we need is to get the Seventh in the field to box in the hostiles, and you're the best Indian fighter we have. I'm sure he'll listen to reason."

Custer remained unconvinced, but really had no choice. "You know the winter camps will be breaking up as soon as the weather warms a bit. If we don't hit 'em soon, they'll be scattered all over creation and we'll have to wait another year."

"There's even more reason to hit soon," replied Sherman. "I'm sure you realize there's growing pressure from misguided clerics all over the east to make peace with the heathen. Grant could change his mind for political reasons and cancel the whole damned operation. No, we've got to get in the field and I need you at the head of the Seventh. See the President on Monday, then get back to your post and get the Seventh ready to move out."

Custer departed, still unsure, to spend a restless Sunday in a town he was coming to despise.

Monday, May 1, 1876.

It was the longest, most boring, and most frustrating day Custer could ever remember. He had presented his card promptly at ten o'clock and had spent the rest of the day in the waiting room presenting a stoic countenance to the steady flow of visitors entering and leaving the President's private office. Editorials in the morning papers mocked Grant with calls to end the hostilities in the west. Even some congressmen were asking pointed questions about the administration policy.

Damn do-gooders stirring the pot, thought Custer. *They ought to spend a few days in Dakota Territory to give them some perspective!*

By five o'clock, the almost constant parade of visitors had disappeared. It was evident that Grant was intentionally snubbing Custer, who still didn't have permission to leave Washington. He penned a quick note to the President and hustled back to the War Department to get permission from General Sherman.

"I'm sorry, sir," explained Sherman's aide, "but the general has gone to New York. Can someone else help you?"

Custer felt a new fear. *Did Grant turn Sherman? Is he against me, too?* To the aide, he gave a curt, "No," then stormed out of the office to find the highest ranking officer he could to get his release. He managed to catch the seven o'clock train to Chicago, turning his back on the city with relish.

General Sherman returned the following morning to find Custer gone. Under pressure from the President, he wired General Sheridan in Chicago with orders to detain Custer when he arrived and to order the Seventh Cavalry to leave Fort Abraham Lincoln without him. The President was adamant. Custer was not to be allowed to participate in this campaign.

Sunday, May 14, 1876. Fort Abraham Lincoln.

"Lieutenant! Jump in here and have your picture taken."

Matt waved off the invitation and continued to stand in front of the headquarters building with other onlookers, but Libbie Custer was not to be put off.

"Don't be modest, Lieutenant. Look, there's room right next to Miss Wellington. Come on."

There was no way to politely refuse, so he stepped forward and joined the officers and wives of the Seventh Cavalry for pictures.

Two weeks of speculation had ended the day before when General Terry and a subdued Lieutenant Colonel Custer arrived at the post. President Grant had ordered Custer detained in Chicago, even threatened to court martial him on trumped-up charges. A series of appeals by Sherman and Terry to the President, followed by abject apologies from Custer himself, finally led to Custer being allowed to return to

Abraham Lincoln. He would be allowed to lead the Seventh into battle, but General Terry would be in charge.

But today Custer was in charge as he moved his officers around for a series of photographs, then excused the ladies for several shots with just his core of company officers. "There'll be no photographer to record our deeds in the field, so we must have a good record. Tomorrow we leave to take the fight to the savages."

No, not tomorrow, thought Matt. *It's going to rain tomorrow and the next day. We won't leave until Wednesday.*

Matt and the other officers sensed an underlying urgency to take to the field. The expedition had been delayed so many times that there was a real chance the winter villages might break up before they were located. After the photo session, Custer met briefly with his officers and added another reason for haste.

"The eastern papers are baying like hounds at the chase. Grant's in real trouble and they're calling for an end to the Indian wars. He may have to oblige 'em." Custer smacked a fist into his open palm. "That won't happen if we get after the hostiles in a hurry, but there's not a day to lose. Crook's ready to move up from Wyoming, and Gibbon's got his men on the Yellowstone to cut 'em off if they move north. All that's left is for us to get out there and seal any escape to the east."

Matt was interested to observe the other officers and their reactions. The command had been sharply divided when they learned Custer had been detained. His supporters, led by his brother Tom and Libbie Custer, had denounced the President with stinging barbs. Major Reno and Captain Benteen led the opposition, supporting Grant while denouncing, albeit softly, their commander. Matt had begged neutrality in the fracas since he was new to the command and not in a position to criticize either party. Custer's return had silenced his critics, but there was still an underlying tension in the command.

Tuesday, May 16, 1876. Fort Robinson, Nebraska.

General George Crook rode west from Fort Robinson in a foul mood. Two days of meetings with Red Cloud had failed to produce even one scout for his command. He had been bluntly informed that no Oglala would help hunt their kinsmen.

Unknown to the general, his party was shadowed by a disgruntled band of young warriors who were looking to assassinate him. Discouraged by the strength of his detachment, the warriors settled for killing an eastbound stage driver before returning to the agency. Red Cloud was not pleased with the killing. Raven had said nothing about killing the general, but the rest of her prophecy had come true.

Wednesday, May 17, 1876.

Final preparations to leave Fort Abraham Lincoln commenced long before dawn on Wednesday morning. By the time the morning fog burned away, the Seventh Cavalry, with its attendant pack train and supply wagons, was ready to roll. Wives, children, and garrison personnel lined the route as the regimental band struck up *The Girl I Left Behind Me* and the famous marching song of the Seventh, *Garry Owen*. Relegated to the end of the procession, Matt waited with a growing sense of anticipation as cavalry units, followed by marching infantry units, trailed to the west. The hair stood up on the back of his neck and he felt a sense of pride in belonging to the Seventh. *I'm embarking on one of the most memorable campaigns in United States history and I'm the only person here who knows how it will end. Well, at least I think I know how it's going to end. The best part is that I get to be there, but I'll be completely safe with the pack train.*

Finally, the pack train moved out. Most of the spectators had retired, but there were still knots of little boys and an occasional woman to cheer them on. Matt tipped his hat to each group and squared himself in the saddle. The sun was out; life was grand.

So, what's going to happen? he wondered. *I haven't heard a whisper about Lincoln Long Trail since he dropped out of sight in Washington. Maybe his cousins never made it and, if they did, what the hell can they do to change anything? If that's the case, I know exactly what will occur. Nothing to do now but take it as it comes. We've got weeks of marching and searching before anything's going to happen.*

Far ahead of the lumbering supply wagons and fractious mules in the pack train, there was a picnic atmosphere to the expedition. Custer was joined by his wife and sister, his younger brother, and a nephew. His other brother, Tom, commanded one of the cavalry companies. It was a family affair.

The next morning the sky threatened rain again as Matt supervised loading the mules. A carriage, carrying Libbie Custer and Margaret Calhoun, passed, heading back to the fort. Libbie gave Matt a jaunty wave. "Good luck, Lieutenant. Watch out for my Autie and come back safely!"

"Yes, ma'am. I'll do that," he answered, forcing a smile which faded from his face as the wagon retreated. He didn't enjoy deceiving a woman who had showered him with kindness ever since his arrival at the fort. *Unfortunately, my job is to preserve history, not alter it to my personal desires.*

FOUR

Thursday, May 25, 2022. Weston, Maryland.

"All right class, you may have the last fifteen minutes of time today to study for the history final tomorrow."

Randy Caldwell almost groaned aloud. Miss Larson, he had decided, was a history *nut*. She really liked the stuff. Randy liked football, especially Redskin's football, but history was only good if you were there. *Why study this stuff, anyway?* he thought as he lazily flipped through his book, moving from section to section: "Revolution", "Civil War", "Opening of the West". The pictures blurred together, familiar names and faces slid under his fingers.

He flipped the page before he realized that something unusual had caught his attention. He flipped back one page and looked again at the grainy picture titled, *"Custer and His Officers Prepare For Action With the Sioux."* No, there was no mistake. "Holy Cow! Wait'll mom sees this! Wow!"

"Mr. Caldwell! Please study quietly!"

"Yes, Miss Larson, but—"

"No buts, just read silently."

Monday, May 29, 1876. Little Missouri River, Dakota Territory.

Matt swore anew as another mule threw its pack in the river, and then jerked free from the clinging quicksand and trotted easily up the far bank.

"Sergeant! Retrieve that pack and reload that God-damned jackass and this time find someone who knows how to tie a God-damned diamond hitch!"

It had been a brutal day. By Matt's count, the trail had crossed and recrossed the river over thirty times. Each crossing was an adventure, with the deceptively swift current, snags and quicksand. Still, he felt a keen joy in being here. The cottonwoods were thick along the shore with deep green hills rising above the river, or steep bluffs where the river had eroded to expose the subsurface of this magnificent land. Game was plentiful and the officers dined on fresh antelope, deer and buffalo almost every night.

Admit it. You're having fun, he thought. He smiled when he thought of his few friends from the future. *I'm probably the only one who's crazy enough to go out with George Armstrong Custer, knowing what I know, and still say I'm having fun.* In fact, there were very few people from that other time that he could even remember clearly. Kimberly and Randy were still vivid images, but most of his acquaintances had faded like an old photograph. He'd even forgotten to communicate with Uncle Demetrius since he left Washington.

Despite the long days and grinding pace of the pack train, the entire expedition had a flavor of church picnic. Custer had bounced back to his occasionally insufferable self once the fort was out of sight. Although General Terry was in charge of the column, Custer treated him like a guest of Custer's Seventh. Matt actually saw little of the main column and command officers. As soon as the march commenced until the end of the day, the pack train lagged far behind the main body of troops. Except for a rear guard, it was almost an independent command.

Matt watched the last of the mules make the crossing, then surged to the head of the column. In the distance he could see white tents blossoming on a broad shelf alongside the river. "An hour to camp, boys," he sang out. "Keep 'em movin' along!"

The same day, General George Crook finally marched his column north from Fort Fetterman, Wyoming Territory. The strong force had one serious drawback—they had very few Indian scouts. Moving blindly north, they were vulnerable to a surprise attack.

Sunday, May 29, 2022.

Kimberly Caldwell sat at her kitchen table and studied the incredible photograph for the umpteenth time. Until three days ago her life had been well ordered and under control. She had reconciled herself to the fact that Jamie was gone. Whatever mission he had undertaken had removed him from her life forever. She had long since given up trying to probe the mystery of his disappearance, which she'd found shrouded in utter blackness.

Her first reaction to the picture was complete disbelief. *Of course not ...There's no way ... Impossible ... Utterly ridiculous!* But something stirred deep inside her. Something told her it was true, however impossible it seemed. *My God! It is him! It has to be. The same crooked smile. The uniform—almost identical to the one he wore last summer when he proposed to me. His eyes—how could I forget those eyes.*

Time travel! That's it! Somehow it's been perfected! I knew we were working on it! We must have beaten the Japanese. Jamie used time to escape. I hurt him so badly he must have volunteered to be a time traveler. He loved the old west, the military—especially the cavalry!

Kimberly's disbelief had turned to acceptance within hours of seeing the photo. Acceptance was followed by anger. *How could I have been so stupid? I drove him away. I hurt him and now I can't ever say I'm sorry.* What made it even worse was the thought that she had driven him to virtual suicide. *Why there? Why Custer? Everybody knows what happened to him. Why, Jamie?* The picture couldn't answer her questions.

Last night had been the worst. The dream returned and now she knew what it was. The milling men and horses were surrounded not by Rebel soldiers, but by screaming Indians. Now she knew why there were arrows in the dream—thousands of arrows raining from a yellow sky above a grassy knoll. *The Little Big Horn. Because of me, Jamie's going to the Little Big Horn to die. He wouldn't do it if he knew. God, don't let this happen. Please, dear God, stop this nightmare.*

Now a new thought pushed through her confusion. *They lied to me! They all lied to me when they made me think Jamie had done something terribly wrong, then continued the lies. Why? Something else must be going on. What is it I don't know? What're they hiding from me, from everybody? Is there another reason you're there, Jamie? I'll bet there is and the sons-of-bitches that put you there haven't buried their secrets so deep that I can't dig them up.*

Kimberly angrily ripped the page from the history book. It was a place to start and she was getting angrier by the minute.

June 7, 1876. Rosebud River, Montana Territory.

Black Feather felt detached from his body. He could step away and watch himself, one of the few warriors left circling the giant Sun Dance pole. Blood from thin cuts on his chest and back had clotted in criss-cross patterns, his breechcloth and legs speckled with rust-colored, dry blood, his moccasins muddy and bloodstained.

He let his mind float free to soar above the packed earth surrounding the pole. As he soared higher, he could see the drummers and singers surrounding the dance ground, then the lodges—over four hundred—dotting the plain by the river. Higher and higher he went, until he could see the herds of horses grazing on the broad prairie, the river winding south to north across lands—unspoiled, unconquered—teeming with vast herds of bison and antelope. Finally, from a great height, he spied the columns, specks of blue, crawling across the plain. To the east, the south, and the north, they inched over a great green canvas, disturbing the tranquility, coming for the thousands of Lakota and Cheyenne celebrating the renewal of life, the spiritual rebirth that was the great Sun Dance. In his ecstasy, Black Feather groaned aloud, then slumped to the ground, complete in his exhaustion.

The voice came from a place far away. "Black Feather, can you hear me?"

"Yes. I know you. I love you."

Raven smiled, then persisted. "If you love me, you'll wake up. The time has come. Sitting Bull's asked for all the council. He wants you and the *akacitapi* there. Wake up, Black Feather."

A light kiss on his lips caused him to stir. "More," he muttered.

"Later, I promise. You have a message to deliver."

The fog cleared slowly. With consciousness came pain. The pain woke him further. "What's happened? How long have I been out?"

"Nothing's happened and you've only been asleep a few hours, but now it's time to share your vision."

Muttering curses, Black Feather reeled to his feet and staggered out of their lodge into blasts from a rogue north wind still lashing the camp. The week had started with two days of snow, followed by three days of rain. The weather had slowed the advance of their enemies, but had not hindered the great celebration of the Sun Dance, feasting, and related ceremonies of the gathered Lakotas.

Under a black sky pierced by thousands of dancing pinpoints of cold light, a great fire burned in the distance. The legendary leaders of the Lakota were assembled with their families and another thousand men and women whose names have been lost in history.

Black Feather was keenly aware of the cold air on his raw skin, but he held his head high and blocked out his discomfort. Raven walked beside him and Bringing-up-the-Rear materialized from the darkness and joined them as they threaded their way through the gathering, finally sitting close enough to the roaring fire to feel the heat.

For long minutes they sat comfortably among their friends. Light banter and joking subsided when *Tatanka Yotanka* stood and raised his hand for quiet. He appeared massive in the dancing light, his arms a series of black stripes where he had slashed himself over a hundred times during the Sun Dance. When he spoke, there was dead silence.

"My people! Hear me! I have had a vision of the future. We know that the blue coats are coming against us. They want to change forever the way we live—to force us to live like disobedient children on their reservations. They want *Paha Sapa*. They want our best hunting grounds. Even now they come from the place they call Fort Fetterman. We have seen them in the distance. They come to fight—they come to die.

"In my vision I saw many soldiers lying on the ground. They were all dead with arrows, many arrows, driven deep in their bodies. Their horses lay like fallen fruit with their legs in the air. I have seen that we will have a great victory! We will drive them from our land forever!"

His speech was greeted by the trilling of a thousand tongues. Raven felt herself caught up in the fervor, but Black Feather sat calmly, his face a blank mask. Behind his apparent composure, his mind was in turmoil. *If I fail tonight, we will fail completely. Tukanhila, give me strength. Do not let me fail our people.*

His breathing came faster as he forced himself to his feet and stepped into the center of the gathering where Sitting Bull had stood. He raised his hand for quiet and began to speak.

"I, *Wiyaka Sapa*, have also had a vision, much like *Tatanka Yotanka*." He risked a sidelong glance at the great Hunkpapa medicine man. If Sitting Bull had any emotions, they were hidden behind veiled eyes.

"In my vision," Black Feather continued, "I saw not one, but two battles. In the first, we were victorious and it was as he described, but not so many soldiers. The second battle was even more powerful." He paused and gathered himself. "In this great battle, Lakota, Cheyenne and Arapaho fought side by side. More warriors than I could count swarmed from a river to the tops of the hills. Many soldiers in blue coats rode in confusion. They fired their rifles to the sky, but we were not hurt. When the battle was over, our lodges covered the soldiers. The great chiefs of the white soldiers came to us. They held their hats in their hands and we told them what they must do to get their soldiers back. This is what I have seen!"

His message was greeted with silence. There could be only one meaning to his vision—the soldiers were to be taken prisoner! How was this possible? This was not the Lakota way.

Sitting Bull himself asked the question. "In your vision, did you see how we were to do this thing?"

"Yes. I have seen it. I will know when it is the time and I will know how to bring this to pass."

Even as he said it, Black Feather knew it was a weak answer. He had not convinced his audience that his vision was accurate. Only the unfolding of events would sway the Lakota people.

As Black Feather finished speaking, a worried General George Crook sat some distance away in his tent on the Wyoming-Montana border. Hampered by the lack of scouts, he knew he was blindly headed north into territory swarming with hostiles, and he had no idea where they were.

The Lakota and Cheyenne knew exactly where Crook's force was located. He was being shadowed every day and his movements were regularly reported to the great Lakota camp on the Rosebud.

The Cheyenne were the more daring. Two days later they made a bold attempt to stampede Crook's horses.

To the north, on the Yellowstone River, Colonel Gibbon penned a dispatch to General Terry to be sent the next day. *"We are at the Powder River. Have not seen any Indians or any trace of Indians."*

The next morning, the great camp of the Lakota started to move south along the Rosebud River. They were heading for the divide to the west where they would cross to the valley of the *Peji-sla-wakpa*—The Little Big Horn.

Thursday, June 15, 1876. Powder River, Montana Territory.

Unfortunately, there was nothing to do but wait and George Custer had never been very good at waiting. "Where the hell is Reno?" he growled to his commanders. "He should have been back by now."

Major Reno had been gone for six days on a scouting mission and now General Terry was waiting on the steamboat, *Far West*, tied up to the bank at the supply depot. As soon as Reno returned, Terry planned to leave on the steamboat and join with Gibbon's command on the Yellowstone. Custer would then be free to move independently in search of the elusive hostiles.

Another five days would pass before Reno returned.

Washington.

President Grant was in no mood for argument. A dejected General Sherman sat across from the President and watched him write the new orders, orders that would change the whole strategy in the west.

"I realize you are not in agreement with these orders, General, however I expect that you will communicate them to your commanders with all due haste."

"Yes, sir. But I still must say that I believe you are making a grave mistake. The consequences of these orders will delay the opening of the west for a generation, or longer."

"The consequences of not issuing these orders, General, could, quite possibly, be the end of this administration. I will not suffer that to happen. The entire winter campaign has been badly executed and has brought us to this turn."

Sherman left the office calculating the chances that a deciding battle might still be fought before the orders reached Terry, Gibbon and Crook. It would take ten days at least. A lot could happen in ten days.

Montana Territory.

For the first time in weeks, Crook had reason to rejoice. Yesterday more than one hundred Crow and Shoshone scouts had joined his camp and they brought news. "There is a great Lakota village on the Rosebud River!" Today Crook made his final preparations.

"We will leave the wagons and pack mules here. Each man shall provision himself for four days and carry 100 rounds of ammunition. We shall take the fight to them, gentlemen! Be ready to ride at dawn."

The next morning more than a thousand soldiers and scouts moved north as dawn broke. Unfortunately, they were headed the wrong way.

Saturday, June 18, 2022. Berkeley, California.

The incessant buzzing of the telephone finally forced Professor Johnson to set aside the article he was reading and stab the connect button.

He was pleasantly surprised to see an attractive young woman on the screen.

"Hello, Professor Johnson?"

"Yes. I'm Johnson. Who're you?"

"You don't know me, Professor. My name is Kimberly Caldwell and I believe we might have a mutual acquaintance."

"Possibly. I know lots of people. Who would that be?"

"Colonel H. Jamison Partridge, the Third."

The name hung in the air. Johnson tried to collect his thoughts, hesitating just long enough to let Kimberly know she was on the right track.

"No. Don't believe I know the name. Sorry. Nice talking to you."

Kimberly bored into him before he could disconnect her. "Wait, Professor. There's more. I think you'll be very interested in what I have to say."

"Actually, I'm quite busy, Miss—er—"

"Caldwell, Professor. Kimberly Caldwell. Remember the name, because in forty-eight hours the information I want to share with you will appear in several major newspapers. I imagine the interest stirred by the article will lead others to ask hard questions—very hard questions—and the American public may not like the answers. In fact, there could be serious consequences to individuals in government and in the scientific community who may have, shall we say, misled the taxpaying public for a number of years. I would imagine tens of billions of dollars have been diverted to ultra-secret research in a highly technical field where you are the leading, nay, only, genius. Now, shall we talk, Professor?"

Kimberly held her breath. Maybe she was wrong, but all her inquiries and research pointed to only one person and she was talking to him.

Johnson chewed his lower lip, a nervous habit Kimberly noted had started when she mentioned tens of billions of dollars. "I'm not at all sure I know what we're talking about, but you may proceed."

"Is your computer running, Professor?"

Johnson glanced to his left. "Yes. Why?"

"What's your e-address?"

"4 D. JOHN//e=mc."

"Thank you. I think you'll find this photograph interesting."

He opened his e-mail and moments later an old, black and white photograph popped onto his screen. In spite of himself, Johnson flinched a little.

"Recognize anyone, Professor? Say, the third officer from the left? Striking resemblance to our mutual friend, wouldn't you say?"

"Where did you get this?" Johnson whispered.

"From a history book. It's a common book. I'm sure you'll be able to locate it and verify the photo." Kimberly let; him dangle, certain now that he was hooked.

Johnson tore his gaze from the photo and his eyes bored into hers. "Who are you? What do you want?"

"I told you, I'm Kimberly Caldwell. I work for the DIA—"

"The girlfriend!"

"So, you know about me. Did Jamie mention me, or was it one of your conspirators? Possibly Mr. Dealey? Or maybe Jordan Phillips?" She studied his face intently on the monitor. "Oh, don't look so shocked, Professor. My boss and our precious Director of the FBI both lied to me. They both knew what was going on, and there were others. I'm sure you'll be quite interested in my article when it appears."

"But you can't do that! You mustn't!"

"Don't lecture me, Professor! Don't you tell me what I can and cannot do! I've been cheated and lied to and so have the American people. They have a right to know and I have every intention of telling everything I know, unless ..."

Johnson slumped a little in his chair. He was pretty sure he knew what was coming. "Unless what, Miss Caldwell?"

"Unless you give me some straight answers now!"

"Miss Caldwell—may I call you Kimberly?"

"You can call me bitch as long as you tell me what the hell is going on!"

"Kimberly, it's just, well, it's not possible. You would need clearances—very high clearances, and even then I'm afraid I would not be able to answer all your questions."

"You have forty-eight hours to get me whatever clearances are necessary, or the lid's going to blow right off the time travel business and I'm the one who's going to do it!"

"That's not very smart, young lady. It could be very dangerous for you if anyone knew what you were planning."

"Forty-eight hours. Don't worry about me, Professor. The article will be printed even if I'm dead by then. It can't be stopped. I'll be in touch."

The screen went blank, as blank as Demetrius Johnson's mind at that moment. He studied the picture on his computer. *So, you made it to Abraham Lincoln. But what's happening? Why haven't you sent any messages? Jesus, what the hell do I tell the President?*

FIVE

Saturday, June 17, 1876. Montana Territory.

When Crazy Horse received word the previous evening of the approaching soldiers, he joined hundreds of Lakota and Cheyenne in preparations for an attack. The hunting party that reported seeing the column moving north were regaled as heroes and now rode near the front of seven hundred warriors loping across the plains to engage and punish the trespassing troops.

Crook was confident that he would find a rumored large hostile Indian village on the Rosebud River either today or tomorrow. Unfortunately, his Indian scouts had not penetrated far enough ahead to pick up the trail of the huge village moving west toward the Little Big Horn. Crook was heading in a direction where he would find only the evidence of abandoned camps. Unless something unusual happened, his strike force would miss any contact with hostiles by more than a wide country mile.

The Crow and Shoshone scouts ranged far ahead of the army column at the mid-morning break. The broken, hilly country shimmered under fierce sunlight. The first sight of masses of Lakotas and Cheyennes bursting over the hills caught the scouts by surprise. A few scattered shots were followed by intense firing as more hostiles appeared.

"Ho-ka-he! Ho-ka-he!" Others took up the command as Crazy Horse strengthened the grip of his legs on his pony, driving him forward toward the hated Crow and Shoshone leading the U. S. Army. Far below, in a narrow valley between rolling bluffs, he could see the main U. S. force. They had been stopped for a rest, but now were milling madly about, resaddling horses and forming up for battle. With the vision of *Tatanka Yotanka* guiding him, Crazy Horse pushed forward without fear.

First infantry, then cavalry units poured out of the valley. The Lakotas countered every thrust with one of their own. Intimately acquainted with the broken terrain, they probed every weakness. After an hour of skirmishing, the beleaguered general still had no idea how many hostiles engaged him, but he knew they must have a village nearby. If he could threaten the village, maybe he could draw off the persistent attackers.

"Orderly! Have Captain Mills and Captain Noyes disengage their battalions! They are to follow the river, find the village, attack and hold it until I get there. Mr. Grouard, you will guide the attack force."

"I don't know, General. We could get trapped in the canyon and we don't know for sure there's a village there."

"Just guide them. I'm certain you'll find a village."

The Lakotas were ecstatic when they saw large numbers of blue coats leaving the field. They redoubled their efforts against the remaining troops. Surely the great victory of the vision was theirs, but there would be no captured soldiers—only dead blue coats.

Crook soon saw the error of his plan. His remaining troops were only barely able to defend themselves. Any hope of crushing the hostiles had gone with the departed battalions. He reluctantly sent a courier to recall the expedition.

The returning force burst out behind Crazy Horse and his warriors. There was no choice for Crazy Horse but to retreat. On the long ride back to the village, he had time to reflect. *We bloodied them, maybe even stopped them, but this was not the great vision of victory seen by Tatanka Yotanka. This was more like what was foretold by Wiyaka Sapa.* It was something to ponder.

Twenty-four hours later, General Crook withdrew to the south, transporting his injured on travois. He sent a report to General Sheridan: " ... *we were obliged to return to the* [wagon] *train to properly care for the wounded ... have ordered five companies of infantry, and shall not probably make any extended movement until they arrive.*"

There was another problem. Most of his scouts were disgusted and drifted away to their reservations. One third of the U. S. forces were now out of the action.

Monday, June 20, 2022. Berkeley, California.

The phone buzzed almost exactly forty-eight hours after the previous call. A weary Professor Johnson punched the button to receive the call.

"Good evening, Professor. Good evening also to any and all eavesdroppers on this line."

"Good evening, Kimberly. Yes, you're right. This call is being monitored by several interested agencies and you should know that they may choose to terminate it at any time."

"I expected no less, however, I would consider early termination a hostile act and might be forced to proceed to take my case to the American people. Do we understand each other?"

"I believe that is quite clear," replied Johnson. "You said you have some questions."

"Yes, but before I ask them, a personal note to Mr. Dealey. I presume you're listening and you know I've been on vacation for the last two weeks and by now you and Mr. Phillips probably know that I've been digging in the fertile garden inside the beltway. What I've found leads me to believe that the DIA and FBI both have skeletons buried in their gardens. Unfortunately, the skeletons are not quite as deep as you might suppose. Additionally, Mr. Dealey, you'll find my resignation in your computer tomorrow morning. Regardless of the outcome of this conversation, I find I can no longer be of service to the DIA."

"I will see that your messages are delivered," said Johnson.

"I think they already have been delivered—loud and clear. Now, presuming you've chosen not to lie to me again, which would be most unfortunate, I want to know just what the hell is going on!"

Johnson cleared his throat. "That might be a little difficult to answer. I—"

"One moment, Professor. Screw the clearances and stuff the bullshit. Answer me one question straight. It'll make it easier to continue in that vein. Is the individual in the photo H. Jamison Partridge, the Third? Yes or no."

"Sort of, actually—"

"Okay, okay. We go to press in the morning. It's really been won—"

"No, you don't understand! Let me explain."

Kimberly looked at the image on her monitor. The face was strained, the eyes sad and tired. "I'm listening."

"Yes, the person in the photo is the man you knew as H. Jamison Partridge, but he is no longer known by that name. He is now Lieutenant Matthew O'Shaunessey."

"Lieutenant? Who'd he piss off? That's a long fall from colonel."

"It has nothing to do with that. It was the identity he took for the mission."

"Bingo! Now you're talking, Professor. And just what is his mission?"

The sad eyes got sadder, the face longer. "I, I'm sorry, but I can't tell you that. Not yet. Maybe soon. Don't hang up. Believe me when I say it is impossible for now."

Kimberly glanced at Randy, sitting out of sight of the monitor. Randy shrugged his shoulders as if to say, *Give him a chance.*

Kimberly plunged on. "Then tell me this. When is he coming back?"

"He isn't."

The finality in the words cut into Kimberly like a knife. "Why not?" she croaked.

Johnson sighed. "It's a one-way trip, Kimberly. We can't bring them back. He knew it when he left."

"Them? How many have you sent?"

"Altogether, four."

"Three others went with Jamie?"

"No, not exactly. They went before he went. He—"

A fuzziness appeared on the screen and the sound died out. Kimberly knew what was being done. Someone was blocking the transmission. She had an answer to that. Savagely, she punched *disconnect.* The monitors at both ends went dark.

Kimberly sat in her hideout, the second in two days, and fumed. There had to be a way.

Seven hours later.

"Am I correct in presuming that the human ears have gone to bed and we're dealing with only the mechanical kind?"

Johnson rubbed his eyes. "Of course, after all it's three o'clock in the morning, at least where I am."

"Very good, Professor. However, my location is not relevant. Can we talk?"

"Go ahead. I'm awake, sort of."

"I think you know what I want."

"It's fairly obvious. You want to join him."

"Correct. And my son will be going also."

Johnson snapped erect. "Wrong! Nobody's going anywhere! It's too late!"

"Wrong, Professor. With time travel, the one thing that's not a problem is being too late. You simply correct time with the gizmo you use."

He couldn't help it. The laughter started in his belly and roared into a life of its own. He hadn't laughed this hard since … he couldn't remember when he'd laughed this hard. When he managed to control himself, he sputtered one word. "Gizmo!" He immediately began to laugh again.

Kimberly waited patiently. This was the last hope. He had to understand.

Johnson finally controlled himself and was surprised to see Kimberly's placid face regarding him on the monitor. "I apologize," he said breathlessly, "but the SSLA has been called everything in the book, but nobody ever called it a gizmo before."

"I don't care what you call it, I just want the next two tickets to the past."

Johnson sobered quickly. "I wasn't kidding. There are at least three problems, any one of which makes it impossible."

"Try me," Kimberly responded.

Johnson heaved a sigh. "First, there are some problems associated with arrival in the past. We don't know exactly what they are, but Matt told us that—"

"Whoa! Matt? You mean Jamie?"

Johnson nodded. "Matt, Jamie, all the same."

"—told you?"

"Well, sort of. He's sent us several messages."

"Messages? How?"

Johnson smiled. "My idea. Personals in the newspaper, only they stopped coming after he left Washington and—"

"Washington? He was in Washington? Never mind. He's there. Whatever the problems were, he overcame them, and I suppose the others did also?"

"Well, one for sure, but we don't know about the other two. Until we saw that picture, we didn't know Matt was at Fort Abraham Lincoln. The others didn't have any way to tell us. Well, I really can't discuss—"

"You mentioned three problems. That's one and I'm willing to take my chances. What are the others?"

"It would be absolutely stupid to make any move until July 6th."

"July 6th? That's, what, three weeks from now? What's so important about July 6th?"

Johnson cocked his head and thought. He decided she deserved the truth, no matter how much it might hurt. "Are you familiar with what happened to Custer at the Little Big Horn?" he asked.

"Sure. Everybody knows—Custer and his entire command were wiped out."

"Well, not his entire command, but we now know that Matt—Jamie—is with Custer. He could be massacred on June twenty-fifth with Custer. The first reports won't be in a newspaper until July 6th."

Kimberly pondered the information. *Jamie was with Custer, but maybe he wouldn't be killed, or maybe he would. So? If he's killed, there's no reason to go, but....*

Kimberly sighed. When she started talking again, there was no hiding the pain in her voice. "Professor, you don't understand. If it weren't for me, Jamie wouldn't even be there. I drove him away. This is all my fault. I have to—to tell him, or warn him. Don't you see? I can't let this happen."

"Kimberly, there are other considerations. There's more involved here."

"So tell me, damnit! Please, I need to know."

Johnson shook his head, touched by her sincerity, her love. "I'm truly sorry, but I can't ... yet. It's all academic anyway."

"No it's not! It can't be."

"I'm afraid so. Remember, there's another problem."

"What's that?"

"A killer. The SSLA is being dismantled. The remaining transport pods are being destroyed. Because of you, certain higher authorities have decided to destroy our capability to travel through time."

Kimberly gasped. "And what are they going to do next, put the atomic bomb back in a bottle?" Her mind raced. *There had to be a way. There must be a way. I've burned every bridge here. Randy, God bless him, wants this at least as much as I do. Dear God, if you exist, show me the way. Help me!* "When is this supposed to happen, Professor?"

"It's already started. A week. Maybe two, then it's history."

Kimberly leaned toward the monitor, intent on her message, willing Demetrius Johnson to action. "I don't believe that will happen, Professor. I believe you can stop it. I *know* you can stop it!"

Demetrius Johnson was staring at a blank screen. She was gone. He knew she was wrong.

Kimberly sat in the darkness, trying to control herself. She remembered the dreams. Men and horses screaming, dying. An arrow in Jamie's chest. Little Big Horn. Now she knew. He was going to die there.

Wednesday, June 21, 1876. Little Big Horn River.

Black Feather strolled through the huge camp in bright, early morning sunlight, gravely acknowledging friendly greetings. He had lost count of how many lodges, how many people, made up the gathering. Over the past few days, the last of the reservation Indians to join the camp had arrived. Representatives from all the major Lakota *oyate* were massed in a camp extending more than three miles along the river. Soon the camp would move one more time, eight miles down the Little Big Horn, where the Cheyennes would be the last to arrive.

Ever since Crazy Horse returned with the news of his victory over the blue coats, Black Feather's status had risen. Scouts had confirmed that the army column had turned back to the south. There was a general feeling that all was well, the danger passed.

Suddenly, Black Feather felt stifled, hemmed in. He changed his course after asking two young boys to bring him two horses. It was too nice a day to spend teaching his students, and there weren't many nice days left. An hour later he and Raven rode west across the valley and into the low hills on the horizon.

The prairie was in full bloom. Luxuriant green grasses that supported the vast herds of bison and antelope undulated in a soft breeze. Black Feather exulted in riding the prairie, a strong Indian pony between his legs. Raven paced him on her own horse, her hair flying behind her, teeth flashing in a radiant smile. They rode for hours, never seeing another human being, or any evidence that men had ever passed this way. They were Adam and Eve in an unspoiled garden such as they had never experienced.

When they found a quiet meadow next to a small stream, they stopped and tethered the horses. Black Feather sat by the stream, lofting small pebbles into the current while Raven stretched out by his side in companionable silence.

"What's going to happen?" she asked.

He was silent for several moments. "Are you also beginning to believe that I truly am a prophet?"

"No, of course not, but I know you have studied everything that happened here. You must have an idea."

Black Feather rolled onto one elbow so he could look directly at her. "I don't know—I've forgotten so much. It just keeps getting worse. I think this may be the day when Custer gets his final orders from Terry. Or maybe it was yesterday, or maybe tomorrow. I don't believe anything I said or did in Washington would change those orders, so Custer will come from the southeast, across the divide from the Rosebud, in a few days. I know it won't be until we move the camp one more time. We're still not down the river to the point where the battle took place." He paused, concentrating to remember.

"Assuming Custer's orders haven't changed, I know what happened, but I'm afraid. Have I convinced the people to trust me? Will they do what I ask? It is not their way of fighting. If they don't have faith in me—"

"They do trust you! You must believe they will do as you say."

"Okay. And if they do? What will Custer do? How can I convince him to work with us, to help us negotiate a fair treaty? It's the question that has plagued me ever since the beginning. I have no control over him. It's all like a big poker game with too many wild cards. God, I wish I had a wild card, or someone in his camp. Maybe the Lakota way *is* the right way. Sometimes I feel, I don't know, primitive. I was trained as a scientist, but more and more I feel capable of … of striking, killing, if necessary. It's not the way Lincoln Long Trail thought."

"Hey, you're just uptight. It'll be alright, you'll see."

Black Feather rolled onto his back and watched a solitary white cloud skip across the sky. "I do know that I'm glad we came. No matter what happens, this time with you, in this place, has been a treasure without price. Lincoln Long Trail was obsessed with time. His studies reduced time to milliseconds, even nanoseconds, but here I don't even know what day it is. Time is seasons, the passing of the moons. If I am to die soon, this is a good place to die."

Raven clutched his arm. "Don't speak of dying. I couldn't stand it if you died. Charlie's gone. You're all I have."

He smiled at her. "OK. I'll stay alive, just for you."

"I trusted you before, the night before we came. You kept me from panicking. Remember what you did?"

"Made love to you?" he asked softly.

She nodded, then eased her body next to him. "Love me, Linc. I'm cold. Make me forget for awhile."

4 p.m. Aboard the *Far West* on the Rosebud River.

Major Reno had finally arrived, two days earlier, from his prolonged scouting expedition. He had seen no Indians, only signs of where villages had been along the Rosebud. The trail indicated that the village had been moving south, but to where? Reno had no answer.

Custer was very satisfied as he reread the dispatch Terry had sent to General Sheridan earlier. *"Custer will go up the Rosebud tomorrow with his whole regiment and thence to the headwaters of the Little Horn, thence down the Little Horn."*

Finally there was action. Terry had already dispatched Gibbon's force up the Yellowstone to the headwaters of the Little Big Horn where they would move to meet Custer. Somewhere between them the hostiles had to have their camp.

The final line of Terry's dispatch caused Custer to smile. *"I go personally with Gibbon."* Custer was on his own, just the way he liked it.

General Terry was anxious to conclude the briefing. "In conclusion, George, I believe it is safe to say that we will encounter a major village at some point within the next week. I expect you, should you encounter hostiles, to use your best judgement as to how and when to launch an attack. Your cavalry will be the primary striking force. If possible, push any hostiles toward the mouth of the Big Horn. We will be coming from there and can crush the hostiles between us."

"What about Crook?" asked Custer.

"We've had no word from him, but he should be moving into the same general area as we are searching. You will be closest to his possible position. Have your scouts be alert for any sign of him. Any more questions?"

"No, sir. I guess that covers it."

"Good." Terry rose and shook hands with Custer. "See you on the Little Big Horn."

As Custer left to brief his officers, General Crook continued his retreat into Wyoming Territory.

Thursday, June 22, 1876. Rosebud River, Montana Territory.

Custer carefully reviewed the dispatch before sealing it. Although one reporter, Mark Kellogg, accompanied Custer, against President Grant's explicit order forbidding any reporters to travel with the command, no reports had been forwarded to his newspaper. However, that didn't mean the nation would be deprived of knowing what George Armstrong Custer was doing. The dispatch he sent was to the New York *Herald* and read in part: "*... Custer should start with his command ... and follow the Indians as long and as far as horse flesh and human endurance could carry his command. Custer takes no wagons or tents ... but proposes to live and travel like Indians.*"

At noon, General Terry stood beside Custer and reviewed the Seventh Cavalry, twelve veteran companies, as they set off up the Rosebud River. Here there were no wives or sweethearts, no band playing jaunty tunes. The Seventh was off to war and Custer had his official orders in his saddlebags. The orders indicated that Terry placed *"much confidence in your zeal, energy, and ability...."* The words, and the freedom of movement and decision-making in the orders, were music to George Armstrong Custer.

Well to the rear, Matthew O'Shaunessey rode with the braying mules in the pack train. By the time Matt passed the spot where Custer and Terry had been reviewing the troops, Custer had already ridden to the head of the column and General Terry had boarded the *Far West*, which was already steaming down to the Yellowstone to catch up with Gibbon's command. The Seventh Cavalry was on its own.

SIX

12:30 a.m., June 23, 1876. Rosebud River, Montana Territory.

A chill wind fanned the flames of dying fires throughout the encampment. Custer sat alone on a folding chair, wrapped in his campaign coat, lost in private thoughts. The motion of a passing officer roused him from his reverie. It was Matt.

"Lieutenant!"

"Yes, sir?"

"A moment of your time?"

"Of course, sir."

"You seem restless tonight, Lieutenant." Custer leaned back in his chair, boots to the dying fire. "You ever do any Indian fighting before?"

"No, sir."

"But I heard you came from the west, before the war, that is."

"That's true, sir, but my brother and I had a gold mine in Colorado. I wasn't in the army then."

"A gold mine? How come you're here if you have a gold mine?"

"I don't have it anymore, sir. I found out after I returned to Washington that my brother died thirteen years ago, may he rest in blessed peace, and the mine is no longer my property."

Custer eyed the Lieutenant speculatively. "Ah, yes, your miraculous resurrection and return to duty. Fascinating." He reached a decision. "Lieutenant, I'm detaching you from the pack train. I want you to act as my adjutant for this campaign. Although you haven't fought Indians, I can always use a man with pluck and luck close to me. Besides, I liked your bloodthirsty attitude at the briefing this evening. You're obviously spoiling for a fight, as am I. If everything goes as I suspect, we'll make history on this campaign. More than enough glory for all and they'll still be writing about our exploits a hundred years from now. Report to me in the morning."

"Yes, sir!" Matt saluted sharply and turned away, his face a wooden mask. *Great. Out of the frying pan and into the fire, but this time there won't be a miraculous resurrection for Matthew O'Shaunessey.*

For the rest of the short night, Matt tossed and tumbled in his blanket. *Less than three days to live. How the hell did I get into this?* For the first time, he hoped that Lincoln Long Trail would be successful. *But you can't let that happen, can you? Can you? But can you stop it? Jesus, what should I do? What can I do? What was it Johnson said? A military man follows orders, but a scientist explores options—all the options? So? So what are my options? Follow my orders – preserve history and ... and die with the Seventh Cavalry. Warn Custer? How could I make him believe me? How would he respond? If he did believe me, I could probably convince him to change his tactics, save my life and lots of others and do exactly what I was sent here to keep from happening. Shit.*

Another thought occurred to him. One that made his options even more difficult. *Hell, what's the plan? We know Long Trail and the Teagues had a plan, but what? Maybe there won't be a camp there. Maybe we'll be ambushed before we get there. Then again, maybe they haven't survived or been successful in implementing whatever the plan was, or is. Christ on a bloody crutch. I may not like it, but I have my orders.* But another part of his mind whispered, ' *Even if they kill you?* '

By reveille, at three a.m., Matt had not slept. He was tired and cranky, lost in dark thoughts when the column moved out at five. The mood persisted for the whole day as they followed the wide trail left by many travois and a large herd of horses. Matt now rode at the head of the column and could closely observe the barely civil attitudes of Major Reno and Captain Benteen to Custer, who seemed oblivious to their rebellious mood.

They passed several old campsites during the day, and with each site, speculation mounted as to how many hostiles there might be. Matt heard numbers from 800 to 1,500 warriors bandied about. *Ha! If you only knew,* he thought. He chafed under his self-imposed silence and it added to his general feeling of ill ease. By early afternoon, he was dozing in his saddle.

When they made camp in the late afternoon, everyone seemed relaxed and confident, except for Matt. When the pack train finally arrived at dusk, Matt looked longingly at the men accompanying it.

The evening meal tasted like library paste. Matt found he couldn't join in the confident banter of the officers after dinner and retired early, but sleep escaped him. He rolled restlessly, scheming to get reassigned to the pack train, or, failing that, to find a way not to be with Custer two days hence. *Face it, short of shooting yourself in the foot, you're stuck. Duty, Honor, Country.* The three words tumbled in confusion in his tired mind. Sometime in the haunting hours after midnight, he fell asleep.

Saturday, June 24, 1876.

Custer scuffed the dust with the toe of his boot. "Ask them what it all means—the red stones, the drawings in the sand, the rest."

Mitch Bouyer, Custer's interpreter, questioned the Crow and Arikara scouts and listened attentively to their extended answers. "They say the red stones mean the Lakota know we're comin' 'n they'll whip us. The drawings show dead soldiers lying in front of 'em. There was a big ceremony here—Sun Dance—'n the Lakota got a strong message. It's like they're sayin' come on."

"When?" asked Custer. "How long ago was this dance?"

Mitch scratched his head, spat in the sand, quizzed the scouts, hesitated, then: "Don't rightly know. Week, ten days, mebbe more. Lots of lodges. They musta bin here mebbe four, five days."

Actually, it was over two weeks ago, thought Matt, *not that it makes much difference.* He looked around the huge, abandoned campsite. The Sun Dance pole in the middle of the beaten center ground looked like a monster sun dial. The shadow cast by the pole pointed straight at the knot of officers and scouts. He shivered, though the day was getting quite warm.

"All right, they've had their big party. What'll they do next?" asked Custer.

"Well, General, they'd probably start breakin' up into smaller camps. They'll be gettin' serious about huntin' buffalo."

Custer took another long look around the camp. "Tell the scouts to fan out ahead, Mitch. Have 'em look for places where they might be breaking up into smaller groups. I want to know where the biggest band is heading. That's the one we'll follow."

There's another option, Matt wanted to scream. *Instead of breaking up, you should be looking for more trails coming in!*

264 Legacy

At one o'clock, Custer halted the column. The trail was a confusion of drag marks extending across the floor of the valley in some areas. Some of the tracks were fresh, others older. It was impossible to tell if they all went the same direction, or if some went the opposite way. Two more abandoned camps, as large as the Sun Dance camp, had been passed. He sent the scouts ahead while the soldiers rested for four hours.

For Matt, the minutes dragged like hours. He watched the sun sliding to the west and wrestled with his conscience. Twice he got up and started to approach Custer, but couldn't bring himself to abandon his mission, even if it meant saving his own life. *Not yet. Not yet. You still have options.*

Late afternoon, Valley of the Little Big Horn.

The last of the hunters were returning to the camp and there were no reports of enemy soldiers anywhere in the valley. *That's true*, thought Black Feather, *Custer is still across the divide on the Rosebud. He won't even be in the valley until tomorrow morning, or later. What day is it? No bands of hunters have been as far north as the Big Horn and Yellowstone, so they didn't see Terry's force either.*

Black Feather felt like a mouse caught in a trap. After all the planning and preparation, he was unsure. It was so different from what the bright, idealistic young university student in another time had proposed so boldly and confidently from the safety of his apartment. *I'm different. I've changed. Now it's real and I'm here. Raven's here and I love her. What about her? She'll be in real danger tomorrow—or whenever. And if she's threatened, what then? I'll kill someone, that's what. Hell, I'll be in real danger. If this doesn't work—I don't want to think about that. It has to work.*

As he surveyed the massive camp, stretching for miles on the opposite bank of the river that snaked its way down the valley at the base of the line of hills below him, he fully realized the complexities, the personalities and the pitfalls. His view, from the top of a hill, east and a little north of the camp, extended to Sitting Bull's Hunkpapa camp, dimly seen through a light haze of smoke and dust, four miles to the south.

And what will you do, Sitting Bull? he thought. *Your vision and mine are not dissimilar, but I know you believe there will be a great military victory, while I seek a diplomatic victory. Your camp will be the first attacked. Will you keep your warriors under control, or will they counterattack as history records? If they don't counter Reno's attack, can they keep him separated from Custer? If so, for how long? How much time do I need?*

The center of the great camp—comprised of Blackfoot, Miniconjou, Two Kettle, Brule and Sans Arc—was easier to predict, but still uncertain. *You will move against Custer when he first tries to ford the river, but will you hold back far enough? Can you push and force Custer to go where he needs to go without direct combat?*

Finally, possibly the most important key to Black Feather's plan: the Oglala and Cheyenne under Crazy Horse's leadership, camped just below at the foot of the hill. *I believe you are an ally, Crazy Horse, but it is so important that you circle to the north and confine Custer. It is here he must be stopped. Then—then it is up to Custer.*

Black Feather heaved a deep sigh. *Yes. Ultimately it is up to Custer and I have absolutely no control over that. Unless something happens, something I can't even predict, it may all fall apart right here. Then what? Then I'm dead and, far in the future, there will be a granite marker here surrounded by headstones to commemorate our greatest military victory.* He glanced down the hill to a level terrace below. *And they'll build the visitor's center right over there.*

Black Feather mounted his horse and swept the valley below one more time. The yellow grass and shrubs on the hills around him waved in a light breeze that also stirred the leaves on the cottonwoods by the river. Across the plain, thousands of ponies stirred clouds of dust that swirled in the afternoon light. A sense of foreboding settled on him. To the south and east, Custer's scouts were approaching the summit of the divide with the Rosebud. Soon, very soon, the great camp of hostile Indians would be discovered. *And there's nothing I can do about it.* The air was suddenly uncomfortably cold.

Aboard the *Far West* on the Yellowstone River.

The arrival of the steamer *Josephine* meant supplies and dispatches. General Terry tore into the dispatches, eager for word of Crook. Where was he? Had he encountered hostiles? If so, with what results? There was nothing in the dispatches to enlighten the frustrated general.

One wire, from General Sheridan, stopped him cold. He muttered a string of curses and sent for Colonel Gibbon immediately. When Gibbon arrived, Terry handed him the dispatch without a word. Gibbon scanned the contents, his face flushing a deep red as he finished.

"By God, Alfred! They can't do this! By all that's Holy! What in the Hell?"

"They *can* do it. It's been done."

"But *why*, for God's sake?"

"It's pretty obvious, John. The President's under a lot of pressure. He's had one scandal after another. He's running scared."

"But this—this is preposterous! What does he hope to gain?"

"Obviously he's listening to the people, and the people he hears are the ones nearest Washington. There's no *Indian problem* near Washington."

Gibbon stood silently, scratching his head. "So what're you going to do?"

"Well, I'm presuming Crook got his own copy and now you know. So, that leaves Custer."

"How do you plan to get word to him, without looking like we're invading the territory?"

"I want you to leave in the morning with three companies and head up the Rosebud. I'll leave tonight on the boat and go as far up the Big Horn as we can. I'll take three companies and march up the Big Horn from there to meet you. Custer almost has to be somewhere in between."

"Three companies? That's not much if we're attacked."

"No, but I don't want to look like an invading force. After all, that's no longer our mission."

As Gibbon opened the door to leave, Terry stopped him. "Oh John, you might ask the quartermaster to supply you with some white canvas. You can use it to make a flag."

Before the sun set, Gibbon was moving south up the Rosebud. The *Far West* was already out of sight, heading west up the Yellowstone, bound for the Big Horn River.

9:15 p.m. In camp, the Rosebud River.

Matt heard the voice, but it was far, far away.

"Lieutenant. Sir, you alive?"

"No. Go 'way."

"Sorry, sir. Officers call. The general wants you."

Matt's whole body protested. "OK, I'm coming." Some reserve of energy kicked in and he staggered to his feet. It was pitch black. He tripped over several sleeping men as he reeled across the camp searching for a beacon to guide him.

A single candle, flickering in an errant breeze, identified the field headquarters of George Armstrong Custer. Matt was the last officer to arrive.

"Ah, nice of you to join us, Lieutenant. I didn't disturb your beauty sleep, did I?"

"No, sir." Matt stifled a yawn and tried to concentrate.

"All right," continued Custer, "here's the situation. The scouts just reported that the trail goes up and over the divide to the Big Horn Valley. They didn't see a camp, but there's a spot on the summit where I've sent a detachment to get a good look at sun-up. They should be able to see the smoke from the fires. The camp may be breaking up, so I want to get closer tonight so we can have tomorrow to plan our attack, and then hit 'em at dawn the following day."

Major Reno immediately criticized the plan. "Sir, we might be spotted if we're up top. Shouldn't we wait a couple of days to give Terry a chance to get closer?"

Custer bristled and snapped back. "Major, my orders are to locate and attack the hostiles, not pussyfoot around waiting for Terry."

Reno was not easily put off. "But, sir, this is a big village we've been trailing—"

"—that's liable to break up any day," Custer concluded. "As soon as we have reliable information as to the exact location of the camp, I want to be ready to move as conditions dictate. It will be safer to approach tonight and lie in concealment tomorrow. At this point I do not want to lose contact with the enemy. Understood?" Custer paused and peered at the assembled officers. "All right. Be ready to move out before midnight."

Matt stumbled away with the other officers. All about were muttered curses and the confusing sounds of gear being stowed, horses saddled, and pack animals braying displeasure as loads were secured. When Matt was ready, he went to the head of the column. Custer was in deep conversation with his interpreter, Fred Gerard, and several Crow scouts.

"Tell 'em to stick to the biggest trail. I don't want any hostiles to escape."

"Don't worry, General," replied Gerard. "There's at least fifteen hundred warriors, mebbe even two thousand."

Custer waved a hand, obviously not taking the estimate seriously. "Ask 'em if we can cross the divide in daylight without being seen."

Gerard received a direct answer. "No."

"All right, then we stop just this side of the divide and hide out for the day. Let's move out."

Somewhere in the dark night, Matthew O'Shaunessey made peace with himself. He rode as if in an altered state. Every sense was hyper-alert. His ears heard every sound—his skin felt every subtle change in the air. He smelled the night, the muted fragrance of crushed grass and the sweet odor of horses and men. *I'm riding with Custer and the Seventh into the valley of death. There's no place on earth I'd rather be. God bless me, forgive my sins and let me die with dignity. Amen.*

Sunday, June 25, 1876. Valley of the Little Big Horn.

"Is today the day?"

Black Feather heard the slight tremor in Raven's voice and tried to make his own statement strong and clear. "I believe so. I may have lost count, but, yes, I think it is today."

"When will we know?"

"Oh, an hour or two before Reno attacks. There should be a report from some hunters who will accidentally discover Custer's camp this morning, and then there are the two boys who will find the pack the soldiers dropped last night in the dark. We'll have some warning."

Raven shook off her blanket and propped her head on a rolled up hide. Black Feather gazed at her naked breasts and felt himself stir. He reached out for her, but she pulled away. "Not now. Maybe later. I, I want you to know something. No matter what happens today, I want you to know that this is the only place I want to be. After all that's happened to us, and poor Charlie, I am happy and proud to be here with you. I will love you forever."

Black Feather had no words. He just nodded his head in understanding. Somewhere, deep in his being, an inner tension relaxed. His love welled up in his eyes and he felt warmth, peace and love. She grasped his hand and placed it on her breast. The sun was high in the sky when Black Feather and Raven emerged from their tipi.

Since receiving word early this morning from his scouts that there was indeed, a large village on the plain not more than fifteen miles away, Custer had immediately ridden to the Crow's Nest lookout and confirmed the sighting. On his return, he found that the entire command had moved up onto the ridge where they could have been spotted from the distant valley. There was more bad news. One of the scouts reported seeing two Indians within 200 yards of the camp who had turned and fled with four others.

The clincher was the news that a squad of troopers had backtracked to locate a case of hardtack that had fallen off a pack mule during the night. "There were already some Indians there," reported Tom Custer to his brother, "but the squad ran 'em off." The morning sun was cool next to Custer's hot wrath. "How the hell could they be so stupid?" he fumed.

Matt watched Custer furiously pace back and forth. All his drive and energy were apparent in his actions. When he spoke, it was almost as if his scouts and officers weren't there. "We should wait. Tomorrow. Dawn is best. But, we've been spotted. They know we're here. If we wait, they'll scatter and we'll have hell to pay to catch 'em this year." He stopped pacing, decisive now. "We have no choice. We'll attack this afternoon. I want every company to assign a squad to draw ammunition and any other supplies needed from the pack train now. Check every man's gear. We'll march as soon as possible."

As the officers dispersed, Custer turned to his Indian scouts. "Gerard, tell them to fight bravely, to run off as many of the horses as they can and then fight beside us to defeat their enemies."

Less than fifteen minutes later the command was on the move across the divide, stirring a large cloud of dust in the dry breeze.

After only twenty minutes, Custer halted the column. "Captain Benteen!"

"Yes, sir!"

"Take three companies and scout the ridges to the left. See if there are any other villages that way, then make haste to catch up to us."

"Yes, sir!" Benteen wheeled his horse calling out: "Companies D, H and K, follow me!"

As the three companies sheared away from the column, Custer assigned three more companies to Major Reno, holding five companies for himself. "We'll advance together until we close on the village." Almost 400 strong, they advanced at a fast walk and, where possible, a trot.

Matt swung easily in the saddle, a smile on his face. Everything was proceeding as history decreed. As he rode, he thought about Linc, Ruth and Charlie. *I guess they didn't make it, or they couldn't convince anyone to make any changes. That means I'll probably die today.*

They were leaving the hills behind. Before them, where two streams came together, stood a tipi. The scouts, riding in advance of the column, were milling around in obvious excitement. As the head of the column pulled up, Matt saw the interpreter, Gerard, on a rise near the tipi. Gerard was waving his hat and yelling to Custer. "General, I can see the Indians. Three, maybe four miles away. There's lots of dust. They're probably running like devils!"

Not likely, thought Matt. *They've probably just found out we're here and they're rounding up horses to attack.*

Custer searched the back trail for Benteen and his three companies, but they were nowhere to be seen. If the Indians were on the run, he couldn't afford to wait. "Major Reno! Take your companies and the scouts. You have the lead! Move out at the trot!"

Black Feather and Raven spent the middle of the day moving from one end of the massive camp to the other, their ears tuned to hear any suggestion of approaching soldiers. Now it was well past the noon hour and they had heard nothing. Black Feather was beginning to believe today was not the day.

He spotted the runner coming from the south and moved to intercept him. He heard the words before the man got close. "Soldiers coming! Soldiers coming! Get your horses. Soldiers coming!"

Black Feather faced Raven, his fists clenched, a bright gleam in his eyes. The long wait was over. "Get our horses. We go to meet Custer at the ford!"

SEVEN

Sunday, June 25, 1876. 2:45 p.m.

With the scout's report that the village was apparently beginning to move away from the advancing troops, Custer increased the pace and ordered a trooper to deliver a message. "Tell Major Reno the village is only two miles above us and running away. Tell him to move forward as fast as is prudent, then charge the village."

The courier sped away and Matt saw Reno's column pick up its pace and angle to the left to ford the Little Big Horn. Custer immediately ordered the five companies left with him to angle right into the hills above the river. "We'll have to circle the village and cut off their escape from the north," he shouted. "Forward at the trot. Let's get 'em before they escape!"

Custer halted his column briefly to water the horses at a small creek, then spurred forward into the line of hills on the east side of the Little Big Horn. A mile further on, he halted again and rode with his scouts to the top of a hill where he could see the valley. From this height he could see more of the true size of the village. Although a few lodges were being knocked down, it was clear the village was not retreating.

Matt watched Custer as he rejoined the column. *He looks grim,* thought Matt. *Guess he realizes now he's got a hell of a bunch of Indians on his hands.*

"Sergeant Kanipe!" Custer shouted. "Find McDougall and the pack train. Tell him to bring 'em straight across to the high ground. If packs get loose, don't stop to fix 'em. Tell him to come quick. Big village. Move!"

The sergeant wheeled and dug his spurs in sharply, racing back the way they had come.

"Reno's charging to the south end of the village," Custer announced to his company commanders. "We have to find a spot where we can get down there and support him."

With that, the column left the ridge tops and was out of sight as Reno engaged the enemy.

Unable to locate a trail leading toward the river, Custer again halted the command, now parallel with the south end of the village, for another look from a high vantage point. Directly below his position, about a mile away, he could see Reno's companies now deployed in a skirmish line and already heavily engaged. He searched to the south, but could see no evidence of Captain Benteen or the pack train. *Where the hell is Benteen? And the pack train? We're going to need that ammo.*

As soon as he rejoined the column, he dictated a note. "Benteen. Come on. Big village. Be quick, Bring packs. P.S. Bring packs." A trumpeter was selected to carry the note to the rear and locate Captain Benteen.

There goes a lucky man, thought Matt. *The last lucky man in this command.*

Again the column headed north, behind a row of hills to the west, the sight and sound of Reno's skirmish was lost to them.

Jesus Christ! thought Reno. *They're not retreating! My God I've never seen so many tipis in one place! There's more damned Indians than we can handle. If we charge into that mess, we'll be slaughtered!*

Waving wildly to his company commanders, Reno halted the charge. "Deploy in a skirmish line! Deploy here. We have to hold 'em until Benteen gets here and Custer can support us! Form a skirmish line!"

Horses plunged and milled in confusion as the three companies came to a ragged halt on the plain, a line of trees along the river to their right, but unprotected on the left flank. One quarter of his men withdrew behind the line to hold the horses. There were only ninety-five men left to face what seemed to be thousands of Indians already starting to move toward them.

"Open fire!" shouted Reno. "Commence firing, by God!"

Black Feather heard distant firing from the south end of the camp. "No! No! They're not supposed to fire!"

"Maybe it is just the soldiers firing, " Raven replied.

Black Feather listened for a moment. The sounds were getting louder. "Go see—quickly! Try to keep them from returning the soldiers' fire!"

Raven whipped her pony away as Black Feather turned back to the men he had been talking with. "Remember, it's important not to shoot back if the soldiers fire. Tell your warriors not to shoot and we will win this day the greatest victory in Lakota history." He moved among the mass of men, almost a thousand warriors, repeating the message. What was happening with Reno's battalion and Sitting Bull's Hunkpapas was out of his hands. Custer and his five companies would soon appear across the river. He had to be ready.

Custer's column proceeded at a fast trot along a shallow valley between the ridge tops. Horses began to give out, putting some troops on foot. A gently sloping shallow ravine angled off to the left, promising an easy route to the river.

Custer halted yet again and gathered his officers around him.

"Captain Keogh!"

"Yes, sir."

"Take your company and companies C and L and continue along the ridge until you reach a point where you can circle the village from the north. Captain Yates and Lieutenant Smith will come with me. I'm going to try to ford the river and support Reno."

"Yes, sir!" Keogh wheeled his horse and immediately started north at a brisk walk.

Matt glanced at the other two company commanders with Keogh. *I wonder if Custer thinks it's safer to send his brother and brother-in-law away from where he expects the fighting to be the worst.*

Matt had no more time to speculate as the two remaining companies followed Custer at a trot down toward the Little Big Horn.

Raven found the south end of the camp in confusion. Women ran between the lodges, gathering children and belongings, then fleeing from the fighting. Some women screamed for lost children; small children wailed, adding to the din. She saw one man and one woman who had not made it to safety. Their bodies were sprawled awkwardly in the dust. A round passed near her and shattered a tipi pole. She realized there was no way to stop the fighting here and raced to rejoin Black Feather. The plan was already failing.

Only twenty minutes had passed, but Major Reno knew his position was hopeless. His left flank was too exposed and it was obvious the Indians were massing to that side. "Wheel the line! Into the trees! Form a new skirmish line!" He realized his position was hopeless without support.

Raven reached Black Feather just in time to shake her head in answer to his quick question about conditions at the south end of the camp. Any further response would have been drowned out by the trilling and shouting of over a hundred warriors as the head of Custer's column was sighted just across the river. Spears, bows and rifles were waved in the air. Horses reared, or spun in circles, adding to the confusion.

Black Feather felt his spine tingling. His mouth was dry. When he tried to speak, he couldn't form the words. *Don't start shooting*, he prayed silently. He focused his attention on the soldiers massing on the far bank of the river, willing them to turn away into the hills. More warriors arrived every minute as they broke off the engagement at the south end of the village, but Black Feather knew Custer would have a good chance of breaking through here right now if he charged.

Custer reined in sharply as the head of the column emerged from the shallow ravine they had followed to the river. A spur of hills to his left had obscured any view of the valley until they were almost at the river. From his position, on a gently sloping shelf of land, he saw that he had not yet reached the north end of the village. Beyond the trees, across the river, lodge poles pierced the sky in every direction and the woods were alive with movement. Mounted Indians clustered between the trees and further north, well out of rifle range, they milled in the shallows of the river in plain sight. The trilling tongues of the warriors sent Custer's heart and mind racing. *To try to ford here would be suicide. There's no room here to adequately deploy my troops. If the Indians get above and behind us, we're dead. Retreat? Get back to Reno. What? How far? Maybe two miles?*

"Sir! Look!" Matt pointed over the trees to the north.

Custer tore his eyes away from the immediate threat, and looked to where Matt was pointing. Dimly visible through swirling dust were hundreds, maybe thousands of Indians moving steadily northward on the plain. Suddenly he knew who they were. "They're moving the families out of danger!" Custer said. "That's it! If we can threaten the families, surround 'em, the rest'll quit."

A corporal on a lathered horse skidded to a halt next to Custer. "General, sir! Captain Yates compliments, sir. He begs to inform the General that Indians have appeared behind our column and on the hills to our left."

Custer swiveled in his saddle and scanned the ridge to his left. Silhouetted against the sky was a line of mounted Indians. The land by the river was quickly becoming a death trap. Any retreat to join with Reno and Benteen would be a fighting retreat, with the enemy in control of the high ground. Ahead, to the right, another ravine angled away from the river to the north. It seemed to offer the only way back to the ridge tops where the command would have a fighting chance.

"Lieutenant O'Shaunessey! Pass the word down the line." He pointed to the ravine. "We'll head up there. Be ready to stand and fight when I halt the column."

"Yessir!" Matt spurred his horse to the rear.

"Corporal, you hightail it up this draw. Find Captain Keogh and order him to await our arrival."

"Yessir!" The corporal spurred his flagging horse, willing more speed.

"Column right," shouted Custer. "At the trot. Follow me!"

We're being herded like buffalo, thought Matt as he reached the far end of the column and wheeled to catch up to Custer. *Is this the way it was, or is something different? We're hopelessly outnumbered, practically surrounded. Why don't they attack?* The sight of so many Indians on the far bank of the river and now above and behind had almost unnerved him. When he glanced at the men around him, he saw fear—pure terror in some eyes—and others who appeared serene—a few whose eyes sparked in anticipation. As Matt spurred his horse and raced up the ravine, his heart beat like a trip-hammer, yet he paradoxically felt detached and calm.

A great shout swelled from the massed Lakota as they saw the cavalry swing away from the river and head back into the hills. Black Feather had only a moment to savor the feeling of relief. Young warriors started a mad dash into the river to pursue the retreating cavalry. Only the presence of seasoned warriors slowed the pursuit. When order was restored, an orderly crossing of the river began. The Lakota split into three forces as soon as they were across and slowly began to advance in the direction the soldiers had gone, spreading into a vast net designed to leave only one course open to Custer and the Seventh.

Raven struggled to keep up with the surging warriors, her heart racing. *It's working! It's working! Oh please, let it continue!*

"Major! They've set fire to the woods! We have to get out of here!"

Even as he heard the shouted warning, Major Reno smelled smoke. Shots were now coming from across the river behind them also. If he stayed where he was, they would be surrounded and wiped out. With Benteen missing and Custer, God knew where, Reno had no choice.

"Retreat! Pass the word! Get to the horses! Back to the ford! Cross the river and get up in the hills! Pass the word—Retreat!"

The troopers nearest to Reno shouted the order to others and began an orderly withdrawal to the rear. Further along the line, it became a wild scramble as men abandoned their positions and raced for the horses. Within minutes most of the troopers were mounted and stampeding for the ford. All semblance of order was abandoned and not all escaped. The warriors who had not left to join Black Feather charged after their hated enemy.

Custer's two companies charged up the ravine to the ridge. The three companies under Keogh's command were just to the left on the flank of a hill.

Custer quickly gathered his company commanders. From their vantage point they could clearly see the Indian families streaming to the north on the plain below. Custer quickly summarized his plan.

"Captain Keogh, I want you to keep your three companies here. Deploy two companies in skirmish lines—one facing south and the other covering that ravine we just left. There are Indians behind us and more coming from the river. Hold your third company in reserve. I'm going to take E and F and cut off the retreating families."

"Yes, sir," answered Keogh. "What about Benteen?"

Custer scanned the hills behind them. Indians, mounted and on foot, were spread across the trail Benteen would have to take to reach this spot.

"He'll have to fight his way through, Captain. *If* he shows up at all." Custer's tone indicated he doubted they would see Captain Benteen this day. "If he comes, give him all the support you can. We need those ammunition packs! Meanwhile, hold this position. Hopefully you will draw off enough warriors that we can safely attack the families."

Custer wasted no time spurring his mount while signaling his two companies to follow. As Matt swept over the crest of the hill, he glanced back to see the two skirmish lines taking shape and, beyond to the south and west, more Indians massing in the hills. The skirmishers were hopelessly outnumbered. *The poor bastards*, he thought. *By the time we get to the river and back, most of 'em will be dead.*

From the hilltop, the horses, flecked with foam and dead tired, followed the ridge to another slight hill before turning down toward the Little Big Horn a half mile away. Ahead, past the trees lining the river, the women and children from the great camp moved north, a great herd of humanity. Only old men and boys, poorly armed and mostly on foot, provided protection. It seemed entirely possible that Custer could lead the two companies through the weak resistance and create havoc among the women and children.

Suddenly, Custer frantically signaled the column to halt. His chief scout was at his side pointing and shouting. Matt looked where the scout was pointing. Emerging from the cloud of dust along the line of march were hundreds of mounted warriors. Silent, purposeful, moving with military precision, the warriors were placing themselves between their families and the suddenly puny threat of two companies of cavalry. It was the most stirring scene Matt had ever witnessed.

My God! That must be Crazy Horse, he thought. *There's got to be three hundred, or more. How many?*

Custer watched the lines of warriors melt into the trees by the river. Soon they would emerge, cross the river and charge. In that moment, he began to believe he might lose this battle. His men were exhausted, their horses played out. This was not the place to stand and fight. The only chance was to retreat to higher ground and consolidate his five companies.

As the Indians began to ford the river and move onto the slope, Custer turned the column and headed for higher ground. The two neat files of horses and men soon disintegrated into a headlong rush. Some horses stumbled. Some men abandoned their worn-out mounts, trusting their own two legs to get them to safety. Those with stronger horses spurred past slower animals. The retreat verged on panic.

Custer led the confused mass up the last slope. At the summit he got another surprise. Captain Keogh and his three companies were retreating in good order and had almost reached the crest.

Matt gasped as he saw the scene. *Most of them should be dead! They were attacked at Calhoun Hill and only a handful was thought to survive to join Custer here! This isn't the way it happened!*

Captain Keogh detached himself and rode quickly up to Custer.

As soon as Keogh reined in, Custer exploded. "What the hell are you doing here?"

"Sir, we had no chance! There're so many damned Indians out there I can't count 'em. If we'd stayed where we were, they'd a surrounded us and picked us to pieces. I figure our only chance is to face 'em with all five companies together."

Custer seemed about to explode again, but then thought better of it.

"Sir, another thing," Keogh continued. "Strangest damn thing I've ever seen. It's like—like they don't want to fight us. Never seen Indians just hold back like they're doin'. It's like they're just herdin' us." His voice trailed off.

Matt was suddenly very sure. There could be no doubt that Black Feather was behind everything that was happening. He stole a glance a Custer who seemed indecisive, almost resigned. *He knows. He knows he can't win. No matter what he does, there's no way out.*

Others were reporting now. Indians everywhere. Command surrounded. More damned Indians than you could imagine. Hostiles were already deployed in a ring to the north and east, part way up the slope. The only area not completely occupied was downhill to the west—directly toward the river and village, but Crazy Horse and his warriors were closing that gap.

Custer sagged in his saddle, his shoulders slumped. "No sign of Benteen?"

"No, sir," Keogh replied.

Crazy Horse had placed his Oglala and Cheyenne warriors where Black Feather had ordered. They waited impatiently until the cavalry stopped above them, just where Black Feather had said they would. Crazy Horse joined the mass of warriors in a great shout of exultation—and then kicked his pony to stretch the line south where he would meet with Black Feather and the Hunkpapas and Miniconjous. Custer and five companies of the Seventh Cavalry were neatly trapped, their fate all but sealed.

Black Feather and Raven led a large band of Miniconjous across the flanks of the hills above the river. Above and ahead of them they occasionally caught sight of blue-clad troopers racing along the ridge. *Soon. Soon you will stop. You're surrounded. You've already lost, but what will you do?* he wondered.

Even as he had the thought, he saw the soldiers begin to circle, then saw Crazy Horse riding straight toward him, closing the circle. Black Feather pumped his fist in the air. "AYIEE! AYIEE!" he screamed. Warriors behind him and those behind Crazy Horse took up the cry as they came together. Several rifles fired into the sky in celebration brought Black Feather back to earth. "Stop firing! Stop firing!" he yelled. It was going so well, but just a few hot-headed warriors could ruin everything.

Black Feather halted and studied the surrounded cavalry at the top of the line of hills. At first, all was confusion, then a semblance of order appeared as the soldiers set a circular perimeter just below the crest of the hills. *Neatly treed, but oh so dangerous!* he thought. *Now for the coup de grace. This had to be fast. Don't let it get out of hand now. We're so close.*

"Raven, do you have the flag?"

"You think I'd forget it?" She reached behind her saddle and pulled out a piece of canvas, three by four feet. The canvas had been bleached to a snowy white. Black Feather hastily attached it to a staff he was carrying. "Are we ready?"

Matt circled the crest of the hill behind Custer and appreciated the neat trap the Lakota and Cheyenne had set. With enough men to completely surround the high point, and enough warriors in any quarter to engulf the 210 men trapped above them, should they choose to try to charge out of the noose, there was no choice but to make a defensive stand right where they were. Make the enemy come uphill, over open terrain, right under your rifles. Obviously it was hopeless. Matt estimated there were over a thousand mounted warriors ringing the position and more were now coming from the south. *I guess Reno's back across the river now, fighting his own little bit of hell, and these guys are coming here to get their share of our hair*, he thought. Two more incongruous thoughts flashed through his mind. *We've been trapped by the very tactics Custer has used against the Indians for years. How ironic. All that gold, safe in eastern banks. I wonder what they'll do with it when I don't come back.*

Order was emerging from the chaos on the hill. Company C, commanded by Captain Thomas Custer, George's brother, was digging in on the west slope. Matt saw Custer's youngest brother, Boston, and his nephew, Autie Reed, hanging close to Tom.

The other four company commanders, including Lieutenant Calhoun, Custer's brother-in-law, were deploying their men to cover the rest of the rough circle they would try to defend. There were no reserves. The battle would be fought by every man available.

Matt had no specific responsibility, so he was the first to spot the unexpected movement of four Indians advancing on horseback up the slope from the west. One was carrying a white flag.

What the hell? He studied the riders through his eyeglass. *Three men and— yes—a woman! What the—*

"General!" he shouted. "General Custer!" Matt found Custer, only a few paces away and pointed down the hill. "It appears the hostiles want to surrender."

Custer raised his own eyeglass and focused on the slowly advancing riders. The man with the flag was waving it above his head, obviously trying to show his peaceful intentions. Custer quickly scanned the line of Indians he could see. They weren't moving. Only the four were approaching the hilltop.

"Get our horses, Lieutenant," he said to Matt. "Ask Captain Yates and my brother to join us and tell Captain Keogh to report to me."

"Yes, sir!" Matt felt his flesh tingle as he raced to find the men Custer had asked for. *The woman's Ruth—what's her name, I'm sure and I'll bet the one with the flag is Lincoln Long Trail. One of the others must be Charlie. Damn! Why can't I remember his last name? I must be getting old. It's getting harder and harder to remember things.*

By the time Matt returned with Captain Keogh, Commander of Company I, the Custer brothers and Captain Yates were in deep conversation. Custer broke off when Captain Keogh arrived. "Captain, you will be in command until we return. See that the men are well positioned and issue any spare ammunition we have."

"Yes, sir. Then you plan to meet with the hostiles?"

Custer looked down the slope where the four Indians had stopped, waiting patiently, halfway between the opposing forces. "Yes, the four of us will see what they want. Oh, and Gerard, you come too. We'll need an interpreter—and bring my guidon. Lieutenant, take some paper. I'll want notes to verify our conversation."

"Yes, sir," replied Matt. *But,* he thought, *you won't need an interpreter.*

Black Feather watched the five riders coming down the slope and tried to control his emotions. He was breathing rapidly, concentrating on the arguments he would use to convince Custer to do the unthinkable—surrender his command. When Custer and his escorts halted, Black Feather raised his right hand in peace. "Colonel Custer, I am Black Feather of the Lakota. This is my wife, Raven Woman, and this is Crazy Horse of the Oglala, and Gall of the Hunkpapas."

If Custer was surprised to be addressed in English, he didn't show it. "You obviously know who I am. This is my brother, Captain Custer, Captain Yates, my adjutant, Lieutenant O'Shaunessey, and my interpreter, Mr. Gerard. What do you have to say to us?"

Black Feather took a deep breath. "Colonel, we believe that you are here under the assumption that the people gathered below us are hostile to the government of the United States. That is not true. We, Lakota and Cheyenne, want peace, not war. If this were not so, we would have already attacked you. We have been forced to defend ourselves against the attack you sent against the other end of the village, and I am sorry for the lives that have been lost there. Those troops are cut off from you. They cannot help you. As for the rest of the army, General Crook was defeated last week and has returned to Wyoming. General Terry is at least a day away. If you insist on fighting us, you will be totally annihilated. The last chance for true peace between our peoples will die with you."

Christ, thought Custer, *how does he know so much? Is it true—Crook defeated? Terry not close?*

Matt had scribbled hasty notes and now watched Custer for his reaction. Meantime his mind raced. *Jesus, he may just pull this off! Where the hell's Charlie? Is he hiding near here with a rifle on us? Do I let this go on, or... What can I do? If I start something, I'm dead too. Maybe that's the way it's supposed to be.* He started inching his right hand to the stock of his rifle hanging in the scabbard under his right leg. *With Long Trail dead, history can be preserved.* Slowly, he slid the rifle out.

Custer finally spoke. "What is your proposal to me?" Then his head whipped around and his eyes bored into Matt. "Lieutenant! Remove your hand from that rifle! Immediately!"

All eyes focused on Matt. He jammed the rifle back in the scabbard, his last chance gone.

"As I was saying, Black Feather, what do you want from me?"

"We want you to surrender your command under the following terms. An area has been set aside for you on the plain where you will have water, and food will be prepared for your men. As a sign of our good faith, your men may keep their weapons, however your horses will be forfeited as payment for invading our land. Also, we will cease our attack on Major Reno and Captain Benteen."

How does he know who they are? thought Custer.

"Early tomorrow I will ride with you, and a delegation from our tribes, to locate General Terry and initiate formal peace negotiations. When he has agreed, your men will be free to leave our land."

"On foot?"

"Yes."

Custer seemed to consider the demands, but Matt sensed his stiffening resolve. When he spoke, Custer left no doubt. "There will be no surrender. Your position, although it seems unassailable, is more tenuous than you think. You cannot win. You will not win!"

Matt swallowed hard. There was no reprieve. The slaughter, slightly altered from a historical perspective, would proceed. His mind whirled. *What if he does surrender? My mission has already failed. I couldn't stop them, history is already altered. If there is a chance for peace, so many will live, so many wives will still have their husbands. There may be the possibility for real justice for the Lakota, Cheyenne and all the others.* There was an alternative, a slim one.

"General, may I have a word with you?"

Custer swiveled and fixed Matt with a steely glare, resolve showing in every fiber of his body.

"Please, General, a private word?"

For long moments Custer glared, then slowly pivoted his horse and turned to face Matt. "What's so important, Lieutenant?" The last word was designed to remind Matt of his vastly inferior rank.

"Sir," Matt spoke in a low voice, quickly, before he could lose his nerve. "I believe you should seriously consider the demands. We're surrounded. There are more Indians here than anyone could have expected. Reno can't help, he'd never be able to fight his way through. General Terry can't possibly get this far south for another day, maybe two. By the time he did get here, we'd all be dead. What good will that do?" Matt knew it was weak, but it was all he could think of at the moment, without revealing the certain knowledge he had which he knew Custer would never believe.

His words obviously had no impact. Custer sat square and tall, his eyes probing, his jaw set. When he spoke his voice was low and scornful. "You don't sound like the same officer who tried a few moments ago to assassinate emissaries traveling under a flag of truce. Just then you seemed quite willing to condemn us to the fate you now say we face. Do you believe that by killing these men and the woman the rest of these savages would slip quietly away? I find your arguments without merit, Lieutenant." He started to turn away.

His last chance seemingly gone, Matt feverishly groped for another argument. A fading memory flitted through his mind. He was on one knee, in full uniform, under a spreading tree facing a beautiful woman. A woman he loved so much. A woman for whom he would have done *anything*. God, how his heart ached for her.

Matt blurted out one word. "Libbie."

Custer's head snapped around. "What about my wife!"

"She loves you, literally worships you. Think how she will feel. Think about the lost years she will have." Custer was listening. "Then there are your brothers, your nephew and your brother-in-law. The other men up there with wives and children. Would you make them widows and orphans when it will accomplish absolutely nothing? You've had a brilliant career—"

Custer raised his hand. "Enough, Lieutenant. That's quite enough." He wheeled his horse to face Black Feather and the others.

Black Feather focused on Custer, but glanced speculatively at Matt, wondering why he was vaguely familiar.

Custer surveyed his situation one more time. *The sun's getting low, but it's still a long time to dark. No help there. What about Reno and Benteen? Is it true, what he said? How about the pack train? How much ammunition do we have? Not enough. Finally, the inescapable thought. Surrender the command? What then? Court martial? Certainly. Cashiered from service? Prison? Firing squad? Christ!*

He looked hard at this unusual man and woman facing him. *Certainly I have never met Indians like these two before. There's something—something different. What? Can I trust them? What about Gall and Crazy Horse? Are they really in control here?*

His decision made, he squared his shoulders and addressed the four Lakota ambassadors. "I will not surrender this command," he announced in a strong voice, "until I have certain assurances."

Matt almost toppled from his horse, such was his giddy sense of relief. He barely heard the short negotiations, but was very aware of the moment when each of the four Lakota solemnly rode forward—Black Feather first, then Gall, Crazy Horse and, finally, Raven Woman—saluting Custer and then shaking his hand. The deal was sealed. History had changed. Matt's mission had failed. He felt elated. It was not a good day to die, he decided.

Matt sensed that he was being closely observed. He glanced around and his eyes locked with Black Feather, who maneuvered his horse alongside Matt's. The short distance separating them from the others allowed them to speak privately for a moment.

"Don't I know you from somewhere, Lieutenant?"

Matt nodded. "I saw you, briefly, last December at the White House."

Black Feather nodded, his eyes showing that he remembered. "Ah, yes, I do remember now, but ... there's something else." He let the statement hang between them.

"Where's Charlie? I don't see him."

"Charlie? He's dead. How do you know Charlie?"

Matt shrugged. "Just heard of him. Heard there were three of you."

Black Feather seemed unconvinced. He started to turn away, then stopped. "Lieutenant, one question."

"Yes?"

"Do you know the meaning of the word *genocide*?"

Matt nodded.

"So—you were sent to stop us?"

Matt nodded again.

"Then it was you. In Washington you tried to kill me." It was a statement, not a question.

"Yes."

Black Feather was silent for several moments, studying the man who had pursued him through time. He seemed to reach a decision.

"We've won, Lieutenant. Will you help us? Please?"

Matt nodded. "Yes, I believe I will."

EIGHT

Monday, June 26, 1876. Along the Little Big Horn.

Matt had never seen a more glorious sunrise. *This is the morning I was supposed to wake up dead, but now I'm riding into history—a new history—and, God, it feels good! No matter what happens when we meet Terry, it can't be as bad as what should have happened yesterday.* Matt still had a hard time accepting the fact that he was alive.

Almost unbelievably, everything had proceeded smoothly the previous night. Once the decision was made to surrender, all nine negotiators had ridden to the top of the hill. The officers and men received the announcement with mixed emotions—obvious relief by some, anger and frustration by others. One modification was made to the surrender. The men were allowed to keep their horses for the ride into the valley. As they left the hill, the Lakota and Cheyenne warriors formed ranks to the right and left, then filled in behind. There were some tense moments when the soldiers realized just how vulnerable they were, but the Indians kept a respectful distance and showed no signs of hostility.

An area near the center of the village had been cleared for them. True to his word, Black Feather had set off immediately to the south to halt the fighting between Reno and the Hunkpapas. Reno's battalion, now supported by Captain Benteen and the pack train, had managed to reach a defensible position in the hills above the river, but there were more than fifty men dead and almost as many wounded. Although badly mauled, Major Reno scoffed at the idea of surrendering, denounced Custer in strong language, and vowed to hold out until "hell freezes over." An uneasy truce settled over the south end of the village as the Lakota held their positions, but stopped firing at soldiers when they slid down the hillside to get water from the river.

Before dawn the emissaries to meet General Terry had left the village. Custer had shown his displeasure with Matt by summarily dismissing him as adjutant and not including him in the party. "You could have gotten us all killed up there," he had said. "And there's something else. How well do you know this Black Feather?"

"I don't know him at all, sir. I saw him briefly in Washington, but we never spoke before yesterday."

Custer had eyed him speculatively, then pounced on him. "You're lying, Lieutenant. There's something going on between the two of you. I saw you talking yesterday. You seemed too chummy to me. How did Black Feather know the names of my commanders? How did he know about Crook and Terry? Can you explain that, Lieutenant, or do you want to wait for your court martial?"

"Sir, I'm telling you the truth. Whatever information he has about this campaign, I can honestly say did not come from me!"

"Not satisfactory, Mr. O'Shaunessey. Consider yourself under arrest until such time as formal charges can be brought against you."

It might have ended there, but Black Feather had other ideas. When he found out Lieutenant O'Shaunessey was not included with the party leaving to find General Terry, he invited Matt to ride with the Lakotas. Custer boiled, certain now that there was a traitor on his staff, but there was nothing he could do.

The sun was still low in the eastern sky when scouts reported they had located a military camp only five miles north. The two hundred warriors accompanying *Wiyaka Sapa* on his historic journey dropped behind when Black Feather unfurled his white flag and proceeded with Custer, Captain Yates, Matt and Crazy Horse toward the camp. They didn't have long to wait. There was agitated motion in the camp before six horsemen detached themselves and trotted toward the Lakota delegation.

General Terry halted the U. S. delegation twenty yards away and signs of friendship were exchanged before he moved forward with another officer. "Good to see you, General Custer," he opened. "I assume a messenger reached you with your new orders?"

"Sir?" Custer looked perplexed. "New orders?"

"You did not get a message from me?" asked Terry.

"No, sir. What was in the message?"

"President Grant has ordered us to cease offensive operations against the hostiles and bend every effort to a peaceful accord. I assumed your presence here with," he waved his hand at the line of Indians spread on the plain, "this many Indians—" Suddenly he realized his assumption was wrong. "If you didn't receive my message, how do you explain this?"

"Perhaps I can explain," interjected Black Feather. "You see, General, there were no—quote hostiles, unquote—until your government so designated us. We are a people earnestly seeking a true and lasting peace with the United States and we were able to convince Colonel Custer of our honest intentions. We are here to pursue that course."

Black Feather's spirit soared. *I must have made some impression in Washington. Why else the change in orders? God!*
"Convinced you, *Colonel* Custer?" asked Terry. "Just how were you convinced?" To Matt it sounded like an accusation.

As Custer explained the circumstances to General Terry, Matt could see the General's lips purse into a sneer. *Oh, oh,* thought Matt. *The army may have its orders, but they don't have to like 'em. This could get dicey.*

"So," Terry began after he had been briefed, "some of your command is surrounded and have not surrendered and the balance is held hostage against the United States? This certainly is a dark day in the history of the United States, Colonel. I cannot imagine it could be any worse, even if you had been wiped out!"

Black Feather moved closer to General Terry, physically imposing himself between Custer and his commander. "General, our people are ready, especially in light of your orders, to offer every assistance to expedite the return of all soldiers to —"

"Thank you, however I doubt *your* assistance will be necessary."

If Black Feather took offense, he hid it well. He continued to act as a buffer between the irate general and Custer and skillfully negotiated the necessary details to begin the orderly withdrawal of United States military forces from the region.

General Terry chose twenty men to accompany him to the Lakota camp. Four scouts rode along with new orders to Colonel Gibbon. They would backtrack over the divide to the Rosebud and turn Gibbon's command around for an eventual rendezvous with the steamboats on the Yellowstone River.

It was mid-morning when they reached the great camp of the Lakota and Cheyenne. General Terry had ridden in stony silence and his face remained impassive as he rode through the length of the village, but Matt could see that he was impressed with the number of lodges. Thousands of Indians lined their route, silent witnesses to the success of *Wiyaka Sapa,* the greatest prophet in Lakota history.

The procession paused briefly at the camp occupied by Custer's men. Terry assured the officers that they would be leaving soon, probably within two days, but the first priority was "the wounded fighting men of gallant Major Reno." Custer cringed in his saddle, deeply stung by the rebuke.

By the time they reached the ford of the Little Big Horn and started to climb to Reno's position, Terry's face had softened somewhat. At one point he swiveled in his saddle and looked back over the plain and shook his head. He would never forgive Custer for surrendering his command, but now he understood what would have happened if he hadn't.

Wednesday, June 28, 1876.

The massed village of Lakota and Cheyenne was breaking up. Matt stood on the spot where he should have died, along with the rest of Custer's doomed command, and watched the lodges melt away on the plain below. Soon the only traces that the village ever existed would be the forty-eight fresh graves containing fallen U.S. troopers and three lodges with the bodies of seven warriors.

The largest party departing the village included Major Reno, Captain Benteen and the companies under their command. General Terry and his detachment rode with them. Custer rode alongside the general, but well to one side. There had been few words between them. Custer was a pariah—a lonely outcast. The rest of his command was also being punished. They would wait another day before starting out on foot and would have to wait at least a week for the steamboats to make the trip to Fort Abraham Lincoln and return to pick them up. Some of the packhorses and supplies were left with them.

Trailing the departing party were most of the pack train and twelve Indian ponies pulling travois with the most seriously injured soldiers. Terry had relented and accepted Black Feather's offer of help when he saw the conditions of the wounded. Black Feather, Raven and a small number of Lakota families brought up the rear.

Matt took a last look around, then trotted down the hill to join the departing soldiers

Friday, June 30, 1876. Big Horn River.

Relieved of any duties, Matt stood apart as wounded soldiers were hustled up the gangplank to the lower deck of the

Far West. The smaller *Josephine* had pulled farther up the river and had taken the most seriously injured, as well as three companies of Reno's command. The more spacious *Far West* would house the balance of the troops, General Terry and his staff, Colonel Custer and the Lakota delegation that would travel to Washington to negotiate the new treaty.

Matt saw Lincoln and Ruth (he couldn't get used to calling them Black Feather and Raven) approaching with a young Lakota warrior.

"Good morning, Lieutenant," hailed Linc. "Nice to see that you'll be traveling with us."

"Probably only as far as Fort Abraham Lincoln," responded Matt. "Custer's planning to bring me up on charges. I'll most likely end up in the stockade."

"Oh, I wouldn't count on that, Lieutenant. I've included your name on the list to go to Washington for the treaty talks and right now I'm pretty much getting what I want."

"Well, I wouldn't get too cocky, if I were you," Matt responded. "It's a long way to Washington and even farther to getting a ratified treaty. It's pretty obvious the military isn't real excited about their orders and I'm willing to bet some western senators won't just lie down and let you carve out a nation in their back yard without a fight."

Linc smiled. "You're right, of course, but if I were a betting man, I'd bet on the new Lakota Nation. In fact, this young man may be the first Chief Justice on our Supreme Court. He's been studying English and law this winter. In Lakota his name is *Kahektabya*, Bringing-up-the-Rear, but he has taken the Americanized name, George Trail."

George extended his hand and Matt found his handshake strong. "Would that be George as in 'Custer,' or as in 'Washington'?" asked Matt.

Linc and Ruth both found this amusing. "We are starting a new nation, Lieutenant O'Shaunessey," replied Ruth. "Why does a name have to be tied to your nation?"

Matt smiled with them. *What can I say? They've already changed history. They're young, smart and energetic. I guess I wouldn't bet against them either.*

"One thing puzzles me," Matt continued. "Where are Sitting Bull and Crazy Horse? I'd think they would be in your party."

"We go to negotiate a treaty for our people. Sitting Bull and Crazy Horse will come to sign the treaty. Meanwhile, they will be more effective here, helping to keep the fragile peace we have obtained."

Sunday, July 2, 1876. On the Missouri River.

Even though the sun had set, it was still hot on the river. Mosquitoes feasted on exposed skin, but being on deck was better than sweltering in the converted closet Matt had been assigned as quarters. He strolled to the aft end of the upper deck, one of the few areas not occupied by soldiers on pallets, and enjoyed the light breeze across the deck. The rhythmic thumping of the engine and splash of water off the paddlewheel comforted him. Half a mile behind them, the *Josephine* plowed in their wake, twisting through the ever-changing sandbars of the mighty Missouri River.

Matt studied the dark silhouette of the shoreline and reveled in the moment. *This river led Lewis and Clark to the Pacific over seventy years ago and has served as an interstate highway, of sorts, for Native Americans for countless centuries. Trappers, traders, adventurers—and now—now a new page in American history. I'm part of the military force that ... lost the west? No, that's not quite right. Maybe we haven't lost, maybe it's more like adjusted, or corrected.*

"Good evening, Lieutenant. Mind if I join you?"

"Ah, good evening, Miss—. I'm sorry, I seem to have forgotten your last name."

"Teague, Lieutenant. Ruth Teague."

"Thank you. I don't know why, but I seem to have trouble remembering things these days."

"We're all having that trouble, Matt. Do you mind if I call you Matt?"

"No, not at all."

"Linc believes it's all part of our journey. Eventually we'll forget everything about the future."

"So you know about me," Matt said quietly.

Ruth slid up to the rail close to him, where nobody could overhear their conversation. "Yes, Linc told me that you were sent after us. But why?"

"Why? How about a dead vice-president and—"

"No! We didn't know anything about that! And what happened, with Charlie and that man—"

"The FBI agent?"

"Yes. That was just an accident. Charlie just reacted. He was scared."

"And the man in California? The car you stole?"

Ruth paused and looked out over the river. "No, that was no accident. It was horrible. We—I—I don't know."

Matt studied her profile. It was a pleasant face. He felt she was telling the truth. "Then there was the letter Linc wrote about changing what happened at the Little Big Horn. Some very powerful people felt history shouldn't be changed."

Ruth laughed and shook her head. "God, that was the joker in the deck. All these years we've fought for our independence, used every device we could think of. That's why NAN was formed, but since everyone knew history couldn't be changed, what difference did it make? Of course, Linc knew about the time travel project, and he was very naughty, given his ultra-secret clearance, and told us about it! I remember it was good for a laugh, but not much more."

"But you must have believed in it to take the chance you did."

Ruth turned her face to him, her eyes large in the dim light. "You really don't understand, do you? After what happened in Nebraska, what were we supposed to do? Every law officer in the United States had us at the top of their hit list. Even if we survived capture, what would have happened to us? Convicted, executed, end of story. What would have happened to our families? Do you really think we had a choice? We didn't have to believe in Linc's crazy theory. The only chance we had was—this."

That's true, thought Matt. *Everyone on our side saw a plot, but all she and Charlie saw was a chance to live.* His mind flashed back to the 'official' government story of how Linc and Ruth had died in the Oakland hills and had to agree with her assessment of their probable fate.

"But how about you, Matt? You were sent to stop us—kill us, yet you now seem to support us. What changed your mind?

Matt thought for a moment, then chuckled. "Remember Professor Johnson?"

Ruth nodded.

"He gave me the key—told me to examine all my options. When we met on the hill, history had already changed. Somehow my mission wasn't as important as living. And, since I couldn't stop you, I exercised an option. Even then, I might not have succeeded, but I remembered a woman who was, well, important to me. That was the key to Custer. Also, I know what the future was and now there's a real chance to make it better for everybody, but it's still an uphill fight."

Ruth nodded. "We're aware of that, but as long as we have our fading memories of the future, we'll fight for every scrap we can get from the government. The future of our people is at stake. We *must* make it better!"

Matt studied the spreading wake behind the boat for a moment. "Of course, there's no guarantee your new future will be better," he said.

"I don't see how it could be worse. Because of what's already happened, we've altered the relationship between our people and the government. If we are allowed to build our own nation I'm sure there will be problems—big problems—but at least we won't end up a welfare state, a third-world people like we were on the reservations. We'll have the opportunity to retain our pride, our culture, our heritage. Those were terrible, gut-wrenching losses under the old system." Ruth brightened a little. "Besides, think how advanced we'll be. We'll have women's suffrage long before the United States!"

Matt had to laugh. "I should have seen that coming," he replied.

They stood by the rail in a companionable silence.

"Lieutenant? A question. Who were you, in the other time? What made you come after us?"

Matt shook his head. "It's getting kind of fuzzy, actually. Besides, it's not important." *Linc brought his woman with him—I came because I lost my woman. Of course, if I hadn't lost her, I wouldn't have come. Now that I'm here, I wouldn't have missed it. And it's true,* she *was the key. How strange.*

Ruth turned away, walking back to her cabin, then stopped. She didn't face him, but asked quietly, "Will they send someone else?"

Matt thought about that for a moment. "No. No, I don't think there will be anyone."

He watched her walk away. *I'm glad I didn't have to kill her, or Linc. They're good people. Maybe they will make a difference. A positive difference all Americans can be proud of.*

Tuesday, July 4, 1876. Bismarck, South Dakota.

Throughout the nation the Centennial Celebration of Independence was joyously observed with parades, speeches and fireworks. The celebrating had started two days early at Fort Abraham Lincoln with the return of many of the missing troops and the official word that the Indian wars in the west were finished.

The mood in Bismarck was more somber. Two special cars had been added to the Northern Pacific train for the delegates heading to Chicago and on to Washington, but the departure had been delayed for three hours now as concerned citizens and local dignitaries gathered and demanded to meet General Terry to voice their concerns. The crowd had reluctantly parted when Black Feather, Raven and six minor chiefs representing the various *oyate* of the Lakotas arrived. Matt sat impatiently in the open end of the rail car as the parade of petitioners met with the general in his compartment. *This is going to be a lonely trip,* he thought. *I'm painted with the same brush as Custer, but even Custer doesn't want anything to do with me.*

The one bright spot was Libbie Custer. When they were boarding the train, she pulled Matt aside for a moment before going to their compartment.

"I know my husband is angry with you, Lieutenant, but I want you to know that I am eternally grateful to you. I surely believe you saved Autie's life. He's been through rough times before. You wait. He'll come back even stronger when this is over."

Matt doubted he would get much chance to talk with Libbie on the trip, *but,* he thought, *at least she won't be trying to match me up with some young woman.*

Finally, the last pleading citizen left the train. With a long blast on the steam whistle, the special began rolling east. Matt pulled his hat over his eyes and went to sleep.

Tuesday, July 18, 1876. Washington.

The first details of the disaster had arrived by dispatch yesterday. Today it was front-page news in all the papers. Matt read the account with a feeling of dread.

HUNDREDS DEAD
IN GREAT STEAMBOAT DISASTER!!
FIRST EYEWITNESS REPORTS!!

Bismarck, Dakota Territory. Two steamboats returning gallant soldiers from the recently completed campaigns in Montana Territory exploded in a gigantic ball of flame visible for miles, killing all on board. The soldiers were from five companies of General George Armstrong Custer's Seventh Cavalry. There were apparently no survivors. Witnesses say it appeared the two boats, the *Far West* and the *Josephine*, were racing under a full head of steam and very close together when the explosion occurred. Both boats were leveled to the waterline and the hulls sank almost immediately. It is believed that over 200 cavalrymen died, including Custer's brothers, Tom and Boston. See page two for a complete list of those believed killed.

The article continued with a recap of the recent military campaign and information about the peace talks just getting underway in Washington.

Matt was stunned. He turned the page and read the column of fine print, men he knew reduced to a list one column long. They were all there. The officers and men of Companies C, E, F, I and L who had ridden with Custer that last day and surrendered to live and fight again.

My God! They're all dead anyway! Why? They should all be alive, or Custer should have died with them.

A cold dread gripped Matt. One shoe has dropped. When will the other one hit the floor?

Thursday, August 10, 1876.

It was oppressively hot and muggy in Washington. The two meeting rooms in the Capitol Building assigned for the peace treaty negotiations smelled like a gymnasium. The air was so thick it seemed to sag from its own weight.

From their arrival in Washington, until today, very little progress had been made. President Grant, in the last year of his second term, was determined to leave office with his peace policy firmly in place, and was pushing hard for a settlement.

George and Libbie Custer had arrived in a swirl of controversy— just the type of situation Custer seemed to thrive on. In a short time he went from being a brow-beaten, dejected man whose career was a shambles, to a fighting warrior, eager to please the President and bedevil Generals Sherman and Sheridan who were calling for his court martial. Custer, along with some eastern senators and the Republican press, seemed to be the champion of peace in the west.

Black Feather and Raven were the toast of the town, invited to every social function, and housed in fine rooms at the Willard Hotel. "What a difference from the last time I was here," beamed Black Feather. Though both were now elegantly dressed in the latest styles and preferred to use Lincoln and Ruth instead of their Indian names, it was the wild Lakotas the hostesses wanted at their parties.

Matt had been reduced to a minor role as a recording secretary for the proceedings, but he enjoyed watching Linc skillfully execute the political art with the senators assigned to the negotiations.

The meeting this afternoon promised to be a boring continuation of the past few days. The Lakotas were proposing what Matt considered a fair bargain. The Lakota and Cheyenne would keep the territory allotted to them in the Fort Laramie Treaty of 1868. In return, they would grant long-term leases for mineral rights in the Black Hills, allow settlement of some tracts of land suitable for farming, and make emigration to the Lakota Nation relatively easy for those who wished to settle there. In return, the United States would assist the Lakota in establishing a comprehensive government roughly patterned after the U. S. Constitution. There would also be material assistance in the forms of loans and grants to establish schools and universities, commercial and manufacturing enterprises, the fabric of a society. It all sounded fair, but it was heavy sledding and real progress was slow.

The meeting was scheduled to start soon. Matt had arrived early and greeted a knot of senators who were huddled with Custer across the room. The men kept their voices low, almost whispering, like conspirators. Matt idly wondered what the conversation was about, then decided it would be a good idea to go to the bathroom before the meeting, and left the room.

Ruth walked down the corridor toward the meeting rooms and nodded to the armed sentry posted at the door. *Seems stupid to have a soldier standing guard over us*, she thought, not for the first time. *The time for killing is over. It's like they don't want the killing to end.*

She glanced into the first room and saw the huddled politicians in the far corner, including the fat senator who was leading the opposition, and decided she wasn't ready to face them yet. She went to the next door and entered the adjacent room. *I'll just have a few quiet moments until Linc and the rest get here.*

The door between the two rooms was partly open. She could hear the whining, nasal voice of the beefy opposition senator. She tried to ignore him, but his words carried plainly to her.

"I tell you George, it's the only way. Grant's a lame duck. Even if this travesty gets to Congress, it'll be voted down. You're the man who can change it."

"Why should I do that?" asked Custer.

"One very good reason. I have here a letter from General Sherman guaranteeing that he will drop all charges against you, restore you to your former rank, and put you in command of the Seventh Cavalry. All you have to do is drop your support for this treaty. Don't worry. We'll throw the savages a few crumbs and then in a couple of years, when all this blows over, we'll pick up where we left off. We get the gold. We get the land. They get what they deserve."

Ruth gasped. *My God! Custer's selling us out!*

Without thinking, she pulled the door open. The senator's eyes opened wide. "What the hell you doin' here?" he demanded. Behind him, Custer jumped up and started toward her.

Ruth blurted, "Damn you! Damn you all!" then turned and fled into the hall, running for the outside door.

Behind her she heard the senator shouting. "She heard us! We've got to stop her!"

Ruth ran faster, as if reaching daylight would save her. She burst through the doors at the top of the Capitol steps. She could see Linc and the other Lakotas getting out of carriages below. "Linc!" she screamed. "Linc, Custer's selling us out! He's making a deal to kill the treaty!"

Linc heard her screamed warning and started to run up the stairs toward her.

She was going too fast when she started down the broad marble steps. By the third step, her momentum was so great that she couldn't move her feet fast enough to keep up. With one final scream, she pitched headfirst down the step, bouncing like a rag doll, her skull crushed from the first impact. When Linc knelt beside her, she was already dead.

"Oh, God, no, no, no." Hot tears flowed down his cheeks as he gently cradled her wounded head. He pulled her tight against his chest and rocked her like a baby. When he raised his head, there was molten fury in his eyes. Like a man in a dream, he rose and pushed through the gathering crowd. Ruth was dead. Nothing else mattered now.

When Matt returned to the meeting room, he found Custer in the middle of an agitated group. Something had happened to break up the peaceful, secretive meeting he had witnessed earlier.

"What's going on?" asked Matt.

"Nothing important, Lieutenant," answered one of the senators.

George Trail followed Linc when he left Ruth. "What are you going to do?" he kept asking as they entered the building and half-ran down the corridor.

Linc charged into the building with no plan. Now, as he approached the door to the meeting room, he half turned to the right and slammed a balled fist into the stomach of the guard. As the surprised sentry slumped to the floor, Linc unsnapped the man's holster, pulled out the pistol, then bulled into the meeting room.

Matt was near the door, the others were across the room. Matt took one look at Linc's enraged face and the pistol in his hand and blurted, "What's happened? Linc, what're you—"

"Ruth's dead!" Linc shouted. "They killed her!"

He brushed past Matt before he could react, raised the pistol and fired twice before Matt could catch up with him.

"NO!" screamed Matt as he reached for Linc's extended arm. Linc's third shot went into the ceiling, then he and Matt were wrestling for the gun. The fourth shot entered

Linc's throat, just below his chin, and exited from the back of his skull, splattering George Trail with bits of bone and brains. Linc was dead before he hit the floor.

Matt stood over Linc feeling the first effects of shock. When he looked across the room, his shock deepened. George Armstrong Custer had taken the full wrath of the enraged Lakota. One shot had hit him in the head, the other in his chest. He was still breathing, but it was clear that he was breathing his last.

Matt looked back at George Trail, now kneeling by the head of his fallen prophet. "Where's Ruth?" Matt croaked. George didn't seem to hear him. "Where's Ruth?" he repeated. *I won't believe she's dead until I see her.* The refrain echoed in his numbed brain.

Numbly, George raised his arm and pointed. "Out front. On the steps." George reached out and gently closed the blank, staring eyes of his prophet. In his mind he began to compose the death song he would sing when the great *Wiyaka Sapa* was laid to rest with his beloved Raven Woman in some secret place only the Lakota would know. His eyes were drawn to a beautiful white arrowhead on a broken silver chain lying near the body. He picked it up and held it in his clenched fist as he began to chant his requiem.

The police were gone, the bodies had been removed, and the blood and bone had been washed from the floor and steps of the Capitol. Matt sat alone in the twilight on the step where Ruth had died. He was numb and shaken, feeling a grief deeper than any he had ever experienced. It wasn't possible just yet to accept that the bright young woman who wanted to bring the vote to Lakota women was dead. His hand rested on the faint, rust-colored splotch which soap and water hadn't been able to erase. The blood of Native Americans stained the very steps of the seat of government of the greatest nation in the world. *And there's not a damn thing to be done about it. They're gone and now there's nothing left.*

"Lieutenant O'Shaunessey? Ah do declare, Ah've been lookin' all over for you."

Great, thought Matt. *Now I'm losing my mind completely. It must be shock.*

"Lieutenant?" The lilting southern drawl was accompanied by a light touch on his arm.

Matt was afraid to look up. He let his eyes rise an inch at a time. A full skirt with a red and white pattern narrowed to a tiny waist. The white blouse was snowy, shapely. Her chin, smiling mouth, nose, eyes and hair were achingly familiar—a face from another world.

"Hi, Jamie. Remember me?" she whispered. The affected southern twang was gone. "I've come a long way to let you know I've changed my mind—if you'll still have me."

For Matt, time stood still.

LEGACY

With the death of George Armstrong Custer on August 10, 1876, the last chance for peace between the United States and the remaining western tribes vanished. Custer was buried with full military honors at Arlington National Cemetery two days later. That same afternoon, Generals Sherman and Sheridan met with a shaken President Grant and pushed for the immediate resumption of hostilities in the west.

Libbie Custer left the cemetery with the firm conviction that her husband was the greatest Indian fighter who ever lived. The travesty was that he was about to become one of the greatest peacemakers who ever lived. She held Lieutenant Matthew O'Shaunessey personally responsible for her husband's death, stating that "he had time to stop that crazed Indian, but did nothing until it was too late." She never spoke to Lieutenant O'Shaunessey again.

Almost immediately, on August 15, Congress passed the Sioux appropriation bill requiring the Sioux to relinquish the Black Hills before the government would provide any further provisions to the reservation Indians. By September, government commissioners had forced the starving Indians on the reservations to sign over the Black Hills and the rest of the disputed territory—then they moved the reservation Indians off the land and back to the Missouri River.

Congress also granted immediate approval for the construction of two military forts on land guaranteed to the Sioux forever by the Fort Laramie Treaty of 1868. They authorized the addition of 2,500 troops to reinforce Generals Terry and Crook. By early September, United States forces were once again invading.

Two new steamboats, named *Far West* and *Josephine* were built and used to ferry troops under General Terry up the Missouri and Yellowstone rivers to continue the pursuit of the two most famous Lakota chiefs still roaming the wild expanses of Montana and Wyoming. Sitting Bull fled before the army and led his people to Canada, where they remained for several years. When he returned, he was confined on a reservation and, on December 15, 1890, he was killed by members of the tribal police while "resisting arrest".

Crazy Horse barely managed to get through the winter of 1876-77, harassed by an unrelenting winter campaign by the U. S. Army. He finally surrendered on May 6, 1877 at Fort Robinson, Nebraska. On September 6, 1877, Crazy Horse was treacherously killed at that place.

George Trail and the other Lakota chiefs waited in Washington for ten days seeking the release of Black Feather and Raven's bodies. They were finally told that the bodies could not be located. Fearing the rise of a cult to follow the martyred Black Feather, the government had spirited the bodies away and buried them in pauper's graves in a Negro cemetery on the outskirts of Washington. The dispirited Lakota were forced to return to their people at the Red Cloud Agency without the prophet's body.

When George Trail returned, he sang the death song he had composed in Washington. He stood before the gathered Lakota and announced in a strong voice, "I was once called *Kahektabya*, Bringing-up-the-Rear, but *Wiyaka Sapa* gave me dignity and I have taken the name George Trail. Now I have been to Washington, a long way from here. From today I will be called George Long Trail. I will work for peace from this day to the day of my dying."

On Sunday, September 2, 1876, Lieutenant Matthew O'Shaunessey married Kimberly Caldwell in a shady grove near a stone bridge in northern Virginia. It was a small, private ceremony. When it was over, Matt, Kimberly, and her son, Randy, sat under the trees enjoying a picnic lunch.

"Tell me again," Matt said, "before we all forget."

Kimberly smiled, reached over and tousled his hair playfully. "Okay, one more time."

"This was the spot where you proposed to me before, only I stupidly said 'no.' By the time I realized I'd made a mistake, you were gone. Then, Randy saw your picture in a history book and I got mad. I got so mad I blackmailed the government into sending us back to you. They didn't want to do it, but then they found out history was changing in spite of all their efforts. I guess they figured it was easier to give in to me than risk exposure."

"They knew I'd failed in my mission."

"Yes. Then they said there were problems with the transporter and they were going to dismantle it, but Demetrius Johnson took pity on us. When the news appeared that Custer was going to Washington, and you were in the party, that wonderful man sneaked us into the accelerator and sent us back before they could pull the plug, or whatever you do to stop a time travel machine from working."

Matt chuckled. "I imagine there's more to it than pulling a plug."

"Anyway, we got here weeks ago, but we were both deathly ill for days. We almost died."

"I talked to Linc about that once. His theory was that a person has to be sort of reborn when they travel through time. We all had the same problem."

"Well, husband mine, it won't be a problem any longer. From now on we travel slowly, very slowly through whatever time we have together."

They returned to Washington and Matt resigned his commission. He made a number of sizeable withdrawls from local banks and the three of them headed west to Montana. "I'll know the place when we get there," Matt assured Kimberly.

Randy Caldwell grew up, married and provided Matt and Kimberly with a lovely granddaughter named Ruth. Ruth eventually married a prominent local rancher named H. Jamison Partridge.

On December 29, 1890, George Long Trail was working for peace between the U.S. Army and Indians on the Pine Ridge Reservation who were participating in Ghost Dances. Tensions were high. George feared the government might overreact to the Ghost Dancers and do something stupid.

His ten-year-old son, Jefferson Long Trail, accompanied him on that freezing morning in December to a place near Porcupine Creek, on the Pine Ridge Reservation, to meet with a band under the leadership of a man named Big Foot. Three hundred men, women and children were camped under the guns of the U. S. Army at a place the Lakota call *Cankpe Opi*. When they came near, George heard guns, including machine guns, firing steadily. When he rushed forward, a stray round slammed him into the snow. His son tried to stop the bleeding, but it was no use. Before he died, George took an arrowhead on a silver chain from around his neck and passed it to his son. "Remember, my son, this once belonged to a great Lakota prophet. In time, it may be found to have strong power. Sometime—in the future."

George Long Trail was the last surviving member of the Lakota peace delegation that went to Washington with such high hopes in the summer of 1876. He is buried with all the others who died that morning—at Wounded Knee.

> *Wi-ca-hca-la kin he-ya pe lo maka kin le-ce-la te han yun-ke-lo e-ha pe-lo e han-ke-con wi-da-ya-ka pe-lo.*
>
> (The old men say the earth only endures. You spoke truly. You are right.)

NATIVE VOICE
Published by The Native American Nation
Issue 4, Volume III   March 5, 2018

Our Pride! Our Downfall!

We, the oppressed peoples of North America, became disenfranchised beggars in our own land largely because of events beyond our control. Historically we were not civilizations that made technological advances—nor did we make great advances in producing machines of war. We neither invented, nor imported, gunpowder or steel. We did not make great voyages of discovery. We did not combine our might to face an adversary. When faced with those who did these things, we were immediately at a decided disadvantage.

The Lakota secured that which was necessary to sustain life from the land we occupied. Within the culture there was no pressure to conquer. No inventors of note arose to bless The Lakota with labor-saving devices. Statesmen made no grand treaties with neighboring nations; freeing us from later breaking solemn promises. We were, in fact, a people largely at peace with our world. We faced it and fought it on even terms.

All of this was irrevocably reversed when we were faced with a numerically superior civilization well versed in the arts of war, the practice of conquest and the artifices of peace. Like small children we attempted to contest the limits imposed on us by those who *appeared* superior. For our efforts we were rebuked and punished. We found we were not equipped to fight and win. Nor were we ready to succumb to virtual enslavement in our own land. Like children we were. Like children we were treated.

It did not need to be this way.

Unfortunately our greatest triumph was our greatest downfall. Until June 25, 1876, there was a chance for peace between The Lakota Nation and the United States of America. Although there had been many unfortunate incidents between our nations, *there were those who spoke for peace and had the power to make a lasting treaty—on both sides.*

Tatanka Yotanka is revered today as a man great in war and strong in peace. Until the day he was assassinated he had the strength to force a settlement between the two nations. Had he but led the great mass of Lakota and Cheyenne warriors at his disposal on June 25, 1876 as a sword to destroy the invading army of the United States at the Little Big Horn, instead of holding them back and forcing the abortive negotiations which followed, our history might be much changed. Today we could control our own destiny. We would certainly control more of our ancestral lands. It was possible that day to deal the United States a crushing military defeat which would have forced that government to deal fairly with us. It was possible that day not only to defeat the Reno-Benteen forces, but also to annihilate the forces under George Armstrong Custer and, thereby demonstrate our resolve to remain free. *Even today, we are punished for our magnanimous gesture to spare 200 men who surely would have died that afternoon.* How ironic it is that they lived for only a short time anyway before being blown away in a tragic accident.

Could only one day in our history be altered—June 25, 1876—our entire existence would be enhanced. We would be powerful and feared. We would be: **The Lakota Nation!**

(Signed) Wiyaka Sapa, Lakota (Black Feather of the Lakota)

Characters - Future

Washington D. C.

Lt. Col. H. Jamison Partridge III, "Jamie"-Asst. Dir., DIA

Kimberly Caldwell - Civilian Employee, DIA

Randall Caldwell - her son

Jordan Phillips - Director, FBI

Kenneth Payne - Head of the Secret Service

Darrin Dealey, Chief of Defense Intelligence Agency

Berkeley, California

Lincoln Long Trail (AKA - Black Feather)

Professor Demetrius Johnson - Director, Project T

Walter Reynolds - Special Agent in Charge, SF Office, FBI

Pine Ridge Reservation

Marie Long Trail - Linc's mother

Amy Long Trail - Linc's sister

Ruth Teague- NAN Activist, Linc's cousin

Charley (Talks Too Much) Teague - NAN Activist, Linc's cousin

Characters - 1876

Washington City (Washington D.C.)

Ulysses S. Grant - President

General William Belknap – Sec. of War (Resigns Mar. 76)

Alfonso Taft - Secretary of War (after 3/76)

Columbus Delano – Sec. of the Interior (Resigned 10/1/75)

Zachariah Chandler – Sec. of the Interior (Appt. 10/16/75)

U.S. Army

General William T. Sherman - General of the Army

Lt. General Philip Sheridan - Commander, Military Division of the Missouri

General Alfred H. Terry - Commander, Department of Dakota

General George Crook - Commander of Department of Platte

Colonel John Gibbon - Commander, Department of Montana

Lt. Colonel George Armstrong Custer - Commander, Middle District, Department of Dakota, 7th Cavalry

Major Marcus Reno - 7th Cavalry, Ft. Abraham Lincoln

Captain William Benteen - 7th Cavalry, Ft. Abraham Lincoln

1st Lt. Matt O'Shaunessey (Jamie): Assigned to the 7th
  Cavalry

Lakota Indians

Lincoln Long Trail is Black Feather (Lakota - Wiyaka Sapa)
Charlie Teague is Charlie
Ruth Teague is Raven Woman (Lakota - Hecala Win)
Bringing-up-the-Rear (Lakota - Kahektabya)
Sitting Bull - Hunkpapa Chief (Lakota - Tatanka Yotanka)
Crazy Horse - Oglala Chief (Lakota - Tashunke Witko)
Gall - Hunkpapa Chief (Lakota - Pizi)
Red Cloud - Oglala Chief. Reservation Indian
Spotted Tail - Brule Chief. Reservation Indian
Note: Bold print indicates non-fiction character.

Glossary
Lakota – English

Akacita	Sub-chief; camp marshal
Akacitapi	Plural of akacita
Ani	Mother
Canke Opi	Wounded Knee
Catku	The man's place in the tipi, place of honor. Opposite the entrance.
Hecala Win	Raven Woman
Ho-ka-he!	Charge!
Kahektabya	Bringing-up-the-Rear
Oyate	Tribe
Paha Sapa	Black Hills
Peji-sla-wakpa	Greasy Grass (Lakota name for Little Big Horn)
Sinte Galeska	(Spotted Tail (Brule Chief)
Sitanka	Big Foot (Teton Chief)
Tashunke Witko	Crazy Horse (Oglala/Teton)
Tatanka Yotanka	Sitting Bull (Hunkpapa Chief)
Tiyospaye	Village or band composed of extended family & other followers.
Tukanhila	Great spirit -grandfather of all grandfathers
Wiyaka Sapa	Black Feather